Young Gods of Kopaz

Start the New Human Race

Young Gods of Kopaz

Start the New Human Race

Book 3 of the Kopaz Series

Dale Groutage

Copyright Material

Dedicated to the Travelers of Life

To my lovely wife, Nancy, and my three exceptional children, Phil,
DaleAnn, and Lane—thank you for your love and support.
We travel our worldly journeys together.
To my Desert Pirate friend, Robbie—thanks! Our adventures in a coal
camp in the 1950s made us who we are today.
We travel on—our journeys are not yet complete.
Two very special people—who gave me life and sent me on the road to
search for hope—are no longer with us. They sit on their lofty thrones
above and smile—their earthly journeys are complete. My father, Fred,
spent twenty-five years in a coal mine. He taught me to never give up.
My mother, Katharine, made our little abode in the desert and our
lives in the ever-present shadow of a bleak existence just a little piece of
heaven.
For all of us who travel on, our journey not yet complete,
there is an old Navy saying:

Fair winds and following seas!

Table of Contents

CHAPTER 1
Red Flash

Startled by the gripping realization that someone or something was stalking them in the nearby thick underbrush, Danny froze. *Oh no*, he thought. *We're not alone.* He thought he saw a shadowy figure. He wasn't sure. His mind raced on. *That flash of red...what the hell was it? Was it a man...a bird...or what?* Something out of the ordinary was going on, and Danny suspected that danger was lurking.

Then it was gone. The thickets of yellow-flowered bushes under the towering vine-draped trees hid nothing out of the ordinary. Danny's eyes stared into the vastness of nowhere. He squinted, but only the fluttering of green leaves filled his view. *Where is it? I saw it. I know I did. Is it hiding?*

The tenseness of his face as he glared with deep-set emerald-green eyes into the dense undergrowth did not go unnoticed by Jeannie. It had not been more than five minutes since she emerged from a pool of calmer water. It was a pool next to the river's bank, and it had a small cut or trench that connected it to the river. That cut in the river's bank allowed freshwater to be constantly supplied to the pool. Jeannie was sitting on a large granite rock not far from the water's edge—her wet T-shirt wrapped tightly around her small breasts gave the impression that she had nothing on. She had washed her blood-soaked clothes, and now her mind was anything but focused on the crazy devil who had shot her and left her for dead not long ago. But Danny and Jeannie's travels through time and space had erased those horrifying moments. Danny had saved her from death with his ring—the ring Jeannie was quite certain came from the finger of Supreme God Viracocha. But their escape from the disciple of Dark God Zuron, Lord Mochcom, in the Scarlet Desert was now only a faint moment in the distant past.

She looked at Danny, a smile creeping across her face. Her eyes sparkled as she contemplated her new focus. She had fantasized about this moment over and over with great anticipation, and now the reality was near. She could wait no longer. It was time for her first intimate, romantic occasion with the boy sitting next to her—the boy who she was positive was in training to become the royal prince of Viracocha. Yet the tenseness of his body made her acutely aware that something other than her was grabbing Danny's attention.

"Danny," she said sweetly, "what are you staring at?" Her hand reached to stroke his massive biceps. She was certain he would lose interest in whatever he was staring at when she brushed up against him with her wet T-shirt. Wiggling to position herself next to Danny, Jeannie was where she wanted to be and was confident of how to get his attention. She had had no problem in the past getting his heart to pound and did not doubt that her flesh pressed next to his would redirect his gaze from the distant bushes to her.

At that moment, a whippoorwill started its serenade. It was the harmonizing sound of the bird with the gentle breeze rustling the tall grass next to the rock on which they sat that managed to pull Danny's eyes from the bush. But just as he started to look into Jeannie's face, she slipped her arm around him and pushed her soaking-wet T-shirt against his biceps— the very biceps she had been stroking.

Holy Mother Mary, raced Danny's mind. It was not her wet shirt that aroused his every sensation but her small, firm breasts that were now causing his skin to ripple with goose bumps.

"Jeannie…ah…er…ah." He stammered and stumbled over his words. Jeannie could tell she had him in the state that she wanted. She smiled at Danny, knowing what was going through his mind, or so she thought. The thought of making love with Jeannie was driving his every emotion, and he wanted more than all the money on earth to let his hormones take control of his body, but making love with Jeannie with an audience—and with their treasure lying next to them—was out of the question.

"Jeannie, we have to do something with the treasure. Also, I think we are not alone," he said in a quiet voice. He smiled back at her. "Jeannie, let's take care of the treasure first and make sure we are by ourselves."

"OK, we need to hide all of this stuff. Let's find a good hiding place. But I don't want to spend a lot of time," she said in reply. "Danny, I've waited for what seems like an eternity to have you all to myself." She paused a moment. "And when I say all to myself, I mean all of you…every inch of your body."

Jeannie, if only you knew what you do to me. Danny's mind raced. *I'd like nothing more than to say to hell with this treasure and spend the afternoon in splendor in the grass with you.*

He pointed to a lone tree on the river's edge not more than two hundred feet from where they were. "That looks like a good spot. Er…let's make it fast! We have something important to do!"

"Yeah, but first," Jeannie blurted out, "we need to open this tin box and find out what crazy LeRoy was hiding."

"Let's carry all this stuff to the tree, and then we'll open Crazy LeRoy's box," Danny said. "I just hope we have something of his that he wants. That evil bastard."

And with his last comment, Jeannie watched his body go rigid. *He's thinking of his best buddy, Tony. He's right. Crazy LeRoy is an evil bastard.*

At the base of the tree, Danny spotted a round, smooth rock. He proceeded to smash the little padlock that was securing the tin box. "Good job, Danny," Jeannie said, also anxious to see what was in the box. Then she continued, "You made fast work, finishing that lock off!" She paused. "When we're done hiding the treasure, we'll see how fast you can get your you-know-what off!" She giggled.

As Danny opened the lid of the tin box, his mind was not still. *Jeannie, you sure have a way of getting to me, I mean, really making me want to see us toss our cloths in the air right now and take a peek!.* His hands on the lid were shaking, just thinking of what would come next.

"Oh my lord!" Jeannie yelled out.

"Just look at that *loot!*" Danny squealed with joy. "We're rich! We're rich! Jeannie, there has to be two to three hundred thousand dollars in that box. Look at those stacks of hundred- and fifty-dollar bills," Danny roared back to Jeannie.

"Where did all of this money come from?" Jeannie said, and she thought, *He never worked. At least everyone in CoalVille never thought he worked. How did Crazy LeRoy get this kind of money?*

"Jeannie, he's evil. Who knows how many people he slaughtered to get this money? I have to say, I think this is blood money." He paused. "But blood money or not, I think it will come in handy, especially if we have to go back to the Scarlet Desert."

Now, his voice became sharp. "Jeannie, I want to go back for one reason and one reason only." He stopped. His glare intensified as he fumbled through the hundreds of thousands of dollars in the tin box. "I'm going to kill him if it is the last thing I ever do!" His final words hung in the air.

Jeannie could tell he was drifting to a place she did not want him to go. She wanted his undivided attention. She wanted to get the Sun Energy Transformer, emerald star, five colored diamonds, sundial key, and LeRoy's money safely tucked away. She blurted out, "Let's hurry, Danny. Do you think we need a big hole to bury this stuff?"

Danny had already taken charge of the situation. "I don't think we could have found a better hiding place," he said as he lifted a large flat rock at the base of the tree. "Look, there is a vault under this rock. We hit pay dirt," he said with excitement. "With that high mountain peak in the distance and the river in this meadow, we have very good landmarks to know where we stashed all of this stuff."

"This is perfect," replied Jeannie as she joined Danny to help him move the flat rock. "All we have to do is put all the stuff in the vault and put the flat rock back in its place as the lid." She pointed to a pile of debris. "We'll put dirt, little twigs, and grass on the rock and then pile dirt on top of the grass and twigs. Finally, we will roll a bunch of these rocks back over the top of everything."

"That sounds like a plan," said Danny.

Danny and Jeannie worked together to bury the Sun Energy Transformer, the box with the bronze bow and bronze arrow, the box with the golden tablets, the sundial key, and the box of money.

"Let's sit here by the river for a few minutes," said Jeannie after the task of burying all the stuff was done. "This is one beautiful place," she said as she sat on the bank of the river and dangled her feet in the water. "This river is so peaceful. It just meanders through this green meadow at the base of those grand mountains. Look at those large birds flying around the high cliffs of the mountains."

"I wonder where this river goes," Danny asked curiously. "It sounds like it makes a lot of noise just around the bend. See how the river wanders through this grassy meadow and then just goes out of sight after it goes around the bend over there." Danny pointed in the direction of the disappearing river.

She wasn't interested in the river, the mountains, or meadows. She had only one thought on her mind—Danny. "Danny, scoot next to me." She reached for his hand and tugged on it. And in moments, they were locked in an embrace.

At that very moment, the piercing sound of *wrrrook, wrrrook* cut through the air, drowning out the serenade of the whippoorwill. Not more than fifty feet from where Danny and Jeannie were locked in each other's arms, there was a giant parrot. Its outstretched head as it strutted on the ground with a humping motion reminded Jeannie of the sage grouse in Wyoming when they were mating. Jeannie's head was next to Danny's as their cheeks brushed together. She looked over his shoulder, gawking at the bird as it gawked back.

"Danny, look at that giant red bird. What is it?" she asked, pulling her head away from his.

Unable to see what was making the loud noise and what had captured Jeannie's attention, Danny snorted. "What the hell is it, Jeannie? A giant bird?"

Seizing the opportunity, Jeannie blurted, "That crazy bird is doing a love dance. Ah…er…maybe," she giggled, unable to refrain from admitting to Danny what she was thinking. "Maybe it's jealous of you and me. Ah, maybe it knows we are about to make love, and it's jealous!" Now her giggles faded as her next question caught him off guard, her voice low and sweet as she asked, "What do you think of that, Danny?"

Caught between three events that were dominating his consciousness—someone or something in a bush not far from them, Jeannie's unbelievable suggestion of an episode of splendor in the grass, and something behind him—Danny's intuition, knowing their vulnerability in a foreign land, pulled at his defenses. Danny paused; his deep-set green eyes were somber as shadows bit into his face, making his cheekbones jut out. He tensed once more.

The sun turned the clouds to a fiery orange. Fully aware of Danny's state, Jeannie struggled for the right thing to say. Her first thought was to ask him why she wasn't the focus of his attention, knowing she had just asked him to make love with her. Their faces were now less than six inches apart. She stared into his eyes in an effort to read his body language. He stared back, and the silence stretched on.

His expressionless face conveyed no message. Then he dropped his arms from her waist and pivoted on the rock to look behind him. For a moment, he said nothing but just gazed. The bird spread its wings as if to fly but started hopping in their direction. Danny winced.

Jeannie's voice was stern. Her message was clear as she spoke with conviction. "Danny, what is your problem? You are either ignoring me or just don't care!"

"Jeannie, I'm sorry! Please forgive me," was his timid response. "You know I'd give my very life to make love with you. God knows I've waited for this moment ever since I laid eyes on you." He took a deep breath and rushed on before she could intervene. "The problem I'm having is that I don't want an audience!"

Now he had her attention. A million questions tumbled through her mind, but two took center stage: *Who or what would watch us? What is he talking about?*

Jeannie knew Danny like she knew herself. His actions were telling her something—something that was starting to frighten her. She blurted out, "Danny, what are you talking about?"

He pointed. "The flash of red I saw in that clump of dense undergrowth was not normal. I don't know what it was." His face was thoughtful, no longer blank. "Do you think it was that bird?" He pointed from the bright red parrot to the thick underbrush and back again.

As Jeannie was about to answer, the bird started hopping in their direction and stopped about ten paces away, cocking his head to the side. She giggled. She clapped her hands, which caused the bird to jump to the side. It then raked the air with its wings and took flight.

Jeannie burst into laughter. "Danny boy…you silly boy! That bird really got you going."

His laughter was quick in response to the flapping gestures she made with her arms, mocking the bird in flight.

They sat motionless, saying nothing as they watched the giant red bird fly down the riverbank and land on the limb of the lone tree about two hundred yards from them. Jeannie spoke first. "I think I know where my family's name comes from. It was Kashom who made the vault at the base of that tree where we hid the treasure. I just thought it was a natural hiding place."

Her smile warmed his heart as she gazed with excitement at the distant tree. It was the only one on the riverbank. "Kashom knew that when we traveled through time and space we would land at this spot. This is Kopaz, his homeland. He prepared a way for us."

She charged on with enthusiasm. "The treasure, the Sun Energy Transformer, and the golden tablets are safe in the rock vault at the base of the lone tree. Yes, my family name is Lone Tree, and now I know why! Just as the tree marks the hiding place for our treasure in this strange land, I'm the one with you as my partner, my love, ready to chart a course for the new human race. We are the 'Lone Ones.' We're gods in the making, and our destiny, at times, will be lonely, but we will be beacons as a new human race is formed from us."

She stopped. The silence was deafening. Not even a breeze competed with her. She had a point to make and watched Danny's every expression as she somberly said, "Our mission is to kill all of the goroms! That is why we are on planet Kopaz!"

Danny nodded. He changed the subject. "Where is your golden medallion?"

She took her boot off and pointed as she said, "It's in here." Pulling on a small obscure pin allowed the heel of her right boot to swivel. She exposed a cutout in the heel that housed her medallion.

He smiled but said nothing. And that was her clue, so she spoke softly. "Danny boy, it was the bird in the bush, and now it is the bird in the tree! So let's make our splendor in the grass a joyous moment as we begin our new lives as gods in the making!"

His reaction was not what she expected. She watched his unease grow stronger as she talked about their new life, their mission as gods in the making.

Her next question was pointed. "You don't believe me, do you?"

Lines of perplexity grew on his face as bewilderment took center stage. Softly, he said, "Jeannie, I don't have a clue what is going on. I don't know if I like this place." He paused for a moment and looked to the sky. Then, stumbling over his words, he continued. "I…I…I don't know if I believe in the g-gods." And with slow, somber words, he managed to say, "My mom is dead. My dad is dead. My best friend, Tony, is dead—killed by a monster. How can there be a god?"

He gave no sign of emotion as he finished his point. "And you and I are supposed to be gods? I don't think so!"

Motioning for her to stand, he grabbed her hands, looked into her eyes, and said profoundly, "I know you believe we are never going to die. You believe we are gods in the making. You believe that this is Kopaz, the land of milk and honey." He paused.

She said nothing but only waited for him to continue.

Slowly, he said, "We're in a predicament, Jeannie. We don't know where we are. In fact, we don't have a clue. At least we had a roof over our heads and food on the table in CoalVille. Here, we have no place to stay. We have no food. But most of all, we have no idea what danger lies ahead."

She had had enough of his feeling sorry for himself. Sternly, her words shot forth. "Danny, I'll have no more of your complaining. You know darn well that a fairy didn't magically wave a wand and send us to this land. My god, Danny, look around! How the hell did we get here?"

So rarely did she use profanity that Danny knew he just stepped into something big time that did not sit well with Jeannie.

He sheepishly lifted his foot and made a motion as he stuck his finger in his mouth. He laughed. "I'm learning! You know me. I'm one hell of a slow learner!"

Squeezing his hands firmly and with conviction, she charged on. "Soon, my love, the great supreme god, Viracocha, will let you know what your role is as his royal prince. And Danny." She stopped momentarily and looked him squarely in the eyes. "Act like a god!"

Whew, he thought, *she can be powerful!* He rolled his head to the sky and continued his thoughts. *We did get here by some strange energy source. Mochcom didn't kill Jeannie. My ring saved her.*

He laughed. "OK, Jeannie, what's next?"

She pointed downriver as she said, "Do you hear that noise?"

Nodding, he answered. "I hear something like water roaring. It sounds like it is only a short way down the river."

Tugging at his arm, she started swinging it back and forth. "Let's walk along the river to that grassy spot." She took her boots off and asked Danny to carry them.

It was déjà vu. As she strolled along the river's edge by his side, new blades of grass brushed across her toes with each step. She wrapped her fingers around his arm, and she peered fondly upward at his face. It was a special moment she was reliving—that moment in time when he had kissed her for the very first time. Her heart pounded as she recalled every minute detail of that day in the Scarlet Desert by the pond at White Face Cliff when they fell in love. It seemed like yesterday, but that was not the case. And just like that day, every minute detail and every movement of his expressions were being recorded in a secret corner of her mind. But this time it would be different. This time they would experience the joys of first love. And just like that day in the desert at the pond, Jeannie had rehearsed her every move for these special moments a thousand times over. But deep in her heart she knew that just like that special day in the Scarlet Desert, the spontaneous moments of young love could never be rehearsed, whether first, second, or…

Within five minutes, their stroll brought them to a place where they had to yell to be heard over the roar of the river. The white water of the river raging over larger boulders created a sea of foam as if it were the mouth of a giant rabid dog.

Curiosity is strange in so many ways, especially when déjà vu is at the heart of it. Jeannie's curiosity tugged at her to look over the cliff and view the water plunging to the floor of the yellow-walled canyon. Who wouldn't want to peek over a scary cliff and get the proverbial adrenalin high? After all, how many times would she be at the top of one of the universe's most giant falls…just waiting for a peek over the edge? It seemed to Jeannie a way to arouse Danny. She had something on her mind, and having Danny excited was all part of the plan.

Jeannie gingerly led the way as she gently tugged on Danny's hand. "Look," she said as she pointed. "The water is a giant stream of roaring foam! Just look at it fall." And then it caught her eye. "Oh my god, the mist from the falling water is creating a rainbow. Wow!"

It was that moment—that instant—that she dropped her guard, and her foot unknowingly landed on an unsteady rock. It rolled. She lost her balance and fell, plunging over the side.

Danny screamed, "*Jeannnnnnnnnie! Jeannnnnnnnnie!*" He watched in horror as she disappeared over a small outcropping of rocks on the side of the cliff. There was dead silence except for the roar of a raging river carving its never-ending mark in the yellow canyon that it had been creating for eons.

A faint sound was all he heard. He was not sure, but he thought he heard something barely audible over the river's roar from the depths of the canyon. He had no alternative. His mind was racing faster than an Indy 500 car on its way to the finish line.

Use your ring! The voice blasted through his mind as if someone were shouting in his ear. With a grip of steel, he held his weight with one arm, lowering himself over the side. His fingers dug into the crack of the rock as if they were a chisel forging a hole for the sole purpose of allowing a man to hang over a cliff. His fingers securing a godly grip on the side of the cliff allowed him to edge himself over the rim and dangle ten feet above a small rock ledge. He lowered himself as far as he dared. Now his feet were less than three feet from the ledge. He had to let go and drop the three feet. Yet he was insecure and continued to hang on, dangling on the side of the cliff.

His mind exploded again. *Use your ring!* This time he knew there was no alternative. With one hand still worked deep into the crevice, he used his free hand to pull the ring from inside his T-shirt. The blast of green light it gave off was next to blinding. It forged a backdrop behind him as if it were a solid wall that he could lean against—a wall that secured him from plunging down the cliff. He released his fingers from the crack, which allowed him to force his weight against the beam of light and slither downward three feet. His foot found the small ledge. He was fully supported, both feet on the small outcropping of rock on the side of the yellow cliff.

Now he had a challenge—should he slither farther down the cliff on a beam of light or look for another means of navigating the sheer rock face? A test of faith was about to take place. He chose the beam of light. Danny gripped the beam of light with both hands. That pillar of green light was his fireman's pole, and it allowed him to slither down the side of the cliff.

He saw her. She was twenty feet farther down the cliff. Her shirt was caught on the limb of a scraggly tree that had managed to spring from a crack in the rocks. She dangled helplessly, only the tether of a bloodstained shirt keeping her from the death that awaited a thousand feet below. The roar of the water plunging to its pool at the bottom of the canyon serenaded the young god making his way down the cliff to reach his love.

Twenty feet was not a great distance, unless it spanned the space from the side of a sheer cliff of rock to a limb of a gnarled old tree jutting out into midair. Danny knew its roots had secured its place for hundreds of years. He had no choice except to use the beam of light as a means to reach Jeannie. Holding on to it as if it were a steel beam high on a skyscraper under construction, Danny slowly made his way to Jeannie. Her eyes opened. His hand stretched out. Gingerly, she lifted her arm and reached for Danny's outstretched arm. Their fingers locked.

"Hold on, Jeannie. I'm going to pull you free." With a strong tug, he yanked her off the limb. She dangled like a large floppy doll at the end of his outstretched arm.

Wrapping his legs around the beam of light, he secured himself and Jeannie. "OK, I'm going to make our way back up the light," he said softly, competing with the water's roar.

There was a tense look on Jeannie's face as she answered, "I love you, Danny."

He winked. "I love you, too! Let's get the hell off this godforsaken cliff!"

Within five minutes, Danny had managed to pull Jeannie up the beam of light to safe ground.

"Jeannie, you scared the *holy shit* out of me!" he said commandingly when they both had solid ground under their feet.

She couldn't resist. "Danny, what did I tell you about cussing?"

All he could do was shake his head, point to his foot, then his mouth, and then wag his finger at the cliff.

As he wagged his finger and turned to face Jeannie, his eye caught the flash of red again in a distant bush. His humor and smile changed to tenseness and a blank stare.

CHAPTER 2
Death on a River's Bank

Maybe it was the strange land. Maybe it was the sudden brush with death that Jeannie had just evaded—a brush with the boatman on the River Styx that once more could have taken her love from him. Maybe it was Jeannie and her unwavering belief that she and Danny were now young gods in Kopaz. One thing was for sure; Danny was gripped by the stark reality that for his entire life he had battled a demon within himself, a demon he perceived made him not a normal human being, a demon he feared would never go away. Maybe he had finally realized he had no demon within him but rather was exactly whom Jeannie knew in her heart he was—a young god in training.

When an Olympian sets his sights on the gold, there is a force that takes over—a force that demands nothing but excellence. That same force of excellence was now taking hold of Danny. Yet when an Olympian sets his sights on gold, he can never let down his innermost guard that wards off every intruder who would steal the gold from under his very eyes while leading him down the pathway of complacency. Maybe that was what Danny was dealing with. Since he had never been a god in training, how could he know the game plan? For Danny, one thing was for sure—he was not eager to agree to a plan he knew nothing about, but now he realized he must be on board. Maybe, just maybe, the magnitude of it had finally hit home. Who knew? Dealing with the unknown, dealing with a plan Danny had no concept of, not knowing the game plan or what being a god in training was all about…maybe that was his challenge.

Danny was certain that something or someone other than a red parrot was in the bushes not far from where he and Jeannie were. The episode—their brush with death—had left them in a somber mood. They were trying to deal with the circumstances they had just experienced. They were comforting each other. Yet Jeannie was fully aware that Danny was preoccupied.

"Jeannie," Danny said, "there is a road or pathway over there." He pointed.

Now he had her attention. "Humans must live close by. Somebody made that road."

Silence fell as his words ended. Raised in CoalVille, Jeannie was street-smart. She was already putting her boots on as she talked. "Danny, did I ever tell you the entire story of what happened at this very spot? This is where Mochcom killed Aerapondes. My god, it was horrible."

Maybe special powers and knowledge were all part of being a god in training. Who could know? But at that very moment, as Jeannie talked about the horrific events that had taken place so long ago when Princess Aeraapondes was murdered by Mochcom, Viracocha opened Danny's mind, and Danny had a vision of the death of the first Neferzul.

King Dalvin and his wife, Queen Neferapondes, had no idea of the evil that lurked in the black hearts of the goroms who made up the quorum of high priests for the royal court.

Prince Kashom, who was eighteen, and Jerzom, his younger brother by five years, loved and adored their younger twin sisters, Princess Aeraapondes and Princess Merapondes. Kashom was destined to be the royal prince of Viracocha—TRPOV. Princess Aeraapondes was the older of the twins. She was destined to be the royal princess of Neferdor—TRPON. Who knows why only one twin had been chosen to become a goddess? Only the gods. She was twelve years old, had long, shiny black hair, soft white skin like the petals of a rose, and sapphire-blue eyes. Aeraapondes, as the keeper of the golden Key of Time, was given the sacred name of Neferzul. This key was a gift from the gods and hung from a gold chain around her neck—it unlocked the Highway of Time and endowed travelers with eternal youth.

The Golden Key of Time

That day was much like so many others that had preceded it, where Prince Kashom would record on his tablets of gold how to use the gifts from the gods to navigate the Highway of Time. His sister would accompany him on his adventures, exploring the Androzes Mountains that surrounded the valley of the Yellshome River.

Aerapondes told her brother she wanted to find the golden flower of the earth goddess, Pachamama, mother of all humans. She walked along the banks of Yellshome River searching for it. Kashom, preoccupied with his own agenda, sat beside the river.

Aerapondes suddenly felt hot breath on her shoulders and the back of her head. Gorom Mochcom's hand covered her mouth. A powerful force pushed her toward the river. She tried screaming, but no sound came out. She felt the chain with her golden Key of Time being torn from her neck. As she was dragged to the riverbank, terror overcame her. She could not understand who would be doing this to her. Where is my brother? Why isn't he stopping this? *Her mind was racing. Her head was forced into the water. Her eyes were open. She could not breathe. She held her breath. The powerful hands tightened on her mouth as they gripped her and forced her under the water. It seemed to last forever. But then the light that filtered through the water started to dim. She became limp. She could not fight any more. She thought of her mother and father as the light grew darker.*

"Yes!" Mochcom mumbled as he strolled from the riverbank, clutching the golden key. "The gods' gift to Neferzul is now in my possession!...It's the only key in the universe that unlocks Viracocha's GAMMAZEL, and I have it. Without it, he can't win the war!"

When Kashom and Aerapondes came to the river, he usually did not pay much attention to her. Usually, after an hour, she would come to his side and quietly say, "My royal brother, it is time to go home." An hour and a half had gone by since Kashom had seen his sister. He was deep in thought about the facts he was recording. As he gazed out over the river, he thought he saw a face drift by under the water. That must be a reflection, he thought to himself. *He continued to record his journal onto his gold tablets, their shining surface reflecting the Androzes Mountains.*

Gold Tablets of Kashom

Then it dawned on him. "Aerapondes! Aerapondes!" he screamed. He raced to the river and ran along the bank. He saw her—drifting quietly under the surface. "Oh my god! Oh my god! This is a dream! It can't be real!" Without taking time to sort out what to do next, he jumped into the river. He swam and tried to grab his sister. He could hear the roar of the falls only one hundred feet from where he was. He reached again, but could only feel her leg being pulled away from him by the river's current. "Oh my god! Oh my god!" he screamed in horror, but his words were muffled by the river's churning water as he swam in vain, trying to reach his sister. He knew if he were not to plunge over the great falls, he must get to the riverbank. As he forced his way against the strong current, his heart pounded to the point that it felt like it would come through his chest. He climbed up over the bank and ran downstream, looking for Aerapondes. He could not see her. The sun was glistening on the river's surface. Kashom ran to the edge of the great falls. At this point, the river's current was roaring as it surged over the massive boulders that were in its path.

A beautiful face—the face of a goddess princess—with flowing, shiny black hair the color of obsidian, soft white skin like the petals of a rose, and eyes of sapphire blue drifted by and was pulled into the rushing current and tossed over the rocks and white water as it moved to the edge of the great falls. Kashom's heart stopped. Time stood still—it was as if everything went into slow motion as he watched the body of Aerapondes fall from the top of the great falls and plunge to the bottom of the yellow canyon and into the turquoise river far below.

Although the events of Danny's vision took up to an hour to transpire, the vision in his mind lasted only a few seconds. Then it hit him. Danny's mind focused on a single thought. It was clear what had gone horribly wrong. Kashom had allowed Mochcom to brutally kill his sister. But more than that, Kashom had teamed up with Mochcom as they traveled together on the Highway of Time to the Scarlet Desert.

Danny mumbled under his breath to himself. "That's why Kashom lost his right to become the TRPOV." He paused, momentarily staring into nowhere.

Hearing his strange mumbling, Jeannie gawked at him in bewilderment but said nothing. Danny looked to the sky. *This is sacred ground I'm standing on. Jeannie has been so right. She is always right. It's me who has so much to learn.*

Yellshome Falls

The enormity of the events that had taken place so long ago weighed heavily on Danny. Those events had forged history and were now forging a destiny that he would play a major role in bringing about. He could not deny that he was central to the establishment of a new generation of humans. Even though Jeannie had told him this truth so many times, he had to find it out for himself. There could no longer be any question why the legends of Jeannie's people had such a profound impact on her. Her legends were now his legends. He and Jeannie were tied together in a profound way that would chart a new course, a new destiny for all human life in the universe.

He continued to stare into the sky as he squinted to block out the intense sunlight. His mind was incredibly clear. The diabolical nature of the goroms and their dastardly deed—killing a young, innocent, twelve-year-old girl—were horrifying. Standing on the ground where that unanswered murder took place so long ago, left Danny eager for justice.

Jeannie's patience was waning with each passing minute. She glared at him.

As he thought about the journey that he and Jeannie were on, something else grabbed his consciousness. His eyes were as still as glass marbles as he stared into an unknown future, looking for anything. But then, that anything just might be the someone or something hiding in the dense underbrush.

Danny mumbled again, "I am the TRPOV—I will not repeat Kashom's mistakes. I will kill all of those horrible goroms. Mark my words."

"Danny," Jeanie screamed, "what is going on with you?" She knew full well that he was lost in the caverns of his mind and that it was something of significance that he contemplated.

Their brief rest as they sat on the large granite rock on the banks of Yellshome River following Jeannie's brush with death was coming to an end.

"Jeannie," Danny said, "we have got to get out of here. We are being watched, and it is not safe for us." She looked a bit puzzled. He picked up on it and shouted, *"We have to go! Now!"*

He jumped to his feet and grabbed her hands. He pulled her to her feet. His eyes darted to-and-fro, looking for safe cover. Yet deep inside, he knew it was too late. Wherever they dashed, they would be followed. For now, his only thoughts were on Jeannie's safety.

He shook his head. Heart-shaped leaves on the tall tree in his direct line of vision were fluttering like thousands of small paper butterfly wings in a windstorm. The sudden change in the wind's direction caused his head to turn. This time he looked directly at a man who was wearing a painted leather skirt covering his groin and upper thighs. A leather band tied around his head secured what appeared to be a headdress made of bright-red-colored horsehair in the shape of a Mohawk. In his right hand, he held a bow. His arrows were in a long circular pouch that hung from his back. His skin was tannish-bronze in color.

My god, thought, Danny, *I knew I saw a red flash, and it wasn't a parrot.*

Before Danny could count to three, there appeared ten more men dressed just like the first. The one closest drew his arrow and let it fly. He lifted his head to get a better look at his target. His arrow found its mark, piercing Danny's chest beneath his collarbone. It was like a flaming sword that cut through him with ferocious vigor. Danny screamed with pain. "*Jeannie, run!*"

"*No, no!*" screamed Jeannie as she watched in horror. It was like the slow motion scene at the Boar's Tusk when Mochcom set out on his rampage of death and terror.

Blood poured from Danny's chest wound. He was all too aware of the severity of his predicament. But what he was unaware of was that the arrow had pierced the chain that secured his ring, allowing it to fall to the ground.

The emerald ring falling to the ground did not go unnoticed by his attacker. He watched Danny and knew that his victim was unaware of the fallen ring.

Danny tried to run but could not. He hobbled to Jeannie, unknowingly leaving his ring on the ground twenty feet away from where he and Jeannie were. She grabbed his arm and tried to steady him. He was faint. He stumbled. She screamed, "*Danny, get up! Get up! They are trying to kill us!*"

Danny put his hand to the base of the arrow in an effort to slow the blood flow. Jeannie managed to steady him as he rose to his feet.

In horror, Jeannie watched the attacker, who she perceived was the leader—the tallest of the eleven men. He directed his subordinates, waving them into position. He pointed at Jeannie and raised four fingers. Immediately, four men made a dash toward Jeannie and Danny. The leader then made a motion to separate Danny and Jeannie and directed six men to attack Danny. In seconds, the ten men descended upon Danny and Jeannie.

First they grabbed Jeannie and dragged her away from Danny. Weak and dizzy from blood loss—and without his ring—Danny was helpless. He watched one of the attackers pick it up from where it had fallen. He thought of his watch. Knowing it had never been used to assert power, he nevertheless thought it might have some powers he was unaware of. He yanked on the chain and pulled it from his pocket. Immediately, one of the attackers spotted his watch and snatched it effortlessly from Danny.

Jeannie did not see Danny lose his watch. She was fighting for her life. The four men easily overcame her. She was totally helpless as they held her like a dying animal—not allowing it to move.

Oh my God! Jeannie, forgive me! Danny's mind was exploding with hatred for himself as he watched the men overpower Jeannie. He whimpered, his voice barely audible. "Forgive me, Jeannie. Forgive me, Jeannie."

As he was mumbling his words of anguish for not being able to spare Jeannie the hell she was experiencing, he was being dragged to the river's edge. He did not know that Jeannie was allowed to see him in his state of peril. He did not know that the four men made it plain to her that the boy she had been with was going to his death. They held her in position and then grabbed her head and turned it in the direction of the warriors dragging Danny to the Yellshome River.

Once they had reached the river, all six men hoisted Danny and started swinging him back and forth. They shouted with each swing. "*Hoyaa! Hoyaa! Hoyaa!*" On the fourth "*Hoyaa!*" they let him fly into the roaring river. Danny hit the water not more than a hundred feet from the brink of the falls. At this point, the river was a raging torrent of white water boiling over the giant boulders that had been marking the brink of Yellshome Falls for eons.

Danny could no longer see Jeannie. His only vision of her was an image in his mind. The raging current as it neared the brink of Yellshome Falls picked up momentum, creating a sea of frothy white water, tossing Danny's body around as if it were a cork on a stormy ocean. Excruciating pain shot through every inch of Danny's body as the pounding water buffeted the arrow shaft protruding from his chest. It was more than he could bear, and now his thoughts were not of Jeannie but were calling to the angel of death to cease his torture.

Jeannie's captors delighted in forcing her to witness Danny's final moments of life. They stood her up and gripped her head with multiple sets of hands, forcing her to look at his body being swept over the falls. To the delight of her attackers, they sensed her heart pounding as they yelled in unison, "*Gorgom! Gorgom!*" Jeannie had no idea what the words meant, but she suspected they were chants of victory.

Her last glimpse of her beloved Danny was his two legs sticking out of the white water moments before he tumbled over the falls. And although the roar of Yellshome Falls filled the air, she heard nothing, only the crying of her soul for the boy she had fallen in love with—the boy she had hoped would be her partner as a young god in Kopaz.

As a river of tears streamed from her eyes, her heart was full of pain as her mind filled with a final thought. *It's over. Good-bye, my love.*

A Hand Reaches Out

If there were a supreme god, Danny certainly didn't believe in it—at least, he was not confident. His mind tried to make sense of it. *Why? Why me? Oh my god, where are you? Are you real?* For all his questions, there were no answers—only a living hell. His body was like a helpless vessel adrift on the ocean, a fierce storm buffeting it in the waves, not unlike a derelict ship on a collision course, headed for the bottom of the endless abyss. For all Danny knew, he might as well have been the *Titanic*. And like the ship of all unsinkable ships, he was sinking fast. The pain was like a white-hot, molten-metal knife stuck in him. The arrow sticking out of Danny's body was a finger from hell, a punishment from a master demon of torment. It had found its mark, and soon Danny would be on the boat traveling down the River Styx. With the current intensifying, the brink of Yellshome Falls less than one hundred feet from where Danny was being slammed into boulders, the foaming waters were washing his body clean of the blood oozing from the arrow wound. It was as if a gate of hell just opened and was thrusting damnation onto a soul just waiting to be rushed into a fiery pit of pain for an eternity.

In those final moments, Danny had no options as he was bounced over the boulders in raging white waters. Without his ring and watch, he was helpless. His eyes, nose, ears, and mouth were full of water. As he approached the brink of the falls, Danny was tossed and turned like a stuffed animal in a washing machine. His last moments of life were slipping away.

The roar of the falls was filling his mind with the anticipation of death. His thoughts turned to Jeannie. *It's over my love. We did not find our dream. I'm sorry. Forgive me, Jeannie, for not saving you.* Now it was not the arrow sticking out of his body that dominated his pain but the arrow in his heart that had been put there a few weeks earlier by the girl who had stolen his heart. She had pierced it with the arrow of love. It was at that moment that the raging waters propelled him over the brink. *Where are you my love?* That was his final thought as his fall was about to begin.

His face rolled over at the edge of the great falls, and he saw the sky for the last time. *It's over!* The roar of the river drowned out all sound, even Jeannie's screams as she was dragged off into the forest. Danny could only imagine his love screaming for mercy.

As he was swept away by the pearly blue waters falling a thousand feet into the canyon far below, Danny felt frozen in time as his spirit gripped his body and took him into a state of slow motion. It was as if time were standing still, but that was not so. Falling like a rock surrounded by the wash of foaming water, he realized that there could be no escape from this situation. What else would it be? The only possible end was death at the bottom of the falls. Danny committed himself to that end. For five seconds, he dropped in free fall at the same speed as the water he was immersed in. The only sound he heard was coming from the bottom of the yellow canyon—the sound of over one hundred thousand gallons of water per second slamming into the massive pool that had been receiving falling water for countless centuries. Although horrifying images filled his mind, he tried in vain not to think of the worst—Jeannie at the mercy of her male captors and what most possibly was happening. *Mighty god, don't let them rape her! Please!"*

By any stretch of the imagination, an abrupt end to a five-hundred-foot fall would most likely be devastating, if not fatal. That would be, of course, if it occurred under normal circumstances. Falling for nearly five seconds and coming to a sudden stop might not seem like a big deal—unless your fall should have lasted an additional five seconds. That was precisely what happened to Danny. Once hurled over the brink of Yellshome Falls by the raging river, he was engulfed in a sea of streaming white water on its way to the bottom of the canyon. The falls was at least one thousand feet high, and it took roughly ten seconds for the water to reach the bottom. So therein was the issue. Why did Danny fall only five hundred feet?

Suddenly, the noise from the bottom of the canyon was drowned out by the roar of water pounding and rushing all around him. This was not slow motion. It was real. Millions of gallons of water were now pounding him like a sledgehammer driving a circus-tent stake into the ground. His head felt as if a watery sledgehammer were driving it into his body. The excruciating pain from the roaring water all around him was masking the pain of the arrow in his chest. His mind was no longer filled with images of Jeannie being gang-raped. No, he was now experiencing something so bizarre that he had no explanation. But the pain of the arrow did not go away. After ten seconds in this most strange situation, Danny was experiencing pain that even a god could not endure. The source of Danny's protective powers—his ring and watch—were gone. He was unaware of the power from some source that had stopped his fall and also the fact he was not being smashed to death by the pounding water. Being caught in a situation beyond reality caused Danny's mind to question the very idea that he was a pawn to the gods in an insidious game of high-stakes cosmic chess. And that was what filled his mind. *My God, my God, where are you? Why am I going through this? Why? Why? Why have you forsaken me, oh mighty Viracocha?*

It was strange. Even while having to endure excruciating pain, Danny could not deny that something solid was beneath his feet. He was standing in midair. He was suspended in the middle of Yellshome Falls. He tried to make sense of it. *What is holding me here? What is going on? Am I dreaming?*

Immersed in the thousands of gallons of water falling over and all around him, he could see nothing. Now the problem intensified. There was very little air around him. He was unable to breathe in his suspended state in the middle of the falls. Gasping ever so slightly, so as not to breathe water into his lungs, he struggled to get one more morsel of air for one more moment of life.

His situation was growing so desperate that he didn't feel the motion at first. Something or someone was edging him forward. It was as if he were standing on a slow-moving platform that was ever so carefully inching forward. The motion was so slow that it was undetectable. But then, just like it would be for a person being repositioned, all things changed. Suddenly, his face started to emerge from the horrific stream of water that had been pouring over and pounding him. He gasped for air. His lungs filled for the first time since his plunge over the brink. He was able to see— and he saw something standing in front of him. *What the hell?* Having no idea what was going on, Danny lurched. Stumbling for balance, staring at the dim figure, he looked down and then at whoever was in front of him. Stiffening his legs to brace himself, he tried to regain his composure. Yet he was shaking from the insecurity of standing in midair, looking down at certain death five hundred feet below, and gaping at someone in front of him. Danny was helpless. He was sure that what he was glaring at couldn't possibly be real.

"*Holy shit, who are you?*" screamed Danny. Not only was he totally caught off guard, he was totally dumbfounded by whatever it was. "*My God, who the hell are you?*" screamed Danny even louder.

It appeared to be a dwarf standing in midair. He reached out his little hand and grabbed the arrow shaft. He yanked it and tossed it into the waterfall behind Danny.

Danny grimaced. Miraculously, the pain from the arrow was gone. There was no more blood. There wasn't even a hole in his chest where the arrow had been. Although there was still the now muffled roar of water behind him, his heartbeat was all that he heard. His eyes darted to the strange smile on the little man's face. Then the little man blinked and burst into laughter—laughter that could be heard so loudly and clearly above the roar of the water surrounding Danny that he thought it was like the roar of a volcano.

Not knowing what to do, Danny squinted. And at that moment of squinting, Danny's vision blurred. The little man was no longer in focus. All that Danny could make out was that it seemed the dwarf was reaching out toward him. The little man motioned for Danny to stretch out his hand. Danny did as he was told. The little man smacked his hand against Danny's, entwining their fingers together and then twisting their joined hands.

The little man's grip was so powerful it felt to Danny like the jaws of hell had just grabbed him. Even with all his strength, Danny was helpless to pull back.

There could be no carnival ride that commanded a more invigorating thrill than what happened next. From his midair position, peering down as if perched on the narrow window ledge of the Empire State Building, his heart pounded as if contemplating a jump. Racing out of control, Danny's mind was as a bomb exploding in all directions in hopes of hitting its mark. *What is happening?* was his only rational thought. What happened next, Danny did not expect. The dwarf leaned forward. Holding onto Danny's hand, he flipped his head down and started a descent toward the collecting pool of roiling water at the base of the falls. Danny and the dwarf were rocketing like a giant bullet traveling twice the speed of the falling water, headed for a pool at the base of the falls.

No, no! screamed Danny's mind as they shot through the air toward the water's surface.

Three seconds of travel later, like an exploding A-bomb, the dwarf and Danny hit the surface, jettisoning a mushroom cloud of frothy blue water, which leaped from the pool's surface as they started their downward descent. The foam-covered collecting basin at the bottom of the falls was no cushion. The explosive slam almost ripped him to shreds. Danny felt excruciating pain as he plunged deeper into the pool. A torpedo fired from a submarine could not have been more like the mass of flesh of Danny and the dwarf as they shot through the pearly blue waters on their way to the bottom, aiming for a target.

The thunderous roar created by the millions of gallons of water finishing their thousand-foot drop was deafening. Danny was helpless. He did not pull back from the little man who was pulling him deeper and deeper. Maybe it was because he had no choice. Maybe it was because his strength was sapped. Maybe it was because he knew he was involved in a grander scheme, a godly venture. Who knows why? But for whatever the reason, he did not fight back. He grasped the little man's hand ever more tightly. He wasn't sure if it were a dream or if he had dived into the depths of hell. But all things change—sometimes for the better and sometimes for the worse. Danny's breath was all but gone, yet the little man continued to pull him down. They went deeper and deeper into the depths of the pool, far below the churning waters at the surface. Light was dimming, and silence was growing. Only a sliver of sunlight made its way through the dense entrapment of liquid hell as a beam of guiding light. It was like a magical beam of light that could be found in Disneyland. The little man followed it down and pulled Danny with him.

As Danny neared the end of his endurance, they reached a snow-white sandy bottom. Danny was sure his lungs would burst. He wanted air. Like an arrow pointing the way through the deep blue waters, the end of the beam of light illuminated a small patch of sand. Just as a spotlight highlights an actor in a Broadway play, the beam of light was focusing its brilliance on something.

Oh my god. I'm dying. There could be no denying the dire situation that he was in. Danny had no air and was without options. Even so, he saw what the light shone upon.

It was the finger bone of a small hand resting on the brilliant white bed of sand. But it was not just the finger bone at the center of the beam of light. The light shone on something else as well. On the sands of the bottom of the pool was something glowing like a strange heavenly light—a giant ruby ring. It was resting like a crown jewel, waiting for something to happen.

Although Danny could see the beam of light reflecting off an engraving on the inside of the ring, the water blurred his vision.

His thoughts were not on an engraving on the ring or the brilliance of the ring's gemstone; he wanted to breathe. He closed his eyes. His mind was fading. *What? Why? I'm…I…I…*

Danny felt a strong pull on his body, and then his hand was directly over the ring. The little man extended Danny's arm as he pointed to the ring.

A voice exploded in his mind. *Grab the ring!*

At the point of collapsing from a lack of air, Danny grabbed the ring. His fingers closed weakly around it.

Then the little man forced Danny to look at the other object. It too glowed with shades of red from the ring's gemstone. No one could deny that the skeleton finger bone was awash in red light from the ring. Why would that be happening? Were the gods at work in a strange way?

Again, his mind exploded. *Pick it up!*

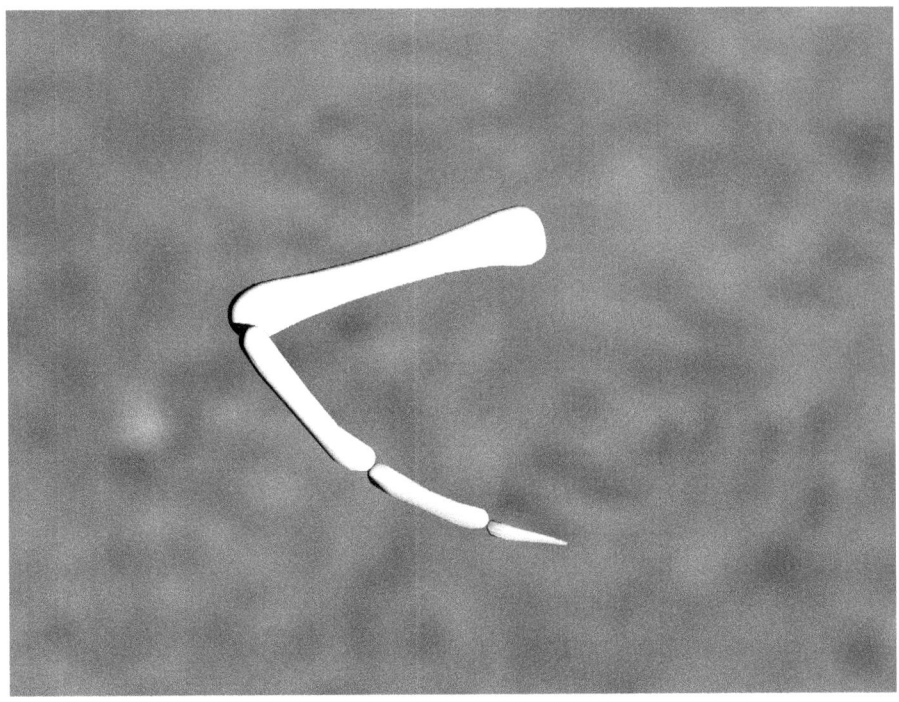

Time was running out. Danny didn't care that he had just picked up some poor soul's last remains. He tightened his fingers around the finger bone in his left hand and the ring in his right as his lungs throbbed for air—air that was nowhere to be found one hundred feet below the surface.

The little man was no longer in sight. Danny was alone and in a state of confusion because of lack of air and trauma. *I'm going to die. I've got to get to the surface.* His only choice was to go up. Like the deep submerged submarine that does an emergency blow to get to the surface in the shortest time, Danny followed the beam of light in a race against time. And like the submarine exploding through the surface, dripping with water, Danny flew out of the water as his race for a lifesaving gasp of air ended. His lungs filled. Heaving, his chest expanded over and over with each gulp of air. The deafening roar of the falling water set the stage for a new chapter in his life.

Not sure of what he was holding so tightly in his fists, he lifted his hands out of the water. Opening his fingers was not an option. He could feel his discoveries: the bone in his left hand and the ring in his right. *It's a ring, isn't it? And a skeleton finger?* He thought as he clutched his unknown treasures. *If I open my fingers, I'll lose them.*

Exhausted and emotionally spent, he turned his attention to the shore. With the pain from his arrow wound no longer an issue, and being in superb physical condition, it was no problem for Danny to swim with both hands clinched tightly around the objects he had just retrieved. As he stroked through the water, he had a few moments to think. *Whatever is in my right hand must be of great value, as it looks similar to my ring.* It took less than a minute for Danny to make his way to the shore. Feeling the sharp point of the finger bone in one hand and whatever was in his right, he knew that he had not lost them.

At the pool's edge, he was finally able to stand up. "Holy shit!" he screamed, knowing he was safe, at least for now. Breathing in and out was a joy. He filled his lungs with air like a baby taking its first breath. The sun broke through the cloud it had been hiding behind. There was a heavy mist that filled the air, created by the waterfall. And the streaming rays of sunlight directly in front of Danny formed the most beautiful rainbow. For the first time since the warriors had attacked him, he smiled. But that was fleeting. The clouds moved on, and so did the rainbow.

His energy was spent. The emerald-green lawn at the pool's edge was a perfect bed. He collapsed. He lay on his back, watching the clouds drift through the sky. Looking upward at a lone silver-lined cloud with the sun behind it, he said in a low voice, "Shit! I lost my ring." His heart started pounding. His mind focused on Jeannie. *How the hell did I let those assholes take Jeannie? Shit.* "Shit!" he screamed aloud. Although he knew his mind had filled with anger and foul words, he did not care. Jeannie was not there. And if she were, she would gently remind him to keep his mouth free from language that offended her. He no longer had Jeannie or his sidekick, Tony. Tony was dead, and for all Danny knew, Jeannie was being gang-raped by an army of heathens. Yelling in agony, he rambled on. "God, why have you done this to Jeannie? She believes in you. She is not the one who does not believe. I am! It's me. Take out your wrath on me!" His words were lost in the roar of Yellshome Falls. The pounding water never ceased. Like endless threads of time, they filled the canyon's floor with the constant booming sound of nothing, both day and night.

He rolled his head on the soft grass, taking his eyes from the canyon walls to look down the river. With the afternoon sun reflecting on it, it looked like to Danny like a silver road. The waters a little way away were tranquil. It was hard to imagine that they had been anything but peaceful, even if just a short while ago they were making their way down a thousand-foot waterfall.

He stood up and walked about aimlessly for a few minutes, gazing into nowhere.

And then it hit him. His attention had been drawn away by his surroundings from something he had retrieved from the depths of a giant pool at the base of the falls. Now, slowly, he opened the fingers of his left hand. No one could argue that the finger bone came from a small hand, and so there it was. Danny stared at it. *It is small. It must be the finger bone of a child*, thought Danny. Who knew how long it had been at the bottom of the pool? It must have been fate. The sun slipped from behind its hiding cloud and showed its face in the expanse of the sky.

Maybe the sun was purposefully shedding its afternoon rays on a brilliant object. Who knows? He opened his right hand. In his palm lay a ring. *You've got to be kidding me*, thought Danny. He stared at it. *I don't believe this.* His mind raced. The flawless, brilliant, thirty-five-carat ruby dominated his thoughts, its beauty overwhelming. His thoughts exploded with questions. *What's going on? This looks identical to mine, except that the stone is different. What the hell?*

The ring was identical in shape and structure to his emerald ring except that it was not as massive. It did not demand to be worn on a finger of extraordinary size as his did. It was dainty, sized to be worn by a young girl.

The engraving was similar to his emerald ring. "Princess Aerapondes. SGN," he read. *Wow!*

And just like his ring, the setting was gold, and the workmanship was worthy of being worn on the finger of a god. Inlaid in the pure yellow gold were the forms of celestial bodies.

Kaboooooooooommmmmm! A loud clap of thunder jolted Danny. It was odd.

There were no black clouds in the sky—only the brilliance of the sun with its rays that were reflecting on the prison walls of his new predicament. He dropped the ring in the grass. Lightning struck again. This time a tree not fifty feet from where he was burst into flames. The tranquil silence had fled. *Kaaabooooooooooooooommmm!* The deafening sound left Danny shaking as he reached to the ground to find the ring. He dropped the finger bone. He bent over. His fingers searched. The ring was there, almost directly where he had been standing before he'd been jolted by the lightning and thunder. He picked it up and quickly put it into his pocket. As he was tucking away the ring, a flash of light caught his eye. It was in the grass next to where he had dropped the snow-white finger bone. Maybe it was an omen. Maybe it was the spirit of the poor soul who was at the bottom of the pool.

Danny bent over and picked it up, along with the finger bone lying next to it. He put the skeleton finger in the same pocket with the ruby ring.

He opened his eyes wide to get a better look at what he was holding. "What the hell is this?" he said out loud. Knowing he did not have to answer to Jeannie, he said smiling, "Jeannie, you were right! I don't know what is going on, but I will cuss 'cause you're not here to scold me."

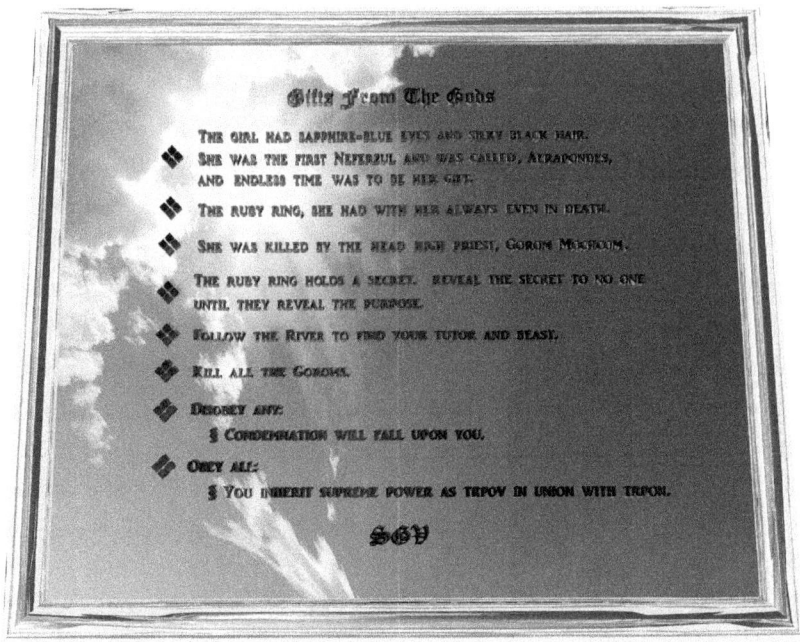

The golden message he held in his hand was almost identical to the gold note his parents had found on the morning after their wedding night at the Boar's Tusk.

The brilliance of the sun reflecting from the polished-gold mirror flashed in his eyes and blinded him. He blinked but to no avail. His eyes had not yet recovered from what felt like an out of control ball of fire in his head. He could only see a black outline of the golden object in his hands. He turned his head away. Slowly, he was able to regain his vision, staring at the steep yellow walls of the canyon. He turned and held the note so it would not reflect the sun.

The roar of Yellshome Falls was deafening, but his mind was silent. From his vantage point, safe on the banks of the river, his eyes now focused on the reflection in the gold plate—the massive falls pouring millions of gallons of water into the yellow canyon in which he was trapped. It was as if the scene he was watching on his private little silver screen was the backdrop for a movie in which he was the star. There was not only a setting but also a plot. *I plunged over that damn thing!* he thought. *I didn't die. That little dwarf man stood in midair, and now he is gone.* He put his hand in his pocket. His fingers felt the skeleton finger bone and the beautiful ring. *Something is going on.* It could not have been a more profound thought. *I'm holding something, but what does it mean?* Danny's early years growing up in CoalVille had given him something he never knew he was getting nor how he would use it—an education from the school of hard knocks. Although the howling winds of fate were blowing up a storm on Danny's journey, his street-smart education was about to pay off.

Glaring at the reflection of the falling water, he looked intently at the golden object in his hand. *I suspect the supreme god is telling me what to do.* Never forgetting his dream of finding buried pirate treasure in the Scarlet Desert, he chuckled as he rubbed his thumb over the letters. The words cut from precious gemstones sparkled as if to add luster to the screenplay for the movie he was starring in.

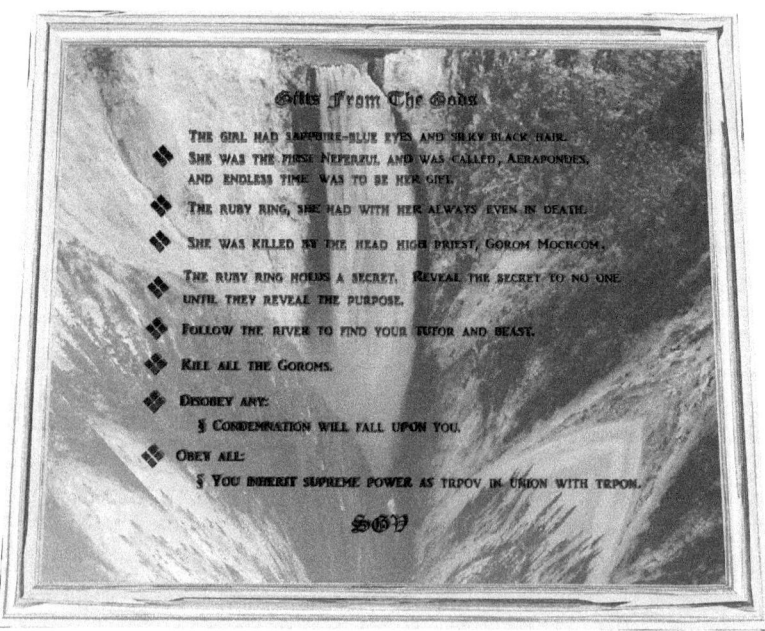

His voice competing with the roar of the falls, he read the message out loud.

Gifts From The Gods

- ❖ The girl had sapphire-blue eyes and silky black hair. She was the first Neferzul and was called Aerapondes, and endless time was to be her gift.
- ❖ The ruby ring she had with her always—even in death. She was killed by the head high priest, Gorom Mochcom.
- ❖ The ruby ring holds a secret. Reveal the secret to no one until they reveal the purpose.
- ❖ Follow the river to find your tutor and beast.
- ❖ Kill all the goroms.
- ❖ Disobey any: Condemnation will fall upon you.
- ❖ Obey all: You inherit supreme power as TRPOV in union with TRPON.

SGV

Jeannie was not here to help him. He could not think what the words meant. It might have been the dire circumstances he was in. It might have been his guilt at not protecting Jeannie. It might have been the weird events that had just taken place with the strange little dwarf man. Whatever it was, Danny could not comprehend the message. Even though it was déjà vu for him, Danny was more heartbroken than ever. It was Jeannie who had made sense of the message when she was furious with him for not revealing who he was the day he saved her from the bottomless pit inside the Boar's Tusk. Danny never denied that Jeannie was his bridge over his troubled waters, but that bridge was nowhere in sight. He was on his own.

Guilt and depression were quickly overtaking him. He felt crushed under a despondent yearning for the one who could never be replaced. He bent to his knees. "Forgive me, Jeannie. I didn't mean to leave you." Lying on his back in the soft grass, he stared at the sheer cliffs on either side of the river. They were ever changing, as the sun's rays would come out from behind a cloud and light them up. Sometimes they were a fiery yellow, and then they would turn orange. The never-ending show of lights on the canyon walls had a beauty. But to Danny, they were a prison. He was trapped in a canyon with no escape except to follow the river to an unknown destination.

It makes no sense. Find your tutor and beast? Hmm! I have no idea what that is about. He held the note tightly in his right hand. The sun reflected off the brilliance of the polished gold, as though it were a grand mirror in a royal palace. The flash of reflecting light hit his eyes once more. "Kill all the goroms," he said out loud, reading every word of the note with intense concentration. "That's clear enough. I just have to find 'em, and I'll cut their beating hearts from their miserable bodies as they witness their last moments of life before they descend into the pit of hell." There could be no doubt what was heaviest on his mind—the band of almost-naked wild men that had taken Jeannie. He assumed they were the goroms, but he did not know for sure. It was unlike Danny to have such awful thoughts about anyone, even his enemies, but his love for Jeannie and the visions of the hell she must be going through dominated his thoughts. "If those bastards are goroms, I'll not only yank their hearts from their chests but also inflict on them with the most miserable pain they could ever imagine."

Lying on his back in a bed of soft grass, his heart fell deeply in his chest. He breathed heavily. He again read the words:

❖ Disobey any: Condemnation will fall upon you.

It was clear what he must do. "Kill the goroms," he said in a somewhat desperate way. His mission was monumental, and he knew it. Failure left his love in the hands of evil men and left him eternally condemned for her suffering. Glimmers of hope were fleeting.

The mind has a mind of its own. Deep in thought about what condemnation might befall him for not obeying the note's warning, Danny found something to chuckle about. It dawned on him. He had pulled the ring from his pocket. Holding it in his left hand while holding the golden note in his right, he read aloud, "The ruby ring holds a secret. Reveal the secret to no one until they reveal the purpose." He laughed. "Well, that is an easy one. How the hell would I know what secret this ring holds?"

So it was at the base of the mighty Yellshome Falls that Danny smiled, knowing that forces of the universe were at work, and he had no doubt Supreme God Viracocha had signed the note of instructions.

Fortunately for Danny, his only option was to follow the river and do as ordered by the god of the universe. Even more fortunately, his boots and clothes were intact, if wet. He jumped to his feet. He kicked at the ground. A clump of sod flew through the air. His smile was all he had to cheer him up. His life on the streets of CoalVille was a good learning experience, and for sure, one thing he had learned was he would never allow himself to be a victim. "I'll figure this stuff out," he said. "I'm not alone. The hand of fate has dealt me a blow, but I'm on this journey under the guidance of the best there is. The supreme god has not abandoned me. He has given me orders, and I will obey."

He started his mysterious journey, following the river.

CHAPTER 4
The Lone Prisoner

She was in a land far away, at a time not yet revealed to her. Jeannie could not have been more locked up in a shell of loneliness. She was in a state of shock, and the direness of her situation had not yet fully dawned on her, but it was coming. During the first moments after the attack, her mind could not dispel the fear that Danny was gone. Deep in her soul, she knew that without his ring he was helpless. He was like a glass bottle thrown from the top of the Empire State Building. That bottle would only be whole until it crashed onto the pavement, shattering into a million pieces. Being thrown over Yellshome Falls by a raging current and plunging a thousand feet to the bottom of the canyon, in her mind Danny could only end like a glass bottle falling from a skyscraper and crashing onto a street.

At first, not quite grasping the deadly predicament she had fallen into, her captivity seemed only a strange circumstance, like the image of a slowly drifting cloud. But that was not the case. One of her captors, a tall man wearing identical clothing to his comrades—leather skirt covering his thighs and groin—reached to touch her side.

"Do you think she's beautiful?" Tangmar asked as his fingers raked over her ribs. Jeannie winced and pulled away, leaving the stranger's hand dangling in the air. She listened to their unfamiliar language and the strange words spoken by the man at her side. She had no idea what he was saying.

The man to her left side answered the man who had just spoken. "She's young," answered Zidmar. "She's not just beautiful. She's gorgeous!" He continued. "She's a bit feisty though!"

Tangmar smiled as he looked at his friend, Zidmar, and then focused his eyes on Jeannie. She gathered from her peripheral vision that the almost-naked man on her right was staring at her as he talked to the man on her left.

To Jeannie, Tangmar's eyes were like daggers penetrating her flesh. Goose bumps erupted all over her body. She was cold, even though it had to be eighty degrees, and the air was still.

"Zidmar, do you think she is innocent?"

Jeannie had no idea what he had just said but guessed from his chuckles that it had to do with her. She did pick up that the man to her left must be named Zidmar.

"Tangmar, you have a one-track mind. You think you will have the privilege of taking her innocence." Zidmar laughed. "You will have to fight me for that privilege, you devil."

Now she knew both of their names. She had no idea the subject of the conversation but somehow realized it was not good. Her experiences in CoalVille with rude boys whose only focus in life was to have sex with the first girl that came along taught her something about the nature of bad boys. Her mind was not on the mountains directly in front of her. Nor was her attention on the beautiful purple flowers that lined the pathway she and her captors were following.

The man who was at the head of the group of captors stopped. He turned and faced the men. At that moment, all twenty men stopped. He bellowed, "Tangmar and Zidmar, if either of you lays a hand on this girl, I will cut your hearts out and eat them for my next meal."

Jeannie's street-smart gift was her sense of communication. But in this situation, she had no clue of what the conversation was about. She had no idea that only by the grace of a stranger who had intervened on her behalf, a man she thought might be the leader, she had been spared the fate of gang rape.

"Do you understand me?" Blackmar hollered. "I can't hear you, Tangmar and Zidmar!" There was silence. "Answer me, you worthless cowards!" Blackmar yelled even more loudly.

Watching from the corner of her eye, Jeannie counted at least fourteen of the men turn their heads to look at Tangmar and Zidmar. She was all too aware that her glances must be inconspicuous, so as not to draw any more attention to herself. What she was able to observe was that, besides Tangmar and Zidmar, only two other men did not move their heads.

At this point, her mind was exploding with thought. *The leader has the trust and support of all but two of these men. My god, I hope I have figured this out.*

The silence pressed on as the leader and his faithful glared at the two men who flanked Jeannie. "Answer me, you worthless *bastards!*" screamed Blackmar. "I'll have your hearts dripping with blood in my hands in moments if you remain silent!"

"We were only having a little fun, Master Blackmar. Zidmar and I will not lay a finger on this girl," Tangmar yelled out.

"Good! Let's move on. We need to get to the palace and present our prisoner to the king," replied Blackmar.

The walk grew lonelier as the dense forest closed in like the walls of a deep cavern leading to an unknown blackness. Jeannie's emotions were tearing at her soul like Japanese knives whacking away at a lean beefsteak. A tear rolled down her cheek as she thought of the only boy she had ever loved—Danny. Her last glimpse of him had been his body being tossed and turned like a cork in the waves of an ocean storm. After his body had been flung over the brink of Yellshome Falls, she never doubted that his next encounter was with death itself. She was all alone, and now she questioned her quest that had started not more than a month earlier. *Oh, Danny, I never meant this to end like this. Why did I insist that we venture on this awful road of horror that took Tony's life, your mother's life, and now yours? Please forgive me, Danny. I meant well.*

She had no idea what lay ahead. Until now, she had been held only by the strong grip of the men flanking her, but that was about to change. The procession stopped. Blackmar, the lead warrior, turned to face his men. "Tie a rope to her. Tie it around her waist."

She did not understand. Tangmar and Zidmar grabbed Jeannie. Zidmar held her hands behind her. A tall, copper-skinned man emerged from the back of the group with a rope made of leather thongs braided together. He walked toward Jeannie.

She was petrified, not knowing what would happen next. With a look of horror on her face, she started to scream.

Tangmar lifted his arm, and like a lightning bolt, he let loose his might, striking her face with a fierce blow. She fell to the ground. Her head exploded with pain. She was sure her eyes were pools of blood. Her mind had nowhere to go. Helpless, she tried to escape the doom descending on her. She concentrated on Danny. *Oh, Danny, if you are a spirit, please help me, my love. I fear that I am going to be tossed into the gates of hell…oh my love, help me.*

And then her cries were not just in her mind. She screamed, "*Help me! Help me! Danny, oh my Danny, help me! Please, please help me.*"

Zidmar's foot came down on her head, smashing her face into the dirt. She could scream no more. Her heart sank. She was sure that hell existed and that her destiny was to venture through its open gates—gates that welcomed all those unsuspecting souls who were bound for merciless torment until the end of time.

The copper-skinned man rolled Jeannie over onto her side so that he was standing directly over her. He reached with his right hand for her still body while holding the leather rope in his left. With one hand on her belly, he wrapped the rope around her. She felt the rope as he pulled on one end. He cinched it up and tied a knot. Grabbing both her hands, he lashed them together with a small length of leather strap. At the time, she didn't know it, but the fact that her hands were tied in front of her would save her life.

Help me…oh supreme god of the universe, please, please help me! Please help me! Her screams were locked deep within her being. She alone could hear her cries for help. Trembling uncontrollably, Jeannie was at the mercy of her captors.

"Keep her down," screamed Blackmar. He was busy making his next move.

Lying helpless on the ground, Jeannie could hear the commands being belted out. Their words were meaningless, yet in her inner soul, she had no doubt that they had something to do with her.

"Drag her," yelled Blackmar. "I do not want the king to get a look at her beautiful face." He pointed to Jeannie. "I want her filthy…filthy as a pig!"

From the corner of her eye, she focused on the massive legs standing next to her. They belonged to the tall, copper-skinned man. Holding the rope tightly in his massive hands, he started walking forward. The rope tightened. As the tall man walked on, Jeannie was dragged along the ground on her belly. She immediately tried to stand. But Zidmar used his legs and feet again. With the force of a brute, he landed a blow on her side with his foot. She felt as if a horse had kicked her. She had no options open. Her only avenue was to be dragged across the ground on her belly.

The sounds coming from her captors were anything but foreign. Laughter in any language was laughter. Their cruel guffaws and snickers filled the air.

They stopped. Jeannie tried to see what was happening. She could not. All she could see were the naked legs of men, whose only garments were thin, tightly stretched leather skirts covering their upper thighs and loins. She could not see where Blackmar was pointing. With his arm held high, he motioned to the others to proceed. The dragging continued. Jeannie was helpless.

Her next deadly encounter did not take long. Although Jeannie had no idea what Blackmar had pointed to, she knew she was now in a large pool of mud, at least two feet deep. She was immersed in thick, black mud. Still on her belly, she could only lift her head so high. It was not high enough. Mud was now penetrating her nose. She could at least bring her bound hands to her face. She was grateful for that. She covered her nose and mouth with both hands in a desperate effort to keep the mud from suffocating her. Fortunately, the pool of mud was finite. The nightmare started to end as she reached the edge of it. Frantically, she clawed at her nostrils and mouth to get as much of mud out as possible.

And fortunately, she felt something wet. She couldn't see because eyes were filled with sand from the mud puddle grinding away at her eyeballs. In her mind, she visualized a pool of water. *Let it be water. Please let it be water.*

With her hands tied together, she scooped at the liquid, fingers cupped together in an effort to get a few drops of water to her face. She was successful. And fortunately, the pool of water was large enough so that she could scoop both hands through the water. Even though her hair was thick with mud, she was able to wash enough from her nostrils so that she could gasp successfully for air.

Now the laughter continued with even more vigor. Jeannie knew it was directed at her.

The procession stopped again. This time she felt hands in her armpits. She was lifted to her feet. Even with her hands as dirty as they were, she managed to wipe her eyes enough to open them. Zidmar and Tangmar were standing next to her.

Barely audible, Zidmar whispered to Tangmar, "Blackmar wants her for his own. I'm not stupid. He wants the king to see a filthy person, and when the king says, 'Get this dog away from me,' Blackmar will have her all to himself. That bastard!"

"Quiet!" yelled Blackmar. He had no idea what was being said but was wise enough to know it was likely to be devious.

A deathly silence filled the air. The procession marched on.

Without an inkling about what Zidmar and Tangmar had said or what Blackmar had been screaming about, Jeannie stared straight ahead. The sun going behind dense clouds seemed like an omen of impending evil. Then it changed. The sun showed its face from behind the cloud it had been hiding under. Jeannie stared on, content that she was no longer being dragged through the mud. And at that moment of brilliant sunlight, they emerged from the thick dark forest to the edge of a valley. There was before her a breathtaking view of splendor. Above her, nestled at the base of a majestic mountain with towering granite peaks, there was a magnificent building. It glistened in the noonday sun like the white marble temples of Rome adorned with gold and alabaster statues. The gardens, manicured to perfection, awaited visitors, proclaiming a royal welcome at the palace gates.

The march across the valley continued for another half an hour.

In Jeannie's mind, the trek was but a moment in time. Then the party stood outside a wall surrounding a decadent palace. King Ludwig's Neuschwanstein Castle paled in comparison to the grandeur of the domicile of the royal family of Kopaz. The announcement at the castle gates was loud and clear—a prisoner was at hand.

"Who goes there?" yelled a gate guard from the inner courtyard.

"We bring an intruder, an enemy of the kingdom of Kopaz. We request that we may present the intruder to King Dalvin for judgment."

Schreeeeeeeeeeeeeeeeekkkk...schreeeeeeeeeeeeeeeeeekkkk! Squealing sounds filled the air as the two large gates started to open.

The end of the day was here. The late afternoon coolness was telling the inhabitants of Kopaz that the sun would soon sleep. The long shadows added to the darkness of Jeannie's predicament. She was at the mercy of those who viewed her as a trophy. She felt as if she were a sleek black panther that had once been free to roam throughout its domain but was now helpless, in its final moments of life, its leg caught in a steel trap, watching a hunter approach to take it as a trophy.

A strange, disfigured little man wearing nothing but a pointed hat and a thin, tightly pulled leather skirt around his loins and thighs nodded his head while holding onto his hat to ensure it did not fall to the ground. "Enter!"

The gatekeeper pointed to Blackmar and motioned for him to step forward. Blackmar walked to a point directly in front of the deformed little man, who looked as if he had had his withered, mutilated legs and hands since birth.

In a voice oddly loud for such a small man, he said, "Take your prisoner to the Hall of the Goroms first. King Dalvin will wait for the goroms to bring the prisoner to the Grand Hall."

CHAPTER 5

The Goroms

T he Hall of the Goroms was massive. One had to wonder why there was such a grandiose meeting room for a small group of religious leaders when there was no congregation who would attend any sort of meeting in it—ever. Maybe it was greed on the part of the goroms. Maybe it was in the name of pomp and circumstance. The fact was that it was there, part of the royal complex, which also included a palace that was not just massive but gargantuan in size. This was where the royal family of Kopaz—King Dalvin, Queen Neferapondes, Prince Jerzom, and his sister, Princess Merapondes—resided. Since the twin sister of Princess Merapondes, Princess Aerapondes, was murdered by Gorom Mochcom, and her older brother, Prince Kashom, was conned by this evil man and hence banished, they were no longer part of the royal family.

The sun had set. Only the silver-orange-lined clouds on the horizon marked the spot where the sun hid its face for one more day.

Bound and tied as a prisoner, Jeannie was brought by her captors—a contingent of the king's royal guard—to the Hall of the Goroms. It had many large rooms, both business and living quarters. The large room where they conducted most public meetings was also called the Hall of the Goroms. Who could say why the building and room had the same name. For centuries it had been that way.

Although the Hall of the Goroms was only a quarter of the size of the royal palace, it was constructed in like manner—of marble, gold, silver, leaded glass, and granite. It sat in a courtyard behind the main castle.

Jeannie was hooded before they entered the building, to blind her to the surroundings leading to where they took her. She guessed that they were walking down a hallway from the sounds of the environment—the nearby walls echoed her captors' words as they walked the long distance. They stopped, and her hood was removed. She could see again, but caked mud disguised her appearance.

She stood outside the door of the Hall of the Goroms, surrounded by guards.

The high priest, Katchcom, was the only gorom in the hall. Stretched out on a couch, his head was buried in a silk pillow, yet that did not keep him from hearing the door open.

"Who is there?" he shouted.

"We bring an intruder. It's Blackmar, Tangmar, and Zidmar, the king's royal guardsmen. The royal family instructed us to bring this prisoner to you." His voice was that of a man anxious to have the proceedings move quickly.

"Bring forward your prisoner," the head high priest yelled as he sat up.

When Jeannie and her captors entered the hall, Katchcom glared at the disgusting sight that was unfolding. He stood and made his way to a massive gold throne at the head of a white-marble table fifty feet in length.

At least thirty gold candelabras, all populated with glowing candles, provided a flickering light throughout the room. It made the hundreds of giant, multicaret gemstones—the rubies, sapphires, diamonds, and emeralds that were inlaid into the solid gold throne at the head of the table—glisten and twinkle with each flicker of the many candles.

Ten windows on each side of the room were draped with large, heavy curtains—each was like a tapestry, woven with a religious scene of some sort, although the images were foreign to Jeannie.

Her short glance at the windows resulted in a swift reprisal. "Slap her head around. She is not to look!" shouted Katchcom.

The guardsman's fist swung, and his blow sent Jeannie tumbling to the floor. Her collapse was short-lived. "Get her to her feet," yelled Katchcom.

The grandeur of the most beautiful room she had ever set foot in could rival that of a heavenly palace, but the bitter reality of being held prisoner by such vile humans clouded any pleasure she might have taken in her beautiful surroundings.

For now, her key was hidden safely in the heel of her shoe, the secret hiding place her uncle had made for her so many years ago, telling her that one day her feet would grow into the boots.

Seated at the head of a large white-marble table, High Priest Katchcom waited patiently. No one moved. Surrounded by guards, Jeannie was helpless. Consumed by fear, she clutched her hands tightly.

Their language left her clueless as to their conversation. After that brutal blow to the head, she was shivering, trying to hold her head motionless. Instant death would be a welcome relief opposed to the unknown certainty of what awaited her next.

Grinding his teeth with each word, he swung his hand, bidding them bring the prisoner forward. Katchcom shouted, "Bring her!"

The caked mud that was clinging to Jeannie's shorts was being dislodged by her movements, leaving a trail of dirt across the beautiful floor.

"How dare you bring this filth into my room?" snarled Katchcom. Irate at what he was witnessing, he growled. "It's late. The servants are gone, and I will have to deal with this mess that you created in my beautiful hall. You sick pigs."

His rant had not finished. Katchcom railed. "At this late hour, who will clean your garbage you leave here?" He glared at Blackmar, the head royal guardsman.

It was what he wanted. Although Blackmar said nothing, he laughed to himself and mocked the high priest. *You're the stinking mess, you mindless fool. You are being tricked, and you are clueless!*

Raving on, Katchcom slammed his fist on the table. "Blackmar, you have some nerve at this hour. I have no patience for a dirty, mud-covered prisoner. You miserable human beings. You come to me with your stinking mess. How dare you bring a filthy dog before me?"

The moment had come. Blackmar spoke. "Your Eminence, we bring this prisoner to you first. She will be brought before the king, and there may be consequences."

Unknown to Blackmar, Katchcom's mind was not on the prisoner. He was plotting to overthrow the royal family. The words of the royal guardsman, Blackmar, fell on deaf ears.

"Out! Get out of my presence. Don't you even think of taking such a filthy pig to the grand hall to present to the king." He ended his rant.

As the royal guards prepared to leave the Hall of the Goroms, Blackmar was happy to exit in haste—he had his trophy in tow, the leather rope attached to her waist and her hands bound together. Excitement grew within him as he fantasized about the pleasure he would derive from her.

Maybe it was convenient, because the sun had gone to sleep and the night was dark. Maybe it was curiosity. Maybe he wanted something in return for what he was about to do. For whatever reason, Zidmar made his move.

As the massive door opened, he cleverly hid in the shadows behind the immense wooden door. The screeching sounds from the iron hinges masked any noise he might have made with his movements. It was the cover he needed.

The door slammed shut. All was quiet.

In the silence, the barefoot footsteps from the shadowy corner of the room were undetected. Katchcom was unaware. Zidmar slithered toward the tapestry-covered window not more than ten feet from the doorway.

Once outside, Blackmar looked at Tangmar and raised his arm, pointing to the quarters of the royal guards, five hundred yards to the north of the royal palace. Tangmar remained standing next to Blackmar and Jeannie. Blackmar held the leather restraints strapped around Jeannie with a powerful grip. He stepped closer to Tangmar so his face was only inches from his fellow guardsman. His arm still pointing, he bellowed, "*Get the hell out of here…now!*"

Tangmar obeyed. He turned to walk away, but he never took one step. On that dark night, he never saw the knife in Blackmar's hand. He felt a blistering hot sensation in his back, but only for a moment, and then he fell to the ground where his legs twitched as his soul tried to leave his body.

From his hiding place, Zidmar was crafty. He watched Katchcom.

Massive rug-like drapes covered the windows. They were excellent to hide behind, as they not only covered the windows but also extended five feet on either side of the window openings. It was a perfect concealment spot for Zidmar.

In the darkness of the early evening and tired from his day's work of plotting the overthrow of the royal kingdom of Kopaz, Katchcom called his manservant. He snorted at him. "Squelch all the candles in the candelabras and then leave. Can't you see I'm tired, you lazy pig?"

Katchcom returned to his couch. It was only moments before it was pitch black in the room. Only a few rays of moonlight managed to filter through the cracks in the curtains—perfect for an intruder to lie in hiding.

Minutes passed. All was quiet, and then the silence was broken.

"Your Eminence." A voice came from the shadows.

Startled, Katchcom bellowed, "Who goes there?"

The peril was real. Zidmar knew the danger. He spoke in a loud, deep voice before Katchcom had time to respond. "Your Eminence, Blackmar has deceived you. He has a Neferzul. The filth on her was Blackmar's plan to hide her identity from you."

Although Katchcom heard the words, they did not register. The starkness of the reality of someone hiding in his inner sanctum was overpowering. Stunned by the sudden outcry from behind the window covering, Katchcom shouted, "Come out from your hiding place, you rat. You must take me for a fool."

Zidmar gingerly stepped from behind the curtain and made his presence. He felt his belt pouch with his right hand, his fingers tracing the shape of Danny's emerald ring.

Staring at the shadowy black figure in front of the covered window, Katchcom yelled, "Who is that?"

"It's me, Your Eminence. Zidmar." His words were spoken in a soft tone that echoed in the stillness of the lightless, marble-walled room.

"What did you say, you treacherous dog?" shouted Katchcom, still feeling vulnerable from the shock.

With even more reverence in light of his fragile situation, Zidmar spoke loudly. "The prisoner that Blackmar brought before you is Neferzul."

That statement left Katchcom more than puzzled. "Gorom Mochcom killed her! How dare you lie to me?" It was at that point that Katchcom realized he misspoke and divulged the murderer of Princess Aerapondes. His mind reacted. *I must fix this unfortunate slip of my tongue!*

"Holy one of Kopaz, I speak the truth. Blackmar has the Neferzul, and she is young and most likely a virgin. The captain of the royal guard is a cunning man who lusts after pleasure." Zidmar started to walk toward the couch.

Not taking any chances, Katchcom shouted, "Wait here."

He then left via the back door, which was situated across the room from where he had been sitting. The stillness of the empty room weighted heavy on Zidmar, who did not know what Katchcom was up to or where he had gone.

Time stretched on. Without the glow of a single candle, the inky-black humid air was like a smothering blanket wrapped tightly around him. Ten and then fifteen minutes passed.

On the verge of risking a sudden exit and cutting what might be his deathly loss, Zidmar took a step. But it was at that moment that the silent room was suddenly filled with the *eeeeerch* of a door hinge. Light from the hallway drifted in. Two figures stood in the doorway. Zidmar could not see his face, but the silhouette of one of the two men in front of the hallway candles appeared to be Gorom Ancom.

The two stepped in. The door slammed shut with a thundering boom that hung in the air like an echo in the Grand Canyon. Blackness took over.

Sandal-clad feet on the green marble floor made footsteps that seemed to Zidmar to be moving away from him. They stopped opposite where he was standing.

Gorom Katchcom flung open the curtains of the window on the west wall of the hall.

Starlight from an unusually bright Milky Way sent a faint glow throughout the room. The name of the ribbon of stars that lights the night sky—Milky Way—was the name that Kashom brought back from his visit to Egypt so long ago and was adopted by official proclamation by the royal family of Kopaz.

Still standing next to the doorway leading to the outer rooms of the high priest's quarters, Gorom Ancom was a man of extraordinary size and massive muscles.

"Come to my table, Zidmar, and tell Gorom Ancom what you told me about the prisoner," snarled Katchcom.

Slowly, Zidmar walked to the far end of the council table of the high priest. He stood next to the throne at the head of the table. He waited next to it for Ancom and Katchcom to meet him.

It took only seconds for both goroms to be at the table—Katchcom to walk from the west window and Ancom to walk from the hallway door.

They stood like three sentinels at the head of a ruling table, just waiting for the others to take their places. That was not going to happen. It was late, and the only business that would be conducted in the Hall of the Goroms on that dread night was not public but secret.

Zidmar stood between the goroms. His head was only inches from theirs. The air was humid, and before any words were spoken, Katchcom's hot breath on Zidmar's face was unmistakable. The high priest hissed, "Seize him."

Instantly, Ancom took a step forward. He turned swiftly and reached out in the direction of the royal guardsman. Like a prey-striking rattlesnake, he grabbed Zidmar's long black hair. His massive arms wrapped around Zidmar neck like a python.

Barely able to breath, Zidmar stared, his motionless head pointed at the face of Katchcom.

Katchcom demanded answers. "Who knows what you have just told me?"

Barely able to breathe, Zidmar was almost helpless to move his head as he made slight motions, trying to communicate.

"Let him breathe," snorted Katchcom.

Ancom released his hold and dropped his arms. Zidmar tried to relax, gasping to fill his lungs with air. His airways were busy taking in lifesaving oxygen, so no words came out of his mouth.

"How many know that name?" growled Katchcom.

Struggling for relief, Zidmar choked out feebly, "Only two others, most holy one."

"Hmm…only two?" rasped Katchcom. His face moved closer to Zidmar's.

The royal guardsman was speechless as his eyes tried to focus on the face just inches from his. His lips moving in slow motion, Zidmar's concentration was shooting all over the place like wildly flung arrows. He was about to say something but was cut short by Katchcom's next question. "Are you positive there are only two?"

Stuttering, Zidmar managed to answer. "Ye…ye…yes, oh most holy priest of Kopaz."

"Who are they?" snarled Katchcom.

Still stuttering, he blurted, "B-B-Bal…Blackmar and Tangmar."

There was a reason for these questions, and only Katchcom knew that most prized secret. His quest to find the leak of this most sacred name would be relentless.

He grilled his captive further. "They are the only ones?"

Nodding his head in the affirmative, Zidmar once more tried to breathe. All his efforts were in vain. He could not still his trembling body. He tensed with each question from Katchcom, the gorom's mouth only inches from his face, blasting it with hot breath.

And once more, looking for any wavering that might be going on, Katchcom posed the question again, in search of a final answer. "You're positively sure?"

It was a mystery to him why Katchcom was so reluctant to believe him. He had no other answer but that which he had repeated numerous times already. "Yes, most holy one of Kopaz, I'm absolutely sure."

Without hesitation, Katchcom looked at Ancom. "Kill him!"

Ancom's massive arms were once more around Zidmar's neck. Ancom's arms squeezed like a giant vice, causing Zidmar's eyes to bulge, as if to pop out of his head. His voice was stifled by Ancom's arms pressing against his throat and vocal cords. Zidmar breathed his last breath and fell limp in Ancom's arms.

Looking completely disgusted, Katchcom snarled, "Take that swine out of my presence, *now!*"

It's funny in the course of destiny when evil events are taking place, how property is transferred from one person to another. Who knows why this happens? Does it matter? Maybe it does, and maybe it doesn't.

Ancom dragged Zidmar's body out of the Hall of the Goroms. Once outside, he hoisted the dead man upon his shoulders. With one arm holding the body firmly, Ancom felt something hard in Zidmar's belt pouch. He reached into the pouch and found the ring. He had no idea of its value or power.

He carried Zidmar's body to the riverbank. Ancom was clever and blew air into Zidmar's lungs, inflating them to capacity. He stuffed mud up Zidmar's nostrils and down his throat to force the air to remain in the dead man's lungs. He threw the body into the river. It floated like a boat and started its journey through the valley to the brink of Yellshome Falls, not more than five miles downriver.

Hmm, this is of great value, I am sure, thought Ancom as he clutched the emerald ring and the chain it was on. *I will tell no one that I have it!*

Zidmar's body plunged over the falls into Yellshome Canyon. Drifting on its final journey down the Yellshome River, not unlike its final ride down the River Styx to the Land of the Dead, Zidmar's body bobbed to-and-fro in the currents and eddies. Soon only unsuspecting travelers who were also making their way downriver would have a chance of seeing the body.

Ironically, Zidmar never knew the power of the emerald ring that was only briefly in his possession.

Ancom returned to the Hall of the Goroms and reported to the priests that all was well. But Katchcom had further plans for Ancom.

In the pale moonlight in the hall, Katchcom gave Ancom sharply defined orders. "Find Blackmar. Cut out his tongue. Take his knife—his gift from King Dalvin—and kill Tangmar with it. Leave the knife sticking in the body. Bring Blackmar and Tangmar's dead body to me. Then get the other goroms."

There was a slight pause, and then Katchcom continued. He snorted. "But before you go, bring me the girl."

For a moment, Ancom hesitated as if he wanted to say something. Before he could speak, however, Katchcom shouted, "Did you hear me?

Go! I want that girl here *now!*"

CHAPTER 6
She Stands Before Katchcom

B oth were on the hunt. One searched for lust and pleasure and the other for blood. It was funny how life's twists and turns brought everyone to the reality of death when all was said and done.

Blackmar's quest for pleasure was just one among many evils that were springing up in Kopaz, especially the clandestine conspiring of Gorom Katchcom. As far as Blackmar knew, his secret was buried deep in his mind for no one to see. His expectations of what he was planning for that unsuspecting, innocent girl excited him. It was sure to be a memorable evening. He was on the hunt, and the right spot would make these approaching moments of ecstasy the capstone of a balmy night on Kopaz. *She will bring me immeasurable pleasure this evening!*

Blackmar was oblivious to the fact that someone else was also on the hunt. He had no clue of the devious nature of the inner workings of the Quorum of High Priests, and that he, the hunter, might be the one who was being hunted.

It is an interesting question. One has to wonder if it ever crosses the mind of the hunter that he is the hunted? Yet even more interesting is this thought. Oh, how the web of evil deeds finds a way of tangling those who march in a direction, blinded by their own ambitions of self-serving gratifications. But in the end, all who carry out their conspiring acts of horror, inflicting terror on others, find the gates of hell wide open with no escape from the hand of destiny that reaches and drags them into the devil's inferno for the eternities.

Not only was Blackmar on the hunt but also so was Ancom. Walking out of the Hall of the Goroms, he was met with pitch-blackness. Although the moon had been shining earlier that evening, it was not now shedding its light on the courtyard of the goroms' massive white-marble domicile.

Ancom's search for Blackmar was underway. A few night birds were chirping as if to serenade with song any passerby who ventured near the trees they were planning to spend the night in. They stopped momentarily, as something was rustling in the bushes on the far side of the courtyard.

Then came a muffled utterance from within the rustling bushes. It sounded like a human trying to scream but who was being prevented from letting that scream escape in full force. On that breezeless evening, even the quietest of sounds carried like the wind, and for the discerning listener, it was not a chore to distinguish from where they were coming.

In addition to the muffled sounds in the bushes, there was what sounded like a light thumping coming from somewhere near the bushes.

Ancom started his journey across the courtyard of the goroms' residence. He made no noise. Once across the courtyard, he spotted the object that was making the barely audible thumping sounds. He walked cautiously toward it. Then he recognized that it was a person. A closer look identified it as Tangmar, a knife in his back. Knowing that he was in the last stages of dying, Ancom finished the job by plunging the same knife deep into Tangmar's heart. There could be no doubt now that no further dying twitches of the royal guardsman would come forth, as his soul had definitely left his body.

Blackmar heard the rustling. He suspected that Tangmar was still alive. He removed his hands from Jeannie's body. Cautiously, he stepped from behind the bush he had been using as his hiding place. He saw no one. He seized Jeannie's rope more tightly. Ten feet from him was Tangmar's motionless body on the ground. He never saw or heard the stealthy figure lurking in the shadows. With calculated movements, carefully, Blackmar approached Tangmar's body.

He had only taken two steps when the lunging figure from the shadows took him by surprise. Ancom's arms were around Blackmar's neck instantly. Anticipating trouble, Ancom knocked Jeannie to the ground and stepped on the leather rope cinched around her waist. With a knife in his right hand and his left arm around Blackmar's neck, he waited for the guardsman to make a sound.

It happened. Blackmar tried to scream but found a hand in his mouth, grabbing his tongue. Within a fraction of second, Ancom's knife had severed his victim's tongue. And to make sure that Blackmar did not bolt, Ancom shoved his knife into the guardsman's thighs. Blackmar dropped to the ground in pain and agony, unable to utter a sound other than gurgling, choking noises.

"Get up, you swine," shouted Ancom.

Pointing to his legs, only gargled utterances emerged from Blackmar. "Mooommoooo. Moouuuuuuuuuuu."

"Crawl then! Go to the goroms...*now!*"

It was one hundred yards from where they were to the main entrance to the hall. Blackmar started his journey across the grassy courtyard, crawling on his hands and knees.

Gorom Ancom needed to carry a dead body, as Blackmar slithered like a snake in tall grass.

It took Blackmar fifteen minutes to traverse the grassy courtyard, spitting out blood to keep from choking. His legs wrenched with pain with each movement of his body.

Once more, Jeannie entered the chamber of the goroms. She was once more hooded, and her hands were retied behind her. Katchcom told Ancom to take Blackmar and Tangmar's body to the dungeon beneath the Hall of the Goroms. He was left with Jeannie all to himself. She didn't utter a sound. Her intuition had told her that death had shown its face already this evening. Even though she had not seen the body of Tangmar, she was sure someone had breathed his last breath. Shaking, she tried to regain her composure but in vain. Her arms quivered. Her hood shook, caused by her uncontrollable motions.

Katchcom yanked her hood off. His face was inches from hers. She screamed. He belted her with his free hand. Unbearable pain instantly jolted through her face and head, and she clenched her teeth in an effort to contain her emotions. She didn't see what he was holding in his other hand. Then he threw a vessel of water on her.

As the mud fell away, he saw the face of a Neferzul. *My god, it is true*, he thought. Katchcom was aware that Ancom knew nothing about the sacred name of Neferzul or her connection to the gods. His face lit up, and his thoughts instantly went to the golden key. *She has it or knows where it is.* He stared intently at her. The core of his being was overtaken by excitement. *The god Zuron has been good to me—he dropped you into my lap. How wonderful.* He smiled at her. His mind raced on. *When I have the golden key, Viracocha will be unable to unlock GAMMAZEL!*

His smiling stare was dreadful. Jeannie blinked, wanting to look away from the hideous man that was violating her with his evil thoughts.

Strange how the mind takes over when a person is placed in an unpredictable living hell. Maybe that's the explanation for what happened next. At any rate, that's what happened to Jeannie. Her mind took off on a marathon chase.

She rolled her thoughts inward to escape. She went back in time to that fateful day when they made their last trip to the Boar's Tusk. Their last trip had been just after they found Eddie hanging on the back of Mochcom's woodshed. He was almost dead. On that day, just like now, there was no stopping the marathon mind chase. She couldn't stop the endless swirling of her thoughts. On that day in the desert, Jeannie had been torn between thoughts of horror and hope for the future. She raced from one thought to another. *I don't blame him—what's there to talk about? What's there to say to Danny and Tony? How do you talk about horror?* Her consciousness kept echoing the chorus of Johnny Bill's song "Danny's Sunday Morning Pain." It had been playing that day as they raced along the dirt road.

I can't hear the music playing, or see the stars of fame
'Cause I'm listening to the silence of a sleeping city's shame.
On a gloomy Sunday morning, on a sidewalk all alone
Makes a body wonder, why I ever left my home.

Just like she had on that day in the desert, that Monday morning in March of 1958, she tried to dispel thoughts of impending horror. She stiffened. And then her mind shifted gears. First one thought and then another drifted in and settled on her. She was back in the desert. *What are we doing? Are we tangled up in a horror episode? Are we going to end up like Eddie—or even worse, like Danny's mother? What is it that we're doing—searching for the Pearl of Great Value from the Kashome legend—eternal youth? Are we searching to find something that's beyond our reach?*

She remembered fiddling with the Sun Energy Transformer. Her soft white fingers had explored every detail of it sitting on her lap. In her mind, she relived every moment of that ride. She gripped a little gold knob and turned it slightly. A golden shutter with a small square hole in it moved. Watching it, her mind raced on. *What's the last part of that song? I know it says something about hope. What is it? Oh yeah—it says, "Through the darkest clouds of sadness, Lord, I'll find my fame tomorrow." Will we find the Pearl of Time today?*

She remembered that she had been the one to break the silence. "Poor Eddie. I can't believe what he went through. Can you imagine hanging like that for an hour? He went through hell! I hate that crazy man!"

It was different now. She didn't have Danny. She didn't have Tony. She was alone, the sole prisoner of the gorom who had replaced Mochcom as high priest. No one had to remind her how evil and dark Mochcom was. Her heart sank. *This monster has me. His reign of terror, inflicting death and horror on his victims…he is no different from Mochcom.* She pleaded, *Viracocha, please help me…please.*

If there was hope for her, she had not yet found it. Her only escape was the cavern of her mind. She filled her consciousness with the words of Johnny Bill's song "Danny's Sunday Morning Pain."

Yes! Hope will make my spirit soar;
Hope will drown the quiet echoes
Of a sleeping city's silent roar.
Oh yeah! In my search, I'll find that hope,
'Cause there's nothing short of madness

That will lift my soul from sorrow.
Through the darkest clouds of sadness;
Lord—I'll find my fame tomorrow.

Jolted by the sound of footsteps on the marble floor, the song in her mind stopped abruptly. Ancom had returned.

"Search her!" shouted Katchcom. His instructions were clear. He wanted the key.

Jeannie was freed of all restraints. She stood helpless. Her innate sense told her what was next. *Oh my god, they are going to strip me naked.* She started to cry.

The goroms laughed, enjoying what Jeannie was going through. Her mental torment and anguish were their pleasure.

"Where is it?" Katchcom screeched. Quite obviously, he was not happy. In fact, he was furious. Despite his outburst, he was careful not to reveal to Ancom what his interest was focused on.

Ancom's hands were all over Jeannie. As she had only a T-shirt and cutoffs on, the search did not take long.

Katchcom knew he must make no mention of a golden key, but his mind exploded. *She doesn't have the key. I have no means of communicating with her. How will I solve this? The key is needed to sit at the council table of the gods, and if Viracocha has no emissaries, he may lose the war. Zuron will kill me if I don't get the key. I will. Somehow, I will get it from her.*

On the floor next to her, her boots stood. They had been removed. Inspecting and shaking the foreign-looking footwear, Ancom's efforts were monitored not only by Katchcom but also by Jeannie, who watched with an undetected glance from the corner of her eye. Despite her great concern, nothing happened. Her golden key was safe for now.

Ancom kicked her boots, and they landed next to Jeannie. He motioned. She put her boots back on.

Katchcom grabbed Ancom's arm and shouted, "Take the girl to the prison beneath the Hall of the Goroms. Tell no one about the girl!"

Katchcom had one more instruction. "If you violate her, I will have your organs…if you know what I mean." Katchcom made his message to

Ancom indelible. "Do you know what a eunuch is? If you touch her, you will be made Gorom Eunuch in the middle of the royal courtyard at noon tomorrow!"

Jeannie was left in a small musty cell down three flights of steps in the bowels of the Hall of the Goroms, with two dead bodies for company. That was her plight…at least for now.

Ancom returned and walked into the Hall of the Goroms. Katchcom was so excited by his discovery, he did not hear Ancom come in. Katchcom was talking to himself as if to congratulate himself. "My god, I've found a Neferzul, and she is mine." Although he spoke barely above a whisper, his words did not go unnoticed by Ancom.

Ancom said nothing, but his mind was not empty. *What or who is Neferzul? Hmm, it must be the prisoner.*

Looking up, Katchcom was startled. Quickly, he asked, "So is the prisoner safely in the dungeon below?"

"Yes, my lord."

Suspecting Ancom had overheard him, Katchcom's focused sharply. *He heard me say "Neferzul." How do I get it out of him?*

"Good." He paused and glared into Ancom's eyes. "Did she talk at all?

That might have seen like a dumb question, as Jeannie clearly didn't speak the language of the goroms, but Katchcom asked it anyway. It was his way of fishing, and not for fish.

"No, my lord."

Continuing to glare at Ancom, Katchcom resumed his line of questioning. "I thought I heard her mumble something like 'Neferzul' or something like that. Did you hear her or anyone say that?"

"No, my lord. I heard nothing. She said nothing."

CHAPTER 7

A Journey to Judgment

Sometimes, even when a journey is short, to the traveler it seems like an eternity. Such was the case on Jeannie's first morning in Kopaz. It followed a night that had been to her a never-ending ordeal in that hellish dungeon beneath the Hall of the Goroms. Her journey started in that inky-black room as she lay wide-awake on a cold dirt floor. The day dragged on. Her activities were nonexistent, except for shivering jerks that seemed uncontrollable and spontaneous. If hell existed, she was immersed in it. There were rats and bugs of all sorts—spiders, hard-shelled black beetles, scorpions, and centipedes—as well as snakes and lizards that slithered to-and-fro as if to investigate the stranger who had entered their domain. Jeannie's position in the corner of the room was her only defense. Lying on the floor and grasping handfuls of dirt, she hurled her sole weapon into the dark. The creatures in the blackness of her prison were her targets, and it was in whatever direction from which came sounds of squeaking, clicking, or slithering that she directed her aim and unleashed handfuls of dirt at the unseen enemy. Jeannie tried to close her mind to the reality of the hell she was enduring.

The goroms set their case on the calendar of the royal court at a most convenient time. They chose to bring the prisoner before the royal family of Kopaz at early evening. There was a reason. With only candlelight flickering from the wall sconces and candelabras in the Grand Hall of the royal palace, it would be easier to keep their prisoner's identity concealed.

The sounds of footsteps coming down the hallway leading to the small room set Jeannie's mind in motion. *How much can I take? Death would be a welcome treat. Someone help me.* Although her journey as a prisoner started that bleak day in one dreadful dungeon, it would end in another.

The visitors walking down the corridor to enter her room were met by earlier visitors. The dank musty room had an attraction, especially for rats. Scurrying along the walls, they kept long tails close to the ground. Their entrance was the crack under the massive wooden door. It seemed they were at liberty to come and go as they pleased throughout the wee hours of the night. They came to see the new resident of this black hole, hidden from the people of Kopaz. Their beady eyes were sharply focused on Jeannie as they stealthily made their way back and forth along the wall furthest from her, squeaking and squealing. It was only the blasts of dirt coming from this new occupant that made them show their teeth and squeal as they darted for the sliver under the door.

As the footsteps got closer, Jeannie's heart pounded more rapidly. The door opened. Ten unexpected rats raced for safety around and among the feet of the black-robed priests.

"Grab her," shouted Ancom. "Make sure she is tied with a lash around her waist. Tie her hands with a thong, and put the ankle chains on her."

The sun had set. All of the hallways and rooms in the goroms' quarters were dark, with only candles shedding their golden glow on the surroundings. Jeannie was taken to the hall once more. Katchcom smiled as she entered the room. The entire Quorum of High Priests was present: Katchcom, Zercom, Ancom, Zidcom, Maycom, Dorcom, Shadcom, Nodcom, and Yellcom. "Take her out and throw mud on her," he shouted out orders to Shadcom and Nodcom. "She has to be filthy!"

This first phase of her journey ended as she was escorted through the massive double wooden doors to be met with a sea of darkness. The moon had not yet risen. Hobbling as best she could with the heavy ankle chains, she struggled to walk, with Nodcom pulling her by the leather rope tied around her waist. She had only walked a short distance, and then a healthy yank on the rope by Nodcom brought her to the ground, and he dragged her to a mud puddle. While Jeannie lay helpless on the ground, Shadcom and Nodcom scooped mud into buckets and tossed it onto Jeannie.

Her face was drawn with lines of fear. Underneath the mud, her captors could not see her horrified expression. *I have to be in a trance, or I will not make it,* she told herself. *I must fill my mind with song.* She chose "Jailhouse Rock," and visions of Elvis shaking his legs in rhythm, his long black hair flying over his eyes with each bob of his head, pulled her mind off the horrendous events that were happening to her.

In her trance, she didn't even comprehend that she was back on her feet and being led under the starlit heavens along a grassy pathway leading from the Hall of the Goroms to the Grand Hall of the royal palace. Her ankle chains allowed her only to shuffle like an old person on the last lap of a long life's journey.

Meanwhile, Katchcom was plotting. He and the other six goroms were strategizing. He ordered Goroms Maycom, Dorcom, Ancom, Zercom, Yellcom, and Zidcom to fetch Blackmar, their tongueless prisoner. Because of his leg wounds, Blackmar was unable to walk. Katchcom yelled, "Yellcom and Zidcom, you are the strongest of the goroms. Carry this traitor, Blackmar, to the Grand Hall."

The party of seven goroms, along with their prisoners, left the Hall of the Goroms and soon caught up with Shadcom, Nodcom, and Jeannie. Within five minutes, all were at the front entrance to the Grand Hall of the royal palace. Katchcom rapped the large iron ring on the massive wood door. The thundering knocks were answered. A square brass window covering was raised, exposing a six-inch-by-six-inch hole. A face appeared on the other side of the hole. "Who is there?" someone shouted.

"Open this door. We have business with the king," yelled Katchcom. A terrible rusty screech ripped through the dark night air as the two wooden doors opened.

Jeannie was escorted in, along with the prisoner Blackmar and the full Quorum of High Priests. At this point, Jeannie was hooded. Her hands were tied behind her. Her waist was tied with a leather rope. She could not see the grandeur of the Grand Hall, but later she would see white-marble walls decorated with a myriad of beautiful paintings of battles, heavenly scenes, portraits of past royalty, and glorious images of the journey of life with humans emerging from beautiful boats afloat on the fountain of life from the Mountain Zor, which formed the River Sloan. Each painting was framed with large, decorative, solid-gold frames that glistened in the yellow light coming from the flickering candelabras. The windows were covered with the most colorful tapestry drapes, woven with gold and silver strands into patterns and designs or scenes of historical events.

The green marble floor was inlaid with imperial jade, diamonds, rubies, sapphires, gold, and silver to form the illusion of stepping into another world. The Grand Hall was three hundred feet long by two hundred feet wide. At the far end, opposite the entryway, was an elevated stage, where four golden thrones were positioned.

When the prisoners and the goroms first entered the hall, it was empty except for the hunchback dwarf doorkeeper who let them in. Once inside, there was an urgency to get all parties in front of the thrones to await the entrance of the royal family.

Even though her captors had hobbled her so that she could go no faster than a shuffle, they were impatient. Nodcom was in front of her, pulling on the cord around her waist. Shadcom was at her rear and held in his hand a leather whip that he now struck Jeannie's back with, swinging his arm in a downward motion. Jeannie's thoughts of Elvis Presley fled her mind, and she screamed as she fell to the ground. Her back was on fire from the laceration from the whip.

Shadcom rolled the whip up and put the handle in a holder on his black robe. He bent over Jeannie, who was lying on her stomach, and put his hands in her armpits. He yanked her to her feet.

Jeannie's arms wrenched with pain. She screamed again, and a powerful blow to her mouth silenced her. Blood smeared on her face and mixed with the mud. She bit her jaws together so tightly that she was afraid they would break. With her teeth grinding, her sounds were no more. Excruciating pain shot through her body. Her arms were like limp silk stockings filled with wet rags. Whimpering, she pleaded for death. *Supreme God, let it end. Give me peace, and bring me home.*

CHAPTER 8
Judgment of a King

There could be no reason to wonder why this grandiose royal court made the Palace of Versailles look like a playhouse. After all, this was King Dalvin's domain, and it was not only the way he wanted it to be but also the way he demanded it must be. He was the Supreme Ruler of Kopaz, and he tolerated no questions from anyone about his authority or his expansive empire. He ruled from the most lavish of lavish palaces in the universe…well, no one could argue. No one would challenge how King Dalvin governed, how he lived, and how he demanded only the best of the best, no matter what—except a crafty gorom who had his eye on King Dalvin's kingdom.

In golden thrones on the elevated platform at the end of the room opposite the ornately carved wooden doors, there now sat King Dalvin and his son, Prince Jerzom.

If one were to compare Katchcom's gold throne to those at the front of the room, one would find a stark difference. Katchcom's was inlaid with hundreds of large diamonds, rubies, emeralds, sapphires, and pearls. These thrones, however, were inlaid with thousands of giant megacarat diamonds of all colors, rubies, emeralds sapphires, imperial jade, and pink, creamy-white, and black pearls, all in artistic designs. Each gem was perfectly placed in the solid-gold seats, which were ten feet tall. The four thrones were unique. Each was subtly different, and each was a one-of-a-kind work of art.

Action-packed scenes of battle and the beautiful bodies of both men and women dominated the enormous paintings that lined the white marble walls. Their beauty, created by artists of unparalleled talent, was matched by the solid gold frames that surrounded each painting.

For the lover of sculpture, one could never find a more prized collection of statues, not even if one went to the ends of all the lands on the planet of Kopaz. Marble, bronze, gold, silver, imperial jade, volcanic crystalline glass, and even solid emerald were but a few of the materials used by the creators of statues and figurines that stood as sentinels on the marble floor of the Grand Hall of the royal palace. They provided a welcome introduction to all who entered, except for Jeannie. She could see nothing.

Bound and tied, a hooded prisoner, Jeannie stood helpless in the middle of the room, not knowing where she was. Her captors had a tight grip on the leather rope cinched around her waist.

Katchcom stood before the king and Prince Jerzom. Both King Dalvin and Prince Jerzom wore royal robes with gold ribbon wrapped around the sleeves, making them shimmer and twinkle from flickering candle light. The kings robe was purple and had precious gems affixed in geometric formation on either side of the chest area. On the left chest area of the king's robe, above the gemstones, were military ribbons that signified triumph and bravery in battle. Jerzom's robe was dark blue. Under their robes, they wore leather skirts that were embroidered with brilliant colored ribbon. Katchcom was no more than ten feet in front of the stage-like platform on which sat the royal family's thrones.

Jeannie never saw the warm, glowing light provided by at least two hundred gold candelabras. The thousands of gemstones inlaid into the golden thrones provided a twinkling light show, which also went unseen by Jeannie.

On that warm summer's night, she shivered as she had on cold winter nights in CoalVille. They seemed so long ago now.

It was customary for all official meetings to be carried out in the language of the goroms. Who knew why? It must have been something the goroms had insisted on at least a century earlier in their efforts to eventually become a puppet government and rule Kopaz as they saw fit.

"Mighty king of Kopaz, it's late. Accept my apologies for this evening proceeding, but the urgency of this matter is so great that I and my fellow priests could not delay the matter further."

Briefly, the high priest paused, and then, looking directly into King Dalvin's eyes, he said, "Please, if I may, let me summarize this case and ask for permission to proceed."

"Please proceed." The king's remark set Katchcom's heart beating just a little faster.

Since prisoners were forbidden to lay eyes on royalty, she remained hooded.

Jerzom had no intention of getting involved with these proceedings or with the prisoner. He was more concerned with a bow that he had been working on and was focused on improving his hunting skills.

The case was clear. Katchcom presented the prisoner as an intruder from some foreign land. He had no idea where the land was, but he stressed that this prisoner posed a threat to the safety and security of Kopaz. Katchcom lied, telling the king and prince that the prisoner had broken into a peasant's home, raped a child, and then killed and stolen a pig, all the food that family had owned. Since the common language spoken was Kopazian, or the language of Kopaz, and not the royal language, Jeannie had no idea what she was charged with or what the sentence would be. In fact, she did not even know she was being tried and sentenced.

She stood, covered with mud. She was so far from the king and prince that they did not have a clue as to her age or identity.

In his summary, Katchcom asked to have sole custody of the prisoner once judgment had been passed by the royal family. Katchcom requested death as punishment.

He was clever. Katchcom motioned for Ancom to bring her forward so that she stood halfway between the center of the courtroom and the king and prince.

His plan was working, as the king shouted, "You bring a swine into my beautiful Grand Hall?"

Katchcom waited. He presented the appearance of remorse, but that was a put on.

"Get her out of here!" demanded the king. "You call me here at his late hour. How dare you then bring a filthy pig to stand before me!"

Yes! thought Katchcom.

As the king's glare intensified, and his words faded, Katchcom waited for silence to descend. It did.

"The reason for the late hour was not the prisoner. It was because of the evildoings of the royal guard!" said Katchcom in a guarded tone.

"What?" shouted King Dalvin.

For Katchcom, everything was so far, so good, and he felt an inner pleasure growing as he cleverly orchestrated the diversion about to commence.

He motioned again, this time for two of his goroms, Maycom and Dorcom, to retrieve the prisoners who were standing outside. They exited the Grand Hall.

Within moments, four goroms reentered—Goroms Dorcom, Ancom, Yellcom, and Maycom. The dead body of the royal guardsman Tangmar was clearly evident, as it was being carried like a sack of potatoes on the right shoulder of Ancom.

Unable to walk on his own because of wounds in his legs, the royal guardsman Blackmar was hooded and was dragged across the floor by Goroms Dorcom and Yellcom.

"*How dare you, you traitorous dog!*" yelled King Dalvin.

Instantly, the high priest, Gorom Katchcom, raised his hands high in the air, the sleeves of his black robe falling down his arms. Waving like a flag in the wind, he shouted, "I have proof." He pointed to the hooded prisoner and said, "Your royal guardsman Blackmar is the thief of royal treasure!"

What Gorom Katchcom was holding in his hand high in the air brought a deathly silence to the courtroom.

Staring at the object in Katchcom's hand, King Dalvin nodded his head. Even Jerzom was now not thinking of his bow and hunting. His attention focused on the proceedings at hand.

"Please proceed, Gorom!" snapped Dalvin.

The procession of goroms and royal guardsmen made their way through the maze of statues, tables, and marble benches, and found places where Katchcom was standing.

Nodding to Goroms Zercom and Zidcom, who were standing guard over Jeannie, they proceeded to move her to where the rest had congregated.

Jeannie was gagged, so her whimpers and soft cries come across as grunts and moanings.

"*Quiet!*" yelled Dalvin.

Words were not required. The hand over Jeannie's gagged mouth as well as the suffocating hood left her starved for air. Her nose, barely able to take in air, was a blessing, as her hot breath on the gorom's fingers pressing the hood tightly against her mouth caused him to relax and withdraw slowly.

Another blessing—the focus was not on Jeannie but Blackmar and Tangmar.

At first, Katchcom's words were soft. "The captain of the royal guard has betrayed you, my king."

But as Katchcom continued his tale of concocted lies, his voice elevated. To Jeannie, who couldn't comprehend a morsel of the foreign language, it sounded like a loud mixture of words scrambled with growling howls.

Katchcom rolled on, having both the king's and the prince's undivided attention. "I ordered my goroms—Maycom, Dorcom, Ancom, Zercom, Yellcom, and Zidcom—to get the prisoner. They went to the royal guards' quarters and entered. What they found was vile and evil. Blackmar, Zidmar, and Tangmar were in possession of the queen's most prized ruby necklace."

The queen's jewels had been stolen on a clandestine operation that Katchcom had ordered a few days earlier. A strange twist of fate had intervened, and the plotting and scheming of the coup by Head High Priest Katchcom to overthrow the royal family of Kopaz had taken a turn for the better—the capture of an intruder. Having Jeannie brought before the king was perfect. It was like she had conveniently fallen into Katchcom's hands, so it was a perfect time to display stolen royal jewels—supposedly stolen by none other than King Dalvin's royal guardsmen Blackmar, Zidmar and Tangmar.

He waved it in the air once more. "They were ordered to give it to the priests, but before my goroms could reach them, Blackmar drew his knife and plunged it into Zidmar. It was not a fatal blow, as Zidmar managed to get to his feet and run outside. Goroms Nodcom and Yellcom followed Zidmar. He was bleeding badly and was growing faint. Zidmar staggered to the river's edge and, unable to steady himself, plunged into the Yellshome River's swift current and was swept away. Nodcom and Yellcom tried to reach him, but all was in vain. Zidmar's body had floated out of sight."

He took a deep breath. Jeannie shook, but no one paid attention or cared. Katchcom's story was center stage, not Jeannie.

"Meanwhile, Goroms Maycom, Dorcom, Zercom, and Zidcom raced toward Blackmar, but it was too late. He had already used his knife again. This time the blow was fatal, and the body of Tangmar lay next to his killer, Blackmar."

Katchcom stopped speaking. He pivoted and walked to Ancom's side. "Throw the body on the floor," he commanded.

Following each facet of the unfolding drama, the king's eyes locked on the knife sticking out of Tangmar's back.

"Do you see, my king? The knife? Does it look familiar?" He let his words trail off as his questions hung in the air.

Katchcom looked squarely into the face of King Dalvin so as not to miss any reaction. A slow nod gave him the go-ahead. King Dalvin's eyes, however, continued to stare at the knife he had once given to Blackmar in a public ceremony for his loyal service to the royal family.

"My goroms asked for a confession, but Blackmar refused, saying it was Zidmar and Tangmar who had committed the sin of stealing the queen's necklace. The problem was that Blackmar was not only holding the queen's necklace but on his fingers were these rings."

Walking to the feet of King Dalvin, Katchcom held out his palms and displayed the royal jewels of Neferapondes. Very gently, he placed them on a silk pillow that had been under his arm, and then he laid the pillow at the feet of the king.

"You know the punishment for lying. Blackmar's tongue is no longer in his mouth."

As his last word—mouth—faded, silence engulfed the royal courtroom.

Katchcom moved between the two prisoners. Jeannie was slightly in front of him, blocking the king's view of the high priest. It was intentional, as he wanted the focus to be on the hooded stranger who had invaded their land.

"We know not who this intruder is. She was found at the brink of Yellshome Falls by the royal guard." His voice boomed out his last utterances at the proceedings. "*She is a spy! She came with another, who was killed and thrown over the great falls! Their terrorist plans to kill the younger members of the royal family are evil!*"

He stopped. He was going to finish with a statement that he, and he alone, had discovered the evil plot, and because of that discovery, the royal family was safe. Katchcom hoped for praise and accolades for his service, but that did not take place. Something else occurred.

Shaking his head wildly, Blackmar relentlessly tried to communicate. His bloody mouth could only utter slobbering grunts. He failed to make any sense. All eyes turned to him.

At that instant, Blackmar squirmed and broke his hands free. They had been tied behind them.

Maybe it was coincidence. Maybe it was fate. Maybe it was the fact that Blackmar was tongueless. Maybe it was the fact that Blackmar was unable to stand on his own. Who knows? For whatever reason, there was an additional twist of fate. The fact that Jeannie was directly in front of Blackmar, blocking the direct line of sight between the king and Blackmar, was a blessing for Gorom Katchcom.

In the commotion, Blackmar, when he freed his hands, tried to pull on a gold chain that was in his belt pouch. That this trial was being held at night and in a dimly lit hall paid off. Katchcom was the only person in the room who noticed the object that Blackmar was trying to retrieve.

Before Blackmar could manage to yank the chain from its hiding place, Katchcom grabbed Blackmar's left hand, twisted it, and prevented him from pulling it out farther.

On the opposite side of Blackmar, his right side, Maycom held the prisoner upright, and Dorcom stood by. As the goroms were restraining

Blackmar's right arm, Katchcom was swift. Without anyone noticing, he quickly stuffed the end of the gold chain back into Blackmar's belt pouch.

Katchcom smiled as he thought, *They saw nothing! Yet I did, and this swine has something of value!*

Twisting Blackmar's arm behind him, Katchcom showed no mercy in yanking the guardsman's arm up his back to the point of breaking it. Blackmar's body wrenched with pain. Not only were his legs useless but now his left arm was also. He was speechless for lack of a tongue and had no option except to bite his teeth around the bleeding stump that was on the verge of gagging him.

Dorcom grabbed the limp arm from Katchcom and held it as he swung Blackmar's right arm to a point where he could bind the man's wrists together with a leather strap. His mission was accomplished. Blackmar's arms were so securely tied no amount of struggling could loosen them.

The disgusting show, not unlike a courtroom of jesters performing a clown act, prompted the king to yell, "*Out…now!*"

Just in case, Katchcom waited for only a moment and then shouted, "Is the penalty *death* for the traitorous dog, Blackmar?" He was not leaving anything to chance, especially the king's final judgment.

"*Yes…go!*"

Katchcom had one more vital point to make. He yelled, "When the goroms convene the court and have tried the intruder, we shall bring the prisoner back for your final judgment."

King Dalvin bellowed louder, "*Yes, I said already! Go!*"

It was like a perfect storm, destroying all that had incurred its wrath. Katchcom's outcome was realized. He now had time to school Jeannie so that she could learn enough of their language to tell him where the golden key was. Even more importantly, Katchcom had control of those who knew her identity.

Not all is finished tonight, but soon it will be, thought Katchcom as he walked across the courtyard, the dew-laden grass brushing across his toes sticking out of his sandals.

On that black night, Katchcom, Jeannie, Blackmar, and Ancom were the only ones to enter the Hall of the Goroms. Katchcom, Jeannie, and

Ancom walked, Ancom dragging Blackmar. Most of the candles had burned out. It was almost dark.

It had been planned that way. Prior to entering the Hall of the Goroms, the other goroms had been ordered to go their rooms in the back of the building.

Katchcom ordered Ancom to take Jeannie to the dungeon under the Great Pyramid, leaving Katchcom and Blackmar alone in the Hall of the Goroms.

Katchcom walked to Blackmar and removed his hood. Blackmar's eyes were filled with terror as he watched Katchcom take his knife from its scabbard. He lifted the knife, and Katchcom slit Blackmar's throat.

Blackmar fell to the marble floor. Katchcom reached into Blackmar's pouch and found an amazing thing. It was Danny's golden watch. Well aware of what it was, Katchcom rolled his fingers over it. *This is needed to give me eternal youth.*

For now, Jeannie was a pawn. She had no idea that Katchcom was busy plotting his coup to overthrow the royal family. At this point, he had Jeannie in his custody and would figure out how to use her to reach his ultimate goal—to topple the government of Kopaz and become Zuron's key disciple.

Katchcom smiled as he whispered, "What a wonderful surprise! Gifts from heaven keep falling into my hands. Soon I will travel the Highway of Time and no longer grow old."

CHAPTER 9

His Beast Yellzor

Abody floating in the river had caught on something. The river's current next to a large boulder flipped the body over. Danny was unaware of the dead person.

Two days in the depths of the canyon with little or no food had left Danny weak. He had fallen asleep on the bank of the Yellshome River, thirty miles downstream from the base of the falls. It had been more than twelve hours since Danny had fallen asleep. He was still restless as he awoke. He threw his arm over his head. Although he was exhausted, he had not lost all awareness. His mind raced as his hand landed on something soft and warm. *What the hell is it?* His instinct to freeze and do nothing was not an option as he could only imagine a wild animal ready to tear out his throat. Yanking his head up and turning quickly, he saw it—a giant yellow beast was lying next to him. Danny jumped to his feet, trying to discern if his mind was playing tricks on him. The beast growled. Danny flinched. "My god, that thing is real!" shouted Danny at the snarling beast.

But Danny wasn't the only one there. "He's Yellzor." The voice came from the river's edge. Danny spun around only to focus his eyes on the little man that he thought he had seen while falling over the waterfall. "Who are you?" yelled Danny.

"Quill." Their eyes locked for a moment. Then Quill said softly, "I am your private teacher—your mentor and tutor. I've been sent by Viracocha to teach you the ways of the gods."

The truth hit him for the first time like a ton of bricks. The way Danny felt, the little dwarf could have been pounding away on his head with a baseball bat. Gripping the reality of being a god was almost more than Danny could comprehend. But now, reality hit him—he was indeed a god. There could be no more denying this most puzzling fact, a truth he had been struggling with his entire life.

"Yellzor," said Quill as he pointed to the giant yellow wolf with emerald green eyes, "is your beast! He is your protector and will be constantly at your side."

The morning sun glistened on the river's surface like a giant mirror behind the little man. It was a mesmerizing force that grabbed Danny's consciousness. The reality of being a god overpowered his mind and drifting into the crevasses of his inner soul was not hard for Danny. The puzzle started to fall into place. He had always tucked away information. He never knew when he would need it. This was one of those occasions. Danny left his contemplation of Quill and ventured deeper into his mind. He dug into something that Quill had just said that sparked his curiosity, and so to the past he went.

Where have I heard the name Yellzor? He did not need to dwell long on that thought. *Yeah, it was in the Scarlet Desert, and Jeannie had mentioned something about her people's legend and the Boar's Tusk. Kashom told his people that his son Yellow Moon no longer had a wild beast within him. He had redeemed himself, and his spirit had befriended the wolf, Yellzor, who reminds us in the stillness of the night when he howls to the moon that the Boar's Tusk stands forever for truth and honor.*

What Danny didn't know was the rest of the story. Jeannie had not shared with Danny everything her mother had taught her. As part of his purgatory, Viracocha told Kashom that if he were to regain his royal status, he must aid TRPOV and TRPON in the fulfillment of their missions and declare to them who they were.

And Jeannie had never had a chance to tell Danny what had happened that fateful day at the Boar's Tusk. Jeannie was no longer listening to Danny and Tony's private conversation. Her mind was no longer on KateLynn's potential pregnancy. She was staring at the last page of Kashom's journal. There it was. Her mind not stopping, her eyes raced on, looking at each Spanish word as she read them to herself, translating as she went:

The royal prince of Viracocha is TRPOV and the royal princess of Neferdor is TRPON. TRPOV and TRPON must fulfill the following conditions:

(1)   They must kill all of the goroms in Kopaz and throw their bodies not yet ashes into the fiery depths of Vulcan—the gateway to hell guarded by CrystalFlame—so their eternity is destined to be everlasting embers in the belly of the outer reaches of darkness.

(2)   They must kill Mochcom and wrap his ashes in the Ancient Shroud of Goroms and throw them into the fiery depths of Vulcan so his eternity is destined to be everlasting anguish in the belly of the outer reaches of darkness.

Then, and only then, shall TRPOV and TRPON sit on thrones of pure gold alongside the gods at their council table of red worox stone and control the gift of eternal youth for all humans throughout the universe.

Beware that the bodies of the goroms of Kopaz remain not outside the gateway to hell past the evening of the high moon, for if they do, all is lost.

And to the TRPOV, his beast, Yellzor, shall devour imposters and throw them into the fiery mouth of CrystalFlame.

Hit with that affirmation, Jeannie was speechless.

Even though she had not fully comprehended the reference to *his beast Yellzor*, there could be no hiding the emotion that surged through Jeannie's body. Her mind erupted with the most unbelievable revelation. *My God! My God! Danny and I are destined to be part of the family of the gods! He's the royal prince of Viracocha, and I'm the royal princess of Neferdor, TRPOV and TRPON.*

She continued translating silently as she read to herself the last entry of Kashom's golden journal. *To the Chosen One: May the gods speed your journey as you embark on your new conquest with the royal prince of Viracocha. I have done all I can to open the Highway of Time. I ask you, as the last Neferzul, to give my regards to my parents when you stand before them in the royal court of Kopaz. Tell my mother, the royal queen of Kopaz, there is still a red ribbon tied around my heart. She will know what that means.*

Danny never knew why a tear spilled from her eye as great joy overtook her heart. Danny didn't even recall that, out of the clear blue, she had turned to him and asked, "What now?" Maybe when she made that comment, she had been about to tell Danny the message in Kashom's journal. Who knows? Events took over that precluded her from sharing with Danny who Yellzor was.

On that fateful day, Danny had been caught by surprise. First came Tony's revelation of KateLynn's potential pregnancy, and that had given their situation a new dynamic, and now Jeannie was asking him, "What now?" with a grin on her face.

Danny's only comeback had been another question. "What's going on?"

Tony's eyes were as large as two full moons. "I will tell you guys what's going on!" he screamed as loudly as he could. *"There's a vehicle racing up the dirt road to the Boar's Tusk!"*

And so it was, on that spring day of March in 1958, at the Boar's Tusk, Mochcom arrived, and chaos took over.

They're all gone, he thought. *Will I ever see Jeannie again? Or my mom, or my best friend, Tony?*

"Are you in a fog?" shouted the little man as he watched Danny. "You're acting like you are drugged. What exactly is your problem?"

Danny lifted his head and looked upward, still daydreaming. For whatever reason, his stargazing demeanor as if he were in a trance lingered. Then his eye caught sight of something strange. It was a body. The eddies in the small estuary cut into the bank of the river had flipped the body onto its back. The sun was brightly shining on the dead man's face. Danny's daydreaming came to a screeching halt. *That is one of those bastards who took my ring!*

He was about to dart for the water's edge but was interrupted by a booming voice coming from the little man. *"Don't bother. It's not there!"*

Danny stopped dead in his tracks. He rolled his head from the river to the dwarf. He almost said something but only stared. His face drew into lines that suggested he was puzzled by Quill's words.

As was fully evident in Quill's expression, he was disgusted by Danny's lack of attention. An onslaught of questions shot from Quill's mouth. "Where are you? Do you not understand the obvious? Are you in a fog? What is your problem?"

Danny was speechless. He just stared, but Quill came to the point. "You have the note…*don't you?*" Quill asked in a forceful voice.

It hit him. "Oh my God!" shouted Danny. "Yeah, the note. I have it and…and…" He stopped for a second. "Quill, I'm slow. But in the end I get it! Holy shit, it is all falling into place," yelled Danny.

Quill wanted to lash out and reprimand Danny for his foul language, but he held his tongue. He smiled, a few thoughts streaming through his mind. *I think he understands what is happening. That is good.*

"No problem, Danny," replied Quill. "I knew it all along. That body in the river doesn't have your ring. You would have wasted your energy looking for it."

Well, thought Danny, *I guess I know who left the note at the base of Yellshome Falls, and I guess he knows a hell of lot more than I do.* Danny gave Quill a smile in return. "Quill, I guess I'm in good hands. I've got you as my private teacher…ah…um, I mean my private tutor. And here's my new friend, my big yellow dog!"

"Danny!" said Quill.

With a smirk on his face, Danny chuckled. "Yes!"

"He's not a dog. Nope. He's a giant yellow wolf…not to be messed with!" said Quill.

And so it was—within the walls of the yellow canyon carved by the Yellshome River—the young god in training met his new friends.

CHAPTER 10
Dungeon in a Pyramid

He knew what he wanted. It was clear in his mind. Katchcom had used the dungeon to accomplish his goals in the past, so why stop now?

His earlier command to Ancom—to take Jeannie to the dungeon—was being carried out.

The night moved on.

Keeping all information from others who might profit from what Katchcom knew was nothing new to him. His modus operandi was no different from that of other evil men since the dawning of time. He wanted something. The significance of the golden watch was not lost on him. He also knew that the golden key was equally as important. He wanted both. He had one but not the other.

It's funny how puzzles linger on when they are not solved. Such was the case with Gorom Katchcom. He had a lingering unsolved puzzle. Before Gorom Mochcom killed Princess Aerapondes and escaped to the Scarlet Desert, he revealed to Katchcom that there was a traitor in the highest inner circle of Viracocha's trusted gods. That god, and Mochcom did not even know his name, was passing vital information to the dark god Zuron, who was at war with Viracocha. And as it turned out, Mochcom had been the conduit for the vital information. Katchcom questioned Mochcom for details, but Mochcom was circumspect and revealed nothing.

Katchcom mused. *The golden watch, the golden key, the answer to a riddle, and how they all fit together—that will solve the mystery that will reveal the two sacred words that Zuron needs to be the supreme god. Hmm. She's got it. I'll find it.* His mind lit up with a burning desire to hasten the hunt.

As he chuckled, his smile grew larger. It had happened many times before. Sooner or later, prisoners talked. The torture of being hidden away in the darkest of solitary holes with no escape had its ways of revealing hidden secrets.

Thousands of years ago, when the original building plans were being drawn up for the royal site, it was because of an oversight on the part of that first group of goroms that the architect made a big mistake. Poor planning by that first group of evil men had been a problem for centuries. From their vantage point at the Hall of the Goroms, they could not monitor activities at the only doorway leading to the dungeon in the Great Pyramid.

Laying out the building sites for the Great Pyramid, the royal palace, and the Hall of the Goroms seemed straightforward. Place the Hall of the Goroms behind the royal palace and at a sufficient distance from it so that their activities could not easily be monitored by the royal family. In essence, they would be out of sight and out of mind of the royals.

The Great Pyramid was one hundred yards east of the Hall of the Goroms. The entryway into the pyramid faced the east. The morning sun lit the entire east-facing side of the pyramid. The royal palace was three hundred yards west of the pyramid and three hundred yards to the south. The Hall of the Goroms was two hundred yards directly to the north of the royal palace.

Katchcom sat on the marble bench next to the east windows. For a while, he could watch Ancom taking Jeannie to the Great Pyramid. Then they rounded the southwest corner, and Katchcom lost sight of them. He was sure that Ancom would carry out his orders and take Jeannie to the dungeon deep in the center of the pyramid. He could not see that happen, so he could only have faith that it did. As they were no longer visible, Katchcom walked to his couch and stretched out.

After they entered the Great Pyramid, Jeannie was led through a long, dark hallway. Centuries of dampness had left the dimly lit hallway reeking from the stench of mold and must.

On the occasions when the wall candles in the hallway were lit, the flickering flames provided only an eerie yellow glow that resembled a dancing light in a Halloween horror house. That was not the case that night. There were only black, dank walls, devoid of any yellow glow.

The dungeon at the end of the hallway was secured by a massive wooden door. The centuries-old iron hinges squeaked and squealed horribly whenever the door was opened to the dark, black dungeon or closed to hide the room of horror.

The prison cell in the dungeon beneath the Hall of the Goroms paled in comparison to the deathly solitude that was the ultimate solitary confinement in the dungeon of the pyramid.

It did not take long. The door swung closed with its squealing sounds of entrapment, leaving Jeannie alone in a pitch-black hole that had been a place of death for eons. As the crashing *boooom* faded into the stillness, she searched for anything…anything that would give her hope.

Time stretched on. The inky blackness closed in. She could see nothing. The hours drifted by. One hour turned into five and then ten. Time mattered not to Jeannie. Her sense of reality was gone. Her sense of time was gone. Her ability to make sense of anything was gone.

It's something that many of us experience when circumstances change and suddenly we are in an unthinkable situation. It could be in the night as you search for something in the darkness. You might feel as if the walls were closing in with a suffocating sensation. The demons come out of the woodwork and smash your ability to cope with what is happening. You descend into a state of hopelessness.

That was what happened to Jeannie.

Her only escape was into the cavern of her mind. She tried to run away and hide with the words of Johnny Bill's song "Danny's Sunday Morning Pain."

Yes! Hope will make my spirit soar;
Hope will drown the quiet echoes
Of a sleeping city's silent roar.

Oh yeah! In my search, I'll find that hope,
'Cause there's nothing short of madness
That will lift my soul from sorrow.
Through the darkest clouds of sadness;
Lord—I'll find my fame tomorrow.

There was no hiding spot in a dungeon of death that had been the last residence of countless poor souls over the centuries. Their only crime had been to be caught by a band of evil men. The helpless victims, their screams of agony, pains of death, and bloodied corpses were hidden from all curious onlookers.

There was no escape for Jeannie. Even her mind could not find a safe haven in a hidden corner.

This most dastardly place of concealment welcomed each new resident with the creatures of the night. Soon, they would search for the one who had just checked in. Soon, Jeannie would make their acquaintance, like it or not.

Sobbing softly, she rocked back and forth. Sitting on the damp dirt, her arms wrapped around her legs, she could not stop the cloud of depression from descending on her. The stark reality of the black abyss in which she was immersed was crushing her more heavily than if the entire weight the world were resting upon her.

There was no hope left. It was all gone now. She was alone. Her weeping grew louder as her mind rushed on, hoping for a miracle that was as fleeting as a starry night she could not see. Silently she mouthed the words that drifted into her mind:

In the stillness of the night, I hear him out there call to me;
His faint voice is like the sadness of a weeping willow tree.
I know the sun is setting in a faraway land of grace.
I fear my love is searching but can't find my hiding place.
Starry, starry night, I hope your lights will point the way,
And bring him back to help me at the ending of this day.
In the darkness of this night, my heart is full of pain.

My love, I hear him call my name—

Jolted by sharp sounds—*sssccccrraattaa…sccreeeeeeeetch*—coming from the dank corners of her prison, the song in her mind stopped abruptly.

CHAPTER 11

A Brother and Sister Talk

Finally, the morning sun peeked over the horizon. The royal palace was nestled in the valley between the Androzes and Vulcan Mountains. The Yellshome River wound its way through the valley. It passed by the eastern boundary and made its way to follow the foothills of the Androzes. Then it plunged over a thousand-foot cliff, forming the mighty Yellshome Falls. Over the centuries, the Yellshome River had carved out Yellshome Canyon, which extended from the base of the falls for a hundred miles. The sun rose over the Androzes Mountains and set behind the Vulcan Mountains.

Morning moved on. The sun was headed for its high point in the sky. Watching the lingering clouds drifting silently across a blue sky, Jerzom was bored. He had been up for over three hours.

He decided to spend some time with his sister. Who knows why? It just happened. She was Merapondes, Aerapondes's identical twin. In the realm of Kopazian time, it had been four years since Aerapondes had been murdered. However, in the realm of the god's time—for Kashome in the Scarlet Desert—it was thousands of years since his sister was murdered. The story was that her older brother, Kashom, killed Aerapondes and then forced the head high priest Mochcom to escape using the gifts from the gods. The mysteries of Aerapondes' death had never been solved.

Jerzom was not aware that his sister was curious about the prisoner, although the news that an intruder had invaded Kopaz had quickly spread to all corners of every village. What Katchcom had said the day Jeannie was brought before the king and Jerzom was the main topic of gossip throughout all the land. Some speculated that the prisoner was an intruder from some foreign land. Many heard from the royal guards who found them that there were two young marauding invaders, that one had been tossed over Yellshome Falls and the other brought before the royal family for sentencing. No one had any idea of where they were from, but for sure, the intruders were a threat.

All sorts of stories were swirling around. The royal guards had their own. They claimed to have fought with a very strong warrior—the one they killed. The fight took place on the banks of the Yellshome River, just before the river went over the falls. The rumor was that the two intruders had broken into a peasant's home and then killed and stolen a pig, which was the only food that family had. No one knew what family. And what was puzzling to Merapondes was how two—only two—young people could cause such a commotion. Even more curious to Merapondes was that few if any peasants lived near the falls, so whose house had they broken into?

Jerzom was unaware of his sister's concerns. He had meandered down the granite hallway leading out of his room. The paintings, golden candelabras, marble statues, and silver dishes sitting on white marble tables all along the way were of little concern to him. He rounded the corner and entered the first door on the right-hand side.

His sister was sitting at her writing desk. "Oh! Hi, Jerzom. What brings you here?" She looked up as she heard his footsteps behind her.

"You don't have to get up," he said as he walked to the marble bench beneath the open window. "I just wanted to come and talk...you know, small talk."

"Hmm...since when was one ever to consider your words small talk?" she asked, giggling.

With the sun shining through the window behind him, the bright light obscured his face when she turned to face him directly. He saw her squinting and moved to the couch across from her desk.

Now the two were across from each other—she sitting on the desk chair and he on the white leather couch.

Maybe it was mental telepathy. Maybe not. Who knows? For whatever reason, she started telling him what was on her mind. "My royal brother, I've been thinking about the young girl held prisoner by the goroms."

"That's precisely why I've come to talk to you, Merapondes!" was his unexpected reply.

No one knew where the information about the intruders came from. Some said the goroms knew the facts, but for Merapondes, something was not adding up. With her eyes locked on his, she said, "The most puzzling aspect about this whole tangled web of gossip is that no one has any real information about the prisoner. And the royal guard never mentioned anything about killing a peasant family's pig!"

Merapondes stopped. Jerzom said nothing. She went on. "The rumor that she is a young girl came from the royal guardsman Blackmar. He was the one who captured her."

Her jaw dropped as she realized what she had said. Her expression changed from puzzlement to concern. She said, "He's missing, you know. No one knows his whereabouts. I hate Blackmar and think he is a wretched, lustful old man, but...missing?"

"I think he's dead," said Jerzom. "He was brought before our father on charges of murder and stealing our mother's royal jewels." He paused.

"Dead...murder...stealing...Mom's jewels?" she muttered.

"Yes!" Jerzom responded softly. "And furthermore, Blackmar apparently lied about it, so his tongue was cut out and his legs stabbed so he could no longer walk."

"Odd. Jerzom, don't you find all of this *odd?*" she questioned.

Shaking his head, Jerzom said nothing.

She ventured on as if she were a trial lawyer searching for answers. "Why would a young girl cause so much uproar that the goroms would concoct such a wild story about a guardsman stealing our mother's jewels? I don't buy it."

He was listening but had a question. "Why? What is wrong with the evidence? Dad's knife was in the back of Guardsman Zidmar, and the royal jewels were in the possession of Blackmar?"

"Aha! For a smart boy, you missed the most important fact!" she snapped back. "You see, my royal brother, the royal jewels were not in the possession of the royal guardsman Blackmar. They were in Gorom Katchcom's hands! And furthermore, the royal knife that Dad gave to Blackmar that was sticking out of Zidmar's back is a joke!" she said.

"A joke? What joke?" was his reply.

"A man without a tongue. His legs severely slashed so he can't walk, and you think he committed the crime? *Yeah*, it's a *joke!* I would think again," she shot back. "For the countless crimes that Blackmar has inflicted on innocent little girls, he deserves what he got, but…"

And without waiting for her brother's interjection, Merapondes rushed on. "My beloved sister, Aerapondes, was murdered by the goroms…not by Kashom!"

Now with tears spilling from her eyes, she told a story she had held within her bosom since Aerapondes was brutally murdered. "The day before Aerapondes was killed, she told me that she had walked just outside the courtyard—near the banks of the Yellshome. She was picking flowers. Mochcom had been stalking her, and she caught him. He wanted to know if she still had her golden key. She asked, 'Why?' and he laughed, saying, 'If you entrust it to me, I'll make you the most important girl in the universe!'"

Jerzom's mind went wild. *My god…could it be true?*

She continued. "Aerapondes turned and ran. She was only twenty feet from the edge of the forest. But as she was running, Mochcom screamed loudly, 'If you tell a soul, your soul will board the boat on the River Styx!' And fortunately, in moments, she was in the courtyard with others. She never looked back."

"What do we do?" Jerzom asked in a sullen voice.

"We go to the Great Pyramid to see for ourselves who that prisoner is."

CHAPTER 12
A Problem for the Goroms

Most often, those involved in clandestine operations say little to anyone. Not all, however, have the wisdom to keep their mouths shut and their actions under control. With damage control foremost on his mind, Gorom Katchcom was oblivious to a problem brewing.

Maybe it was quite by accident that Merapondes convinced Jerzom to go with her to see the prisoner in person.

It was past lunchtime when Merapondes and Jerzom set out on their mission. Their conversation was nonexistent as they walked briskly from the royal palace on the diagonal pathway across the courtyard to the Great Pyramid. However, their walk did not go unnoticed.

As they rounded the southwest corner, Katchcom lost sight of Merapondes and Jerzom as they walked closely to the base of the east wall of the Great Pyramid. But Katchcom wasn't even the only one who spotted them.

It never occurred to them that they'd be stopped, and yet he was there. Walking fifty yards, half the length of the pyramid, Gorom Dorcom was a lone guard, sitting just outside the giant doorway leading into the pyramid.

Dorcom watched the royal youth approaching. His position behind a large dense manoa bush kept him out of their sight.

"What brings you here?" he asked, still hidden by the bush, as Jerzom and Merapondes came closer.

Startled, Jerzom whirled to face the direction the voice came from. "Who are you?" he yelled.

The gorom stepped from his hiding place. He walked to the doorway leading into the Great Pyramid.

"Step aside," shouted Jerzom. Saying nothing more, Jerzom walked to the pile of torches lying next to the entrance. He picked up two and lit them with the flame from the already smoldering firepot just to the left of the doorway. It remained constantly burning for that purpose.

Holding their torches, Jerzom and Merapondes ignored Gorom Dorcom and walked down the dank hallway leading to the dungeon.

The footsteps behind them made it clear that Gorom Dorcom was following them.

Why are they here? he wondered. *Members of the royal family have never entered this place of death!*

Making sure to not get too close, Gorom Dorcom paced his stride. *Highly unusual…highly unusual.* The thought kept racing through his mind like a broken record on a turntable unable to stop.

It would seem odd, if by chance a casual observer could have seen the procession. *Why do those in front look back every so often?* they might wonder. *Why is one hesitating as if stalking its prey?*

Even though there were scattered candles on the walls of the hallway, they were not burning. The only source of light was from their torches— two held by members of the royal family and one some distance behind, held by a high priest.

Onward they went.

They stopped. The massive wooden door was bolted shut from the outside.

Grabbing the iron ring on the bolt, Jerzom pulled on it. Its years in a damp, cold tunnel of death had left it rusted, and with each movement, it sounded off. *Ssqquuuuueeellll!*

Jumping to her feet, Jeannie screamed. The walls had closed in on her, and terror was her first instinctive reaction to the horrific sounds coming from the door.

The old wooden door was being pulled open. Now it was not the lock that was sounding off but the iron hinges under the heavy weight of a door. *Eeeeerrreerrrrcchhhh! Eeerrrreeerreeecccccchhhh!* It could have been the devil calling his next victim for all Jeannie knew.

The blinding light from the torches cut through the air and obscured the faces of those standing in the doorway.

The light didn't blind Jerzom or Merapondes. It shed its radiant glow on the face of a frightened girl.

Jerzom didn't make the connection, but Merapondes did. Jeannie's incredibly filthy state did not mask the resemblance that Merapondes immediately noticed. *My god, is this my sister?* Something that unusual was beyond coincidence. The silence was short-lived.

Merapondes asked, "Who are you?" She used the common language of Kopaz.

Jeannie, still scared, shuddered. Knowing the light was blinding her, as her eyes were used to the dark, Merapondes gently grabbed Jerzom's arm and motioned for him to lower his torch. She did likewise.

Jeannie took a cautious step forward. Nothing like the devil she had imagined moments earlier, there was a girl standing in front of her, her features identical to her own.

At first, Jeannie was at a loss as to what to do. She could not comprehend the language of Kopaz, the language the girl was speaking, so she had no clue what this girl had just said. She suspected it had to do with her appearance.

Jeannie answered in English. "I'm Jeannie. What is your name?"

Merapondes stared at Jeannie. The girl's language was foreign to her. The situation grew uneasy. Tension was building, and Merapondes was not sure what to do. If the girl she was looking at was a demon from the underworld—a demon who was impersonating her sister, Aerapondes— then there were big problems. If that were not the case, then something very strange was going on, something equally weird.

Dead silence fell in the dungeon. Merapondes and Jeannie continued to stare at each other. Their eyes locked. A million things were rattling around in Jeannie's mind. She did not know if the girl before her was real or a demon from hell. It was as weird for Jeannie as it was for Merapondes.

A million questions flashed through Jeannie's mind. Merapondes could sense the tension in Jeannie. The situation grew dire.

Gorom Dorcom waited fifty feet down the hallway. He could hear bits and pieces of the conversation. *What is going on? This is not good.* He grew uneasy as he waited for Jerzom and Merapondes to exit the dungeon.

He walked to the open doorway of the dungeon. His torch in hand, he glared at Jeannie. He shouted, "Talking with prisoners is not allowed. Conversation between royalty and prisoners is absolutely forbidden!"

Merapondes turned to Jerzom and asked, "Why can't we talk to her?"

She then turned to the gorom whose eerie silhouette in the doorway caused goose bumps to race up her spine. "Who are you to tell the royal family who we can or cannot talk to?" Merapondes snarled.

The window of opportunity for Jeannie to say something of significance was quickly closing.

"Quiet! *No talking!*" yelled Dorcom. Jeannie's bare face was a problem. "Why is her hood removed?" Dorcom asked.

He threw his torch on the ground. It landed just outside the doorway leading into the dungeon.

He ran toward Jeannie and Merapondes. His stature was large, and his movements caused a tenseness to come over Merapondes.

Dorcom stepped between Merapondes and Jeannie. He saw the hood lying in the dirt at her feet. He bent over and picked it up. With both hands holding the hood open, he forced it over Jeannie's head.

Then the gorom turned to Jerzom and Merapondes and yelled, "Get away from the prisoner!" Dorcom glared as he shouted at the princess. "She is evil and has killed already. She killed a twelve-year-old boy and will not hesitate to kill again, even a member of the royal family!"

Killed a twelve-year-old boy? This was news to Merapondes. No one had said anything about a murder. *Something is fishy*, thought Merapondes.

The prince and princess hesitated. Dorcom yelled louder, "Stand outside! It is not safe to be near this prisoner!"

Maybe it was fate. Maybe it was evil intervention. Maybe it just happened. Who knows? The torch that Jerzom was holding went out. Shades of darkness consumed the dungeon.

Tensions were rising. There could be nothing but conflict. A decision was fast in the making.

Instinctively, Jerzom grabbed his sister's hand. Her story earlier about the murder of Aerapondes by Mochcom made him uneasy. *We have to get out of here.* He tugged on his sister's hand. She felt his pull and the tenseness of his hand. His body was rock hard.

He lifted his other arm and pointed. Jerzom and Merapondes walked out of the dungeon and into the hallway. Fifty feet from the dungeon doorway, they stopped.

The eerie creaking and squealing of the dungeon door filled the air as Dorcom pulled it shut.

With Gorom Dorcom behind the closed door, alone with Jeannie, Jerzom and Merapondes could only speculate what was happening within the confines of the prison.

Darkness intensified in the dimly lit dungeon as the entrance was closed off. Void of candles in holders on the walls, the only source of light that penetrated the room was from the smoldering torch on the ground. Dorcom yanked her hood off.

"Turn around," Dorcom yelled. Jeannie had no idea what he just said. He grabbed Jeannie and yanked her. She did not know what he wanted, so she did nothing. He yanked again. This time Jeannie started to cry. Dorcom lifted his arm and slapped her with the full force of his confusion and vengeance. She fell to the ground. Lying helpless at his feet, her face was in the dirt. He took a leather rope from the pocket on his black robe and held it over her. He rolled her over so that she could see what he was doing. Even though she could not see him clearly, his dark shadowy image hovering over her was vividly clear, and he knew it.

She screamed over and over, "*No! No! No!*"

The sound of the screaming girl made Merapondes panic. She raced back to the door.

Jerzom was caught off guard by his sister's reaction. He hollered, "What are you doing?" Merapondes stopped. She was five feet from the door. She was torn between her brother and the screams coming from the dungeon.

"This is not our business, my sister. We must leave!" the prince yelled.

Caught on the horns of a dilemma, Merapondes shook her head, signifying no. She shouted, "We must help her!"

Her dilemma was how to help the girl without herself becoming a victim at the murderous hands of a wicked gorom. She wanted to stay, and she wanted to leave.

Petrified, Jeannie was helpless, knowing nothing but fear of what would happen next. The heavy breathing right above her was chilling. His shadowy figure was real. She could not see his smile. She could not see the saliva dripping from his lips, but she felt his nasty slobber hitting her face.

She next felt his massive hands on her body. His hands found their target. He stopped and used his fingers to explore. Jeannie was terrified. She was expecting the worst event ever in her life. She felt his massive arm lift her limp body. He used his other hand to force the leather rope underneath her. The cinching of the rope was almost more than she could bear. Once it was secured tightly around her waist, Gorom Dorcom tied a knot.

On the other side of the dungeon door, all was quiet except the faint rustling noises coming from the closed-off prison.

Merapondes walked closer. Her heart started pounding.

Meanwhile, Jeannie's mind exploded with horror and terror. *No, no! What is he doing? Oh my God, help me!*

With the knot securely tied, Dorcom rolled Jeannie onto her stomach. With her face in the dirt, her hopes and dreams were all gone. She was sure this was the end and she was going to join Danny in the Land of the Dead.

Dorcom grabbed both of Jeannie's hands. With fine grit digging into her skin, he pulled her arms behind her. She felt the slimy sensation of wet leather straps being laced around her wrists. In moments, her arms were securely tired behind her back, the strap cinching her stomach.

There could be no denying it. Merapondes knew what was happening to the girl trapped in the dungeon.

Sensing his sister's anxiety, Jerzom rushed to where Merapondes was standing. Racing past her, he grabbed the iron ring and pulled on the door. Once more, the squealing sounds of a dungeon door opening filled the air.

In the faint light, Jerzom and Merapondes could see the silhouette of a man standing over the prisoner on the floor.

Dorcom's leg came back.

Merapondes screamed, "Stop!"

There was no stopping him. Dorcom's leg was moving already swinging toward the prisoner in the dark. Merapondes eyes could only focus on his brutal attack. The helpless girl lying in the dirt got the full force of his powerful kick.

The blood-curdling screams that filled the dungeon were more than Merapondes could bear.

The treatment of Jeannie was so horrifying that Merapondes blocked it from her mind. She drifted into a state of subconscious behavior. In slow motion, she grabbed Jerzom's arm and tugged on it for him to step away from the terror that was occurring on the dungeon floor. "My brother, let's leave," she whispered.

Gorom Dorcom could not make out her words. He stepped back. His hands pulled on the leather strap tied around Jeannie's waist. He lifted her a foot into the air. He released the tension on the rope. She fell to the floor. Her head slammed into the dirt. She screamed, "*Help me!*"

Dorcom lashed out at her. "Quiet!" he yelled as he kicked her limp body.

For Jeannie, it was more than she could take. Her crying was now muted with sobs of terror. The pain in her side was unbearable. The gorom's foot had hit her with such force she was sure her ribs were broken.

Jeannie heard footsteps. She did not know what was happening. At that point, she forced her mind to think of only one word: *Danny, Danny, Danny, Danny.*

Her one-word train of thought quickly vanished.

Consumed with fear, Merapondes's body broke into an uncontrollable state of shaking.

Jeannie heard talking start up again.

"Jerzom, let's go," Merapondes said.

The massive wooden door was moving as Merapondes and Jerzom pushed on it in their exit. The squealing sound of the old iron hinges filled the dungeon with the horrifying serenade of *schreeeeeeeeeeeekkkkkk.*

As the voices started fading, Jeannie was left with a desperate thought. *The girl is leaving.* She whispered so quietly that she could not even hear her own voice. Her lips mouthed the words: "Please come back. I need someone to help me."

Tears streamed from Jeannie's eyes as her mind went somewhere safe. It filled with images of her beloved cat, Zanzee. She was sure he was there. She was positive. She tried to reach out and touch him. Even if he had been there, her arms were securely tied behind her back, and it would have been impossible. She could touch nothing. Her reach for Zanzee was only in her imagination.

It was one of those inexplicable situations. Merapondes had only walked ten feet from the dungeon door when she stopped. She pulled on Jerzom's arm to stop. She said nothing. She turned and looked at the dungeon. Her heart sank. She knew the fate of the girl.

There was not even a wisp of air in the dank dungeon and hallway, and the door remained open just a crack.

Through her tears, Jeannie tried to say his name. "Zanz...oh my kitty, Zanzee."

The sharp slam of Dorcom's fist against her face muted her cries, and all that came out of her mouth was "Zanzch—" Her sobs drifted into silence.

Merapondes was about to run, but the strange sounds caused her to turn and listen.

The massive door was almost closed, but the words piercing the air— *Zanz* and *Zanzch*—did not go unnoticed by Merapondes. Her memory seized on something—a black cat that had once roamed the halls of the royal palace.

She put her hand on Jerzom's arm. "My brother, I'm uncomfortable leaving that girl in there with Gorom Dorcom. Something tells me that all is not right."

"What do you mean, Merapondes?" He was puzzled by his sister's concern. "I don't understand."

"Jerzom, that girl is not a bad girl. I know it. Please believe me." Merapondes grabbed Jerzom's hand. "Jerzom, Gorom Dorcom is the evil one, not the girl!"

She did not wait for his response. "You have to go back in and tell Gorom Dorcom to leave. Have him untie the girl and have him leave immediately."

It was something Jerzom did not want to get in the middle of. Although he loved his sister, politics was at the core of his hesitation. Starting a fight with the goroms was not a good idea.

"Merapondes, it is not our business," answered Jerzom. "Let's go. We do not want to be in the middle of this."

Maybe it was something Jeannie did. Maybe it was the words she had uttered as they were leaving. Maybe it was her age. Merapondes suspected that the prisoner was her age. Maybe it was genetics. Who knows? For Merapondes, she could not choose to do nothing.

She grabbed her brother's arm firmly. They stood in the hallway of the Great Pyramid that led to the dungeon. With a firmness and strength in her voice, she said, "Jerzom, would you go back if it were me in that girl's place?"

He said nothing. Their torches lit the granite walls with flickering light.

She asked again. "Would you abandon me? That girl is someone special. I know it. I think she was trying to tell me about her cat, Zanzee."

That got his attention. He had no idea who the girl was, but he could not argue with his sister. She had a sixth sense that he knew was not natural.

"OK, we'll go back," said Jerzom.

As they neared the door, they heard loud screams coming from the dungeon. Jerzom dropped Merapondes's hand and took off at a sprint. It was only seconds before he was at the massive dungeon door. With all his might he pulled on it.

Schreeeeeeeeeeeekkkkkk. The riveting sound once again filled the hallway and dungeon.

"Leave her alone," screamed Jerzom. "Out!"

Startled by Jerzom's entrance, Gorom Dorcom, who was standing over Jeannie, yelled, "This is my business! Not yours!"

"And it will be my business to kill you if you don't get away from that girl and get the hell out of here!" yelled Jerzom.

Dorcom walked to Jerzom and smiled. The dancing shadows on the walls from the bouncing flames of the torches also fell on Dorcom's face. His smile was cruel in the faint light. "You have no idea what you've started."

Jerzom snarled, "If you lay one hand on that girl, I personally will cut your beating heart out of your chest." He smiled at the gorom. "That's what I will start, and that's what I will finish."

Well aware of the situation he had just created, Jerzom drove home his point. "You can tell Katchcom that I'll be visiting this girl daily, and if she is harmed or touched in any vulgar way by any of the goroms, there will be war!"

CHAPTER 13

A Gorom Plots

There's an old saying—knowledge is power—and this must be a pretty old saying, as Katchcom was well aware of it. If and when the royal family gained knowledge of the dirty business of the goroms, all hell would break loose. Their plot to overthrow the ruling family of Kopaz and replace it with a religious government run by Katchcom and his band of evil men would end. The goroms would lose, and the ruling king of Kopaz would win. That would not be good for Katchcom, as he was plotting an overthrow of the government of Kopaz, planning on doing away with the entire royal family.

Dorcom's encounter with Prince Jerzom and Princess Merapondes had thrown a spotlight on something that might have grave consequences for the high priest.

His question was this. "What to do about it?"

Fuming with outrage, Katchcom contemplated damage control. For as long as Dorcom had been a member of the Quorum of High Priests, he had been a problem. It had been one thing after another, but this was the final straw. Throughout the kingdom of Kopaz, gossip about Dorcom's lust for teenage girls had, in the past, been just an embarrassment. While Mochcom was high priest, and now for as long as Katchcom had held that position, they had been able to hide Dorcom's nasty little secret. With no evidence ever surfacing, both Mochcom and Katchcom were always able to shove under the rug all allegations made by his victims, or the parents of his victims, of rape, indecent actions, and even murder. At the very least, it had been an annoyance to Katchcom. Now, however, it had escalated. Dorcom had dragged the royal family into his dirty little habit, and that was a problem.

This time, not only had Dorcom placed his filthy habit of lusting after teenage girls on a public stage for all to see, but he had also illuminated the nasty business of the goroms. More importantly to the high priest, Dorcom had dragged the royal family into the middle of Katchcom's personal plans to claim a seat at Zuron's council table once the dark god became the supreme god.

Damage control was the name of the game, and deception was his plan. He pondered. Not only was the insubordinate gorom on his mind but also Prince Jerzom and what to do about him. He invited Goroms Ancom and Dorcom to join him for dinner.

Seated at the massive marble table in the Hall of the Goroms were three goroms: Katchcom, Ancom, and Dorcom. The smell of spiced roast duck permeated the atmosphere.

Gnawing on a leg dripping with grease, Katchcom looked intently at Dorcom and asked, "So what happened today in the Great Pyramid?"

Katchcom waited for the man to answer, quietly studying Dorcom's body language, his physical reaction to the question.

Fumbling for words, Dorcom muttered, "Ah er…ah whaa…what do you want to know?"

"Just what happened!" demanded Katchcom in a direct voice.

"Well, you know—"

Before another word dropped from Dorcom's lips, Katchcom snorted. "*I know what?*"

Tensions were on the rise. Gorom Ancom cringed just watching his colleague squirm under the questioning of their leader.

Silently, the moments dragged on. Then Katchcom broke the void of sound. "I'm listening!"

"Well, I…ah, just checked on the prisoner. And, ah…you know." He stopped, knowing he was repeating the words he had fumbled around with earlier. Then Dorcom shot back, trying to justify his actions. "It's my job to make sure she does not escape!"

"Hmm...I see," growled Katchcom. "And did she escape?"

Feeling he was at last digging himself out of the hole he had dug for himself, Dorcom answered forcefully, "*No, my lord*, she did not escape!'

"Good!" Silence took over as Katchcom's face transformed to a sullen scowl, his jaw rigid as he glared intensely at Dorcom. He put both hands on the table. The food on everyone's plate was growing cold.

Opening his mouth in what appeared to Dorcom to be almost slow motion, Katchcom offered some words of warning. "If you go near her again, I shall cut off your right hand!"

Dorcom said nothing. Ancom lifted his head and rolled his eyes at his fellow gorom.

As his face intensified into lines of anger, Katchcom changed his tone. "*No!* I'll not cut off your right hand." There was a brief silence. Then Katchcom unleashed his foreshadowing wrath. "If you touch that young girl ever again, I shall cut off not only both your hands but you will howl and scream as you journey from man to *eunuch!* Am I clear?"

No more words were needed. The threat laid down by the high priest could not have settled more profoundly on Dorcom. He was now on probation, and he wondered, *What's next for me? I don't trust him.*

Fully aware that Dorcom was a problem that was not going away, Katchcom brushed off any more of his inquiry and changed the subject. "Let's finish dinner. I have an assignment for you when we are through."

Winning was the only feasible outcome, and Katchcom needed just a little trust from an unsuspecting victim. Now one thing dominated Katchcom's mind as he rolled the corncob in his teeth—Jerzom and how to deal with him.

Like a wild animal walking into a trap set by a cunning hunter, such would be the fate of Jerzom. Katchcom's idea for a trap raced around in his mind. It was a plot with jaws of steel, where, long after the point of no return, deception would grab Jerzom and leave him blind to what the goroms were up to. And equally important to Katchcom's clandestine, twisted web of deceit was his ability to drag out of Jerzom, without provoking any suspicion, some much-needed knowledge. Katchcom had to know whether or not Jerzom suspected who Jeannie really was, and garnering that information was imperative.

It was midafternoon. Despite there being no conversation, the three goroms had not left the table. Leaving without permission was absolutely forbidden, as went without saying.

Cracking into the air like cherry bombs, Katchcom's words broke the silence, and he commanded their full attention as he rasped, "Ancom, get the prince here within the hour!"

Snapping to attention, Ancom fired back. "Yes, my lord!"

Then nothing—no one spoke.

A sharp knife could not have cut through the tension. Tired of waiting for an answer that did not come, Katchcom asked, "How do you plan to get the prince here?"

"I, ah…er…ah well, what should I ask?" replied Ancom sheepishly.

"Tell him we've retrieved a golden object—an object that the goroms find strangely puzzling. Tell him it was on the prisoner, that it appears to be of royal provenance, and that we need the prince to look at it!"

CHAPTER 14
Jerzom Spots a Golden Watch

The knock on the iron ring alerted the doorman. "Who goes there?" he asked through the peephole in the wooden door of the Grand Hall.

"It's Gorom Ancom. I bring a message from Gorom Katchcom for the royal prince."

The door opened. Ancom was met by the deformed man whose only job was to open and close the main doorway leading into the royal palace.

Stretching out his arm, Gorom Ancom handed a handwritten note to the little man. "Please give this to Prince Jerzom and tell him Gorom Katchcom would like the prince to visit the Hall of the Goroms within the hour, if possible."

"OK," said the dwarf, and he grabbed the door to close it.

It was only a matter of minutes before that note was passed to the head of the royal guard for delivery to Prince Jerzom.

Meanwhile, all alone in his sanctuary, Katchcom mused. *He won't be able to resist talking to me about the girl...especially if he thinks I've found something. He's not dumb and knows damn well she has the appearance of a Neferzul.*

The prince arrived in less than an hour. The meeting started as planned.

Something had transpired between Gorom Dorcom and the high priest, Gorom Katchcom, during the forty-five minutes it took Ancom to request the presence of the prince and for Jerzom to show up at the Hall of the Goroms.

Cleverly, Katchcom started the conversation. "I've talked to Dorcom about his treatment of the prisoner. He has been severely punished."

Sitting at the far end of the table, Dorcom waited.

"Dorcom, show Jerzom your back," yelled Katchcom.

Sure enough, blood still dripped from Dorcom's back, undeniable evidence that he had been punished. His skin was laced with lash marks from a severe beating by a leather whip.

Looking for signs of anything out of the ordinary, Katchcom followed Jerzom's movements and expressions to detect what, if anything, Jerzom's body language was revealing. With focused attention, Katchcom saw Jerzom wince a bit when he gazed at the deep, fleshy lacerations on Dorcom's back.

"I've commanded my goroms not to lay a hand on the prisoner until she is brought before the royal court for her final judgment," said Katchcom, as he went on to assure Jerzom that the girl would be treated civilly. "She was brought before your father, the king, to make him aware that a spy had invaded our land. So now we enter the next phase of this legal process—the trial and interrogation!" Katchcom did, however, have a point to make. "She is a prisoner of the state, and prior to a royal proceedings and final judgment, she will be brought before a hearing in the Hall of the Goroms, where all goroms will take part in a trial, questioning her and reviewing all evidence. After the hearing before the goroms, she will be brought to the Grand Hall of the palace, and final judgment will be passed by King Dalvin and you, Prince Jerzom."

Jerzom nodded his head in agreement. Katchcom was satisfied.

Jerzom remained still. Katchcom become uneasy with the prince's behavior. He puzzled over the mood that had just descended. *What is he waiting for?*

Maybe Katchcom had forgotten his instructions to Ancom. Maybe it was intentional. For whatever reason, Katchcom had not yet shown Jerzom the golden object of interest.

Then the unexpected happened, quite by accident. Katchcom had a nervous habit of fiddling with things he had placed in the pocket of his black robe, and he had been doing so throughout the meeting. As Katchcom sat at the table, studying Jerzom's reactions as well as his body language, his hand tangled in the golden chain attached to the golden watch.

It was a warm summer day, and the bugs were out in force. A large black wasp landed on Katchcom's nose. It was in the mood to sting a victim, even the high priest. And that it did. Letting out a scream, Katchcom yelled in pain and quickly pulled his hand from his robe's pocket in an effort to kill the wasp.

The golden watch and chain landed on the table.

The prince's eyes shot like darts to the golden object. "What's that?" Jerzom asked.

Caught off guard, Katchcom had no quick answer. He had planned to show Jerzom a worthless golden coin that the goroms had in their custody for centuries. It was a coin the royal family knew nothing about. Katchcom suspected that Jerzom would not be interested in the coin and brush it off as something of meaningless significance, even if it were discovered on the prisoner. That plan never happened. By accident, Katchcom grabbed the wrong golden object in his robe pocket—the golden watch instead of the golden coin.

He fumbled over his words. "Ah…er…ah…er…it…it is a just an object I've had for a long time."

"Where did you get it? And from whom did you get this most unusual piece of fine gold?" hissed Jerzom, dragging out his questions.

"Inherited. It belonged to my father," shot back Katchcom.

It was obvious. By now, Katchcom could read Jerzom's body language like a book. The prince was not buying a word of it.

And if things could get even worse, well, they did.

Ancom blurted out, "Maybe the Neferzul owned it."

As the sound of the word "Neferzul" faded away, silence filled every inch of the Hall of the Goroms.

With the silence pressing on like a stealthy thief in the night, Katchcom had no choice except to change the subject and hope the entire conversation would vanish like the sounds of the words just spoken and be hidden like so many events in history that get lost on the pages of time.

Although Jerzom had only heard the term once when Aerapondes was alive, his memory was crystal clear. The name was sacred and had something to do with the gods. This strange behavior of Katchcom piqued Jerzom's interest.

If one problem wasn't enough, Katchcom's other problem was that he was not the only gorom that knew who the prisoner was. Although Katchcom knew that Ancom was aware of who Jeannie was, he was waiting for the right moment to take care of that problem. Now he had two problems—the Ancom problem of knowing who Jeannie was and the royal prince problem of Jerzom knowing that Katchcom had the golden watch.

Katchcom had a new challenge. He must confine the news of the prisoner's identity. His mind erupted with concern at her sacred name being exposed, *Ancom knows, but does anyone else? It's crucial…oh so crucial… that I find out!*

Katchcom was hungry. "Will you eat with us?" queried Katchcom, hoping that Jerzom would say no. He'd had enough surprises to last a lifetime without having his enemy hang around.

As he expected, Jerzom declined. "No, not now…I have business to attend to!"

Beady eyes glared at Jerzom from around the room—not just Katchcom but also Goroms Dorcom and Ancom all suspected the prince's rebuff of the high priest's invitation had a hidden meaning. Slamming the door as Prince Jerzom exited the Hall of the Goroms, the royal prince wandered into the late afternoon air with a mind full of questions. *Something is amiss. Katchcom is up to something, but what?*

After he told Dorcom and Ancom to get out, Katchcom ate alone. His fingers pulled pieces of well-cooked goat meat from rib bones. His mind was filled with thoughts about what to do next. The goat meat was not mutton, but that was OK. Katchcom was not in love with stewed sheep, no matter how well they were seasoned. The name Neferzul, a golden watch, and a seat at the council table of Zuron—those were the topics foremost on his mind. He was sure if all went as planned, Zuron would become the supreme god of the universe. What troubled him now was how and what to do to insure that all would go as planned.

The sun had hours left to shed its light on Kopaz, and the tall grass in the gardens brushed across Jerzom's toes with each step. His sandals left his feet all but bare, and the walk in the soft ground cover in the courtyard between the royal palace and the Hall of the Goroms was a welcome treat as he contemplated his next move.

The Fiery Pit

Humans exist throughout the universe, reaching even the most obscure corners in the outermost reaches. Those who lived on Mother Earth were but a mere speck of sand on an ocean's endless beach. The whereabouts of Kopaz had never crossed Danny's mind—at least not until now. He just assumed it was someplace on the order of an earthly land. He was about to run into a creature that was not earthly, yet the creature had been fully introduced to humans not unlike those he had known from the moment he was born, so in that case, where was he? If there were no beasts such as this on earth, logically, he was not on earth, and therefore, the thought that dominated his mind was this: *Where am I?*

His days with Quill had been long and hard. Learning the ways of a god was not for the faint of heart. Maybe that was why Viracocha had picked Danny as his royal prince. Who could say? For whatever reason, Danny was a young god in training, and Quill was his tutor.

The sun had just shown its face above the highest peak of the Androzes Mountains. Yawning, he lay half-asleep and half-awake, with his head on his newfound friend, Yellzor. Suddenly, Danny was doused by a cold bucket of water. He jolted awake.

"Quill, what the hell are you doing? I'm tired. We did not get to bed until the wee hours of the dawn. I do not need a bucket of cold water as an alarm!" Danny shouted as he jumped to his feet.

"Good morning, my royal prince," said Quill with a strange puzzled look on his face.

"Good morning, my hind end," shouted Danny as he lifted his soaking wet T-shirt over his head. "You certainly have a strange way of greeting someone you call your royal prince!"

"Well, you were snoring, and I did not want to use my hand to shake you for fear of getting snotted on or spit upon by your vibrating mouth and nose!" Quill said as he snorted, trying to keep his laughter from taking over.

Danny rubbed his eyes. He looked at Yellzor and asked him, "Do you like to get doused with cold water at the crack of dawn?"

"Gaarraaaa gaaaaarrarrrrraaar," replied Yellzor.

"I thought so," said Danny. He looked west, away from the Androzes Mountains, and saw a billowing pillar of black smoke making its way to the sky.

Still staring at the rising black smoke on the western horizon, he asked, "What's on the agenda today?" He laughed and then added, "Except throwing water on your new friend." He paused for a moment, and then with a straight face, he looked directly at Quill and asked, "Am I your friend?"

It was a fair question. Quill hadn't ever thought of his relationship with Danny as friendship. It had been in his mind a teacher-student matter, and that was the extent of it. Yet over the past several weeks, things had changed. He had been told by Viracocha to ready the royal prince to sit at the council table of the gods, and he took that assignment seriously. He had had reservations, thinking he would be dealing with an immature teenager who might be wet behind the ears and a real brat, so Quill had started with his guard up. He looked at Danny as he thought, *Boy, did I miss the mark about you!*

"Danny, there has to be a level of respect in our relationship. You are the student, and I am the teacher. That will never change." His face lit up as he charged on. "Yet I have come to love you as a dear friend. The quality that defines the core of an individual, god or human, is the attribute of trust." He stopped and just stared at Danny. A silence fell between Danny and Quill. It was if time had stopped. Quill took a deep breath. "Danny, I have an uncanny ability to discern the character of an individual by how he treats animals." He stopped again. And when he continued, he nodded his head as if to not only voice the feelings that he had for Danny but also convey them with his body language. "Yellzor would lay down his life for you. I know that. I know Yellzor. He has been with me for centuries, and you have only known him for a few brief days. Yellzor is your best friend, and that is good enough for me. His sixth sense of trust is way beyond mine."

Danny looked down. He had just heard something that should have made him elated, but it did not. His mind started rattling on, trying to compose something to say. Quill cut off the response that he was in the process of making.

"Danny, you could have looked at me as a flawed man. I am not large and built like you. You are handsome and muscular. I am small and thin. Yet your respect for me has been unwavering. I know that. You have never questioned anything that I told you. That is good. You have never doubted me. That is good. You have placed full trust in me." Quill stopped. He looked at Danny. Then in a quiet voice, where his words competed with the sound of a slight breeze rustling the tall blades of grass in the meadow where they had spent the evening, he said, "Do you know what creates friendship and is also the bonding force that keeps it going?"

Danny's eyes opened wide as he waited for more.

"Do you remember your experience as you were thrown over Yellshome Falls?" Quill asked.

Danny nodded.

"You put full trust in me as we plunged downward and dove into the deep pool at the bottom of the falls. Not once did you jerk or yank your hand or arm in an effort to get away from me as we together faced what could have been your final moments of life. For me, I knew the outcome. You did not. It was then I got a glimpse of the core of your being. And I must add, I liked what I found."

For a few moments, the two friends looked fondly at each other. Then Quill broke the silence. "Danny, the force that creates friends and the force that keeps them together is trust. For without it, no relationship will survive."

Danny made no response. What could he say? He looked at Quill, put his index fingers to the corners of his mouth, and pulled upward as if to make a smiley face. Then he said in a strange-sounding voice, his mouth stretched to its limit, "Shall we charge on?"

Although Danny had just signaled that they should get started and face the chores that Quill no doubt had scheduled for the day, he did not stay standing. He sat down on a nearby rock and asked, "Did you see the full celestial body that was reflecting light from whatever sun this planet is circling?"

"Yes," answered Quill. "The humans on this planet, Planet Kopaz, call that celestial body you referred to the moon."

Danny's face went blank. Quill ventured on. "We know the humans on Earth call the celestial body that circles Earth by the name of *moon*. Is that a coincidence that the two planets have the same name for their respective moons?"

Danny waited as his facial expression suggested to Quill the question "Why?"

Quill continued. "When Kashom visited Earth, he asked the Egyptians what they called the celestial bodies that they could see in the night sky. They told him that *moon* was the name of the orb that circles the earth. They also told Kashom that the ribbon of stars that light up the black sky that can be seen on a clear night was called the Milky Way.

Danny was all ears. Quill forged on. "The star at the center of Earth's solar system was called *sun*."

Quill was comfortable in his role as teacher and instructor. In fact, he liked it. Danny was comfortable with the role that Quill played. Danny nodded. Quill proceeded. "Now here is the interesting part! Planet Kopaz is four time bigger than Earth. And by four times bigger, what I mean is that in earthly lingo, the diameter of Kopaz is four times the diameter of Earth."

This started to grow into too much of a reenactment of Danny's school days. He laughed and added, "Quill, I got an *F* in Mr. Hall's geometry class, so you just lost me!"

Quill paid no attention to Danny's interjection. "OK, here is the part I wanted to get to!" said Quill, beaming. "Planet Kopaz spins on its axis four time as fast as Earth spins on its axis, so the length of daytime on Earth is essentially the same on Kopaz. So Kashom adopted the earthlings' names of *moon*, *Milky Way* and *sun* to be used here in Kopaz, in honor of the Egyptians. Of course, the name *sun* on Kopaz refers to our star, Kolar, at the center of our solar system."

"Quill, you sound like Tony. He was my best buddy and would get off on tangents of mathematical and scientific bullshit!"

Quill chuckled at Danny's remark. "Yes, I know of Tony! He was a wonderful, brilliant human being before Gorom Mochcom killed him."

With that comment, the mood shifted. Danny started to think about his best friend who now lived in the Land of the Dead. Quill detected the mood change and changed the subject. He stood and walked to a rock that he had placed a large leather bag on earlier. He reached in it, grabbed two objects, and threw them at Danny. They landed at Danny's feet.

"Danny, put those on!"

Danny stooped and picked them up. Instantly, he said, "You have got to be joking! I would not be caught dead in this shit!"

"Yeah, well your clothes are all but finished, so do you want to go around naked?" Quill shot back.

"This is a leather skirt! What the hell do I wear under it? You know to cover my you-know-what!" Danny snorted.

"Like I said, Danny, you can wrap the leather loin garment around your you-know-what and put on the leather skirt on over it or go naked! It's your choice. There is also a leather belt that keeps the skirt in place."

"Shit," said Danny, "this sucks!" He told Quill to turn away, and then, reluctantly, Danny started to change his clothes. He knew his Levi's were all but shot and so full of holes that they weren't covering much. It made sense to get rid of his old garb.

As Danny was finishing, Quill added, "One hour of Kopaz time equals four hours of Earth time, so in effect we are on a twenty-four-hour clock just like you have on Earth. Sunrise was at five thirty here on Kopaz and someplace on Earth it was also five thirty!"

Danny said nothing. Standing with his new leather skirt—the identical clothing that was worn by the Royal Guard when he and Jeannie were attacked—he flipped Quill a middle-finger salute, grinned, and added, "There ya go with the bullshit schoolwork stuff again!"

Quill laughed. It was a time for fun and a time for two friends to get to know each other.

The half hour the two newfound friends spent sharing their inner souls with each other was worth the time. It was clear that they were friends bound by trust, yet Danny was aware that Quill was his superior at this point in their relationship, and respect would not be compromised.

"The smoke you were looking at a few minutes ago is where we are heading," said Quill. "Let's get started. We will stop and eat at noon. We have much to do at the Pit of Vulcan."

As the sun kept climbing Danny, Yellzor, and Quill walked vigorously on their trek to the western mountains, the Vulcans.

Noon came none too early. It was time to rest and eat. Fortunately, they did not have to look far for a perfect spot, one with a cold brook, seat-sized granite rocks in a grassy meadow, and plenty of wild fruit and nuts. Nor did it take Yellzor long to have his mess of wild hare to feast on while Quill and Danny had all the fruit and nuts they wanted and, for a treat, a few slices of cheese from Quill's carry bag.

"I think I could lie down in this soft grass and take a nap. How about you, Quill?"

Shaking his head, Quill said, "That is out of the question! Evil is afoot, and time is not on our side."

The day moved on. The sun started its descent. It was late afternoon, and there were at least five miles left in their journey. Thinking ahead, Quill and Danny picked a few extra apples, and each filled a satchel of almonds and filberts. They could eat on the run.

The smell of sulfur permeated the air. The gurgling sounds coming from the bubbling lava of the volcano they were approaching let them know it was not idle.

Finally, they made it. Standing at the rim of the volcano, Danny was puzzled.

Quill noticed and asked, "What?"

"Ah…er…ah, ah…well…" Danny's struggle for words was obvious. He knew something was up but wasn't sure what it was.

Still staring at Danny, Quill blurted, "Well, what?"

"What the hell are we doing here?" snapped Danny. He had no clue.

There are times when a student hates math. It is written all over his face. He thinks, *Who in the hell will ever use this crap? But here I am stuck in a boring math class that I hate.* This was one of those symbolic math situations for Danny. After all, he was the student, and he had no clue what was going on.

At that moment, the ground on which he was standing moved. "Holy shit, what is going on?" yelled Danny. The little movement in the beginning only lasted a moment. The next movement was beyond Danny's comprehension. He and Yellzor were suddenly a hundred and fifty feet in the air, swinging back and forth from something, but from what, he had no idea.

Looking down from so high up, Quill looked ever so small—not unlike an ant—which prompted Danny to weigh in big time on his current predicament. Even though Quill was having a huge laugh, it was not funny to Danny. "What have you done now?" shouted Danny. "Give me a break. I want to know what is going on."

For a little man, his voice carried. Still laughing, Quill shouted back, "How do you like CrystalFlame?"

"Who?" ripped Danny back.

"She's the dragon who guards Vulcan, the volcano, and keeps it red hot. Neat, huh?"

CrystalFlame was the length of two football fields, longer than six hundred feet. Danny was perched on her head. She opened her mouth and shot out a flame that could rival the explosion of an atomic bomb. From his perch in the sky, now at two hundred feet, as CrystalFlame lifted her head still higher, Danny bellowed at the top of his lungs, "Holy shit, Quill. What the hell is going on? What is this?"

"I told you, it's a dragon. What do you think? Nice, huh?"

Danny had had it. "Yeah, nice my butt! Quill, you've really gone off the deep end with this thing! *Get me and Yellzor down!*"

Yellzor let out a yowl—*yoooooooooowwwwwwwllllll!*—letting Quill know he was in agreement with Danny.

"Well, you see, my young god, you will only sit at the council table of the gods when you have killed off all the goroms and thrust them into the fiery pit of Vulcan. It is the entrance to the blackest abyss of hell, and no one who enters this perdition will ever leave. CrystalFlame makes sure of that."

Sometimes when a teacher instructs a student, the best learning mechanism is a reality lesson. Coming from CoalVille, Danny had fond memories of his days in Miss Carter's class. He recalled the time he had been fantasizing about pirate treasure at the Boar's Tusk and was caught by Miss Carter.

In those few minutes on CrystalFlame's head above the mouth of Vulcan, those CoalVille school memories flashed through his mind.

He recalled staring at his yearbook. *There's a pirate standing at the Boar's Tusk. They buried something there—I know they did! Yeah, they put it near the Boar's Tusk—it's a perfect marker.*

Standing behind her desk, Miss Carter tapped her pencil. "Mr. Roberts, can you enlighten us as to where your mind is and what you are thinking about?"

Danny flinched. He said nothing.

"I'm waiting," she snapped as she leaned forward.

Shit, lady, Danny thought. He hesitated, then blurted out, "Yes, Miss Carter. I think there's treasure around here!"

"Oh? I had no idea, Danny. Just what on earth are you talking about? Are you here—or someplace else? I thought the subject was transportation! Evidently, Danny, you want to study something else during this hour—is that not so?" Miss Carter fired back at Danny with a smile on her face.

Swaying back and forth on CrystalFlame's head, Danny remembered what happened next. He had rubbed his tongue across the edges of his upper teeth. "Farts and outposts," he leered. "Miss Carter, if the wagons had not come through Wyoming, we wouldn't have the farts and outposts."

Silence engulfed the entire class. He slapped the side of his cheek with his hand—mouth open. All students heard the loud pop. Not waiting, he snapped, "I mean *forts* and outposts."

Danny knew what was on Miss Carter's mind. *You smartass,* her expression said. *You're playing with me. All right, two can play. This is my territory!*

"Yes, Danny, we all know what you meant," Miss Carter said, looking at Eddie. "Next time, choose your men wisely. I mean…ah, ah…choose your words wisely."

I've got her! Danny grinned from ear to ear. *Too bad, Miss C!*

"Men? Choose what men, Miss Carter?" Danny shot back as he noted that she was looking at Eddie. "Touché, Miss Carter!"

Although there should have been an outburst of laughter from every student in American history class, there was dead silence. The laughter was bottled up inside everyone. If silent laughter was golden, Danny found his treasure—he knew what everyone was thinking. Then his eye caught a quick glance from Miss Carter.

Why'd she look at Eddie and then at me? He's her pet. Is she comparing me to him? Is she wanting a new conquest—she's not for me!

Those thoughts brought Danny mind to a strange place. He started thinking of Jeannie. *Is she dead? I let her down.*

High in the air, above the mouth of a volcano, on the head of a dragon, Danny's mind was racing. Recalling the fun days he had had with Jeannie and Tony brought a bitter sadness to his soul.

Quill noticed his change of mood and motioned CrystalFlame to lower her head so Danny could get off. "I think you have found another friend. She would give you a lick with her tongue, but that might not be a good idea." Quill watched Danny maneuver his way around CrystalFlame's eye and wiggle down her scales to get his feet safely on the ground.

And so it was that he was a student learning a lesson from a new teacher on how to become a god. His memories of his old school days when he dreamed and searched for buried pirate treasure in the Scarlet Desert with his school friends were the only treasures that he had left—memories of his adventurous days with Jeannie and Tony as they stumbled onto a priceless treasure that opened the Highway of Time. But the past was gone. His schoolroom was not in a school building back in CoalVille but in a strange new land with creatures he had no idea existed. As he stood at the doorway leading to the pit of hell, guarded by a Herculean dragon, he realized he was no longer on earth. The bitter sadness that had overtaken him as he remembered the days when he lived in the Scarlet Desert pierced his soul. *My old friends are gone*, he thought. *I have no idea where I am, and all I have now for friends are a giant yellow wolf, a fire-breathing dragon, and a peculiar little man with a weird sense of humor.*

Quill was reading Danny's mind. He knew what to say. "Danny, you and I are in a time warp. The time you and I are in is not the same time that Jeannie is in. All we can do is hope that we finish your training and do what we need to do so you are a strong god ready to unleash a wrath of vengeance on the evil goroms that have taken Jeannie."

Danny listened, and Quill spoke softly. "When we come out of this time warp, we shall enter the time realm that Jeannie is in and pray she still lives."

Solemnly, Danny said to Quill, "I hope so."

CHAPTER 16

The Meeting of a Prince and a Princess

Considering the stakes at play, Jerzom leaned into his elbows on his desk with his head in his hands. Deep in thought, he looked out the window directly in front of him. Having a clear mind and a full comprehension of impending doom was paramount. However, little did Prince Jerzom know that if ever the royal family of Kopaz was headed for troubles with the Quorum of High Priests, nominally the spiritual arm of the government under the rule of King Dalvin, it was now.

Up until this point, the goroms, the Quorum of High Priests, had successfully manipulated their influence upon the royal family under the guise of spiritual leadership. But it was more than that. Political influence is the name of the game in any government. And most would agree that was a true statement. But manipulation under the cover of holy and moral justice was quite a different story. Namely, the brutal murder of Princess Aerapondes by Gorom Mochcom and then his masterful shifting of the blame so that it fell squarely upon Prince Kashom—all took place in the name of cleansing evil from Kopaz to please the supreme god of the universe. The goroms were masterful and successful liars. The Quorum of High Priests proclaimed that the supreme god must be pleased, or all would face his wrath, and his punishments would affect all the people of

Kopaz if justice were not allowed to prevail.

And so it was. The Quorum placed the blame for the murder of the first Neferzul, Princess Aerapondes, on her older brother, Prince Kashom.

The king had bought it hook, line, and sinker. King Dalvin declared that his beloved son—favored by Viracocha to become his royal prince at the council table of the gods—was a traitor, and thus it was proclaimed throughout Kopaz by an official royal decree.

This time, however, Jerzom knew he was falling into the same kind of trap. But up to now, the trap was still being set, and Jerzom, unlike his brother, Prince Kashom, was a bit more suspecting.

The golden watch on the gold chain was a puzzle. And even more puzzling was the word "Neferzul."

It was the day following the meeting that Jerzom had had with Gorom Katchcom, and he was deep in thought about what had transpired. *What are those bastards up to? I do not trust Katchcom! What is that gold object on the gold chain all about? I've never seen anything like it in Kopaz.*

Noon was approaching. Lunch would be served within the hour.

As Jerzom walked down the Grand Hall on the way to his room, the aromas of the mouthwatering foods being prepared by the cooks in the kitchen of the royal palace filled the air. Jerzom mused, *That disgusting mutton Katchcom was gnawing on last evening is shit. My palate will enjoy something far more excellent. I will have a royal meal fit for a prince in less than two hours.*

On most occasions, the royal prince ate lunch with his sister, Princess Merapondes. Today, that was not the case. Jerzom had scheduled lunch with his most trusted friend, Peizar.

Jerzom walked to his sister's room. He had at least half an hour before his lunch engagement with Peizar.

"Merapondes, do you have a few minutes?" asked Jerzom as he walked into Princess Merapondes's room.

"Yes, my royal brother. What is on your mind?" Merapondes answered.

Even though Merapondes was alone in her room, she elected to discuss strategy privately, in a more secluded room.

They selected the reception hall in the royal palace to talk. It was a large room but much smaller than the Grand Hall. It was at the far end of the palace, and rarely, if ever, did anyone visit it. It was reserved ahead of time for special dignitaries or heads of state from other lands.

Merapondes was delighted to meet with her brother. She was so proud of him for confronting Gorom Dorcom.

Their encounter with the evil gorom in the dungeon had weighed heavily on Merapondes's mind. And the girl being held prisoner was foremost in her thoughts.

Jerzom did not want a drawn-out meeting, and so his questions were direct. "Do you know anything about a golden watch on a gold chain?"

"No" was her simple reply. Then she added, "Jerzom, what is a watch?"

That was all the prince needed. He moved on. "Have you ever heard the word *Neferzul*?"

This time, his question was followed by a deathly silence. Merapondes stared at her brother, saying nothing.

His sister's stare caused Jerzom to press the issue. "Do you know anything?" he whispered. "Is it a name or just a word?"

She answered, "I don't know."

Her guarded response left him more puzzled. At first, all Jerzom could say was "Hmm."

Her body language told him she might know more than she had said. He wanted to get to the bottom of the mystery, so he widened the scope of his questions. "Do you know anything about the word or name *Neferzul*? Do you know the source of the word or name?"

For a moment, Merapondes stared at him. She took a large breath. "Once, long ago, our beloved sister, Aerapondes, mentioned that word by accident. She clammed up immediately afterward and hemmed and hawed when I asked her what it meant."

Merapondes waited for her brother to respond. He said nothing, so she continued. "I have no idea if it is the name of a thing, the name of a person, or the name of a place. The only thing I know is that Aerapondes would not talk to me about it. I asked her at least three times. She always brushed me off."

Jerzom studied Merapondes's facial expressions. He knew she was not telling him what she knew about the name Neferzul.

Jerzom was about to say something, but detecting that she was holding back, he waited.

For good reason, Merapondes was hesitant. Her sister told her that grave consequences would follow if the sacred name of Neferzul was ever revealed or that Aerapondes was the Neferzul.

Jerzom was persistent. He queried, "Well?"

Finally Merapondes blurted out, "Aerapondes told me the name of Neferzul is sacred. She told me that the goddess Neferdor personally gave it to her and told her under penalty of death never to reveal it."

That made more sense. Jerzom now knew why she was hesitant—and he knew that it was a name and not just a word. More importantly, it was a sacred name, connected to the gods.

It concerned Merapondes that he had even asked the question. She asked, "Why do you want to know?"

More than willing to get it off his chest, he explained. "Last evening I had a meeting with Goroms Katchcom, Dorcom, and Ancom. The word *Neferzul* came up, and a gold round object on a chain was inadvertently placed on the table." Jerzom looked at Merapondes, making direct eye contact, and continued. "I didn't think anything of either one at first, but it was the way the goroms reacted. They seemed really concerned that the golden object, which Katchcom called a watch, was exposed and that the word *Neferzul* had been revealed. Their fidgety behavior alarmed me."

"So now what?" she snapped.

"I don't know!"

CHAPTER 17

Two Friends—A Royal Prince and a Commoner

It was now early afternoon. Jerzom and Peizar were finishing their lunch. It had been a time to relax, and that gave the royal prince an opportunity to collect his thoughts and strategize with his best friend.

The food had been wonderful. However, that was not foremost on Jerzom's mind. Keenly aware that something was up with the goroms, his mind was running helter-skelter to find answers.

Feeling as if the passing of each moment strengthened his enemy, because a conniving group of evil men were conspiring to overthrow his kingdom, Jerzom decided there wasn't a moment to be wasted. He needed answers and quickly.

The sun's warmth had taken the chill out of the royal palace. The two young men sat at the white marble table in the visiting dignitary conference room of the royal palace.

The bond of a true friend was stronger than the walls of the royal palace. Peizar had stood the ultimate test of strength for Jerzom, and he was Jerzom's most trusted friend.

For those who had experienced true friendship, the story of Jerzom, a royal prince, and Peizar, a commoner, was heartwarming and sincere. Jerzom would kid around with Peizar and say to him, "If I fell off the boat in the raging waters of Yellshome River, who would throw me a life ring?"

Peizar would laugh and say, "My royal prince and most loyal friend, I would not throw you a life ring. I would dive into the waters with the life ring in my mouth and save you from plunging over the falls."

"Yes, I know that. That is the mark of a true friend. Trust."

Then Jerzom's face drew into to unfamiliar lines of concern as he looked at his most dear friend.

The royal prince's expression of concern left Peizar with no options. There was only one question he could utter. "What is troubling my prince?"

Jerzom laughed. "When strange situations are occurring, and intelligence is required to get the bottom of what may be an insurmountable calamity, then who better to gather intelligence than one who can be trusted?"

"I see," said Peizar. "And what is it that my prince would have me do?"

Now it was not lines of concern that stretched across Jerzom's face but a look of fear. It did not go undetected by Peizar. "You're troubled, my prince. What brings you to this state of fear?"

In a quivering voice, Jerzom proceeded with a line of conversation he had never expected. "Peizar, I fear that what I am about to ask you may cost you your life."

Silence engulfed the friends. The profound compassion of this royal prince for a commoner could not have weighed more heavily on Peizar.

"If I must give my life for you, my prince, I could not find a more worthy end." He paused and stared into the eyes of the disturbed prince. Then he continued. "Jerzom, you have given me a place of honor in this kingdom unlike none other in centuries."

He stopped and looked to the sky. "When my family was accused of treason by the goroms, it would have been easy for you to accept the death sentence dealt to me by that evil group of men." Now tears rolled down his cheek as he rushed on. "You saw something in me that was not evil. How great you are for being a man of principle."

And now there was a flood of tears spilling from Peizar's eyes. He recalled a story. "You could not save my dear mother and father." He choked up at his own mention of his parents. "Mochcom was well too aware of your intervention to thwart their evil conspiracy to bring death to the peasants. My mother and father were simple people who only wanted happiness for their only son. They put others first and then themselves. They had not done a morsel of harm to another living soul. And the knock on the door of our humble house was the last sound they heard. When they opened their home to whoever wanted in that fateful night, death walked in."

Now Jerzom could not hold back his tears. He had never forgotten what had happened five years ago. His mind went over every detail. *On that awful night, I had sat through a hearing in the Grand Hall of the royal palace. Mochcom told a story of lies, which my father believed. It was about a family that had killed a white stallion pony that belonged to the royal family because they wanted to overthrow the kingdom of Kopaz. In so many ways, it was absurd. How could a peasant family, whose most precious gift was their small boy—a child who would smile at a prince riding on a black stallion—be able to overthrow a mighty kingdom by killing a white pony?*

In so many ways, Jerzom blamed himself for not acting sooner.

Perceptive like no other, Peizar watched the royal prince deep in thought. He knew without asking what he was thinking. Maybe it was because he also was thinking of that fateful day and his beloved parents.

A tear rolled down Jerzom's cheek. His mind filled with the events of that dreadful evening. *My father was only concerned with the appearance of being a forceful king and did not listen to my pleas. He could have cared less about the plight of a peasant family. I pleaded with my father to send the royal guard. His only focus was playing a stupid game of garish cards. He spent countless hours fumbling through cards, as if they held the secret to life itself. How foolish.*

A lump formed in the young prince's throat. *It was I who ordered the royal guard to go to Peizar Vassar's house. It was too late. They found a scene of horror—the mutilated bodies of the father and mother of young Peizar.*

Prince Jerzom turned his head so his friend could not see his tears of sadness and remorse. *When the royal guard reported back to me, I raced to the Vassar house on my faithful black stallion, Zar. When I walked through the open door onto that dreadful stage of death, I heard the sound of sobbing. I lifted several boards on the floor and found a hole in the dirt. And when moonlight streamed through the open door, it illuminated a half-naked boy, shaking and crying. I vowed never to let the goroms' rule again bring death to the innocent people of Kopaz. And now, I'm about to ask that boy I found so long ago to put his life in peril and maybe even give his life for me.*

Peizar decided it was time. He could not let the prince think any more. He knew Jerzom's heart. He knew that gods and kingdom came before self-interest.

Peizar charged onward, putting into words what was heavy on Jerzom's mind. "There can be no solace. There can be no remorse. There can be no sadness." He smiled at Jerzom. "My dear friend and savior, I would lay down my life for Supreme God Viracocha. I would lay down my life for my royal prince who someday will be the greatest king Kopaz has ever had. And that is that."

The sounds of silence filled the visiting dignitary reception room as two young men plotted a course that would influence Kopaz for eternity.

"What is it, my royal prince, that you would have me do? You know my heart. Your decision for me is my pleasure to carry out!"

Jerzom fumbled for words. His mind was full. *The most difficult thing I will ever do in my life is send my best friend, who has a heart larger than life itself—who would lay down his life for me—on a mission he may not return from alive.*

Gathering his thoughts, the young prince said, "My dearest friend, we need to know the mind and soul of the evil ones who are plotting the demise of our kingdom."

It was an eternity of silence when the prince stopped speaking. He wrung his hands. He stared into nowhere. A stillness seemed to descend on every fiber of his being. Jerzom then said, "Will you be my spy and find a way to listen to the plans of the goroms?"

There could be no other answer from Peizar. "*Yes, my lord. I serve you with all my heart and soul!*"

Their eyes locked. Jerzom said, "There is something I must show you."

Jerzom reached for a wooden box that had been sitting on the table. "Three years ago, on my thirteenth birthday, my older brother, who was eighteen at the time, gave me a present. This is it."

As Jerzom opened the box, Peizar's anticipation mounted.

Whenever Jerzom showed him something, well, it was worth the wait. This was no exception. "Oh my golly," yelped Peizar. "That is beautiful!"

Jerzom smiled, knowing his friend was pleased. "This brass bow and arrow"—he stopped and placed his finger on the bow—"is the handiwork of Kashom. He wanted to give me something special. He was a master craftsman in the art of forging beautiful items from gold, silver, brass, bronze, and gemstone. You see here?" Jerzom's finger tapped on the gemstones inlaid in the brass. "Jerzom, Prince of Kopaz!"

"Wow!" said Peizar. "How beautiful!"

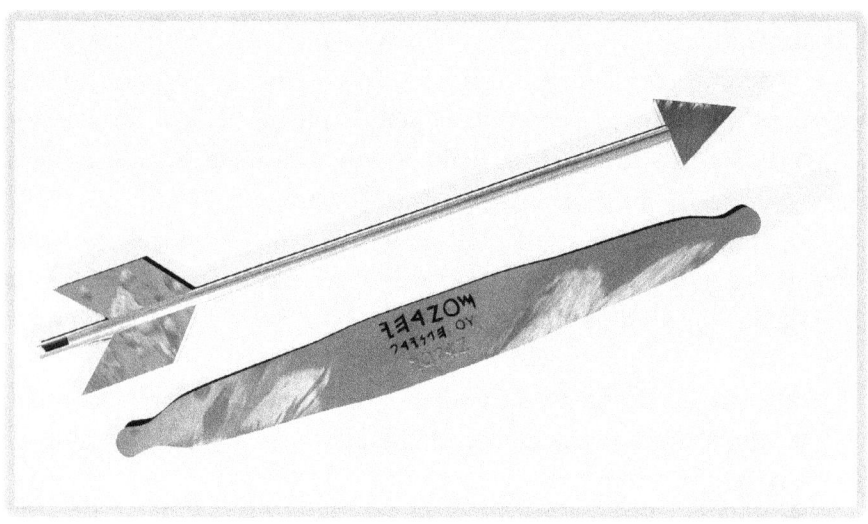

"I agree," said Jerzom, "but here is what is really neat. This brass bow and arrow are a set of keys. They open a secret passageway to not only the Hall of the Goroms but also the Grand Hall of the palace."

"You're kidding me?" replied Peizar as he laughed with delight.

"It's dark in the secret passageway below the first level of the palace. Getting to them is the trick. We need to go outside, walk around the southwest corner of the Grand Hall, and then walk north along the west side of the royal palace."

Taking a deep breath, Jerzom continued. "We're fortunate that this room, which we normally use to receive dignitaries, has a back door. It's hidden from the sight of the goroms. They do not have a direct line of sight from the Hall of the Goroms to this place."

Peizar listened intently. No one had to tell him the gravity of the mission that he was about to embark on. The peril was clear. He sat at the table across from the prince, listening to each word with deep concentration, his hands folded in his lap.

"Since I fear that our voices will carry outside, I must say what I have to in this room."

Nodding his head, Peizar lifted his hand as if to make a motion of approval and whispered, "I understand and will follow your wishes."

"OK, let me continue. We will go out the back door. That puts us on the south side of the palace. We walk to the southeast corner. We're fortunate that the forest is only ten feet from the west wall of this building."

Again, his breathing increased as he thought and talked at the same time. "Once in the forest, we walk two hundred yards north. That will put us halfway along the palace wall. It's there where we enter the secret passageway. I can show you how this all works." Jerzom pointed to the back door of the visiting dignitary conference room of the royal palace.

Jerzom was about to open the door, but Peizar didn't move. He suspected Peizar had suddenly got cold feet. He looked at his friend still sitting at the polished, cobalt-blue, volcanic-glass table.

"What?" asked Jerzom.

"Before we leave, tell me about the secret passageway. Where do I go? What do I do? Are there multiple passageways that I need to be aware of? Do you know?"

Slapping his forehead as he said, "Daaaa!" the prince walked back to the table.

The meeting between the friends stretched on for another half hour. Jerzom laughed as they wrapped it up. "God, I hope I got it all!"

"I think you covered more than all the details needed. I'll be fine!" said Peizar.

It was those words—"I'll be fine!"—that hung in Jerzom's mind.

With a surge of hope, his mind still concentrated on a single thought. *Gods be with my loyal friend.*

The sun was headed for the mountaintops. It was two thirty in the afternoon. The two boys left the palace and walked along its southern perimeter.

At its southeast corner, they waited. All was clear. Only a buck deer noticed them. They dashed across the ten feet of open space to the forest.

Safe in the woods and out of sight from any and all onlookers, they proceeded to walk north two hundred yards.

Fifteen minutes later, Jerzom put his hand in the air and motioned a stop. They now had to dash back across the ten feet of space that separated the forest from the west wall of the palace.

Fortunately, over the centuries, the undergrowth had grown over the open space, so their movements were concealed from anyone.

Along the base of the royal palace, a plethora of vines snaked their way up the first several layers of large rock that comprised the foundation of the structure. Jerzom pulled on several of the vines but did not break them so as not to disclose any intrusion.

"*Ah!* Here it is," whispered Jerzom with glee. He used his hands to scrape away loose dirt that had been gathering for years as the winds of time had blown a natural cover over two small holes in the base rock.

"Watch this, my friend," Jerzom said as he put the bow in a slit that was the shape of the brass bow. He then put the tip of the arrow into the keyhole beneath the bow. He turned the arrow just as if it were a key.

The massive rock moved backward, exposing a doorway into a tunnel.

"Holy shit," whispered Peizar. "What is this?"

"I told you there was a secret passageway. Well, here it is."

Jerzom removed the bow and arrow from the rock and motioned for Peizar to follow. "Step in."

When both boys were inside the passageway, Jerzom used his fingers to feel for another set of holes. He found them. He put the bow and arrow into the appropriate slot and keyhole. He turned the arrow clockwise. The massive rock closed, leaving the two boys in complete darkness.

"Holy crap, how do we get out of here?" whispered Peizar.

The arrow was still in the keyhole, so Jerzom turned it counterclockwise. The rock moved again, opening a doorway to the outside.

Once out, Jerzom motioned for them to sneak in the shadows and go back to the dignitary room in the palace.

The meeting turned into another hour of discussion about what to do and how to do it. Their conversation touched on all aspects of the emerging doom, and that included a young girl held captive by the goroms in the dungeon of the Great Pyramid and the plots to overthrow the royal family. The two young men forged a clandestine mission to uncover the evil conspiracies of the goroms who were seeking absolute control of not only Kopaz but also the universe.

"The hour is late, my friend. May the great god of the universe, Viracocha, abide with you as you embark on this most dangerous mission."

As the door closed, and Peizar walked into the darkness of an unknown future, Jerzom's heart sank as he thought, *Will I ever see him again?*

CHAPTER 18
Peizar Hears All

Gently tapping his fingers to the rhythm of the thoughts of grandeur that were streaming through his mind, Gorom Katchcom sat at the head of the table and envisioned the blood and gore spewing from the fallen royal guardsmen in a final triumphant battle. Surveying the faces of the priests whose attention was fixed on him, his smile was not unlike that on the face of Leonardo da Vinci's *Mona Lisa*. He gazed with delight at his Quorum of Goroms, knowing the end of King Dalvin's reign was at hand.

The end of day had not yet come, and the sun's rays still left a shadow on the courtyard dial, telling all it was now four o'clock. Katchcom's agenda for the meeting was twofold. One, his plans to overthrow the royal family must be understood by all, and he must secure their complete loyalty. This was the open element of the meeting's agenda. Two, there was a hidden element. He had to know for sure who among his goroms knew about the sacred name of Neferzul and the golden watch.

There was also someone lurking in the secret passage just on the other side of the wall, but that spy was known to no one except Prince Jerzom and the spy himself—Peizar. Moving his head closer to the marble wall, Peizar was able to press his ear tightly against it. It was perfect. The sounds of the meeting transpiring in the room on the other side of the wall were transmitted flawlessly through the stone. Leaning into the wall, his foot kicked a stone. It rolled into the wall and made a loud thump.

"What was that?" blurted Gorom Ancom. "I heard something."

His hand went instantly to his face. Katchcom whispered, "Shh," his index finger erect against his ruby-red lips.

Silence descended. All eyes were on Katchcom. He motioned with his other hand as he pointed in the direction of the thump.

Maybe it was coincidence…and then, maybe not. Who knows? Katchcom's cat had a small furry toy that she had believed was lost, but miraculously, she had found it again. Batting the toy with her front paws, she was playing a cat-and-mouse game. Racing after the toy, she slid into the chair leg that the toy just scooted under. Pointing to the decorative, gold-inlaid chair, Katchcom's Mona Lisa smile seemed more relaxed than ever. He said, "Zatchie is busy, I see. She has her lost toy. That's good. She's not howling as her mother, Zona, did."

He grinned and put his hand face down on the white marble table as he finished his remarks. "Zona is no longer with us and will cause me discomfort no more."

It seemed like a plausible explanation, or did it? Ancom's facial expression seemed to display a doubt that provoked Katchcom's ire. "Have you a question? Or do you question?" rasped Katchcom.

No one at the table spoke. The stillness of the voiceless group dragged on. Tension was mounting.

"What?" asked Katchcom, looking at Ancom with a stony face. "Have you nothing to say?"

"No, my lord," spoke Ancom in a cowardly voice. He jerked slightly under the intense glare of the high priest. "I have nothing to say. I question not your wisdom."

"Hmm," mused Katchcom, still glaring. "Let's get to the business of this gathering!"

Peizar took a deep breath and gave a sigh of relief. He managed to relax yet realized his caution was of the utmost importance. *Oh my God, that was close!* he thought as his lungs filled again between his timidly controlled efforts to breathe.

Taking the prize from the former high priest, Gorom Mochcom, whose position Katchcom now held as the leader of the Quorum of Goroms, was not his supreme goal. Katchcom's blinding zeal to rule was in all of his plans and schemes. For now, he could only imagine the thrill of being the disciple of the dark god, Zuron. To reign in blood and horror, twitching with ecstasy with each act of evil that was inflicted on defenseless victims—it was within his grasp. His soul leaped with joy, but his composure at the head of the table remained steadfast as befitted the leader of this band of evil men.

"Who is with me?" he rasped, looking at each gorom individually for a moment as he rolled his head so as to judge their confidence or lack thereof.

It was Yellcom who first raised his hand, his palm facing Katchcom, fingers erect and thumb spread. Instantly, the others followed suit.

"Good," said Katchcom as he leaned forward and put his elbows on the table. "We shall overthrow the king. Maybe even this evening!"

Once more, his eyes moved to survey each Gorom. There was silence.

Peizar's heart pounded. *Oh my God! They are going to kill the king.* No longer could he control his shaking. *Oh my God…oh my God.*

He pressed his ear more tightly against the cold rock wall. The dank, dark corridor left him shivering. Musty air that had not been circulated for centuries defined the atmosphere. The words coming through the stone could not have been. His fingers touched the wall and trembled as if to proclaim the state of mind Peizar was in.

With not a word from any gorom, Katchcom proceeded. "Cleverness is of the utmost priority. We shall entrap the prince, using him as our pawn to bring down this rotten ruler."

Once more, he stopped and took notice of the goroms' body language. It wasn't clear that he knew for sure if all were on board with his plan. "Is it clear?" he growled.

Now it was Shadcom who moved for a motion of approval by raising his arm to the square. And again, the motion was supported unanimously by all goroms with their arms to the square.

"I want you all to give me your sworn word that secrecy prevails and that what we say and do here does not leave here!" His voice rose as he continued. "All of the royal family will be gone, and their memory will fade into the blackness of oblivion throughout this land."

Their nodding heads reassured him that they were listening. "Here is the plan. First, we gain the trust of Jerzom at all costs. Second, we will lay a trap for him. Third, we will confront King Dalvin and Queen Neferapondes with an ultimatum. Fourth, in the confusion, we attack, using our army of bodyguards to kill all of the royal guard and then the royal family. Fifth, we will govern with horror and bloodshed, taking all from the people of Kopaz to ensure they are poor and can never challenge our control."

His glare intensified. "Am I clear?"

All heads nodded again.

"I have not heard what I desire!" Katchcom snarled.

It was clear at this point what he wanted. Gorom Dorcom quickly offered him assurances. "My lord, I swear to you that your will is safe, and I will never divulge your secrets. I will lay down my life to preserve your trust in me!"

Following suit, all proclaimed allegiance to the high priest.

Katchcom relaxed. He had the reassurance he needed, at least from most.

"Good," said Katchcom. "Our goal to dethrone Jerzom will leave the king and queen vulnerable, since the king has already demonstrated his inability to comprehend the workings of his kingdom." Katchcom laughed loudly. "The king's leadership has been an abysmal failure, and not having his son to point the king in the right direction on crucial issues will be our prize as we plot our coup."

There could be no denying that a victory dance would top off the meeting in grand accord, but victory was not yet in their grasp. Katchcom must have been satisfied, as his spirit was lifted just watching the joyous faces and uplifting conversation that was taking place at the council table.

As a personal vendetta against the queen, he made a parting remark to the group. "When King Dalvin falls, Queen Neferapondes, a woman without her man, will be defenseless against the Quorum of Goroms. Ha-ha to that old bitch!"

Drawing the meeting to a close, Gorom Katchcom dismissed his goroms with a challenge. "Bring me your plans on how we shall proceed with our overthrow of the kingdom of Kopaz! I want them no later than tomorrow evening!"

The secret meeting to plan the coup ended.

In light conversation, eight goroms walked toward the back door of the hall. Bringing down the royals was on all of their minds. It was as if they all had a new game to play and found pleasure in how to orchestrate it with zeal.

Cutting through the air like a sharp knife, Katchcom's voice elevated high above their small talk. "Goroms Dorcom and Ancom, stay!"

Frightened by what he heard, Peizar wanted to run to the prince. But the new development kept him frozen in place. *Goroms Dorcom and Ancom…hmm!*

"I've asked my cook to bring in dinner," said Katchcom as he motioned for Dorcom and Ancom to retake their places at the table.

Puzzled they were, but loyal they must be, so they obeyed. The meal was served.

It was not only the gnawing of mutton meat on rib bones that occupied Katchcom's time. His mind raced with each bite. *That idiot Gorom Dorcom could not have failed me more miserably than by letting his lust for a young girl cloud his vision of a grander future.*

The rippling goose bumps on Dorcom's skin were obvious to Katchcom. The dagger-like gaze of the high priest weighed heavily on Dorcom, and his uneasiness gave Katchcom total control of the situation.

Pulling small pieces of sinew and foul-tasting tendons from bones was not Dorcom's problem. It was that he was under the microscope. He was clueless. Growing tenser by the moment was his only response to Katchcom's silent inquisition.

Katchcom's face muscles roiled in disgust as his mind ventured on. Dragging the royal family into the goroms' business had long been forbidden, an unwritten code of honor among the priests.

Something was up. Unfortunately, neither Ancom nor Dorcom knew what it was. The foolish actions of Dorcom—dragging into full view the nasty business of the goroms, putting it center stage for the royal family to see—was only half the problem.

The inadvertent disclosure of the golden watch and sacred name of Neferzul Katchcom could blame on no one except himself. His problem was what to do about it.

At first, Katchcom played dumb. He pulled something from the pocket of his robe. As Ancom's mouth was full, Katchcom asked, "Do you know that this object, called a watch, has magical powers?"

Behind a solid stone wall, Peizar could not see how Katchcom's body language told a story of its own as the high priest fished for answers. Yet more than his own body language, the high priest was also fishing for the messages betrayed by the body language of the others at the table. He studied how Dorcom and Ancom answered his questions.

Ancom's hesitation to answer his leader's question did not go unnoticed by the high priest. He did not let that stop the questioning. "Dorcom, do you know what magical powers this object holds?"

"No, my lord," replied Dorcom. "I have never in my life seen this object that you hold before me. I can only guess what powers it holds, but you know my guesses. Well, pathetic!" He laughed as he answered.

Ancom's mouth was empty. His appetite was gone. Katchcom rolled his head and looked squarely into Ancom's eyes. "Ancom, is there a name associated with the magic of this object?"

"My lord, I have no name to associate with the watch, other than Neferzul." There was a hesitation, and then something strange happened. "My lord, it is not only the watch but also a golden key!" He smiled at Katchcom as he made his statement.

Ancom's answer was not what Katchcom wanted to hear. *He knows more than he tells me. He knows the girl is a Neferzul, and the watch is connected to her. How does he know about the golden key? Hmm!*

"Ancom, how wise of you! Do you know more?"

Never would he have expected the answer that followed. What happened next was beyond anything Katchcom could or would have suspected might come from Gorom Ancom.

"The golden key is the prize Mochcom sought after. Mochcom discovered that it would be required to win the War of the Gods. It unlocks GAMMAZEL," said Ancom. "He murdered Princess Aerapondes to get the golden key and prevent GAMMAZEL from working."

Listening to every word, Katchcom said nothing. He motioned with his cupped hand, fingers flipping out and then in, for Ancom to proceed.

"He knew…Gorom Mochcom knew that Aerapondes was TRPON and that her golden key would allow her to sit at the council table with Viracocha and the ruling gods. He ripped the key from her neck, drowned her, and then tricked Kashom into using the emerald star and five rainbow-colored worox stones to travel the Highway of Time."

Katchcom thought he had been the only one in whom Mochcom confided. He was wrong. His mind raced. *Mochcom told the other goroms. I wonder how many know the story?*

Ancom went on. "I was told by Mochcom that the golden watch has magical powers. It somehow is connected to the golden key. The entire story of the key and the watch remains a mystery, but what is known is that the two are somehow the connection between TRPOV and TRPON and the operation of GAMMAZEL, which is required for Viracocha to win the war of the gods!"

"What do you know about TRPOV and TRPON?" asked Katchcom, holding his body still so as not to inadvertently reveal his secret aspiration to sit at Zuron's table.

It worked. Ancom raced on. "The Neferzul in possession of the golden key becomes TRPON when the golden watch, which is a personal gift by Viracocha, is given to TRPOV."

"I see," said Katchcom, as he thought, *He didn't admit that his knowledge is limited. Hmmmm, I don't know the connection and I wonder if Ancom does?*

When it came to the connection of Danny's golden watch to Jeannie's golden key, Katchcom knew nothing. Although Danny and Jeannie were the only humans who know the secret that the golden watch holds with its connection to the golden key, that bit of information was unknown to Katchcom, but it did not stop the high priest from his quest to discover all of the secrets held by the gifts from the gods.

Out of character for a subordinate of Katchcom, Gorom Ancom boldly asked, "What's the connection between the golden key and the golden watch?"

Listening to Ancom break protocol, Katchcom felt that he had no choice but to respond, as he wanted Ancom to shut up. With thoughts racing wildly through his head, *You know not how foolish your actions are, and soon you will pay dearly!* Katchcom took lead in the conversation and told Dorcom and Ancom. "The golden watch is needed by TRPOV, and without it, he is powerless. At least, that is what Mochcom told me."

Hearing a story he never expected, Peizar's focus was heightened to a level that surely would have lifted him to the clouds where eagles soar. He heard the words. Peizar did know not what the word "TRPOV" meant. And even more confusing to Peizar was that the goroms knew the power of TRPOV and they controlled TRPOV's power because they had his watch. They were confident they were on the path to controlling all Kopaz by destroying the royal family.

Leaning into the wall, Peizar lost his footing and fell. This time there was no cat to blame for the *thump*.

Ancom lost focus on what Katchcom was saying. *There is something behind that wall, and for damn sure, it is not a cat.*

Maybe it was his concern about who knew about the watch, the key, and the sacred name of Neferzul. And then just maybe it was Katchcom's focus on what to do about two of his goroms—Dorcom and Ancom. Maybe it was just the way it was. At any rate, Katchcom ignored the noise behind the wall.

Not wanting to drag the meeting on for more than an hour and a half, Katchcom was through. He'd learned what he wanted. Ancom's loss of focus was not unnoticed. Katchcom used the interruption to end the meeting.

For Ancom, the night was yet young. He elected to stand outside the hall in the shadows.

CHAPTER 19
Peizar Warns a Prince

Throughout the ages, there has been a defining quality that sets some people apart—it's called trust. Loyalty can only be genuine when it is accompanied by this most intangible thing called trust. It is the defining quality that brings two people together in the bond of friendship. Without it, a friendship is in name only and can be cast off as frivolous. However, when a friendship is real and endures through the most devastating of crises, it can only be attributed to this most prized element that cannot be seen, cannot be felt, but yet has an everlasting effect that all in the friendship can attest to. Such was the friendship between the commoner, Peizar, and the royal prince, Jerzom.

Maybe the secret entrance to the catacombs leading from the royal palace to the Hall of the Goroms had been positioned on the west wall of the palace by accident. And then again, maybe not. Who knows? The fact was that the secret door was where it was, and Ancom was hiding in the shadows near the hall—the location where Gorom Ancom thought he heard the thump! He never saw Peizar exit the catacombs and make his way to the front door of the palace.

Dropping below the horizon, the sun had just settled in for the night. It was not quite dark. The palace candles had not been lit, so twilight was settling in. The doorman recognized who knocked. "Jerzom waits for you," he told Peizar as the commoner entered the massive doorway and started his journey to the opposite doorway across the Grand Hall. It was the doorway that led to the main hall of the palace and the rooms of all of the royal family members. Standing and holding the door open, Jerzom was anxious for his best friend to make his way to him.

"I'm so glad you are OK. Oh, was I concerned for your safety!" were the first words that left the prince's mouth as he hugged his friend.

"My royal prince, we have a crisis on our hands. It will destroy the royal family and devastate all who live in Kopaz. We must hurry. Things are taking place even as we speak," Peizar said urgently. Unlike Helen of Troy, who had a face that launched a thousand ships, Peizar's face could launch nothing. Grieved, he stared at Jerzom. "I fear I am too late! Forgive me, my royal prince."

"Hurry, I've cleared my desk in my room. We can spend as much time as required," said Jerzom as he hugged his friend once more and then pointed for the two to hurry down the hallway to the prince's private room.

Peizar found a smile hidden someplace in his being as the prince hugged him for the second time. "I will lay down my life for you when you ask!"

Words were not needed to describe the bond of friendship between these young men as they walked down the long hall to the prince's study.

"We're here. Come quickly. Let's sit on my couch. It will be more comfortable than if we hunched over my desk," said Jerzom as he pointed to the massive leather couch that stretched across the entire twenty feet of the back wall of his study.

Lifting his eyebrows, his face concerned, Jerzom locked eyes with Peizar. "OK. What happened?"

The words poured from Peizar's mouth. "I fear we are doomed!" His statement left Jerzom without words. Expanding his bare chest, his ripped muscles tightened not for lack of air but in shock at why he hadn't seen it coming. For quite some time, the actions of the Quorum of High Priests had left a feeling heavy on Jerzom's mind. He had sensed that the goroms were up to evil.

He breathed and, without a word, nodded for Peizar to proceed. The lines of disbelief that stretched across the young prince's face displayed the gravity of the unfolding events, which had to be handled with the utmost urgency.

With the cool evening upon them and the study windows open, letting the night air drift in, Peizar should not have been sweating. That was not the case. His bare chest was wet with perspiration as he started his tale of deceit, deception, death, and horror.

For all his desire to have it be something other than a tale of doom, there could be no fabrication of facts that would lead to any other conclusion. "My friend, my prince, with my own ears I heard the conversation of the goroms." He took a deep breath and continued. "Your brother, Kashom, was once in possession of the golden watch, a gift from Viracocha. He was TRPOV."

Jerzom stopped his friend in the middle of his sentence. He repeated the word with a question. "TRPOV? What or who is that?"

Peizar's jaw dropped. He asked, "How do you mean?"

It was obvious that a mystery had just been exposed. "Did they say what 'TRPOV' means?" queried Jerzom.

With a look of distress, Peizar answered, "I don't know. All I know is that there is a godly significance to the word 'TRPOV.'"

Knowing that the prince was most interested and wanted answers, Peizar waited. Jerzom nodded slowly. "What else, my friend?" He now knew for the first time who had killed his beloved sister and the fate of his brother.

Taking this as his cue, Peizar continued. "Your murdered sister, Aerapondes, was in possession of the golden key and had the sacred name of Neferzul." He went on. "The Neferzul in possession of the golden key becomes TRPON when the golden watch, which is a personal gift from Viracocha, is given to TRPOV."

Totally dumbfounded by the dump of information, Jerzom shook his head in bewilderment. "Did they mention any connection between my brother and this devious plot?"

"No, my royal prince. They only said Kashom was conned," said Peizar, knowing the pain in Jerzom's heart because his brother, Kashom, had been blamed for the most horrific crime ever to occur in the Land of Kopaz—

the murder of Princess Aerapondes.

"What else, my friend?" Jerzom asked.

"Nothing good," replied Peizar. He looked away to collect his thoughts. "They have put in place a dreadful plan to overthrow the royal family and begin a reign of horror on the people of Kopaz." A tear spilled from Peizar's eye as he continued. "They spelled out the plan, and simply put, it is this. First, they gain your trust, Prince Jerzom, at all costs. Second, they will lay a trap for you. Third, they will confront your parents, King Dalvin and Queen Neferapondes, with an ultimatum. Fourth, in the confusion, they will attack, using their army of bodyguards to kill all of the royal guard and then the royal family. Fifth, they will govern with horror and bloodshed, taking all from the people of Kopaz to ensure they are poor and can never challenge the goroms' control."

"*My God!*" yelled Jerzom. "This is the blackest evil I've ever imagined in my wildest dreams of these horrific bastards." His look of helplessness could not be overlooked.

"Can you tell your parents?" whispered Peizar, afraid Jerzom's last outburst might have alerted the personnel working in the palace.

"I thought of that, my friend…but no! If I brought this matter to my father without proof and told him a commoner passed this information to me, he would have me tried for treason!" Jerzom's heart sank as he said, "I know my father."

"We must find a way to stop them, my royal prince. It is bigger than you can imagine." Peizar stopped and looked at his beloved friend. "They have something, the golden watch. I know not its powers, but the magical powers of the watch are at the center of their deception."

Peizar gathered his thoughts and tried to recall how the watch was connected. "The golden watch, my royal prince, is needed to work with the golden key. The golden key and watch are used to open the Highway of Time. The golden key is required to unlock GAMMAZEL."

Jerzom's ears could not have been more focused on the words dropping from Peizar's lips. "My royal prince, if they have the golden watch and golden key, Viracocha will lose the war of the gods! The supreme god needs the golden key to unlock GAMMAZEL in order to win the war!"

"My god!" said Jerzom. "We are center stage on the battlefield of the gods!"

Slowly and with calculated words, Peizar continued. "My royal prince, on several occasions you told me that Kashom had explained to you the war of the gods is a winner-take-all contest. I suspect the goroms are plotting to ally with Zuron. Your family has been allied with supreme god and goddess, Viracocha and Neferdor. I don't know for sure, but if they succeed in overthrowing your father and mother, we are in trouble, and who knows where it will all end? I have an awful feeling in my gut." He stopped. The young men looked in each other's eyes. "If they succeed, all could be lost, not only for us but for the entire human race!"

"Let us learn more. It is late, so on the morrow, let us find a way to stop this," said Jerzom as the meeting came to a close.

Jerzom's mind raced on as he watched Peizar walk out the door. *Where did the watch come from?* It was a mystery to him. But even a larger mystery filled his thoughts. *Hmm. If my brother once owned it, what does it have to do with the prisoner? Does she have the golden key?*

CHAPTER 20
Zanzee in a Dungeon

Sitting on the dirt floor, Jeannie wrapped her arms around her knees, squeezed tightly, and rocked back and forth. Her mind was filled with song. It was Johnny Bacon's smash hit "You're My Angel Divine." The last verse echoed loudly as it dominated her every thought.

> Pretty pretty blue eyes from the gods above
> You fell from the heavens to bring me your love.
> Now you're my beautiful angel divine
> You're sixteen and you're all mine.

It's funny how minds drift when there is nothing else to do. That drifting can, however, be a demon in disguise. When you least expect it, in your mind, things happen. That is, when you are in a horrific situation with no foreseeable way out, your mind takes over, like it or not.

Her Danny boy would sing Johnny Bacon's song to her. She loved it. She would say, "If only Johnny B could sing like you, Danny, he'd be ten times richer!"

If Danny had one talent that shone like the one and only Hope Diamond, it was his ability to belt out a song like no other. Jeannie would say, "You have the voice of an angel, and not just any angel! You have the voice of the Archangel Michael, and when you sing, you command listeners throughout the universe to listen."

Danny would laugh and reply, "I think I detect a bit of a bias in your analogy!"

But she would shoot back, "I don't think so, Danny. If an agent worth his salt ever heard you sing, Elvis Presley would have to move off stage to make room for you!"

Tears burst from her eyes as she thought about those adventurous days in the Scarlet Desert when she fell in love with the boy who she discovered was the royal prince of Viracocha, the one the supreme god called TRPOV. But it was all gone now. Jeannie was sure that her lover lay someplace in the depths of a pool at the bottom of Yellshome Falls.

She cringed as an uncontrollable thought crept into her mind. *He's food for the hungry flesh-eating fish. They pick his bones clean.*

Another horrifying reality hit her. *Has Viracocha replaced Danny with someone else as TRPOV?*

Sobbing loudly to block those awful thoughts from entering her consciousness, she found that only a conversation with herself would keep the demons away.

"He's gone," she whimpered. "Why did it have to happen?"

Not all in the musty, dark cold room were paying attention to Jeannie's conversation. As her sobbing raced on and she was about to say, "Why? Why? Why?" something bit her bare leg.

She screamed, kicking her folded legs, and jumped to her feet.

"Get away! Help, help! Get away!" Her spontaneous yell for help echoed in the dungeon as if to say, *Who are you asking for help?*

Yet over her screams to find help and get the creature away from her, her ears filled with animal sounds. *Eeeerrrreeerrrree, sssqqeeeqqqeeeqqqlll, ssscchheeeeeeee!* Then they stopped.

Having no concept of time, she had no idea that it was late in the afternoon and that darkness was settling on the outside world. It was that time of the day when creatures of the night came out, slithering to-and-fro in search of prey.

It was not the slithering creatures of the night, but the sounds of footsteps in the hallway outside the heavy wooden door that filled the air and sent a chill up her spine.

Then, terrible *sssssrrreeeeeeeekkkk, sssssrrreeeeerrrreeeekkk* sounds drowned out the sound of footsteps.

The bright light of the torch blinded Jeannie. Her eyes were used to the dark, and they could not compensate quickly enough to see past the flickering brilliance of the red-hot flames.

In a language she did not understand, a deep voice behind the torch said, "How's my sweet little baby doing?"

There were chuckles of glee, which Jeannie did comprehend. She froze. Her heart raced. Her rigid body felt to her like granite.

"I've come to keep you warm. It's cold in here. Your tender body next to mine will bring warmth to your soul!" The words made no sense to her. Yet her intuition was far more revealing than the man's words, and she knew there could be only one thought dominating the gorom's mind. *My little girl…pleasure awaits me!*

His evil thoughts might as well have been broadcast on the silver screen so all who were sitting in the theatre could watch the episode and hear them loudly.

Oh no! It's him! The terrible thought exploded in Jeannie's mind. *Help me…Please God, help me!*

Her pleas for help faded as she hugged her body with her small arms. Pulling them tightly around her, Jeannie could only hope her arms would give her protection from the man she recognized as the gorom who had visited earlier. If fate had not intervened and two strangers had not shown up, this same gorom standing in front of her would have taken her innocence and left her to die. But now there were no strangers to help.

In her mind, she could not even comprehend that fate existed, let alone that it would be a defining force that would change an impending outcome. This time it was clear to Jeannie that there were no others. She was all alone with a monster with one thought on his mind. She was defenseless before this evil gorom who wanted to take his pleasure from a helpless teenager in a dungeon deep in the bowels of an ancient pyramid. There was no escape. She was doomed.

The bright light moved closer. Now she could see his outline. His eyes glared. They sparkled behind the light. She cringed with each step he took. For Jeannie, time had stopped. She was frozen in space. Not a muscle could she move. She waited.

Another sound ripped through the dank dungeon air. *Grrrrrrrarrrrrraaaarrrrrr!*

Then there was silence. The gorom stopped. The torch no longer moved. The flame flickered in place. The gorom's image was like that of a demon from hell with the flickering light of the torch in his hand dancing across his grotesque bearded face.

Ggggrrrrrrrggggggggrraaaarrrrrr! Again, the sound echoed through the cold musty dungeon and filled every void.

She could not see. Her eyes had not adjusted. She was helplessly waiting for the next episode of terror to strike.

Then something happened.

Rrrraaaarrrrrr!

"Hel…help…oooooowwwwwwwwww!"

The torch dropped to the ground, its light shining upward. There wasn't much light coming from the torch on the ground, but enough so that she could see not only the man's face but also his entire body.

Thrashing like an alligator with its prey in its mouth, he was reaching, struggling to dislodge whatever was at his throat. He failed. His throat was torn open, and blood shot out with such force that it splattered Jeannie.

She screamed. The man dropped to the ground. He rolled violently to thwart the creature that had a death grip on him. His efforts were to no avail.

The eerie sound *gaaaaadddaaadd* could only be the blood gargling in his throat.

Then she saw him, the man's attacker.

She screamed, "*Zanzee…Zanzee!*"

Her black cat—her protector—released his hold on his prey.

Dorcom slapped his hand over his bleeding jugular. Frantic, he had only one option left—pressure would stop the hemorrhaging. At least momentarily, it worked. He managed to get to his feet. His stare was not to find Jeannie but the door. He did. He stumbled toward it.

She no longer was terrified by the monster who had had only one objective—to find pleasure in a helpless teenage girl. Yet she knew deep in her soul that fate had not intervened. No, it was not fate—it was her protector, Zanzee. Purring loudly, he was at her side, brushing against her bare legs.

In a panic, Gorom Dorcom tried to get out before he died. He needed to escape from whatever had just ripped his throat out before it attacked again.

Still faithfully producing light, the torch lay on the ground. Gorom Dorcom left it there, lighting the room as he staggered through the door into the long hallway leading from the center of the Great Pyramid. He only hoped his strength did not give out before he reached the doorway out of the Great Pyramid.

Zanzee was now in her arms, purring loudly. She pulled the cat tightly against her body. She said nothing. Her mind flashed back to a night she had spent talking to her mom.

She recalled as if it was yesterday—her mom smiling, their conversation on the culture of her people. *We don't know much about Zanzee's former life. We do know that he lived with the royal family of Kopaz. Zanzee was Kashom's cat and comforted him in times of trouble. Kashom was going to give Zanzee to his sister, but then she was murdered, so later he gave him to his daughter, Moon-Of-Day. Since that time, the eldest girl in the LoneTree Family is the one whom Zanzee comforts—that has been tradition for centuries. He has special powers. Clearly, he never dies. Zanzee was my cat for twenty-eight years—now he is your cat and comforts you.*

Jeannie's tears of fear were now tears of joy. She snuggled Zanzee, rocking him against her quavering body as she spoke softly. "Oh Zanzee, I love you so much. You did hear my cries for help. You are my special gift from the gods."

It's funny how sometimes time seems to be meaningless and stretches in circles, bringing back the past as if it were the present. That must have been the case for Jeannie as she drifted into the past to some memorable moment with Zanzee.

Snuggling Zanzee there in the dungeon, Jeannie remembered the night as though it had just happened. It was a night long ago at her home in the Scarlet Desert when she had walked through her bedroom door, still with Zanzee in her arms, stroking his shiny black fur as she teased him.

Ironically, Jeannie remembered verbatim her words. She repeated them now as she stroked his soft black fur and he purred even louder. "Zanzee, my friends all ask me where you came from and who put the earrings in your ears. They want to know why you have two in your right ear and only one in your left ear. And all you can say is meow? Zanzee, you're a good kitty—but I'm still trying to figure out what you're good for. Oh, I'm sorry! *Just kidding!* I know—I don't want to hurt your feelings. You're my best friend. You keep me company all night long, sleeping right by my side."

And as she had done so long ago in her bedroom, now in a dungeon, Jeannie lifted him to her face and kissed his nose. She giggled and asked him a question. "Do you know what I tell my friends, Zanzee, when they ask me where you came from? Well—I tell them that the Egyptian gods gave you to me to guard my path through life and keep me company. What do you think about that?"

And just like always, Zanzee gave Jeannie that familiar look that he always did when he had an answer to her question. He looked at her eyes. "Meow, meow."

His meowing, as well as his loud purring, faded into a dead silence.

Cautiously, still holding Zanzee, she made her way to the open door, glancing hither, thither, and yon as if there were other monsters lurking in the shadows of the dungeon.

Stepping through the doorway, she was able to look down the long hallway. It was as if she was peering into a long tunnel. Squinting, she was able to see the dying gorom.

Partially plugged by his finger, Dorcom's gaping hole in his jugular was still bleeding, but not as profoundly as it had been, now only squirting a few inches with each beat of his heart. He stumbled on, at least three hundred feet from her. He was nearing the exit doorway from the Great Pyramid, and she lost sight of him as he rounded a bend in the hallway.

Dorcom's problem was real. In his condition, losing his grip on reality from loss of blood, his hand was not covering his wound completely. His strength was being sapped with each beat of his heart, squirting blood out of his torn jugular. He could not stop it. He was less than one hundred feet from the pyramid's exit. He didn't make it. He fell to the ground.

Jeannie watched and waited. She pulled Zanzee closer. Because of the bend in a hallway, Gorom Dorcom's dead body, which was lying not more than fifty feet from the fresh air of the great outdoors, was concealed from her. Without knowing if he was alive, dead, or waiting for her to venture out, she, figuratively speaking, was in the dark.

Zanzee's shiny black fur and sapphire-blue eyes had set him apart so long ago when he had been Kashom's cat living in the royal palace. Kashom no longer lived in Kopaz. Zanzee was no longer Kashom's cat. He was Jeannie's protector. He purred loudly, knowing she was safe.

The song in her mind that she had been humming earlier now took on a different meaning. Holding Zanzee, she sang softly,

Pretty pretty blue eyes from the gods above
You fell from the heavens to bring me your love.
Now you're my beautiful angel divine
You're Zanzee, and you're all mine.

CHAPTER 21

A Princess and a Friend Meet a Goddess in Training

C all it coincidence. Call it fate. You may call it what you may. The fact is—it happened. The mystery of why this intruder in the land of Kopaz looked identical to herself and her twin, Princess Aerapondes, was haunting her. Princess Merapondes had to know for sure who the prisoner really was. Her curiosity about Jeannie was gnawing away at her. Oh yes, for sure, there would be risks, yet for Merapondes, sneaking into the Great Pyramid felt like her only option.

It might have been curiosity that was the driving force of Merapondes's plan. But attempts to outsmart the insidious hand of fate were tenuous at best. Did Merapondes fully comprehend the danger of gambling with the hand of fate? Maybe not. Sometimes that unknown entity called fate, which cannot be seen, surely can be felt when least expected. Can anyone deny that fate is wielded and controlled by the forces of coincidence? Or are there hidden forces that catch us by surprise and are wielded by pure evil? Did Merapondes know what devious schemes the evil men, the Quorum of High Priests, were plotting, all in the name of righteousness? Maybe she didn't, and then again, maybe she did. Who could say?

Yet unlike the calculated gamble with fate that Princess Merapondes was about to take, sometimes things happened that could not be explained by reasonable thinking. Those involved, blindsided by the unforeseeable forces of the insidious hand of fate, were in actuality oblivious. One event that might be considered a coincidence was the death of Gorom Dorcom, the evil man who had been looking for pleasure from a teenage girl. Her name was Jeannie LoneTree, but no one on Kopaz knew that except the young man she feared is dead. Dorcom had no knowledge of her real name. He was merely seeking pleasure and was caught.

However, the death of one might be a twist of fate that benefited another. The dead body of a man, lying in the dirt hallway not far from the doorway leading out of the Great Pyramid was, to some, an unexplained mystery. Questions would arise: How did he die? Who killed him?

Ironically, however, while such a death might be considered fate by some, Gorom Katchcom would likely have a totally different view. He might call it opportunity. The fact that Gorom Dorcom was dead, to Katchcom, might not matter at all. And so those questions—How did he die? Who killed him?—would be tossed aside as other devious schemes were put into place. Katchcom might be glad that Gorom Dorcom was dead and say, "I shall deal with him no more. Thank god, he's dead."

So there you had it. The fate of an evil man, killed by a cat, was of no consequence to the man who cared not how his subordinate died, only that the untimely death had given him an opportunity that could be useful to him.

On the other hand, the girl in the pyramid, who looked identical to a member of the royal family and her murdered twin sister, might be another story. The mystery behind that question—Who is that girl who looks identical to me and my twin sister?—was real. The answer was of vital importance to Princess Merapondes, who was probing the meaning of this mystery. One can only ponder: Was it coincidence? Was it fate? Who knows?

Whatever the reason—coincidence, destiny, or who knows what—the insidious hand of fate steps on the stage of life when least expected. Most often it strikes unsuspecting victims with a sword of death that comes from nowhere. Merapondes's calculations were nonexistent as to the unseen twists of evil forces that wielded their will on innocent, unsuspecting seekers. And so it was on that balmy day in Kopaz.

Jeannie waited. All was quiet. She had a decision to make. She held Zanzee next to her. He lifted his right paw and gently touched her cheek. She smiled down at him. Questions filled her mind. *Where is that evil man? Is he dead? Is he hiding someplace so he can jump from the shadows and strangle me?* Letting her imagination run wild left her heart pounding.

Time stretched on. No one came into the Great Pyramid. The sun started its descent in the western sky, shedding warmth across Kopaz and all the inhabitants of the small villages that dotted the countryside. Unfortunately, the sun's warmth did not make its way to Jeannie in the unholy sanctuary that had been the scene of so much torture and murder, that had been a living hell for unsuspecting souls who had had the misfortune of ending up there over the centuries as sacrificial lambs.

Jeannie did not know that the evil gorom would never return. How could he? Gorom Dorcom's black soul had been shipped to the outer reaches of darkness in the Land of the Dead.

Katchcom was yet not aware of the death of Dorcom, but his problems with an insubordinate gorom were no more. Dorcom had already revealed the nasty business of the evil Quorum of High Priest to the royal family. The damage had already been done. Even if Katchcom knew of Gorom Dorcom's untimely death, the high priest could not roll the clock back and undo the damage. Dorcom's encounter with Prince Jerzom and Princess Aerapondes was history. Other than that, all was quiet on the eastern wall of the Great Pyramid.

Back at the royal palace, the start of a lazy afternoon left Princess Merapondes pondering various questions. *Aerapondes never mentioned a golden watch, but she asked me if I knew anything about the name of Neferzul. What was she talking about? What does the prisoner have to do with Neferzul? Does she have the golden key?* Her meeting with her brother only heightened her curiosity.

Aerapondes said Neferzul means "beautiful blue," and that is all she said. Hmm, I wonder what the blue is?

In the early evening, most of the servants were busy cleaning and making preparations for the next royal meal that would start in several hours. She had time. She slipped out of her room, sneaked out of a side door in the reception room of the royal palace, and planned how to get across the courtyard between the palace and the Hall of the Goroms. It would be tricky because she would have to walk almost a mile to get to the east wall of the Great Pyramid. Doing that entirely undetected by the goroms was her challenge, yet the twilight would give her cover. Once outside the palace, she eyed the situation to select her course.

The architect's mistake when the Hall of the Goroms and the royal palace were being designed two centuries ago might now be a blessing in disguise to Princess Merapondes. Since the entrance to the Great Pyramid was on its east side, all she had to do was navigate her way to the thick forest that lined the eastern boundary of the courtyard. And since the front entrance to the Hall of the Goroms was seven hundred yards from the side door of the diplomat room in the palace, she was comfortable that the goroms would have trouble discerning who was in the courtyard, and the many trees and garden hedges would block any onlooker's curious view. Her course was set. Her plan was to walk directly east six hundred yards. Then she would select her path so that the Hall of the Goroms was always out of sight. Once at the edge of the courtyard, Merapondes would use the cover of the forest and thick undergrowth to conceal her journey to the Great Pyramid six hundred yards due north.

Since the Great Pyramid was a hundred yards east of the Hall of the Goroms and the entryway into the pyramid faced the east, the evening sun was on the west side of the pyramid and the hall. This was convenient because it left little light to expose anyone entering or leaving the pyramid.

Merapondes left the royal palace and embarked on her planned journey.

Slithering among the well-manicured hedges and flowering trees, Merapondes must have felt as though she were a giant salamander lying low to escape the view of a beady-eyed predator. It was working. At least that was what she thought. *OK, I'm halfway across the grand courtyard. I haven't been able to see the Hall of the Goroms, so I'm sure they haven't seen me.*

She did have one concern however. *What if someone from the palace sees me crouching out here in the bushes?*

Her heart started pounding. She took a deep breath and stopped. Her mind was searching. *OK…I've got it!* She smiled. *I'll just say what I'm trying to discover is whether the large red parrots that live in the trees speak the language of Kopaz or the language of the royals. No one will be the wiser.*

Satisfied, she pressed forward. The last three hundred yards across the courtyard took her half the time the first three hundred had.

Upon reaching the edge of the forest, she sighed with relief. *I made it! Whew! Halfway there.*

Lifting her arm to wipe the sweat from her brow, she took a deep breath. Smiling, she was confident that her choice of dress was perfect. Her silk blouse and loose-fitting silk pants flapped gently against her breasts and legs in the afternoon breeze. *I can't imagine my brown blouse and pants with a green leaf pattern woven into them would stand out. I think I made the perfect choice for a nice camouflage. I blend into the forest!*

Pressing onward, she could see that she was almost directly across from the east wall of the Great Pyramid. She moved closer to the edge of the forest. *Yes, I'm almost there. I can see the pyramid.*

Now she faced her most challenging leg of the journey. The Great Pyramid was fifty yards due west of her. One thing in her favor was the result of an oversight by the architects who laid out the locations of the palace and the Hall of the Goroms. Seeing only a corner of the northeast wall of the palace and not able to see the hall at all, she felt safe. She thought about her last fifty yards in the open without the cover of the forest. *I only have a short distance to go!*

Waiting at least five minutes before venturing out of the forest and onto the open grassy lawn, she looked at every possible hiding place that a gorom might be stationed. *I don't think they are here. The door to the dungeon in the pyramid has a sliding bolt lock.* She paused. She rolled her head, all the while looking at each and every possible place a gorom might be standing guard. She found nothing that would concern her. She commenced her silent planning. Nodding her head with each thought, she continued. *OK, if the guards are not on the outside, they for darn sure are not on the inside. They're not stupid. They would not subject their bodies one minute to the filth, dankness, spiders, bugs, snakes, and rats that make their homes in the hallway of the pyramid.*

It was almost dark, and the twilight was dimming. The night creatures started their serenade.

"What are you doing here?" came words from the dark.

Totally surprised, she froze and squealed, "Who's there?"

Spinning around instantly, as if she were an Olympic ice-skater doing her final twirl in front of the judges, she blurted out again, "Where are you?"

Stepping from behind the bright yellow-flowering bush with large fig-like leaves, Peizar restated his questions. "What is going on? Why are you here?"

Quite sure her heart had flopped over at least twenty times, she took a breath. She pointed at him. "I'll ask you the same. Why are you here?"

He lifted his finger to his lips. "Shh! We may have company!"

He motioned for her to follow him to a rock not far from where they stood. A little deeper into the forest, it was fifty feet from them.

In moments, they were both relaxing, sitting on the rock.

"I'm on an assignment that Jerzom has instructed me to carry out. I can't talk about it," said Peizar. He pressed her again. "What are you doing out here?" He knew the danger of being out late at night anywhere near the pyramid. "You are in danger just being here!"

"I want to see the prisoner," Merapondes whispered. "She looks exactly like me and—"

Cutting her off in the middle of what she was saying, his face instantly changed into an expression of total concern. "You can't, Merapondes. It is so dangerous just being near this place, let alone being in the dungeon. Your life is at risk."

"You have no control over me!" she snapped. "You have a choice to help me or just go about your business. Which will it be?" she fired at him.

Clearly, she was not to be reasoned with. "OK," he said. "Let's figure how we get across the lawn undetected and then into the pyramid."

"Good," she yelped in a hushed tone. "Let's do it!" She stood and motioned for him to follow.

The final stage of their journey began. They hadn't gone twenty feet when something snapped a twig on the ground, breaking the silence with a loud *crack*!

Spinning around, they saw nothing. They stood motionless for at least four minutes. All was quiet.

For whatever reason, Ancom had set up a watch site. Maybe it was because he had heard the thuds behind the walls of the Hall of the Goroms when Katchcom was having his planning meeting. Who knew?

He waited. He listened.

Although moments earlier, their conversation was carried out in hushed words, Ancom had heard all. His hiding place on the edge of the forest just east of the pyramid was only thirty feet from the rock where Merapondes and Peizar had been sitting.

Convinced it was nothing, Merapondes and Peizar turned and started walking in the direction of the Great Pyramid once more. The doorway, which looked like a large black square hole, was getting closer with each step.

Although the sun was shedding its final rays of faint light on the west wall of the pyramid, the full moon was up early that evening. It lit up the grassy courtyard like football stadium lights, so convenient for a stalker who had his prey in sight.

He watched their every move. Ancom was deep in thought. *Hmm. What shall I do. Why is she here? Why is Jerzom's friend here? Something must be up*. Then the unexpected happened.

At least a half an hour had gone by since Jeannie had walked out of the dungeon door holding Zanzee. Dorcom never came back. She had lost track of him but feared to leave.

The passing of time must have influenced her or convinced her not to stay. Maybe she felt it was safe. Maybe Zanzee gave her courage. Maybe she felt it was her only chance to escape. Who knows?

It took her five minutes to walk cautiously down the long dirt-floor hallway. The inhabitants—rats, spiders, snakes, and the like—did not faze her on her journey. She rounded the corner. The massive doorway opening leading out of the pyramid came into sight. She first saw the bright rays of the moon. In the darkness of the hallway, she tried to gingerly walk forward, making her way to the door when it happened.

Tripping over something on the floor, she fell. She dropped Zanzee. He raced for cover. She broke her fall with her outstretched arms, so her head did not slam into the ground. It made a soft landing on the arm of a dead man. The full moon shed its light on something startling. Staring into a dead face not three inches from hers, she screamed, "*Noooooooooo! Nooooooooooooooo!*"

Sssssrrrrrrrrkkkkkkkkk!

When Jeannie screamed, Merapondes seized Peizar's arm and yanking, she unconsciously ripped his shirt. He stopped. Pointing frantically, Merapondes said, "It's her! I know it!"

Consumed with fright and unable to move, Jeannie stared into Dorcom's blank, open eyes. The sight of his bloody throat left her paralyzed.

CHAPTER 22
Caught and Murdered

Screams coming from the pyramid? What was happening? It wasn't much of a puzzle. How could it be? They could be coming from no one other than the prisoner. To say that Merapondes was startled would be an understatement. Either it was time to hightail it and run or it was time to make a mad dash and come to the screaming girl's rescue.

Evidently, Merapondes and Peizar chose neither of these two options, as they neither ran toward nor away from the pyramid. Their first thought was that someone was in the dungeon, causing the prisoner harm. But the screams sounded like they were coming from just inside the doorway. They were too loud to be coming from the dungeon itself, deep in the bowels of the pyramid. No, the screams were coming from just inside the entrance to the Great Pyramid.

"Peizar, something is wrong! She's not in the dungeon. I think she is just inside the door," said Merapondes.

It was not only Merapondes and Peizar who heard the screams. Skulking in the shadowy forest not far from the doorway leading into the Great Pyramid, Ancom heard the same screaming. Knowing she had not left the pyramid and that no other goroms were around or guarding the dungeon, he waited. He watched. He listened.

Only moments from leaving the Great Pyramid, Jeannie didn't even have time to compose herself and get off the dirt floor. She rolled reactively as instinct took over. Now lying ten feet from the dead gorom, she lifted her head to the see the silhouettes of two people standing in the doorway.

The air was still, and the night was breezeless. Without competition from Mother Nature, the sounds coming from the hallway leading into the Great Pyramid traveled effortlessly.

With his hand cupped behind his ear, Ancom heard the sounds of talking. It seemed to be coming from inside the pyramid. He looked and squinted. He saw two human shadows just inside the doorway.

Stymied, Merapondes and Peizar were initially at a loss. She asked Peizar, "Should we see what happened?"

Peizar answered her with a whisper. "Yes, give me your hand, we must… let's go really quietly. We don't know who it is or why they screamed."

Princess Merapondes answered in a whisper. "We do know who it is and why she screamed. She needs help! Yes! Let's go!"

Watching his prey like a cat, Ancom's mind raced on. *Sounds like the prisoner is out of the dungeon, and now there are the princess and Peizar, the prince's friend. What are they doing with her this evening?*

Rubbing his eyes and squinting, he struggled to make out what was happening. Ancom could make out that Merapondes motioned to Peizar that they should go in. Then they were out of sight.

Cautiously, Merapondes and Peizar ventured through the opening into the blackness of the hallway. Their eyes not yet acclimated, they walked slowly.

Then they spotted her. She was on her knees, fumbling to get to her feet.

Not knowing who was on the ground next to her, Merapondes and Peizar walked ever so slowly toward her.

Jeannie watched them move toward her. Now she was on her feet. She stepped back and stood as still as a marble column on the Greek Parthenon—a temple in honor of the goddess Athena.

Merapondes and Peizar continued to walk toward her. Prepared for the dark hallway, Peizar lit a torch. It was perfect.

The moon had moved farther west in the sky. Now behind a cloud, it was no longer visible. The dank hallway went a few shades darker.

Peizar's torch was good enough. Even without light streaming through the doorway, Jeannie could see their faces. She recognized the girl. At that point, Jeannie started running toward them.

Shaking and out of control, Jeannie wanted help. Merapondes reached out to Jeannie with outstretched arms.

Words were not needed. There could be no more welcome gesture than outstretched arms. Jeannie's heart felt like it might one day be whole again.

It's strange how things happen sometimes, even when you are not aware of your actions. Zanzee had bolted for cover when Jeannie tripped over the dead body. He didn't go far. Jeannie was unaware that he had even left, let alone raced back to her as she lay on the dirt floor next to the gorom's dead body, a gorom that Zanzee had taken pride in killing.

Out of instinct, Jeannie had picked up Zanzee and squeezed him like a baby tightly to her small breast.

Reaching Jeannie, Merapondes stopped. Although her arms were outstretched, Jeannie was unable to return the welcome gesture because she was holding a cat.

Merapondes heart soared. *"Yes! I knew it! Yes, yes!"*

Merapondes's excitement was not normal, and Jeannie realized that this girl who looked identical to her knew who Zanzee is.

Using signs and gestures, Jeannie proceeded to tell the story of how Zanzee protected her and killed the man on the floor.

It is kind of interesting how fate played a role when least expected. Merapondes, without even realizing what she was doing, started speaking. "Oh my god, it is Zanzee. How in heaven's name did he get here, and how does he know you?" This time she spoke in the language of the royals.

Totally caught off guard, Jeannie yelled, "You speak the language of the royals?"

"My God, who are you?" squealed Merapondes.

They were now just inches apart. Peizar stepped back a few feet. Jeannie lifted her right hand and touched Merapondes's face. Still holding Zanzee in her left arm, she said, "I'm Jeannie LoneTree, the great-great-great-great-granddaughter of Kashom. Who are you?"

Words could not describe the emotions that exploded in each girl. Never in a million years did Princess Merapondes ever dream that the prisoner was a member of the royal family of Kopaz. How could she? Maybe it was the cat. Maybe it was fate. Who knows why, but it must have been something on a divine order that lifted this cloak of mystery.

Now at stake was not only the mystery of who the prisoner was but the far greater mystery of what had happened to Princess Aerapondes, Merapondes's twin sister, so many years ago.

Words could not come out of Merapondes's mouth fast enough to get the answers she had longed for. "How did you get here? How did you get Zanzee? Where is my older brother, Kashom?"

It was at that point—the moment when she had asked where Kashom was—that Merapondes froze and become rigid as a statue. She asked, "Is Mochcom there or here? Where is he?"

There must have been a sixth sense among all three. Hanging around in a dirty hallway filled with creatures of the night was something none of the three wanted to continue to do.

Not knowing what was being said mattered not to Peizar. For him, not speaking the language of the royals did not keep him from knowing what was going on. Peizar pointed to the doorway and told Merapondes that they quickly leave.

Maybe it was instinct. Maybe it was fate. Maybe it was just time to leave. They all turned and ran as fast as they could toward the doorway of the Great Pyramid.

Just before they were ready to bolt through the door and exit the dungeon, they stopped. Princess Merapondes grabbed Peizar's arm and whispered in the language of Kopaz, "Let's make sure it is clear before we go out into the open!"

Princess Merapondes then turned to Jeannie and repeated her words, this time in the language of the royals. Jeannie nodded.

Slithering like a large python despite his immense physical stature, Gorom Ancom hugged the base of the pyramid, making his way to the doorway. He did not hear the conversation between Princess Merapondes and Peizar but was now close enough to hear a muffled string of words.

Since he could not understand the words of the royal language, he did not know what they were up to, but that did not matter. He was no more than ten feet from where he wanted to be. He moved to the middle of the doorway

Never in a million years did these three teenagers expect what happened next.

Expecting an open doorway, Peizar, holding onto Merapondes's hand as she was holding Jeannie's, ran smack dab into a massive wall of human flesh.

"What are you doing here, my little sacrificial lambs? Why are you meddling into the goroms' affairs?" rasped Ancom.

At first, Peizar was dazed and did not know what was happening. He cringed from the horrifying sounds coming from the dark shadows just above his head. *Woooooop...woooooop...woooooop.* A giant black bird fluttered his wings from its perch on top of the arched rock that framed the opening into the pyramid. The howling squeals from the bird sent blood-chilling chills crawling all over Peizar's skin. "*Rawaarrrrr...rarrrarreeee,*" it screeched as it watched its master, Lord Ancom.

A hand with long fingers clutched him tightly, the sharp fingernails puncturing his skin. Peizar lunged in an effort to get away—he couldn't. He saw the long, outstretched black wings of the huge bird and felt gusts of wind from his fluttering just above his head. He had no idea what was going on and was not ready for the scuffle that occurred during the early hours of that fateful evening.

Crimson blood oozed from beneath each of Ancom's nail and made tiny red rivers flow down Peizar's arm.

Swinging his head away from the giant bird directly above him, Peizar never dreamt whose face would be inches from his.

"*M-my God! It's y-you, Aan...Ancom!*" Peizar screamed—his eyes rolled from the black bird to Ancom's steely blue eyes. The gorom's face was so close he could smell the sour-milk breath coming from him.

Ancom, who was holding Peizar just inches from his hot breath, reached and grabbed Merapondes with his free hand.

Merapondes let go of Jeannie's hand. Petrified, Jeannie did not know if she should run or help these two people who had come to help her. She stepped back and fumbled on the ground in the dark in search of a rock or anything she could use as a weapon against this monster.

Ancom growled. "Trusted friend of the prince. What brings you this way on this moonlit night?"

Then his massive arm immediately swung around Peizar's neck.

Ancom's hairy forearm covered Peizar's mouth, but his nostrils were unobstructed, and so he tried to breathe. But that was short-lived.

Ancom tightened his hold on Peizar's neck.

Merapondes screamed louder and managed to break loose from the hairy hand holding her. She scrambled to get away from the monster who was killing her brother's friend.

She lunged backward. She stumbled but caught herself and tried to pivot on one foot—still screaming in absolute terror. Her pivoting body was like a top that was trying to spin but could not because an anchor was stopping it.

Maybe it was a twist of fate. Who knows? For whatever reason, her foot had got wedged and was anchored between two granite rocks that had been used at one time to secure the massive wooden door of the pyramid in a closed position. Merapondes's twisting motion lodged her foot more firmly.

Peizar's eyes began to budge as pressure mounted. His head felt as if it were exploding in slow motion. His sight dimmed. Now he could no longer see.

Merapondes had no concept of the pain that Peizar was experiencing, but she was deep in her own pain. As she pivoted and her foot caught, anchored solidly between the rocks, her leg snapped, the broken bone breaking the skin. Blood squirted from the hole in her leg caused by the protruding sharp leg bone.

Unable to hold herself upright, she fell backward. Her screaming stopped.

In excruciating pain, Peizar tried to scream, but Ancom's hairy forearm muffled all sound. Ancom gave one last massive squeeze of his arm, and like a dry stick under a heavy foot, Peizar's neck snapped. It was over. Peizar lived no more. His dead body fell to the ground.

In the dark hallway, Jeannie saw two eyes glowing like fire. Zanzee leaped toward Ancom. His teeth sank deep into the gorom's arm.

Ancom belted Zanzee with his free hand, knocking Zanzee to the ground. Ancom swiftly brought back his foot and planted it squarely on the black cat.

Zanzee took off like a football on the first play of the game when the kicker sends the ball flying toward the other end of the field.

Jeannie screamed as Zanzee howled.

There was no option left for Jeannie. Ancom stood smack in the middle of the doorway.

With the two strangers lying lifeless on the ground, Jeannie turned and ran back into the pyramid.

Ancom looked at Merapondes. He walked to the motionless princess lying on the ground not more than ten feet from him. Her face was turned up, and her eyes caught the moonlight. They were open, but her body was motionless. He rolled her body over and saw a sharp rock covered with blood. In her fall, Princess Merapondes had hit her head on that rock, which had split her skull wide open. She breathed no more.

"Hmm, she's dead," Gorom Ancom rasped.

With no time to lose, the gorom overtook Jeannie with little trouble. With his arms grasping Jeannie tightly, he dragged her from the Great Pyramid. Gorom Ancom tied Jeannie securely with a leather rope and took her to the Hall of the Goroms.

What Gorom Ancom did not see before he parted with his prisoner was Zanzee. Jeannie's cat was not far from the entire episode, watching for the right opportunity. When all was clear, Zanzee, like a thief in the night, made his way to the bodies of Peizar and Merapondes.

CHAPTER 23

The Fiery Pit—Day Two

No longer did Danny question where he was. He didn't care. He wanted Jeannie. He was waiting to unleash a reign of death and terror on those who had taken her and left him for dead. He had no idea who they were. He knew, however, he would find them and would expend his last ounce of energy on revenge. It was his single focus.

Maybe Quill knew that there was a canker of hate in Danny's heart and maybe not. He didn't care.

Danny's days with Quill continued to be long and hard. The constant workouts had made Danny's body matchless among humans, with bulging muscles fit for Superman. Danny's training to become a god was hard, but he had learned much in a short time. He was obedient and, if needed, would continue to learn and work as long as required.

Well aware that that Danny did not have a faint heart, Quill was pleased with the young god's progress. The boy was of strong mind and body and had a will as solid as the Great Pyramid of Egypt. That could very well be why Viracocha picked Danny as his royal prince.

The sun had just hid its face behind the highest peak of the Vulcan Mountains. Yawning, Danny rested his head on his newfound friend, Yellzor, tired from the exhausting work that Quill had had him doing for days on end.

Danny had dosed off. His mind was on Jeannie, and so were his dreams.

As he lay in the soft grass next to a rock that he had been using to set his belongings on, the dream he was having intensified. Someone was calling his name. "Danny! Danny! Help me! Help me!"

Half dazed and not fully awake, he shot up to a sitting position. He started swinging his arms wildly as if to be fighting an evil force.

Then it happened again. Danny was jolted by a cold bucket of water dousing him.

"*Holy shit*, Quill! Stop that! What the hell are you doing?"

Danny had left a pail of water on the edge of the rock next to his bag of things. It didn't take much of a swat with his swinging arms and hands to dislodge it and cause his own soaking.

Quill was at least fifty feet from Danny and had not been paying attention. Darkness had set in, and the fire near Quill did not shed much light. He had been sitting on a small rock near the fire. He had been deep in thought as to what the next moves should be to thwart the army of evildoers that had a stranglehold on the land of Kopaz. But the sudden actions of Danny caused him to swing his head quickly and look in the direction where Danny was. Because of the blackness of the evening, he could not see the royal prince of Viracocha. Alarmed, Quill yelled, "What? What is happening?"

Wide-awake and soaking wet, Danny realized what was going on. Danny shouted as he jumped to his feet, "All is cool, Quill! This time it was me who doused myself with a bucket of cold water!"

Quill raced to Danny, still not sure what was happening. "Hmm, my royal prince," said Quill with a strange little puzzled look on his face as the two stood next to one another. "Why are you soaking wet? It wasn't me!"

A smile started growing on Quill's face as he looked at Danny shivering in the cool of the evening, and he said, "You look like a wet dog!" He laughed.

The smile on Quill's face was brief. As he looked at his friend, he knew something was troubling him.

"What troubles my dear friend on this cool night?" asked Quill.

Danny said nothing. Yet Quill was aware if what was consuming Danny's every thought and emotion. "It's Jeannie," said Quill, answering his own question.

Danny nodded as he said, "Yes."

Quill wanted to spend time talking to Danny, but events were unfolding at a lightning-fast pace elsewhere that were taking center stage. He said, "Much is happening in the land of Kopaz." Quill stopped. "The forces of evil are at work." His face grew serious. "Viracocha is concerned now that Merapondes has entered the Land of the Dead, and Jeannie could be next on the list of boat riders on the River Styx."

"Who?" queried Danny with puzzled look on his face. "I've never heard that name. Who is it…and what does that person have to do with Jeannie?"

"You had a vision, Danny! Do you not remember? Merapondes was the twin sister of Aerapondes," spoke Quill reverently.

There was a moment of concentration, and then Quill said, "I'm sorry for being curt. You knew nothing of Merapondes…only what you learned in that short vision of her when you stood at the brink of the Yellshome Falls, where Aerapondes was murdered."

There was an eerie silence for a few seconds as Danny stared at Quill. Then Quill said something that gave Danny comfort.

"Viracocha let me know a few moments ago that the Neferzul yet lives!"

Now with conviction, Quill said with power in his voice, "The balance of the universe is teetering, and you will soon be at the center of it. Viracocha wants us both to be ready!"

Danny wiped the water from his face and eyes. Lines of concern drew across his high cheekbones as he said, "Do we know what to be ready for and when it will happen?"

"No," replied Quill. "All I can tell you is 'be prepared!' When the call comes, we will move quickly."

"I figured that," said Danny. He looked at the mouth of Vulcan. It belched a plume of sulfur smoke into the air.

Quill was anxious to take Danny's mind off Jeannie. Nodding his head as he looked at Danny, Quill changed the subject. "Danny…" He stopped. He wanted Danny's undivided attention.

"Yes, Quill," replied Danny. He waited for his tutor to speak.

"I wasn't going to tell you, but you have performed way beyond my expectations. I've had you lifting that heavy rock"—he pointed to it—"for hours on end, day after day."

Quill paused. Danny listened. "You have developed into a human fighting machine that I never expected. You never argue with me. You do not complain. You just keep lifting that two-hundred-pound rock as long as I ask you to." Quill smiled and continued. "Yes, I know you started with a fifty-pound rock and moved to a hundred-pound rock and then to one weighing a hundred and fifty pounds as your muscles developed. And holy cow, you can run," said Quill laughing. "I got tired just watching you race up and down the side of the mountain." He pointed to the highest peak in the Vulcan Mountains where it rose behind the mouth of hell.

Patiently, Danny remained quiet. He didn't know where Quill was going, so he just listened.

"That is what I like about you, Danny. You are obedient, and by the way, Viracocha thinks highly of you!"

Danny smiled as he said, "It was all so foreign to me, but you gave me the strength to go on."

"No, Danny, it wasn't me. It was you. Just look at you. Your muscles would qualify you for Mr. Universe, as earthlings would say, without competition! The schooling, the exercise, the listening, the waiting, and now it will pay off!" said Quill with confidence. "You have learned the language of the people of Kopaz, and holy shit, as you say." Quill paused at that statement, and he couldn't hold his laughter in. "*Holy shit!* Those are your words I'll never forget!"

Danny laughed and chimed in, "*OK, Quill! Holy shit!* And?"

Nodding and smiling at his best friend, Quill said, "You never complained when I told you that you needed to learn not only the common language of the people but the language of the royals as well, and you learned them both in record time."

Danny laughed more freely. "Yeah, and the bucket of water fits in this training someplace, doesn't it?"

This even got Yellzor howling, as he was usually a target of Quill's dousing whenever Danny was.

There could be no denying that Quill was pleased. No, he was more than pleased. He was ecstatic with Danny's development into a young god. "Just look at you, Danny," said Quill beaming. "You are no longer a young god in training. You are in the final stages of earning your seat at the council table of the gods! It is late, Danny. I don't know the exact time, but I believe we will have to move shortly," Quill said as he smiled willingly. "You are ready…more than ready, and soon the goroms will feel your wrath, a specter of death that will haunt them for the ages," said Quill. Then he pointed to Yellzor. "Get a good night's sleep, you and your friend. You will need it."

Maybe it was instinctive, and maybe not. Yellzor was tired and knew Quill had just given them the go-ahead to hit the sack.

Snuggled next to Yellzor, Danny watched the night birds flying in the twilight sky, as the silver and orange clouds from the sunset began to fade.

Watching Danny watch the birds, Quill lifted his arm and pointed upward. "Soon we will join them."

CHAPTER 24

A Trap is Set

C atching an innocent creature in a snare might be the scheme of some who have evil on their minds, but not all practice this devilish way of existence. In many cases, it is difficult, if not impossible, to distinguish between those who are waiting in the shadows to pounce on their victims when they least expect it and those who are not. How could anyone tell the difference? Is there something about them—some evil and some not—that is a defining characteristic? Something that would alert even the most unsuspecting soul about what secret evil hides in someone else's heart? Maybe there is.

It was late. The moon was making its way to the center of the sky. Katchcom was in his night-robe, ready for bed. He was lying on his couch, his nightclothes not yet tied. They fell in folds from his chest, abdomen, and legs, leaving his half-naked body exposed. With only a single candle to bring light to the expanse of the room as well as the heavy tapestry drapes solidly blocking out the glow from the moon, Katchcom was safe from the view of any curious eye.

Someone approached. Katchcom heard the footsteps. He fumbled to grab his robe, which was unevenly folded in small piles on each side of his ripped muscles. These were toned by a rigorous fitness routine. He had no idea who was coming.

As he jumped to his feet, his red velvet robe dangled around his masculine physique. Now, the ends of the braided rope belt, made from gold and silver strands mixed with silk lace, were easily grasped. He quickly found them. Pulling tightly, he made sure he was properly covered.

He moved to his throne and waited. The doorway to his chamber opened. Ancom dragged Jeannie in, a leather thong around her waist.

Katchcom could not see Ancom's face, but the sounds of heavy breathing—characteristic of Ancom when he was under stress—so raspy that it almost sounded as if the man were gasping frantically for a breath of air, told Katchcom who it was. *What the hell is Ancom doing with the prisoner?* The question raced through Gorom Katchcom's mind.

"Why did you bring her to my chamber at this ungodly hour?" howled Katchcom as he stared first at Ancom then at Jeannie.

Their silhouettes, backlit by the hallway candles not yet extinguished by the servants, could not be mistaken for those of random intruders.

Why did it happen thus? Why would a person suddenly get, figuratively speaking, tied in knots for no clear reason and utter random bursts of sound mixed with gasps of air? Who knows? It just happened when Ancom was placed in a compromising position.

Ancom had a nervous habit of choking on his words with his heavy breathing, and no one who knew him could deny who was putting on this display of audible gibberish.

Frantically, Ancom fought for composure, as if left unchecked he might fall victim to a seizure and completely lose control.

He expanded his chest and held his breath. It worked. He relaxed. He delivered his message. "The princess is dead. Dorcom is dead. What do we do?"

Drifting through the open window, a nightingale's song to its lover was the only sound that hung in the air. And in between its burst of serenading melody, deathly silence fell like a heavy hand quenching any signs of life.

At first, Gorom Katchcom was filled with anger, but then his face lit up with a smile. His mind was searching. *Aha! We can use this to overthrow the prince.*

Katchcom responded, "Do you know what you have done?"

For some reason, his words were different than his thoughts. *We will take advantage of this for our good!*

"M-m-m-my lord, I...I...I...it was an accident. The...the...the princess fell. She died."

"So what about Dorcom?" rasped Katchcom.

Jeannie understood nothing—not one word. It was a warm night, but goose bumps covered her body like a disgusting rash that even a leper would complain about.

Katchcom stepped from behind his golden throne, letting the candlelight from the hallway get caught in the gemstones. It created an unusual mood in the hall.

Not understanding the conversation, Jeannie's eyes rolled slightly as she saw what could have been a hundred colored eyes on the gold throne blinking randomly.

Unable to talk, her mind took over. *God of the universe...on this night, let my soul find comfort in the land where my love has traveled, for I do not know how much more I can bear, and I long to be with him.*

The sight of a feeble gorom whose seizures took over when calmness must prevail was something that Katchcom was unable to deal with, especially in light of the grave consequences that would follow if he were exposed as the mastermind behind the murderous plots against the royal family.

"Get her out of here! *Now!*" growled Katchcom. "I want her in the dungeon of the hall, not the pyramid. Do you understand? Or should I paint a picture for you?" Katchcom howled as his fist slammed onto the table, casing Jeannie to jerk.

"Ya...ah...ah...yes, my l...ah...er...ah, my lord!" Ancom finally managed to get his message out.

He tightened his rope and yanked. Jeannie lunged forward and was about to fall. She threw her leg out to catch her balance.

Turning, he started walking toward the doorway, pulling Jeannie closer to him as he gathered the rope.

"Stop! I'm not finished!" shouted Katchcom.

It was clear in his mind. As his plan fell into place, Katchcom's grin intensified, knowing he was masterminding the coup of coups, and soon he would be the ruler. He had waited long for it, and he knew it was at hand.

Still as a statue, Ancom waited. Turning slowly, he faced Katchcom.

"Here's the plan. Pay attention!" shouted Katchcom. "Take her to the dungeon below our hall. I want her close to us," he snapped.

It was clear in Katchcom's mind. *It's a secret prison that no one except a very select group of the goroms knows about. Since Dorcom is dead, it's only Ancom and one other high priest—Gorom Zercom—who know of the goroms' special dungeon.*

"Listen closely!" yelled Katchcom.

Each word from the mouth of the high priest cut through the still night's air. "Bring the other two bodies here." There was a pause, and then Katchcom said, "Tell no one you killed the princess!" Selecting his words carefully, Katchcom hissed slowly as he talked, knowing that was a warning to Ancom to keep his mouth shut.

"Yes, my lord, I'll talk to no one. I'll have all three bodies here shortly."

"Three bodies?" snorted Katchcom.

"Yes, my lord. Prince Jerzom's friend is the third."

Once more Katchcom made his point. "So be it. Bring them all here. Tell none of the other goroms about our plan, as we risk being prisoners ourselves if the real killer of the princess is revealed. You have committed murder at the highest levels. Do you know the price you will pay if exposed?"

Fully understanding what Katchcom's words meant, Ancom's body tensed as hard as a block of steel as he said softly, "Yes, my lord!" He knew he would be the fall guy if it came to that.

"Good! We need to take care of this by putting the blame on someone other than the real killer!" Katchcom smiled.

Ancom left with Jeannie.

Not five minutes passed before Katchcom summoned Zercom to his quarters.

A private meeting took place in the Hall of the Goroms on that starry night in Kopaz. Gorom Zercom was Katchcom's most loyal and most trusted confidant. Ever since Gorom Mochcom had left and Katchcom had been named the new high priest, Zercom had been the brains in the background. Zercom was up front with Katchcom and made it quite clear he did not want the leadership role. What he wanted was the chief-of-staff position and would carry out any assignments in that capacity.

The time had come for Zercom's most important assignment. The clandestine meeting commenced. Orders were given. Zercom listened.

"Watch Ancom closely. I don't trust him. We must lure the prince from his room and wait in hiding. This must happen this evening. When the prince comes out of his chamber and leaves the palace, grab him! Bring him to me. We'll throw him in the secret dungeon also—there are three small cells, and one has his name on it!"

Then Katchcom said nothing.

He turned, walked to his desk, and stopped. He turned his head, looking over his shoulder at Zercom. Standing next to the council table, the gorom waited for his master to make his next move. Katchcom smiled, the gleam in his eye not unnoticed by Zercom. He then turned his head back around to focus on his desk. He opened the long drawer that stretched the entire length of the ornate wooden desk. He pulled out an object, turned, and walked back across the hall to Zercom. Standing next to him, Katchcom grabbed Zercom's hand and slid something into it.

"Plunge this knife—it's a royal knife—into the body of Merapondes."

Zercom nodded with each instruction from his master.

"When we have the prince, go and tell the king that there have been horrendous murders committed in the kingdom and that the killer is a high-ranking citizen of Kopaz."

If ever there was urgency to carry out the most heinous of crimes, it was now.

"Go quickly! The hour is late. The night comes upon us. Go! Get the prince!"

Zercom left.

Alone, Katchcom waited by the doorway to the hall. He heard someone in the hallway. He opened the door and asked, "Who goes there?"

"It's me, my lord. I bring you the dead bodies of Dorcom, Peizar, and Princess Merapondes."

The moon shone through the hallway window, revealing the silhouette of Ancom with a body over each shoulder and one in his arms pressed against his chest, making him look like a giant hulk.

Katchcom held the door open.

Ancom was strong, but the weight of three bodies that he had carried over three hundred yards had left him exhausted. He stepped in, not looking at Katchcom but looking for where he should place the bodies.

He did not see Katchcom's arm rise into the air.

He felt the blade of a knife plunge into his back. He dropped the bodies.

He had enough strength to turn around.

He tried to defend himself, but it was in vain. The second stab of Katchcom's knife found Ancom's heart. The fight was over before it began.

Hmm, thought the high priest, undoubtedly pleased at the turn of events. *That miserable mess of humanity is no more! Fortunately, his meddling into what he had no business in has left the princess dead, and that will be the perfect snare to trap Prince Jerzom!*

Katchcom gave a sigh of relief. "No one knows but me. The secrets are safe now," he mumbled to himself. "Whatever Ancom knew about the golden watch, the golden key, and GAMMAZEL, he will keep with him, locked up in the eternities. Good riddance!"

CHAPTER 25
A Royal Prince is Prisoner

*B*ang! Bang! Bang! Bang!

    The clash of the iron ring on the door of the Grand Hall of the royal palace cut through the night air.

"Who goes there?" shouted the doorman.

"It's Gorom Zercom. Give a message to the prince. Tell him there is a problem with Princess Merapondes and Peizar at the Great Pyramid."

There could be nothing else that would arouse the prince so quickly other than the possibility of the clandestine activities of his friend being exposed, but the mention of Princess Merapondes took over his mind.

It worked. Jerzom came to the door quickly.

Zercom was patient. When he had Jerzom's attention, Gorom Zercom said, "Peizar is injured. He is near the Great Pyramid and asked for you, my royal prince."

Fortunately for Zercom, the doorman closed the door to the Grand Hall. For whatever reason, Jerzom had stepped out. Still, he was not about to go with Zercom. Something did not sit well with him.

Zercom waited for Jerzom's reaction. It was not a long wait. With only the moon for light, Zercom was swift. He used the club he had been holding next to his leg. Swinging the club, he scored a perfect hit.

Instantly, before the boy could recover from the blow, he got a stranglehold on the prince. Zercom's hand was over the prince's mouth, muting any unwanted sounds. In seconds, Zercom had a leather strap tightly around the prince's head snuggly binding his mouth, stifling any screams for help.

He slammed the prince to the ground, and in seconds, Zercom had pulled Jerzom's arms behind him and strapped his wrists together.

Making sure that the prince was immobilized, the gorom placed extra straps around the prince's hands, legs, and arms to ensure that Jerzom had absolutely no way to escape.

The night was dark, and so, unseen by anyone, Zercom carried the prince like a sack of potatoes to the Hall of the Goroms.

Katchcom was waiting.

Blood was everywhere around the doorway. However, Ancom's body was nowhere in sight. Katchcom had disposed of it to cover up his coldblooded murder of his religious brethren in order to advance his journey to ultimate power. Only three bodies were on the floor.

Katchcom had the torches lit, so as to shed light on the bodies.

Feeling quite sure that the end of power for the royal family of Kopaz was near at hand, the head high priest snorted. "Look! Four wretched souls board the boat on the River Styx headed for the Land of the Dead. They were miserable in life, and I'm sure they are the most miserable passengers on the boat traveling the River Styx this evening, don't you think?" he said. He lifted his head to glare at Jerzom.

The gag was removed. Jerzom swallowed with relief when the leather strap was removed from his mouth. Not concentrating, at first the royal prince did not recognize the corpses.

Katchcom was delightedly anticipating Jerzom's reaction to seeing his best friend and beloved sister no longer with the living.

He did not expect Jerzom's reaction. "Where is the fourth body, Katchcom, or are you seeing ghosts?"

"What are you talking about, my prisoner prince?" snapped Katchcom.

"You said four, not I!" shot back Jerzom.

At that point, as if things weren't going downhill for Katchcom fast enough, Zercom blurted out the next challenge. "Where is Gorom Ancom, my lord?"

Now the cat was out of the bag. Reacting instantly, Katchcom goal was to divert attention from himself to the death of the royal princess and the most loyal friend of Prince Jerzom.

Motioning to Zercom, he said, "Look, my royal prince!" Katchcom sneered as he had Zercom force Jerzom to look at the two people that Jerzom loved more than any other in this world.

Zercom delighted in feeling the prince's body wrench with emotional pain, yet it was short-lived, as the prince snarled at the gorom, "Your ass will be aboard the next boat, and you can make light talk with the boatman, you bastard!"

Now there was a new challenge for Katchcom. Katchcom knew that Zercom had just asked the most damning question. With the question still hanging in the air, Zercom seized on one thought. *Where is Gorom Ancom?*

Damage control was of the utmost priority as Katchcom snarled, "Ancom is on the boat traveling to the Land of the Dead with that miserable bastard Dorcom, the princess and Peizar, as he betrayed me and wanted to expose our coup."

Now, looking directly into Zercom's eyes, his face not more than six inches from Zercom's, Katchcom yelled, his breath hot on the face of his loyal priest. "Take this wretched prince to our dungeon. Return quickly and get these bodies from my sight!"

Ten minutes later, Zercom returned to get the dead bodies. As he was picking them up, the moonlight glinted off something lying on the floor, something that Katchcom had missed when he thrust his knife into Gorom Ancom's back. In his final dying moments, Ancom must have retrieved the object he had in the pocket of his robe. It was a ring on a gold chain.

Zercom picked it up. The green stone was so massive, he knew it must be a gemstone of great value. Secretly, he stuffed it into the inner pocket of his black robe and went about his business of removing the bodies from the floor of the Hall of the Goroms.

Oblivious to what he was getting into, Zercom had no idea that it was not just an ordinary ring. He had only thought, *Surely, the ring has to be of great worth!*

Gorom Zercom had never passed up the opportunity to further his own greedy lust for the finer things of life, even if they were acquired by malevolent means. For him, it was his gain and someone else's loss. Yet he had no idea that those tangled webs the greedy wove so often thrust them into a twisted maze from which there was no escape except the final exit—death. Could it be that this ring was such an object?

CHAPTER 26
A Royal Matter

I t was late. Katchcom sent his first lieutenant, Gorom Zercom, to tell the king what had happened and to announce that they would be at the royal court in less than an hour.

The entire Quorum of High Priests, the goroms, even the two dead ones (Katchcom, Zercom, Ancom—*dead*, Zidcom, Maycom, Dorcom—*dead*, Shadcom, Nodcom and Yellcom), all assembled in the Grand Hall

Also, Jerzom and Jeannie, both shackled and hooded, and the dead body of Peizar were brought into the courtroom.

The king was waiting, sitting on his throne. The goroms threw the dead body of Peizar at his feet. The king hollered, "Call the guards. How dare you bring slime to my court?"

Dalvin's focus was on the dead body at the foot of his throne. He did not see his hooded son in shackles.

With time of the essence, Zercom motioned for Gorom Maycom to come forward. "Show our mighty King Dalvin the gifts from the gods," he shouted. Gorom Maycom displayed the golden watch on a silk pillow, golden threads embroidering the insignia ROHP, which stood for the "Royal Order of High Priests."

The time was ripe. Katchcom stepped forward. His purpose was to lay out his fabricated evidence that would suggest there had been a royal murder by one in the royal family. "My king, you know the legend of the golden key. Your oldest son, Kashom, killed his sister Aerapondes for it. But what Kashom did not know was that this golden object, sometimes called the golden watch, is needed to open the Portal of Time, along with the emerald star and rainbow-colored worox stones."

Succeeding in capturing the king's attention, Katchcom sprang the trap. "My royal king, we bring you sad news. Your youngest son, Jerzom, has repeated the dastardly deed of murder, as his brother, Kashom, did."

Caught off guard, the king shouted, "What did you say?"

Then lifted his head to the prisoners. He recognized his son. His face was like that of a wild man. He yelled, "You shackle my son?"

Instantly, King Dalvin lifted his arm and motioned to his guards as he bellowed, "Seize these traitorous dogs who committed this crime against the royal family!"

As planned, Gorom Yellcom stepped forward, holding a body that had been covered with a blanket. He let the bloody covering fall to the floor, revealing the dead body of a young girl.

The king looked at it with horror. Speechless, he stared in unbelief at the gorom holding his daughter Merapondes in his arms.

At this point, the king was not yet aware that the princess was dead. He yelled, "How dare you imprison my son and touch my daughter? *Take them!*" he screamed to his royal guards.

Zercom was ready. "Oh your royal highness, we do no such thing. Your son is the evil one. *We have the proof!*" he yelled, each word getting louder.

"On your knees, swine. Your head on the floor. Your blood will water the ground of Kopaz. Your evil is through," shouted King Dalvin.

On his knees, Zercom looked down but then lifted his hand. He pointed to Yellcom and belted out his message. "Jerzom's knife is in the heart of his sister."

Silence fell for a moment as Dalvin's heart sank. Now he saw the crimson blood dripping from the limp body in the arms of Gorom Yellcom.

Zercom screamed out, "Where's your knife, Jerzom?"

Caught in the tangled web of the unfolding nightmare, the king glared at his son. In a low, harsh voice, he said, "Where is your knife?"

Bound with leather straps, Jerzom was unable to move his arms. He was gagged and could only make strange, guttural sounds. He shook his head wildly but could make no meaningful attempt at communication.

Zercom, still on his knees, looked at the king. The king said, "Rise!"

With a pounding heart and a tense face, King Dalvin asked the royal guards to have the queen brought to the royal courtroom. His words stammered out. "Did Jerzom aid his brother, Kashom, in the brutal murder of Aerapondes? The royal family will deal with this matter."

CHAPTER 27

A Message for a Mother

An urgent matter in the Grand Hall so late at night was most unusual. Neferapondes was brought to the courtroom. She looked past her son who was tied up, his hands bound behind him. Racing to Gorom Yellcom, she touched the face of her dead daughter.

She was wearing a silk dress with beautiful embroidered floral decorations. And like her husband, she had been wearing a robe that matched his, except hers was not purple but violet. The gemstones affixed to Neferapondes's robe were arranged such that they resembled floral arrangements. In her haste to reach her daughter, the queen had flung her heavy robe to the floor so as not to be hindered by its weight. And like Merapondes, the royal robe lay lifeless on the cold marble floor.

Bitter sadness wrenched her soul as her fingers gently stroked the face of her daughter. Ever so gently moving her fingers to the open eyes of Merapondes, she closed the lids so no one could look into the spiritless body of her daughter again. The need to fight back her emotions as the queen of a nation was more than she could bear. Tears streamed from her eyes as her fingers moved softly over the face of Merapondes. The lines of deep depression moved swiftly over her face and conveyed the utter helplessness of a childless mother. Deep in her heart, she knew they were all gone, and no one had to tell her that Jerzom was at the bottom of the horrific crime. She turned, and her body shaking, she walked to her husband's side. She knew not what to say or do. Using the language of the royal family—that language that was only spoken and understood by the members of the royal family of Kopaz—she quavered, "What shall we do, my husband?"

The deathly silence that had fallen over the Grand Hall was deafening as emotions beyond description engulfed the royal family.

Stammering, King Dalvin managed to speak in the royal language. "Our sons are evil. They killed our precious daughters. First Kashom, maybe even with the help of Jerzom, killed Aerapondes, who was Neferzul, and now Jerzom has killed Merapondes. Our family was destined to become part of the family of the gods, but our sons are evil and have brought disgrace upon us. The gods are not pleased with the royal family of Kopaz. They will vent their anger upon us!"

He issued orders to the goroms. "Take them away!" screamed Dalvin. His words hung in the air as silence took over once more.

That deathly void of sound pressed on all in the Grand Hall for a moment. Then something happened from out of nowhere. The voice of the hooded girl prisoner filled every corner of the hall with a stunning announcement. Yelling at the top of her lungs in the language of the royal family of Kopaz, Jeannie made her presence known like the crack of thunder following a bolt of lightning. "Kashom still has a red ribbon tied around his heart! Mochcom killed Aerapondes, and Ancom killed her twin sister, Merapondes. Your two sons, Kashom and Jerzom, are innocent. The goroms have betrayed you."

But unlike cracks of thunder and bolts of lightning that fade away as nothing more than brief occurrences during a passing storm, Jeannie's explosive revelation would go down in the history of Kopaz as the start of a war that would change the destiny of all mankind.

Stunned by the words of the royal language coming from the prisoner, the queen was in shock. The only words she had heard were "Kashom still has a red ribbon tied around his heart!" And in a similarly explosive voice, the queen shouted, "Dalvin, who is the prisoner? She knows something that only our son Kashom and I know. What is going on?"

The king, on the other hand, heard it all. His mind erupting with the memories of what he had said and done to his sons, accusing them of the most heinous crimes, his heart filled with revenge. *My god in heaven, it's never been my sons. How could I have been tricked in such an evil way?*

Blasted with the reality that he had been conned by the goroms, Dalvin screamed, "Bring the prisoner forward! Remove her hood! We must see her face!"

And with the power and forceful might of an angry king, Dalvin shouted commands in an unquestionable display of authority. "And untie my son, you evil creatures!"

CHAPTER 28

The Fiery Pit and a Dragon's Roar

Having dozed off while snuggling close to the belly of Yellzor, Danny was now wide-awake, thinking of what Quill had told him earlier. And with the giant wolf's paws gently wrapped around him, Danny's mind was like a racehorse on its last stretch of the Kentucky Derby.

"Quill?" said Danny, as if asking a serious question. "I can't sleep."

Saying nothing, Quill just looked on. He heard Danny but was silent for some reason. Danny stood and walked to where Quill was sitting. Yellzor didn't move. He must have been tired.

The night was still. Stars twinkled as they were displaying silver threads woven into the ribbon of the Milky Way across the backdrop of a black sky. Danny took a seat next to Quill on a large granite rock. They said nothing for at least five minutes. Words were not needed. To anyone, it would have been obvious. These two friends sitting at the mouth of hell contemplated the scheming activities of the goroms, disciples of the dark god, Zuron.

Now Quill spoke. "Yes, Danny? What is your concern?" Quill relished the warmth radiating from the molten lava while sitting on this rock with Danny. The rim of the fiery Pit of Vulcan on that cool night was cozy.

Yellzor elected to move. He stood, walked to where his master was sitting, and curled in a ball next to Danny's legs, which were dangling down the face of the large granite rock.

"Ah…er…ah…"

As Danny fumbled for words, Quill cut him off. "Speak up!"

"What do you think the goroms have done to Jeannie?" mumbled Danny.

Now that was a serious question that caught Quill by surprise. Although somewhat vague in tone, the question had a deeper meaning. All too aware that Jeannie's innocence was at the root of the inquiry, Quill could only speculate. "Only those evil creatures that hold her hostage and the supreme god and goddess know the answer to your question, Danny. Although Viracocha and Neferdor know all…it is up to you to bring justice to the evil ones who have taken the Neferzul. You and I do not know what the goroms have done to your beloved Jeannie. We can only hope she has been spared the vile actions of lecherous men."

"Quill," asked Danny, "why can't Viracocha stop the evil that is being brought on Jeannie?"

"He can't, Danny! Who do you think you are to question the actions of the supreme god?"

He looked at Quill. *Hmm*, thought Danny. *Boy, did I stick my foot in my mouth.*

Then it happened. Quill pointed to Danny's foot and made a motion of him lifting it to his mouth. Smiling, he said, "You are learning!"

Holy shit, can this guy read my mind or what? Danny thought.

Now it was Quill's turn to really have some fun with Danny as he remarked, "Danny, there is no such thing as h— s—, if you get my drift!"

"You win! I lose! Good grief, how did I end up with a guy that can read my mind? This is way too *cool!* How can a guy have any dignity if everything he thinks is on a giant silver screen for all to see and hear?" asked Danny. He screwed up his face, lines of sadness pulling the corners of his mouth into a frown. He put his hands over his face, blocking it from Quill, and then, slowly letting them drop, he revealed lines of happiness pulling the corners of his mouth up into a smiley face.

The fiery pit roared on, belching globules of molten lava as if it were a popcorn kettle shooting the newly popped kernels into the air. The moon had just broken over the horizon. It was late in the evening. Danny had thought it would be an evening of relaxation under the stars with his trusted friend. That would not be the case.

"The moon will be at its high point next to the Milky Way in five hours," said Quill as he watched Danny gazing into the western sky at the rounded sliver of light just peeking over the outline of the Vulcan Mountains as the moon started to show its face during the beginning of its climb for the evening. "Who knows, we may be on a tight schedule this evening," mused Quill.

"What are you talking about?" asked Danny most seriously. "What schedule are we on?"

"As I said, who knows?" remarked Quill. "We are governed in our mission by the moon, and so we must be vigilant at all times." He stopped as silence took over. The only noises were the rhythmic plopping sounds coming from the Pit of Vulcan in its never-ending boil.

Shaking his head, Danny was more confused than ever. "Quill, this is all just mumbo jumbo crap that I have no clue of what you are talking about. *Governed by the moon?* Good grief, guy, you are making me feel like an idiot!"

Danny reached to touch Yellzor and took his soft ears in his hand. "Yellzor, do you have a clue?" asked Danny. But before Yellzor could utter a growl, the Pit of Vulcan roared like the blasts of a thousand jet engines all in unison. The deafening sound from the fiery pit was not the only roar. CrystalFlame, breathing out fire, was creating a din on par with that of the pit.

The earth moved. The giant head of CrystalFlame was now next to Danny, Quill, and Yellzor. "Danny, she is here! It is time. The hour is late, and we must make haste or our mission is lost forever."

Things were not all that clear to Danny. Actually, he didn't have a clue. Earlier in the day, he was learning—or perhaps more precisely, he was being taught by his tutor from the gods—about dragons. At this point, however, Danny could not grasp what he should be learning. One could question if he were justified, as he was dealing with the teachings that focused on becoming a god. He had managed to get through the earlier episode. Now he had a question. "Quill, the last time CrystalFlame started her antics…well, you remember how Yellzor and I ended way in the hell up in the air. What's going on now?" yelled Danny over the twin roars of the pit and the dragon.

This time the answer to Danny's question did not come from Quill, Yellzor, or CrystalFlame. The bowels of the fiery pit roared even louder. "The peril is imminent! *Go now!*"

"Go where?" shouted back Danny. He spun around to see who had spoken, as Quill hadn't. No one was there. He looked at the belching lava from the Pit of Vulcan, but saw no one. *Hmm*, he thought.

The time for explanations had expired. Only precious moments separated death from glory.

Quill shouted, "Death is afoot. We fly—grab my hand!"

The fiery pit roared once more. "Fail and your endless hell will be this pit!"

Holy shit, thought Danny, *that volcano can talk. And Quill, I don't care if you hear me say the s-word, so there!*

Quill's ring erupted, emitting the green beam of transport.

In moments, Quill, Danny, and Yellzor were on the head of CrystalFlame.

For the second time in his life, Danny flew through the air at supersonic speed, but this time it was not on a beam of green light but on the head of a dragon.

And so it was in the stillness of the evening, the moon barely peeking over the mountaintops, that Danny and his friends headed to the capital of Kopaz. The moon's light was faint at best. With the full moon low in the sky shedding little light, it was the backdrop of the Milky Way that invited people to look to the sky in wonder. Some people who lived in Kopaz thought they had seen something strange flying high in the sky, something that had the shape of a dragon. But that seemed out of place, so it became a discussion among the inhabitants of the scattered villages about who saw what or who thought they saw what.

CHAPTER 29
Chaos Reigns

"**D**alvin, who is the prisoner?" shouted the queen for the second time in just a matter of moments. "She is speaking our language!"

Events were happening that Katchcom had never expected. At first, he was caught off guard.

The queen shouted louder, "The prisoner knows something that only I and my son Kashom know. Who is she?"

Like a ship in a hurricane smack dab in the middle of the Bermuda Triangle, Katchcom was at the center of a raging storm. His evil had just been uncovered. Yet instinctively, Katchcom screamed at Zercom, "*Kill him!*" and he pointed at the king.

The gorom reacted, readying his bow, setting an arrow to the string. The face of the king was enraged. "You traitorous dogs! *Untie my son!*"

Over the thundering voice of King Dalvin, Jerzom filled the Grand Hall with his booming command. "Guards, *react! Cut me free. I'll kill the goroms! Kill them now!*"

Yellmar, the royal guardsman who was in command, raced to Jerzom. He used his knife and slashed at the leather thong that secured the prince's hands behind him. In seconds, Jerzom was free.

There could be no silence in a room with so much horror and evil. Yellmar placed a sword in Jerzom's hand. The young prince was no longer a boy as he raced toward Gorom Yellcom, who was still holding the body of Merapondes.

With the full force of a football linesman, Jerzom slammed into Gorom Yellcom. All three, Jerzom, Yellcom, and the body of Merapondes, ended up on the cold rock floor. Quickly, the gorom rolled over and over to escape the lunging knife of Prince Jerzom.

It was at that point that Jerzom came face to face with his dead sister. The knife in her heart was glistening as the light danced on the precious gemstones in the solid gold handle. *My god*, thought Jerzom, *it's my dad's knife.*

In a state of unbelief, his mind exploded. *My father's knife has pierced my sister's heart. It makes no sense.*

Yet in the madness of it all, Jerzom was a loyal son and knew in his heart that King Dalvin was at the center of a con. Unable to make sense of his father's knife in his sister's heart, and in a state of confusion, Prince Jerzom yelled out orders to the royal guard. "Take Katchcom prisoner, and protect my father from this evil!"

Jerzom's actions were in vain. Zercom's arrow had found its mark. The king stumbled and fell to the marble floor. Jerzom looked on with horror. His father was dead—an arrow had pierced his heart.

The king lay face down at the foot of his throne. Gorom Zercom responded immediately and ordered the coup to proceed. "Imprison them!" he screamed. "Kill the prince. Take the queen and the intruder to the dungeon of the pyramid—*now!*"

The second arrow from Zercom's bow struck Jerzom's right thigh. The tide was turning, and the royal family was losing.

The young, buff royal guard, Bobmar, was not convinced that Katchcom and Zercom were commanding the situation. Bobmar shouted, "*Halt! I'll give the orders, not the goroms!*"

Bobmar's words were short-lived. His next utterance was muffled gurgles of nonsense as his internal organs belched out blood. It flooded his airways and spilled from his mouth. A gorom's arrows had found their marks, and Bobmar was on his way to meet the boatman on the River Styx.

On cue, the goroms' bodyguards burst into the Grand Hall and shouted,

"Hail, Katchcom, we are here!" Their bows were strung with arrows. Their targets were the royal guardsmen. Their instructions paid off. In seconds, ten of the noblest royal guardsmen were joining Bobmar on his journey to meet the dreaded boatman.

Outnumbered two to one, control of the situation was swinging to the goroms. In moments, if all went as planned, the rule of the royal family would fall to the Quorum of High Priests. Katchcom's smile was lighting up his face. His dream was becoming a reality. Screaming at Yellcom, he shouted, "Kill the prince. Take the queen prisoner…*now!*"

United, the remaining goroms (Katchcom, Zercom, Zidcom, Maycom, Shadcom, Nodcom, and Yellcom) stepped forward, flanked by their personal army of fifty bodyguards.

Arrows flew, hitting their marks. It happened again. Fiery pain pierced Prince Jerzom's side. Although Prince Jerzom fell to the floor, two arrows protruding from him, the one in his side had missed his vital organs, and the other was in his thigh. He was not dead but immobile. He reached and grabbed the arrow in his side. He yanked it free from his flesh.

Strangely, there was one watching Jerzom. It was his mother. Fraught with emotions and struggling at the sight of her last son rent with pain, her heart sobbed. Although the raging chaos unfolding in the Grand Hall of the royal palace was a relentless roar of human misery and death, the queen's mind was silent except for a mother's troubling focus on her remaining son. *Did you take part in the crime of murder? I…I…I don't understand. Oh Jerzom, how did you leave your sister helpless to the evil goroms? Did you betray us?*

Staring, her eyes could not be drawn from the agony of her son. Neferapondes wept in bitter sadness, watching her son lying on the floor, watching him as he reached with his free hand and grabbed the arrow protruding from his leg. Fortunately for Jerzom, the arrow was in his thigh muscle and had not pierced an artery or major vein. For the second time, he yanked and managed to pull the arrow from the wound.

The madness of the mayhem gripped her soul with a force more painful than a thousand arrows striking her heart. Recoiling from the unfolding scene of horror, the queen's body hardened until it was like a granite rock on a high mountain just waiting for a nudge to get it rolling down the embankment, smashing everything in sight. But that nudge that would give her that smashing momentum to change anything was nonexistent, and she knew that whatever royal influence she had as a ruler over Kopaz was over. She was caught in the center of a storm that had been raging since the death of Aerapondes, and she was left only to helplessly watch the fall of her empire.

Jerzom was her baby boy. Her swirling thoughts were bittersweet. Did he kill his sisters? How did Dalvin's knife end up in Merapondes's heart? *No, no. He's an innocent little boy. He's always been my cute little baby!* The images of horror and death just kept racing through her mind. Yet she could not take her eyes off her son as he quivered on the floor, blood spilling from the wounds in his side and leg.

With each moment, another soul boarded the boat on the River Styx. Unfortunately, they were not the souls of the goroms or their bodyguards. The dwindling numbers of the royal guard were evident. With only twenty guardsmen remaining, the fifty warriors in the personal army of the goroms were using their swords to slash off heads like they were dicing up liver for stew.

Standing at the center of the raging battle, the sounds of death permeated the hood that kept Jeannie in the dark. She heard the dying screams of valiant men who had served the royal family of Kopaz for decades as they performed their last acts of loyalty to an empire that was being crushed by a group of evil men.

The unrelenting grinding of her teeth was her only defense against the sheer hell that surrounded her.

CHAPTER 30
The Fury of a God

Z ercom never saw it coming. Zanzee raced toward Zercom, and the cat could not have been more on the mark with his razor-sharp claws. Landing on Zercom's face, it looked like the gorom wore a furry ski mask over his face to keep the bitter cold wind from freezing his skin. He looked like an Olympic downhill skier ready for competition. But that was not the case. It was Zanzee stretched over Zercom's face, and like a surgical doctor with a sharp scalpel, Zanzee's claws ripped into his targets—the eyes of Zercom. Not just shredding them, he ripped Zercom's right eye out of its socket. The gorom's screams of pain filled the hall as he staggered, one eyeball dangling on his cheek.

Blinded by a cat, Zercom did not see what happened next—a vengeance-riddled young man with sun-colored hair and emerald-green eyes bolted through the entrance to Grand Hall and swung onto the battlefield of chaos and death.

Danny, Quill, Yellzor, and CrystalFlame had just arrived on the scene.

Although the courtyard between the Grand Hall of the palace and the Hall of the Goroms was mammoth, it was tiny for CrystalFlame. Her tail had smashed the east wall of the Hall of the Goroms, leaving rubble where moments earlier there had been walls.

"*Go!*" shouted Quill to Danny as the dragon, CrystalFlame, was doing her thing.

As Danny slammed the giant wooden doors against the marble walls of the Grand Hall, the thundering booms alerted everyone except the hooded prisoner that someone new was joining the battle. Jeannie could only hear the noise and had no clue that someone else had just entered the battlefield.

Standing helpless in the center of the courtroom, Jeannie's heart dropped. She could only speculate what was causing the horrifying sounds that exploded through the Grand Hall.

For those heavily engaged in the fierce battle, Danny's thundering entrance caused them to pause and take notice. Soon, however, they would discover that he was not just another warrior who might join the ranks of those boarding the boat on the River Styx.

An uninvolved onlooker might say that the timely actions of a black cat strangely caused the event that changed the outcome of the battle. Certainly, the goroms who were in the midst of overthrowing the royal family had no idea that a black cat would ultimately be their demise. Would anyone suspect that the stranger who just burst into the battlefield and the black cat had something in common? How could anyone put two and two together and make the connection that only the supreme god Viracocha could orchestrate this? But an even more puzzling question would be this: who could know that there was a connection between the stranger, the black cat with sapphire-blue eyes, and the hooded prisoner standing at the center of the raging battle? And perhaps even more profound would be this question: who could know that this newcomer to the battle would be the defining factor that would change the course of destiny for all living creatures in the universe throughout the eternities?"

Danny yelled in the language of Kopaz, "The time of reckoning for your evil is upon you." He pointed to Katchcom.

Smiling, the high priest mouthed the words, "We shall see. Time is not on your side, whoever you are. The fall of the royals is almost complete, and soon you will join them!"

Time was of the essence for the young god in training. Zanzee used his teeth and paws to get the emerald ring on the gold chain from the inside pocket of the blinded, screaming Gorom Zercom. The ring and chain in his mouth, the cat bounded across the blood-covered marble floor to Danny's side. "Good work, Zanzee," said Danny as he found a brief second in the depths of the mayhem to thank Jeannie's protector. Watching the entire episode and being surrounded by chaos, Quill, speaking in the language of Kopaz and not in the royal language, immediately joked, in a booming voice so all in the Grand Hall could hear, "He has seen enough already, and now, thanks to Zanzee, he will see no more forever!" That caught Danny's attention, and with a quick glance at Quill, Danny gave him a high five wave.

Danny's shared joke with Quill lasted but an instant. Jeannie was never the wiser that her protector, Zanzee, was helping her lover, Danny. Within seconds, Danny's body hardened with the energy of the gods. He sprang from the doorway into the middle of the battle erupting in the royal court. The explosive voice of Viracocha cracked through Danny's mind. "Use your ring!"

With his ring of godly powers, Danny's eagle eyes followed the flaming finger of the supreme god and saw the beating of a throbbing heart under a blinded gorom's black robe. Instantly, a deadly green dagger shot from Danny's ring, piercing the heart of the foolish gorom. Gorom Zercom shook his head in pain. The two bloody holes that were his eyes stared into space. He fell to the ground. His chest was no longer throbbing with a beating heart. Now, it was smoldering with a circle of glowing cinders that just moments prior had been flesh but was now was a red hot clinker.

Katchcom stared at his comrade's chest. It looked like it had just been disintegrated by a meteorite streaking down from the heavens to hit a fleshy target, its final resting place. The supreme god had intervened, and Katchcom was not about to be the next dead man.

Now the ring lay visible on the chest of the young god. It was not only Gorom Katchcom that took note and paused but Gorom Zidcom also watched his trusted companion meet a horrifying death. It dawned on both of them that Danny was no ordinary human.

Gorom Zidcom was standing next to Katchcom. A backup plan was needed. Katchcom grabbed Zidcom's arm. He turned to face Zidcom so there faces were only inches apart.

"You are second in command. The prisoner is Neferzul. She must die…do you understand? said Katchcom.

Zidcom nodded and replied, "Yes!"

Katchcom pointed to where gorom Maycom was standing and said to Zidcom, "Go!…take command!"

With Zidcom no longer standing by his side and in the frenzy of confusion, Katchcom took cover. Cleverly, he leaped so as to cushion his fall. He chose as his landing point the soft body of a dead guardsman. Unfortunately, the royal guardsman whose soul had since departed did not take his sword with him as he ventured to the Land of the Dead. Landing on the dead body, that sword sliced deep into Katchcom's leg. Biting his tongue was his only choice to keep himself from howling in pain. Pulling his robe over himself securely, he waited for the right moment to make his escape.

Gorom Zidcom took charge and commanded the remaining army of goroms. "Kill the Neferzul. It's our only hope!" Zidcom pointed to Goroms Maycom, Nodcom, and Yellcom. Staring at the three goroms, Zidcom froze, seeing his brave comrades in arms but not their leader, Katchcom. Zidcom had drawn his bow. His target was the hooded prisoner, Jeannie. With his arrow ready to fly, Zidcom stopped briefly. Looking around wildly, he searched for the high priest. He did not see Katchcom anywhere. *"Where the hell are you?"* Zidcom yelled.

In the confusion, Zidcom's intended attack was too late. Allowing himself to be distracted by looking for the lost gorom was a mistake. Danny took advantage, and like a lightning bolt striking in a fierce storm, he flew through the air and landed by the man, snapping the neck of Gorom Zidcom and ripping off his head. His fury was all-consuming. Nothing could hold back his wrath. He instantly surveyed the position of the remaining goroms. Their black robes made them sitting ducks. His first targets were those with weapons. Instinct took over. Three of the remaining goroms reacted. They separated. Goroms Maycom, Nodcom, and Yellcom shifted their attention from Jeannie to the queen. She was only half the distance from them, and they were all too aware that the superhuman among them was tilting the balance of the battle.

Gorom Maycom waved his arm at Gorom Shadcom, motioning him to attack the hooded prisoner. He thought it a wise decision, as Shadcom was the youngest of the goroms and could run a mile in less than three minutes.

Never in a million years did Gorom Maycom expect the gory death that would befall him and his comrades. But as fate would have it, they were destined to endure a living hell in their final moments.

Gerrroooewelllll…geeerrroooooweellll…rarrrrr! Blood-curdling screams filled the Grand Hall of the royal palace. Not seeing what monster had made such booming sounds, Gorom Maycom was frozen, terror ripping through his trembling body, and he squealed in fright, *"What is that?"* Instantly, he and Gorom Yellcom bolted in the direction of the queen, leaving Nodcom standing in bewilderment.

Gorom Nodcom froze. Never suspecting his comrades, Goroms Maycom and Yellcom, would desert him, Nodcom was left alone. He wheeled around for an answer to the question that Maycom had just squealed out. What was making that terrible noise?

To Gorom Nodcom's surprise, he found himself glaring into the emerald-green eyes of a giant wolf. It looked as if death had already come. For him, time went into slow motion. The silence that greeted him in the expanding jaws and flesh-tearing teeth was the only answer he would ever have.

It was too late. The *gggrrrrrrrarrrrgggarr* was the last thing Nodcom heard in his mortal life. A giant yellow wolf crushed Gorom Nodcom's head as though it were a Wiffle ball. It was painful for but a moment, and then the lights went out. His body went limp and fell to the floor. Yellzor howled as if baying to the moon on a cold winter's night. Nodcom's soul was now ready for the boatman to load as cargo for his next voyage down the River Styx to the Land of the Dead.

Crouching behind her massive gold throne, the queen was hidden from the oncoming goroms. Her vision of the king's throne, however, was unobstructed. It was only fifteen feet from hers. There was Gorom Yellcom. His race for cover had been successful. He hid behind the massive gold structure of King Dalvin's throne.

Glancing for a moment at his colleague, Gorom Maycom witnessed a moment of terror—Nodcom's head in the vice-grip jaws of a giant wolf. It sent him racing for cover. He reached the king's throne and joined Yellcom.

"Shh," whispered Maycom to Yellcom. "That beast, that animal, did not see where we are hiding. Let's crouch low to the ground and then at the right moment attack the queen."

It was not only the mounds of dead bodies on the savage battlefield that hindered Shadcom's advance on Jeannie but also the swarms of warriors in fierce hand-to-hand combat. Being savvy and without hesitation, Shadcom's survey was quick. He noted the hiding place of Maycom and Yellcom. He was about as far from Jeannie as possible within the room, more than a hundred and fifty feet. He spun around and screamed at Yellcom. "You kill the queen, and I'll kill the Neferzul. It's our only hope." Their plan was to lodge an arrow in Jeannie's heart and likewise place one in the queen's. Yet Shadcom's problem was his distance from Jeannie, and there were two dozen warriors raging a bloody fight between the prisoner and himself.

In the middle of the mayhem, Jeannie stood like a statue, frozen with terror. Maybe it was instinct. Maybe it was fear. For whatever reason, she was frozen.

The tiny bit of space between her face and the hood was hot with the trapped air from her convulsive breathing. Blind to her surroundings and hearing the howls of Yellzor and the screams of dying men, Jeannie felt helpless and at the mercy of whatever the outcome might be. It was fortunate that some of Katchcom's bodyguards had moved in front of her. Ironically, those whose only function in life was to protect the priests were serendipitously protecting Jeannie from the evil goroms.

Those brief moments as they huddled behind the king's throne gave Maycom and Yellcom time to regroup. The problem they faced was what they should do in the face of these unnatural enemies. They'd watched the savage deaths of their fellow priests at the jaws of a yellow monster and a superhuman. Whoever it was had flown through the air on a beam of green light, landed on his target, Gorom Zidcom, and literally ripped his head off.

Who are they? Where did they come from? And why are they in the middle of battle that is not connected to them? Or is it connected? These were the questions flooding the minds of Gorom Maycom and Gorom Yellcom. Yes, challenging questions for goroms, but they also must have felt triumphant that they were successfully hiding from the savagery of the young man with yellow hair and emerald-green eyes and his terrible beast. They clutched their bows, waiting for a clear shot. They could not see the queen. She was on the other side of her throne. Their only option was to sit tight and wait for the queen to show herself as a target, as moving from their hiding place would surely mean their deaths.

The events unfolding in his palace were not unnoticed by Jerzom. At least his mother was still alive. The superman in their midst was no ordinary intruder. Handmar, Jerzom's most trusted guardsman, was not only hesitant but also observant. Even in the midst of the chaos that was engulfing the Grand Hall, Handmar noticed that the stranger with superhuman strength was focusing his vengeance on those who wore black robes.

Jerzom motioned to his personal bodyguard, Handmar. He was only ten feet from the fallen prince. Racing three steps, he knelt over Jerzom. "My royal prince, we must help the stranger kill the evil goroms and their guards and—"

Handmar stopped. Collecting his thoughts, he made his point clear. "I know not the reason why, but the intruder and his beast are not our enemies."

"Yes, my loyal guardsman. Order your forces to intensify their efforts to kill the goroms and their bodyguards. Tell them to save my mother. The mighty one and his yellow beast are turning the tide against the evil ones," uttered Jerzom.

Pressing his hand to the wound in his side, Jerzom managed to stop the bleeding at the hole where the arrow had pierced his side. "Go, my royal guardsman, and if possible let your actions—yours and those of your fellow guardsmen—against the goroms and their bodyguards be known to the stranger and his beast!"

At that instant, Handmar roared, "Kill the goroms and their bodyguards!" as he swung his arms forward, motioning to the royal guard. "*Help the stranger and his beast!*"

Danny took notice. He waved his arm above his head and yelled in the language of Kopaz, "*Carry on! I know you are sincere!*"

The battle raged on, and a body flew through the air.

Why did a dead body fly through the air? As it turned out, Yellzor was the culprit. He had spotted Zellom, Katchcom's personal bodyguard, and feeling playful after crushing the man with his powerful jaws, he swung his head, let loose, and flung the dead body through the air.

Screaming in utter terror, Jeannie had no idea what had landed on her, but it knocked her to the floor. Thrashing and squirming in his last moments of life, Zellom lay across Jeannie, kicking his hairy legs with each dying twitch.

"*No! No!*" screamed Jeannie. "*Whooo…whooo…who…what is it?*"

Her breathing intensified in short, erratic intakes of air as she tried in vain to push the quivering two-hundred-pound body off of her.

Jeannie's screams were lost in the roar of noise from the raging battle.

Maybe Goroms Maycom and Yellcom thought they had no choice. Maybe it was their only choice. Maybe they thought the queen would never move from her hiding place. For whatever reason, Maycom and Yellcom elected to charge the queen.

Even as Handmar was belting out orders, Danny was flying through the air once more. This time, he landed next to the queen before the two oncoming goroms had time to nock their arrows. Not looking at her, Danny reached behind and gently touched the queen's arm, motioning for her to lie still on the floor. She dropped to the floor.

To get to the queen, the charging goroms had to get through Danny. Only ten feet from the young god and charging forward, Maycom and Yellcom were unable to draw their bows and charge at the same time. They dropped their bows and instead drew their swords. With swords high in the air, their arms ready to fall with full force on Danny, they must have been sure that two against one would give them the upper hand.

Neferapondes, from her prone position on the marble floor, rolled her head and watched Danny, who stood no more than three feet from her. She witnessed his hand like an ax fly through the air. The gorom out in front was no match for his lightning speed. Yellcom never had the chance to wield his sword even one inch before Danny's rigid hand landed on the charging gorom's throat. Although not literally an ax, nonetheless, Danny's hand cut through the neck of Gorom Yellcom like it was hot butter. The queen watched in horror as the body of Gorom Yellcom, its head half-severed, slammed to the ground next to her. Instinctively, she rolled over to distance herself from the body squirting blood from a slashed jugular.

Maybe it was the gentleness with which he motioned the queen to lay on the floor. Maybe it was his supreme strength that could only come from the gods. Maybe it was the vengeance he was wreaking on those who had orchestrated the coup, killed her husband, and devastated her life by killing her beloved Aerapondes. Who knows? Whatever it was, she caught Danny's attention with an upward glance and a faint smile.

Stopping his momentum was impossible. Gorom Maycom was right behind his colleague, but Yellcom's swift death left him to face Danny alone. Towering above the oncoming gorom, who was helplessly trying to arrest his forward motion, Danny grabbed Maycom's hair. In one powerful motion, he slammed the gorom's forehead onto the solid gold chair back of the queen's throne. The head cracked open like an eggshell. Blood and brains flew from the smashed head of Maycom and splattered the queen with unthinkable matter. She screamed.

There was no time to waste. Leaving the queen on the floor, Danny leaped over the back of the throne. His hands were wide open, his fingers tight together. Yellzor was at his side. Their target was the group of twenty bodyguards moving toward Jeannie. For the army of bodyguards, time stopped. For Danny and Yellzor, the perception of time was also in slow motion, giving them the advantage. Danny wheeled his arms through the air, and like an executioner's ax, he struck the necks of the fear-gripped men. In essence, they were defenseless. He best friend and beast, Yellzor, was at his side, part of the killing brigade.

The army of bodyguards blinked at the smashing blows falling on them from a god venting his vengeance on the evil men who had taken his precious Jeannie. Their necks snapped like matchsticks.

Howling in rage, Yellzor was a giant killing machine. No one there was a match for a six-foot wolf who knew no fear. His jaws ripped off heads and flung them like bowling balls striking pins at the end of the alley.

From the floor, Jerzom cried feebly, "Find and kill Katchcom!"

The prince's words fell on listening ears. Handmar did not need to be convinced. Handmar had already pledged his allegiance to the superhuman and his beast. He just witnessed this superhuman negate any effort by the goroms to kill the queen, and he had stopped the swarm of warriors trying to kill the hooded prisoner.

"It shall be done, mighty prince!" yelled Handmar, following Jerzom's order to find and kill the high priest.

Jerzom spotted a blood-soaked robe moving. He screamed, "It's him!"

Katchcom was at least seventy-five yards from Jerzom. Yet the innate wisdom of the young prince let him know who was hiding, pretending to be a dead man under a black robe.

Confusion reigned. The battle was raging in all directions. Jerzom's efforts to kill Katchcom were not without challenges.

Ten of the remaining bodyguards eyed the doorway and made a mad dash to escape. Their speed was like that of a turtle compared to Danny. Like a flash of light from a gunshot, Danny was standing in the doorway long before the goroms' army reached it. His body blocked their exit. The lead guard, Zatchem, shoved his subordinate in front of him in an effort to shield himself from Danny.

Gripping his hands into a tight fist, Danny struck his target. The thundering blow to the face of the pawn, who died to preserve Zatchem, left one more body on the floor. Those few seconds gave Zatchem a chance to retreat, and so he was successful in preserving his life, at least for a short time. As Danny and Yellzor focused on the eight guardsman trying to flee the Grand Hall, Zatchem raced as fast as he could to get away from Danny.

It was at that brief moment in the raging battle when Katchcom made his play. Hiding under his robe, Katchcom was able to get the attention of Zatchem. He pointed to Jeannie lying on the floor, trying to get out from under a dead man. Katchcom made a motion. Zatchem watched closely every movement. His master, Katchcom, used sign language and gave orders. Together, they orchestrated a plan. And so the plan was set. Zatchem nodded his head. Katchcom slithered back under his black robe and lay still, like a dead body.

Growling in rage and standing erect on his hind legs, Yellzor towered ten feet in height. Fighting at Danny's side, his mighty front paws were deadly, and he quickly killed four of the bodyguards. The other four met their fate at the hands of the young god. It was like the bodyguards were ducks in a barrel being blasted by a shotgun.

And when that short fight was over, Danny and Yellzor turned to determine their next move, having dispatched eight more souls who were no longer in the battle.

Jeannie was helpless on the cold marble floor, under the weight of a two-hundred-pound dead man. She was covered with blood and was desperately trying to get him off of her. Jeannie remained in the dark, still a hooded prisoner, as she struggled with her hands tied behind her.

Jeannie did not know that her lover was unleashing his wrath, his desire for vengeance like no other, on the evil that had hung over Kopaz for decades.

For the warriors left standing, who followed the gorom's lead, their defeat was imminent. Danny focused on their leaders. His vengeance now narrowed down to the three leaders: one lying on the floor under a bloody robe; one standing fifty feet him and staring him in the eyes; and one trying to get to Jeannie before Danny could. Danny could not know that the man staring at him was Zatchem, once Mochcom's most loyal partner and his personal bodyguard. But that was years ago when Mochcom was still in Kopaz. In Scarlet Desert time, it was centuries ago.

Danny's aim was vengeance for what these evil creatures had done to Jeannie, and his goal was to avenge the hell they had inflicted on his girl—his lover. The lonely bodyguard stood his ground, fifty feet in front of Danny. Neither flinched. Turning his head cautiously, and with the glare of an outraged god, Danny's eyes surveyed the mayhem. Not only was the young god looking at the battle, he was also looking for someone. He did not see her face. *Is she here?*

In the middle of the screams and moans of those dying all around her, the lone prisoner under a dead body was in the dark, now trying to be inconspicuous. Danny did not have a clue who was left standing in the mayhem.

Briefly, silence enveloped the hall as the superwarrior assessed the scene.

That respite was short. Mayhem erupted again on the other side of the hall: a group of warriors fighting between Jeannie and Gorom Shadcom.

Watching Danny from his place of cover, Katchcom's eyes followed the young god's movements, trying to detect if he knew who he was looking for. Katchcom was convinced Danny was unaware of who was who in this battle for power. He made his move. Katchcom slithered out of his hiding place and rolled around, knowing his only chance was to reach Jeannie. He tried to stand but fell, and his sword clanked on the marble floor. The clatter of his hasty movement dominated the room. Zatchem nodded his head again as Katchcom grabbed his sword from where it had fallen next to a body on the floor. Zatchem was halfway between Danny and Shadcom. Katchcom knew if he could get the sword to Gorom Shadcom, that all would end in victory. Danny could not know what their purpose was. It was like a Hail Mary pass in a football game, where deception was necessary to outmaneuver the opponent. Katchcom threw the sword to Zatchem. He hit his mark, and Zatchem caught it. Their teamwork was perfect. Zatchem skillfully tossed the sword high in the air. The blade flipped over and over, like the propeller on a prop plane. Shadcom swept his arm through the air and grabbed the twirling sword by its handle.

Katchcom smiled as his mind raced. *So far, so good.*

Gorom Shadcom's target was Jeannie. His sword would cut through whoever was in its way. His mission was set, and he charged. As the most skillful swordsman in Kopaz, he raced to his target like a skilled athlete in the Olympics. He wheeled his arm back and, with all his might, sliced into his first victim. He cared not if it was a royal guardsman or one of the gorom's bodyguards. It was collateral to him, and he had to reach the hooded prisoner at any cost.

Danny was caught off guard. He had to use his ring before it was too late. Then it dawned on him. *It's Jeannie they are after! Where is she?* His eyes searched. He did not see her.

Zatchem howled with laughter, but that was cut short as Danny pointed to Yellzor.

It was only a microsecond before the head of Zatchem howled no more as Yellzor's jaw crushed any laughter that wanted to escape the guardsman's body in his dying moments.

Now only two leaders were left.

The swiftness of Gorom Shadcom put him right where he wanted to be—in the mix of human bodies behind Jeannie. He was between Jeannie and the queen—ten feet from Jeannie and also ten feet from the queen. The royal hall darkened as the moon hid its face behind a cloud, and little light came through the massive wooden doors. In the dim light, Danny was unable to discern where Jeannie was. He could not risk the deadly beam of light from his ring missing its mark and destroying his love. He had to kill the gorom with his hands.

Jerzom was lying on the floor. Watching the drama unfold, he realized the target was the Neferzul. Jerzom lifted his head. Time was everything. Loss of blood had left him weak, yet he knew the clock was the enemy, and he reacted quickly. Jerzom was only able to use one arm, but that was enough. He threw his sword toward the melee. The clanking of metal as Jerzom's sword hit the marble floor cracked through the air and startled the queen.

The clank of metal stopped the onslaught for a moment. Shadcom's eyes darted to see what it was. His mind raced as he saw Jerzom. *A deception, you fool? You must be the dumbest prince in all of Kopaz if you think you can distract me from my mission!*

Watching Shadcom ready his sword, Neferapondes felt her body grow even more rigid. She had no idea that Shadcom's target was Jeannie, and she braced herself for death.

The queen had already come under attack and had been saved by the young warrior. This time, however, he was on the other side of the Grand Hall and was in no position to save her again.

Maybe it was just too much for Neferapondes to handle, but the queen started to scream in uncontrolled howls. Shadcom flinched and turned, startled.

An opening arose. Neferapondes bolted for the side door of the Grand Hall. The queen's movement momentarily diverted Danny's attention. Shadcom, who had been tracking Danny's every move with beady eyes, took advantage of this diversion. He was close enough now. He had two choices. They raced through his mind: *A knife at the throat of the most prized person in the room would be a huge bargaining chip. Slitting her throat would be more positive and would foil Viracocha's grand plan, but it might mean my death.*

Shadcom was positive he had the upper hand. He chose the first option, as he wanted to save his own hide. He jumped over the dead body at his feet and raced to reach Jeannie. Drawing his knife from its leather sheath as he sprinted, he made it to Jeannie's side. He grabbed the dead body and rolled it off Jeannie. He seized her and yanked her to her feet. He held her tightly and thrust his blade to her throat. With one quick motion, his knife was precise, making the initial cut on Jeannie's throat. Holding his knife tightly, his fingers wrapped around the ornate gold handle inlaid with precious gemstones, his eyes deepened to a squint.

He rolled his hand to soak his fingers in the trickle of blood oozing from the cut on Jeannie's neck. "Back off, or she is *dead!*" shouted Shadcom. He lifted his knife, dripping with blood. He firmly held Jeannie in his left arm, and his strength was overpowering. She was without options. She stood hostage, a sacrificial lamb.

All eyes were on Shadcom. The battles stopped. Silence fell throughout the Grand Hall. This would be the defining moment of the gorom's coup.

At first, Danny thought the situation was hopeless. Schooled by Quill, one thing dominated Danny's mind. His heart was pounding, knowing that if a gorom killed a Neferzul with a knife from the black god, all was lost. Jeannie's soul would travel to the Land of the Dead forever.

Maybe she was meant to stop momentarily and look back. Maybe it was just a coincidence. For whatever reason, the queen on her way through the doorway stopped and turned. She had just enough time to witness the horrifying episode unfolding. She screamed as the image of her daughter's throat being severed by the evil gorom flashed through her mind. Shadcom blinked. Her shrill screams were the only sounds in the silence that had descended and filled the entire hall. Shadcom turned his head to the direction of the screams.

That's all it took. That brief moment of Shadcom letting his guard down gave Danny the opportunity he needed. Propelled through the air in an instant on a beam of green light, Danny slammed into the gorom, knocking Jeannie to the ground. She let out a scream, not knowing what was happening. Terrified, she huddled in a fetal position, her hands still tied behind her.

The sound of Shadcom's knife hitting the marble floor was music to Danny's ears. In his collision with Gorom Shadcom, Danny had grabbed the gorom's arm with his enormous right hand. Yanking the gorom up with a powerful jerk and dragging him three feet from Jeannie gave Danny the sight he wanted to see. Glancing quickly at her, he felt relief. Her hood had lifted slightly, exposing the cut on her neck. *She's alive, and I don't think she's bleeding anymore.* Danny's massive hand clenched around the arm of the gorom and literally ripped it from its socket. Howling in pain, Shadcom dropped to his knees. A set of bloody fingers twitched on a detached arm that no longer held the knife from the black god and then went still. The gorom who once took orders from Gorom Mochcom pressed his remaining hand over the bleeding socket. He slithered backward on his knees, trying to distance himself from the superhuman. He stopped as his feet bumped into the body of the king lying face down, an arrow protruding from his back.

Danny waved to Yellzor. In seconds, his beast was at his side. Yellzor knew what to do. With Jeannie lying on the floor once more, the giant wolf took his position and stood guard so no one could get near the Neferzul.

Jeannie lay still on the floor listening to the low, growling sounds coming from Yellzor as he made his presence known. *Goooogggll grroowww.*

Jeannie's mind exploded with images of terror. *My god, what is it? What is going to happen to me now?*

Slowly, Danny walked to Shadcom. Jeannie heard footsteps. Her body went rigid like a rock.

In measured tone that balanced authority and harshness, Danny growled in an unfamiliar voice, speaking in the language of Kopaz so that Jeannie failed to recognize him. He delivered the sentence. "For you and your kind, the treachery and deception is over!"

The loud snap of the dying man's neck echoed off the walls of the Grand Hall of the royal palace. Jeannie's heart pounded so fiercely that for that brief moment she never connected the voice as coming from a familiar person. The sounds of death and the growls of a giant wolf overpowered the silence in the room once more.

The tide had turned. Only one gorom was left alive, and he was no longer in a position to lead. Only four of the goroms' bodyguards were left standing. They laid their weapons down and were quickly made prisoners by Handmar and his men.

And now, at the final moment of revenge, Danny stared at the gorom beneath the bloody black robe. Unaware that Katchcom had fallen on a dead warrior's sword and severed a vein in his leg, Danny was taking no chances with this prized specimen of evil. He instantly traveled on the beam of green light emitted by his ring. Danny stood over Katchcom.

Danny was uncharacteristically angry. Maybe he knew how evil Katchcom really was. Standing over the gorom, looking down at him, the young god growled with vengeance. "Your journey to hell is about to begin. You will face the eternities in misery, torment, and pain that will smother every moment of your endless imprisonment in darkness!"

Maybe it was revenge for Tony. Maybe it was revenge for his beloved mother. Maybe Danny finally realized the prisoner, his only love, Jeannie, was safe and wanted to be certain no one would ever harm her again. Who knows? For whatever reason, those few moments of reflection were brief. Danny's mind was fixed on the thought of killing the evil man who had gripped the kingdom of Kopaz in a reign of terror.

In a booming voice, Danny roared, "You bastard, I hope your death is beyond the description of pure hell!"

There was a brief moment of silence.

Then the hall echoed with screams. Katchcom, howling in the face of his final moments, begged for his life. His cries for mercy were to no avail. Danny's massive hand gripped the gorom's throat, crushing his final words as he ripped out the gorom's jugular, exposing a gaping hole of raw flesh. The pure hatred in his eyes dimmed as death overtook the high priest with each pump of his heart, squirting blood from his neck and throat.

CHAPTER 31
The Mayhem is Over

There could be no feeling more heartrending than the despair that was tearing the soul of Queen Neferapondes into a million pieces. Her world was shattered beyond comprehension. Her beautiful daughters were no more. The chaos had ended. The cries of the dead and the dying in the Grand Hall had fallen silent. She turned around and slowly walked down the hallway leading back to the most beautiful room in the palace. Its beauty, however, was camouflaged with lifeless bodies. It was now a stage of death, a battlefield of good against evil. The fact that the goroms were no more was not foremost on her mind. She had to know more, and the answers were in the room she had just walked out of.

As hard as it had been when Aerapondes was murdered by (as the queen thought at the time) her elder son, Kashom, the death of Aerapondes's twin sister, Merapondes, was more than a mother could take. To lose her husband and have him lying on the floor next to his dead daughter left the queen in a dark corner of hopelessness. She had one son left, but she no longer knew if Jerzom was the sweet boy he used to be or if he was the monster he seemed to have turned into. She could not even bear to look at him, lying on the floor of the Grand Hall, so filled with death.

The scene in the Grand Hall was like a battlefield, bloody corpses lying in their own pools of blood. On this stage of darkness, even the Angel of Death would refuse to swoop up the fallen victims. No angels would want the souls of these evil men. Why would they?

A deathly silence descended on the room. Jerzom stood unsteadily. He was shaking with pain, but he mustered enough strength to walk. He said nothing. Retracing her steps back down the hallway, Neferapondes stopped in the doorway. She looked at Jerzom. Their eyes locked. He dropped his head as he hobbled in the direction of the body of Gorom Katchcom.

Maybe it was curiosity. Maybe she was searching for hope other than in her son Jerzom. Maybe she wanted to know more of the stranger who had just killed the quorum of evil men who had strangled the life out of the royal family and thrown a veil of darkness over the land of Kopaz for decades—all in the name of religion. Who could say? For whatever reason, the queen turned her attention to the center of the royal courtroom.

The only sounds Queen Neferapondes heard were whimpers coming from a helpless child lying on the floor, the hooded prisoner. She watched the young man with ripped muscles, shaggy blond hair, and emerald-green eyes make his way to the young girl. He picked her up as if she were a weightless baby and held her in his arms, pulling her tightly against his body. Jeannie had no idea who was holding her. Her body was tense.

Neferapondes was bewildered. She had no idea what was happening or why the stranger was holding the girl.

Danny gently stood Jeannie in front of him, making sure her feet were firmly placed on the floor. He turned her around. She froze.

Helpless, her hands tied behind her, Jeannie felt the blade of a sharp metal instrument. She started to shake. Danny said nothing, but very gently, he used his knife to slice through the leather straps that bound Jeannie's wrists. They had been strapped together so tightly, they had lost all feeling.

Then her hands were free. Her mind raced. *What are they doing now? Oh my god, why is it so quiet?*

With one arm gently on her left shoulder and the other on her right side, Danny turned Jeannie around to face him. She heard no sound. She did not know who was standing next to her.

Danny reached and took the hood. As he lifted it from her head, his face was the first thing Jeannie laid her eyes on. Emotion exploded within her entire body. She lifted her hand trembling to touch his face. Even locking her eyes with his, she could not believe who was standing in front of her. She feared it was a dream. She moved her hand and stretched out her fingers. Tears streaming down her face, she slowly touched his face with her shaking hand. Still not believing it was Danny, she slid her fingers into his shaggy hair. Her fingers tingled with uncontrollable emotions. She stared. They slid to his cheek. Danny was motionless as his lover and partner explored the reality that he was not dead. Slowly, she put a finger on his lips and pressed gently. His smile erupted, and in the same fashion, Danny gently put his finger to her lips. His other hand found her cheek. He sweetly caressed it with his fingers, rough with calluses from months in a time warp of wilderness survival. He whispered, "It's me, Jeannie. I'm not a dream!"

Her emotions could no longer be contained. Her crying was no longer from fear, and tears of joy swelled in her eyes. The words that burst from her mouth were far from collected, as she tried to speak through her tears. "Is-is it y-you? A-am I dreaming? Oh, my love, is it really you?"

"It's OK, Jeannie," said Danny, speaking in the language of the royals, trying as hard as he could to be strong, shaking with emotions of his own, and knowing that she was alive and safe. He pulled her quavering body into his arms and pressed her next to him, his arms wrapped around her.

He whispered, "I'm so sorry, Jeannie, that I could not defend you. My world ended when I lost you." Now with tears streaming down his face, he whimpered, "Never will you be alone again."

The pawing at his leg sent a sweep of joy through him. "There's our cat, Zanzee! He thinks he needs to be picked up!" said Danny as he reached and picked up Zanzee.

The queen watched the emotional scene play out on the stage of the Grand Hall from her vantage point. There was little doubt now for Queen Neferapondes. The young man speaking the language that was reserved for royalty confirmed something was going on that was not evil. Her elder son's cat, Zanzee, was back in the royal palace, and the young man had just called Zanzee by name. Memories of Kashom playing with Zanzee in the palace so long ago, running up and down the halls, trying to find a hiding place from a cat that knew all secrets, caused her to swell with joy. She watched events take place that only the gods could have orchestrated.

With each passing moment, as the queen watched and listened to Danny, Jeannie, and Zanzee, her heart swelled with joy.

"Here, Jeannie," Danny said as he held Zanzee for Jeannie to take. "He has been waiting for all of us to be together again." She snuggled the cat next to her face. For a few moments, his purring was all that cut through the silence of the scene of death that surrounded them. At that moment, Jeannie's composure returned, the comfort of her two protectors settling her to a state of ease.

Her question could wait no longer. "You speak our language?" she asked, her words full of curiosity. "How?"

He wouldn't let her ask any more. He was anxious to introduce her to his new friend. Holding his arm straight out, he pointed. "Quill."

Jeannie looked in the direction Danny was pointing and saw the dwarf man smiling back at her. Jeannie realized who the man must be. "He's your teacher…sent from the supreme god Viracocha to teach you the ways of the rulers of the universe!"

Enjoying the warmth of every word that came from her lips, Danny followed her gaze, watched her survey of every inch of his bare chest. Then she rolled her eyes downward and lifted her arm as she spoke. "My god, Danny, I thought you were the biggest hunk in the world before, but just look at you now…"

He had no control. He reflexively tightened his already rock-hard muscles even more as she placed her outstretched fingers on his abdomen. She gently let them slide down with a feathery touch and sweetly said, "You…you…oh my *God*, Danny, I can't wait!"

He nodded, his beaming smile in no way containable. Her face wore a smile bright with innocence, letting Danny know that the goroms had not molested her. The swelling of his heart matched hers, and they squeezed each other's hands, knowing their journey had taken a giant turn and was now leading to golden thrones at the most powerful table at the center of the universe.

Jeannie's eyes focused on the aftermath of the mayhem that had engulfed the royal court. At first, her heart pounded with joy, knowing that Danny was responsible for the destruction of the evil that had gripped Kopaz. His vengeance against those who had taken his love from him was painted in blood in all directions. Squeezing his hand more tightly, she knew he was not human, no longer a young god in training but a powerful young god carrying out his mission. He was the young god that had meted out justice to the group of evil men that had had a stranglehold on the land and people of Kopaz.

Then she saw the body of King Dalvin lying at the base of his throne. His golden crown was lying next to him on the marble floor. Her eyes searched for the queen and Prince Jerzom, but to no avail. She motioned with a shaky hand. "Save the king!"

"He's dead, Jeannie. His soul has taken its journey on the River Styx. There is nothing I can do at this point."

CHAPTER 32
The Queen Leaves

I f ever there were a case of a broken heart and a joyous heart coexisting in a body crushed in spirit, such was Queen Neferapondes. In that state of mixed emotions defined by the gods' intervention to rescue Kopaz from evil, there was a hesitation deep in her consciousness that left her in doubt as to who her son was. *Could it be he is not evil? Could it be he was deceived by evil? Could it be he is indeed evil?* Her mind drifted, searching for answers, as she moved her attention from a scene of joy to a young man struggling to walk, the only son she had left. He moved toward the still body of the dead gorom.

"The hour is at hand." A voice rang through the air in the Grand Hall as Quill stood on the king's throne and declared that all was not finished. He was all too aware that joyous reunions were needed, yet intense emotional soul searching had to take second place to the chore that could not wait any longer. "Danny," shouted Quill, "the bodies of the goroms must enter the gateway to hell this very evening—before the moon is ripe, or all is lost!"

Now the dwarf had everyone's attention. It was not only Danny who was looking at the dwarf standing on a golden throne but also the queen, Jerzom, and Jeannie. Zanzee would have none of it. He lifted his paw and gently let it slide down Jeannie's cheek.

"Danny, what does he want?" whispered Jeannie as she tried to ignore her cat insisting that he should be the focus of attention, not a little man on a golden throne or her lover, the royal prince of Viracocha.

Although her question caught him at a moment of weakness as his own emotions were tugging at his soul, telling him to ignore Quill and focus on Jeannie, he was all too aware that time was not on his side and that the will of Viracocha must be done. "He thinks we need to get busy," said Danny.

Jeannie giggled freely as she said, "He was sent by Viracocha to teach you the way of the gods, so I guess we had better do as he says!"

"Yes, we have much to do this evening," said Danny as his look grew solid with concern. "The moon cannot reach its high point in the sky before all the bodies of the goroms are ushered into hell through the gateway guarded by CrystalFlame."

His concerned face broke into a gentle smile as he moved his mouth to her ear and softly spoke. "It is not I alone who must do this, but we together must take the disciples of Zuron to the Mouth of Vulcan and let them be ashes as they start their journey to the outer reaches of darkness for the eternities."

His words were for Jeannie and Jeannie alone. They conversed as gods in training. And as he spoke, her mind drifted momentarily as their eyes locked in silence. He waited. He did not expect what she had to say.

"Danny, at the Boar's Tusk, on that fateful day, when Mochcom vented his rage on you, me, and Tony, in those final moments prior to us venturing on the Highway of Time, I looked at the last page of Kashom's journal. Remember what I said to you then? The royal prince of Viracocha is TRPOV, and the royal princess of Neferdor is TRPON. Only when TRPOV and TRPON have killed all of the goroms in Kopaz and have thrown their bodies not yet ashes into the fiery depths of Vulcan—the gateway to hell guarded by CrystalFlame—so their eternity is destined to be everlasting embers in the belly of the outer reaches of darkness of hell, and only when Mochcom's ashes are wrapped in the Ancient Shroud of Goroms and also thrown into the fiery depths of Vulcan so his eternity is destined to be everlasting anguish in the belly of the outer reaches of darkness; then, and only then, shall TRPOV and TRPON sit on thrones of pure gold alongside the gods at their council table of red worox stone and control the gift of eternal youth for all humans throughout the universe. Beware that the bodies of the goroms of Kopaz not remain outside the gateway to hell past the evening of the high moon. And to TRPOV, his beast Yellzor shall devour imposters and throw them into the fiery mouth of CrystalFlame."

"Hmm," said Danny, and he smiled.

It wasn't at all funny, but at that moment, Danny laughed softly. "How the hell did you get that far ahead of me, Jeannie?"

And in response she just smiled and said softly, "Danny boy, you have a lot to learn."

He broke into such loud laughter that all in the Grand Hall could hear as he managed to say through his chuckles. "Jeannie, I believe I've heard that 'Danny boy, you have a lot to learn' statement before! And oh, by the way, you are the only one who can get away with calling me 'Danny boy'!"

Quill at that point said, "Danny boy, get busy! And oh, by the way, you forgot me." He laughed. "I am the only *other* one who can call you that!"

He stopped. And then, like a dam bursting and loosing a flood of water, so his voice echoed in the silence of the Grand Hall. In the booming voice of a god's tutor, he bellowed, "*No one, I mean no one, shall address these two*"— he lifted his arm and pointed to Danny and Jeannie—"*except by the titles of TRPOV and TRPON! Is that clear?*"

For a moment, there was a stillness like that in a glen on a quiet evening. Quill continued. "Until there is further notice from me, the new king of Kopaz is TRPOV, and your new queen is TRPON!

If there had been silence prior to that proclamation, it was a roar compared to the silence that now filled the courtroom in the Grand Hall of the royal palace. All eyes were on Quill. He stood erect on Dalvin's golden throne. He rolled his head. His eyes searched. He stopped and glared at Handmar. "What is your name?" he shouted.

"Handmar, my lord!" the guard roared back, like a soldier answering his sergeant.

"And why are you here?" yelled Quill.

"I'm the new captain of the royal guard!" shouted Handmar in the same manner.

There was a long silence that seemed to drag on forever. "Hmm…" Quill mumbled. He looked at Danny. "Is that correct?"

Way ahead of Quill, Danny laughed and motioned for Handmar to approach him.

Slowly, the guard walked to Danny. Neferapondes, no longer royalty, and her son, Jerzom, looked on. When Handmar reached Danny, he said, "At your service, my king!"

"Who appointed you head guard?" said Danny sternly. Handmar's face tensed as Danny glared at him. "Answer me!" said Danny.

Beside himself, Handmar started shaking, knowing he had no answer. He knew not the next move of this superhuman who had just rained death upon the goroms. He was about to speak when Jeannie screamed, "Danny, what is this *dog* doing here?"

Totally amused, Danny jerked his head from Handmar to Jeannie. He burst into laughter. "Jeannie, you just said he'll devour the impostors. Do you not have a clue of what you speak?"

Bursting into laugher, Jeannie reached her hand and started petting the giant wolf standing no more than six inches from her. "Good boy, Yellzor!" she said very gingerly as he growled in reply.

"Well, it sure seems that we are all one happy set of rulers: you, me, Zanzee, and Yellzor. Can't get any better than that!" Danny laughed.

Maybe it was because a little humor was needed and Danny knew it. Maybe it was because the scene of death that dominated the Grand Hall was so powerful that a change of air was needed. Maybe it was Danny just being Danny. Who knows? But whatever the reason, Danny felt justified in bringing a little laughter to the stage of horror that surrounded them as he joked about him, Jeannie, the cat, and the wolf being the new rulers of Kopaz.

An intense look from Quill changed the tone of the conversation. He didn't have to say a thing. Danny knew the gravity of the situation and that they must proceed in haste.

With a quick wink directed at the royal guardsman, Danny said, "Handmar, as the new chief of the royal guard, have your men, the royal guards, collect all of the bodies of the goroms. Make sure you have all nine of them. Put their bodies on a wagon and prepare to take them to the Pit of Vulcan!"

Taking Danny's order at face value, Handmar's hand swung to his forehead and saluted, shouting, "Your will be done, my lord!"

"Wait!" said Danny to Handmar. "Let me make it official!"

There was a puzzled look on Handmar's face. Danny shouted so all could hear, "You are officially the captain of the royal guard, and so do your duty with a heart full of joy!"

At that moment, Handmar hesitated. He looked at Danny. "What about Prince Jerzom?" He knew the pain in the prince's heart must be growing as he was the guardsman closest to Jerzom.

Since they were speaking the common tongue of Kopaz, Jeannie was totally in the dark about what they were saying. Jeannie was clueless about the words of the conversation, but she had a sense of what was transpiring. Her lack of knowledge of the common language did not leave her without an uncanny sense to read body language.

Perceptively, Danny said, "What about Prince Jerzom? Well, he is a brave man who has both witnessed and been subjected to much evil. He and his family have suffered much. He has my respect!"

There was a bit of tension growing. Jeannie said nothing. She had caught the queen's reaction to Handmar's question. *Only a mother in pain would flinch and give her son that look.* Her mind searched. *The prince…the queen…something is not right.*

She stared on. Watching the queen and knowing her heart was broken beyond what most humans could bear, Jeannie wanted to do something. She didn't know if she should try to talk to Neferapondes or help Danny.

As it turned out, it was the queen who made the decision to walk toward Jeannie. As Neferapondes started making her way to the center of the Grand Hall, Danny gave orders. "You may have Prince Jerzom help in any way he desires. Go and make haste to collect the bodies of the goroms!"

Danny took a moment to watch the interaction between Jeannie and the queen. Jeannie spoke first as the queen approached her.

"Hi…ah…I'm Jeannie." That was all that came of Jeannie's mouth.

Usually Jeannie was the one who knew what to say and do. In this case, however, Danny was not so sure. He decided to go to her side.

There was much to be done. Quill motioned for Danny to come to him. Danny replied by putting two fingers in the air, telling Quill he would be just be a few minutes. Danny gently put his hand on Jeannie's shoulder, and in the language of the royals, he said, "I have much to do. You talk to the queen, but when we are ready to transport the bodies to the Pit of Vulcan, I will come and get you."

"Danny, that's fine. That will give me a few moments alone with the queen of Kopaz."

Jeannie saw what might have been a slight smile start to form on Neferapondes's face. No one could deny the grace with which the former queen was presenting herself. She didn't know Danny. She didn't know Jeannie. The battle that had just erupted in the Grand Hall had taken its toll on her, not only emotionally but also in the physical loss of her beloved daughter and husband. Maybe that was why she was gracious but also guarded.

Quill was nervous. For him, time was moving too quickly. "We have at most three hours to get these bodies to the Pit of Vulcan. The problem we have is that I see only seven dead goroms. Where are the other two?" said Quill to Danny as he remained standing on the throne so that they stood face to face.

Quill looked around the Grand Hall and shouted, "Find the missing bodies!"

The scramble was on. Jeannie talked to the queen, and the others looked for bodies.

Although Neferapondes was now nothing more than an ordinary citizen, the thought of being a commoner was furthest from her mind. Standing next to Jeannie, she was cautious. She was not focused on losing her royal status. Her mind was drifting. *My husband has gone to the Land of the Dead. I must not have been a good mother...my sons...*

The former queen had not yet spoken. Jeannie started getting nervous. Neferapondes looked away. Her attention was not on Jeannie. She was watching her son, Jerzom, who was talking with Danny and Quill.

Jeannie did not know that. Caught in a state of bewilderment, she wondered, *Why? What now?* She could only guess. The tenseness of Jerzom's mother was evident, but the reason was not. She had shared with her own mother many tense conversations, and Jeannie knew something was going on with Neferapondes that she was not privy to. Jeannie was about to speak, but then she didn't. She just waited. She did not look to see what Neferapondes might be staring at.

The rest of those in the hall were hunting for two dead bodies, as Quill had ordered just moments ago, but Neferapondes was not watching that.

It was her son she was looking at. Handmar was busy instructing the royal guardsmen to collect the dead goroms after visiting briefly with Jerzom. What Neferapondes did not hear was that Jerzom told Handmar he knew the whereabouts of the bodies of Goroms Ancom and Dorcom.

Having spent time in the dungeon beneath the Hall of the Goroms, Jerzom knew exactly where the bodies were. Their stench had permeated the dank cell where he had been a prisoner. His roommates had been the bodies of two dead goroms.

Neferapondes did not hear Handmar say, "Thank you, Jerzom, my loyal friend. I'll get the two bodies and have them here within the hour. I know the time frame we are working with."

What Neferapondes's concentration was on was what her son was doing. He was dragging the body of Katchcom to the door of the Grand Hall. A trail of blood marked the path, and yet it was not the blood she was looking at, nor was it the body of Katchcom. It was at an object that had fallen out of the gorom's robe and was now lying in the trail of blood. And as she watched, Jerzom was keenly aware of his mother's glare.

Jerzom glanced back at her. It wasn't her face but the direction of his mother's stare. He looked in the same direction. He saw it. Dropping the legs of the gorom he had been dragging along, he hobbled the five steps back to the golden watch. He stopped. He bent over and picked it up. He put it in his belt pouch, turned, walked to Katchcom's body, and his excruciating agony evident on his face, he began dragging it to the doorway once again.

Watching her son, the queen tensed as her mind took off again. *He took something from a dead man. That object Jerzom picked up and put in his pocket is not Jerzom's. What is going on?*

At that moment, the former queen reached, grabbed Jeannie's hand, squeezed it tightly, then let go, turned, and walked away.

Jeannie didn't know why. She didn't know what to do next. Jeannie was concerned that she had offended the former queen. On impulse, she ran a few steps and stood by Neferapondes's side. "Is there anything I can do?"

Neferapondes smiled and said as she quickly glanced at Jerzom, "I'm sorry if I offended you. Please forgive me. I…ah…this is so difficult for me."

Unaware that Neferapondes was wondering if her only son was evil, Jeannie moved closer to the queen. Jeannie's smile grew as she gently extended her arm. She took Neferapondes's hand.

Maybe that was all that was needed. Tensions fell, and the conversation started.

The queen started. "You speak the royal language. It is reserved for only a few."

There was a pause, and then Jeannie said, "Yes, I do."

Neferapondes didn't question Jeannie's answer. "You also have my son's cat."

Jeannie softly said, "Yes, Zanzee is now my kitty!" She swung him gently as he purred in her arms.

The queen then locked eyes with Jeannie. "Are you Aerapondes?"

As unrehearsed as she had ever been, Jeannie spoke in a clear, solid voice. "No, and yet I am of the royal family of Kopaz, and you are my great-great-great-great-great-great-grandmother!"

Even though the Grand Hall was filled with commotion and loud noise, Neferapondes could have heard a pin drop.

"I knew it. I just knew it," said the queen beaming with a glow of joy. "My son, Kashom, do you know him? Where is he?" asked Neferapondes.

Jeannie threw her arms around Neferapondes and hugged her tightly. Exciting words were about to fall from Jeannie's mouth when the queen said, "You know that only royalty can hug royalty, so I welcome your hug…I needed that!"

"Oh, my gracious queen." Jeannie stopped abruptly and then said, "Or do I call you 'Grandma'?"

"'Grandma' is an endearing name that warms my heart, so you can call me what you desire, but I'd love it if you called me Grandma," said Neferapondes, a tear rolling down her cheek.

Jeannie could not hold back her words. "We have both endured so much. Long before I came to Kopaz, Gorom Mochcom's reign of terror was real in the Scarlet Desert. He…I…I…can't…"

Her emotions took over. The queen listened as Jeannie went on. "When I arrived in Kopaz, I became a prisoner of the evil high priests." Jeannie stopped. "I can't talk about it."

The queen's personal knowledge of the evil Jeannie was touching on brought a chill upon her as she thought, *My children, all of them, have suffered horrific crimes of monsters…and it even reached my grandchildren…and now…*

The queen diverted her attention from Jeannie and turned to look at Danny as her thoughts continued. *Now, maybe it will be over.*

As Jeannie's last words hung in the air, Neferapondes pointed to Danny and asked, "Is he TRPOV?"

Jeannie nodded her head.

"You must be TRPON!"

Again, Jeannie nodded.

"I knew it! My heart is so full it is ready to burst out of my chest." Neferapondes beamed with such a delightful smile that her radiance at that moment could compete with the sun's brilliance.

"Grandma, we have much to do before the moon is at its high point. When all is finished, we will talk and talk and talk."

"Yes, we will, but for now, that young man you are in love with needs you! Go!"

It was Quill who said what had to be said. "Jeannie, tell Neferapondes that all will be OK."

Neither Danny nor Jeannie comprehended Quill's full meaning. How could everything be OK? They did not know that Quill knew the whereabouts of the golden watch, which was essential in the grand scheme of the eternities.

"It is almost time, Jeannie. As soon as the two bodies are retrieved, we leave for the Pit of Vulcan. And there you will see a new friend!" said Danny.

It was Danny's way of diverting her attention. Usually, it didn't work. Who knew this time if it did or didn't. Time would tell.

"Oh, a new friend! And who might that be?" Jeannie replied. Still holding Zanzee, she shot back, "Will my new friend like my old friend?"

Fencing with Jeannie was a game for Danny. He knew he would never win, but he did not care. "My love, you will just have to wait." He smirked at her. "Ah…er…ah, which friend are you talking about? I'm not old!"

The balance of the new human race teetered on an action yet to happen.

Humor was Danny's way of coping with messy situations. His fencing was finished, and that was fine with Jeannie. She was behind Danny every step of the way. Even before he moved on, she knew what he was about to say as he spoke with the voice of a god. "The hour is late, and the Mouth of Vulcan waits to devour the bodies of the goroms."

And so it was that Kopaz had new rulers. The goroms were gone. News of that magnitude traveled swiftly across the land, even in the late hours.

CHAPTER 33
All Aboard

When there's work to be done and there are willing hands, the job is much simpler. The spirit of camaraderie takes over, and all jump in. That was the case on that night of death. Maybe it was a way of clearing their minds of the horrors they had seen. Maybe it was the start of a new life free of evil. Maybe it was just good old hard work, and many hands make the job just a little easier. Whatever it was, all pitched in, and the work was underway.

Four men grabbed the heavy door leading from the Grand Hall of the royal palace to swing it open.

Handmar was anxious to get to the secret dungeon that his friend Jerzom had just disclosed. As soon as the door opened far enough for him to fit through, he bolted out into the royal courtyard.

He didn't stay there.

Racing back in, he screamed, "*The devil has come! Run!*"

He might have alarmed some, but not all, especially Quill.

"*Stop! All is well! It's CrystalFlame, and she belongs here!*"

That was enough to calm the fears of some, but certainly not Handmar's. "Yeah, you go out there. That damn thing is spitting fire everywhere."

"I want five men. Two will help Jerzom, as he is hurt, and the others follow me," yelled Quill.

They did as they were told.

CrystalFlame was curious. She snorted bursts of flames randomly as the men walked cautiously around her. Her gargantuan body filled most of the courtyard. The remains of what used to be the Hall of the Goroms lay in rubble after CrystalFlame's tail destroyed it.

Quill and his workers had to make their way through the debris to get to the entrance to the secret dungeon. The horrifying scene they stumbled into would have made the souls of heaven weep.

The piles of skulls, broken bones, weapons of torture, and fingers filed to half their size told a story of horror revealing the dark and evil nature of the vilest humans who had ever lived.

The stench of death led them to the corpses of the two goroms. The bodies already in the process of decay, the workers vomited as they dragged the bodies through the courtyard. Fresh air helped, but the lingering smell that permeated the still air helped them make haste in getting the bodies to the Pit of Vulcan.

Their task was almost finished.

Danny motioned for all—except Neferapondes—to come outside and gather around him. "Listen up," he shouted. "Follow Quill's orders!" He motioned for Quill to take over.

Instantly, Quill was no longer next to Danny, but using his own ring and beam of light, he was standing on the head of CrystalFlame. He commanded their attention.

"OK, we have nine goroms' corpses in the wooden wagon," shouted Quill. "Those who will go to the Pit of Vulcan are: TRPOV, TRPON, Jerzom, Handmar, and three of his faithful guardsman. Handmar will choose who he wants to go. That's a total of seven."

The next round was in play. It was a show worth watching. One by one, those named were beamed to the head of CrystalFlame. The last to board this most unusual mode of transport was a wagon full of dead bodies.

Danny helped Quill, and together, Danny, Quill, and the wagon were beamed onto the dragon's head.

There was no delay. The moment the wagon was on board, CrystalFlame took off, flying high in the dark sky.

Most spectacular was Yellzor, standing erect at the front of all. On his back was Zanzee, who also stood on all fours.

Their faces to the wind, the giant wolf and black cat were like a sailing ship's figurehead, pointing the way as the ocean winds carried the vessel to war.

Once more, CrystalFlame's silhouette against the backdrop of the Milky Way was the talk of villagers across the land of Kopaz.

CHAPTER 34

The Fiery Inferno—A Harsh Encounter

The hour was late. The moon was climbing, though it had not yet reached its high point. Like clockwork, Quill had all on the ground, and CrystalFlame had taken her position.

Curiosity is a funny thing, especially when you're standing on the brim of a volcano. It may be fun if you're at the Black Volcano, which is nothing more than a bubbling mud pot, where scooting closer to take a peek may be interesting and of no consequence. But at the mouth of a giant pool of molten lava that doesn't so much bubble as boil violently into the air, giving off eruptions of white-hot liquid rock, getting too close is not advised, as curiosity would have severe consequences.

"Get back," screamed Jeannie to Jerzom as his footing gave way, and he slipped, falling with his head over the brim of the Pit of Vulcan.

Blistering heat from the molten lava burned his face. Not severely, but he was rather red—like a beet.

Jerzom's close call set a tone of caution as the next phase of the operation got into full swing.

"OK," shouted Danny. "The goroms are ready!"

A wagon full of dead bodies next to a volcano would be out of place at most volcanoes, but not at the Pit of Vulcan. This moment had been in the making for many centuries. The time had finally come to turn the tide of the war of the gods.

All was not finished, but Vulcan swallowing nine of ten goroms was a good start.

No one knew what would happen next—that is, no one but Danny and Quill.

Danny signaled, and Quill gave the order. "CrystalFlame, it's all yours!"

As the head of the dragon lowered, there was a scramble to move away from her fire-breathing mouth.

The wagon never moved, and CrystalFlame's jaws clamped around it in a spectacular display of fireworks as she lifted her head high in the air.

All eyes looked to the sky. CrystalFlame belched out the wagon full of dead bodies, her head high above the Pit of Vulcan.

Rarrrrrrraarrrrrrrrarrrrrrrrrrrrr! The dragon's roar squealed through the air as she watched nine bodies—now white hot and glowing like giant Chinese fireballs at a New Year's parade—descend into the Pit of Vulcan.

Breaths were held. Hearts pounded. Some clapped. Others shouted. But all were cheering for the same ending that they were witnessing—an end to the evil that had oppressed Kopaz for centuries.

The mouth of the Pit of Vulcan opened wide. The pool of white-hot molten lava was no longer contained like a lake of fire but was a giant sinkhole, a flaming inferno.

They were gone. On their way to hell, they would cause terror no more forever.

It seemed that all was done. That was not the case.

Jerzom was no longer at the brim of the mouth of Hell but was standing fifty feet from it.

Yellzor roared in anger.

Jeannie screamed. "Jerzom, *give it up!*"

What was a mystery to the four royal guardsman and Jerzom was not to Jeannie, Danny, or Quill.

Flashing through Jeannie's mind was the message of an angry god, the supreme god Viracocha.

She remembered it from that fateful day at the Boar's Tusk. It was the last page of Kashom's golden journal. At the time, they were just puzzling words.

Things change.

It was oh so clear. And to TRPOV, his beast, Yellzor, shall devour imposters and throw them into the fiery mouth of CrystalFlame.

Maybe it was her basic nature not to want to see bad things happen to someone who might not deserve it. Maybe it was the longing love of a mother for a son that weighed heavily on Jeannie. Who knows why Jeannie intervened. For whatever reason, she did.

"Jerzom, throw the golden watch!" screamed Jeannie frantically. It was the statement in Kashom's journal that she recalled that caused her to scream out at Jerzom:

And to the TRPOV, his beast, Yellzor, shall devour imposters and throw them into the fiery mouth of CrystalFlame.

If Jerzom continued to seize possession of the golden watch, he would be an imposter, and it would be Yellzor that would devour him and throw his remains into the Pit of Vulcan.

Equally puzzled, Jerzom did throw the watch. He threw it toward the volcano. All eyes watched as it streaked through the air—and stopped.

The golden watch hung in midair. The problem was that it was hanging in midair right smack over the Pit of Vulcan.

Quill looked at Danny. Danny made a motion.

Quill took center stage. He was once more on the head of CrystalFlame. Quill shouted in proclamation, "Well done, Royal Prince of Viracocha."

The golden watch did not move.

Quill looked directly at Jeannie. "The royal princess of Neferdor has proven herself worthy to be the partner of the royal prince of Viracocha throughout time and for all the eternities."

He shouted louder. "You are not finished. You have one gorom to deal with, and that will take a special effort. Once you have dealt with Mochcom, your seat at the table of the gods will be waiting for you."

"*Hail TRPOV and TRPON!*" The dwarf's voice boomed through the air. Every living creature in Kopaz heard Quill's words. "Let this proclamation go forth to the ends of the universe, so all mankind will know that soon there will be two new seats at the table of the gods!"

It was a breathtaking sight, how the golden watch remained suspended in midair. But that was not to last.

CrystalFlame lowered her head. Quill stepped to one side of her head, next to her giant eye. She blinked. Jeannie laughed. Danny said, "Shh! Quill is not finished."

Stretching out his hand, Quill grabbed the golden watch and threw it.

Like the great New York ballplayer, number forty-two, Jackie Robison, Danny caught it.

Laughing, he said, "Thanks, buddy!"

Danny's laughter subsided as he looked in the direction of the young man holding his leg, his head hung low.

Danny walked to him. Jerzom looked up. The two were less than a foot apart. Putting his hand on Jerzom's shoulder, Danny asked, most seriously, in the language of the royals, "How are you doing?"

Saying nothing, Jerzom shrugged his shoulders.

"Is there anything I can do?" asked Danny.

This had been a concern to Jeannie also. She was just happy that Danny was the one to address the situation. *Guys can do this better than gals*, thought Jeannie with a lump gathering in her throat.

"It's OK. Let's go home," said Danny, a smile trying to emerge on his face.

Jerzom hadn't said a word. Danny tried to get the young prince to talk. Jerzom remained silent. The hour was late, so Danny turned to walk away.

Jerzom said, "I'm OK, but I miss Peizar!"

Spinning around, Danny asked, "Who?"

"Oh, you don't know him. He was just a person I used to know," Jerzom said, still with his head hung low.

"Hmm," replied Danny as he grabbed Jerzom's hand. He gave it a tug and pointed to CrystalFlame. "We're going home, and you, my dragon friend, must stay. For the eternities, you cannot leave. The mouth of hell must never be left unguarded."

A blossom of flame streaked from CrystalFlame's mouth as she blinked at the young god who had given her a lasting purpose that would stretch through the ages.

"We fly, Danny," said Quill. "You take Jeannie's hand and travel on the beam of your ring. God speed."

Streaking across the sky, the young gods of Kopaz were gone.

Quietly, Quill motioned to all who were waiting to step aboard for a flight on a beam of light. "My ring will guide us back. All of you grab hands, and then take mine."

CHAPTER 35
The End of a Long Day?

It was not the winds of time that changed the landscape of Kopaz. It was the young god who had vented his wrath and vengeance on a band of evil men who now lived in hell.

On the ride back from the Pit of Vulcan, Danny had some time to think. Maybe it was good, and maybe it was just his way of filling idle time.

As part of his months of training, Quill told Danny that there was a fundamental law that governed the universe. The law was this: "The arc of justice is long, bending so that in the end good triumphs over evil." It had been decreed by the supreme god Viracocha, and it was and always would be the law that ruled.

Could there be a double meaning? Sure, the obvious interpretation was "Good triumphs over evil." However, was there an even more powerful subtle meaning?

High in the sky above the kingdom of Kopaz, two young gods, Danny and Jeannie, were traveling back to the royal palace on a beam of green light. Danny's mind fumbled for answers. He rattled questions around, looking for something that made sense. *Is Viracocha absolutely positive that he will win the war of the gods? If he lost, then could the arc of justice bend toward evil?*

"We're home, Danny." Jeannie's words startled him. He hadn't noticed that they were back in the courtyard.

Quill arrived right behind them with his party of travelers.

Along the hillsides of Kopaz, little stargazers must have let their youthful imaginations run wild, watching beams of green light streak across the night sky, mingling with the ribbon of the Milky Way.

All were safe and sound.

Filtering though many windows, light from the candles in the royal palace made a soft glow on the lawn.

Danny brushed away his thoughts on the arc of justice, as Jeannie was anxious to move on.

The Grand Hall had been cleaned. It was not perfect, but the scene of death that had dominated it was gone.

Jeannie was tired. It was so late at night that it was morning. Most of the staff at the royal palace had retired.

Neferapondes had waited for the return of Danny, Jeannie, Quill, and all who took part in the disposing of the goroms' dead bodies.

Watching the two young lovers walk across the Grand Hall, Neferapondes stood silently. In the stillness of the night as they walked toward her, she could make out their conversation.

They hadn't noticed her standing in the far doorway leading to the hallway and private rooms of the palace.

"Danny, we have a challenge on our hands. I fear that Neferapondes's heart has been so badly smashed that it may be broken to the point of no return," said Jeannie, squeezing his hand tightly.

His heart sank, knowing the literal hell Jeannie had endured as a prisoner of the most evil of humans. Yet her compassion for the lady who was going through a literal hell of her own that might not be fixable made him shiver. He said, "Jeannie, it will be OK for Neferapondes. I believe with all my heart that this too will pass, and a brighter future is on the horizon."

It was only a moment, and they were only fifty feet from Neferapondes.

Wiping the tears from her eyes, Neferapondes spoke softly so as not to surprise Danny and Jeannie. "You make me want to be young again. I see you are so much in love."

Not expecting to see her, Jeannie was surprised, but she dropped

Danny's hand and ran the last twenty feet. She threw her arms around the most gracious lady she had ever known. "Thank you!"

Neferapondes smiled with delight, and tossing away her customary dignity, she threw her arms around Jeannie as she said, "I must know more about you. You look identical to my daughters. I'm longing for your story!"

It warmed Jeannie's heart. For some reason, Neferapondes was beyond life, and that captivated Jeannie in a way that caused a bond of friendship to grow from the first moment she had laid eyes on her not so many hours ago.

That must have been a mutual feeling, as Neferapondes said, "I'm so glad you are here. You have no idea what you have brought into my life."

There was no doubt. She was motherly. "My staff has made arrangements. You have a complete new wardrobe, as does TRPOV. Tomorrow, with new clothes and a new day, things will seem brighter." Neferapondes stopped. "What do I call you? What do I call the royal prince of Viracocha?"

Throwing a crosswise glance in Danny's direction, Jeannie's look said she was in charge, having heard Neferapondes's question. He nodded.

Squeezing her hand softly, Jeannie said, "I see. I agree. The royal princess of Neferdor and the royal prince of Viracocha are titles way too awkward for a queen."

Not wanting to drag on the conversation, Jeannie said, "Privately, when you and I are alone, I'm Jeannie, and that is that," making her point clearly that she, Jeannie alone, would determine how people addressed her. But as far as Danny was concerned, she was not sure. "Ah…" Jeannie stammered. She was unsure what to tell Neferapondes. "I guess you can call him"— she looked at Danny—"prince of Viracocha. In public, as Quill said, I'm TRPON, and he's TRPOV."

Another glance at Danny caught his nod. Then he added, "My dear queen, you may call me Danny when we are not in the public."

"OK, good. As I said, my staff has prepared your rooms." She pointed. "That room at the end of this long hallway is yours, Jeannie. It was Aerapondes's room many years ago, but she would love to have you have it."

Tears spilled from Jeannie's eyes, listening to this mother talk about her daughter. As the tears rolled down her cheeks, the queen lifted her hand and gently brushed Jeannie's face, wiping away her tears.

She looked at Danny and pointed. "That room—two doors down—is yours, Danny. It was Kashom's room long ago, but he would be happy knowing you now have it."

The night had fallen heavy on Neferapondes also. Sleep was the escape she wanted. "We shall rise in the morning on a new day. Until then, may the blessing of Viracocha abide with you."

Jeannie was unaware of just how grief stricken the queen was. While Danny and Jeannie were at the Pit of Vulcan, the queen had instructed her servants to take the dead bodies of her husband and daughter, Merapondes, to a sanctuary in the royal palace to be readied for their funeral. It would be a private funeral, where she and Jerzom would say goodbye to her husband and daughter. The queen's mind drifted with mixed emotions. *I send my daughter and husband to the Land of the Dead, which pulls my heart into a hole of sadness, but my newfound granddaughter will surly lift it from that state of grief.*

The queen turned and walked to her room. The door shut and signaled the end of a long day.

Danny and Jeannie retired.

He couldn't sleep. His eyes wide open, Danny lay on the royal bed. It was made of gold and inlaid with precious gemstones. It was ever so comfortable and inviting, quickly lulling whoever spent the night on it to the land of sleep.

Who knew why, but Danny could not sleep.

His mind kept rattling around past events. For some reason, his father's funeral was on his mind. The words of Mochcom, masquerading as Pastor Duncan, flashed through his head, over and over. *The winds of time blow through the vast expanse of endless space, picking up souls like a storm picks up grains of dust, forging the landscape of a fleeting life not unlike the ever-changing dunes of the desert. Would it not be wonderful if, by some gift from our supreme god, the ravages of time could cease? Our mountains of hope would stand for an eternity rather than be blown away like tiny mounds of dirt. How beautiful will be the day when a life's journey is endless, stretching through time and space.*

He tried to make sense of it all. The actions of the young man, Jerzom, at the volcano, who almost joined the goroms, weighed heavily on Danny.

Something is wrong. How does that statement, that the winds of time blow through the vast expanse of endless space, picking up souls like the dust of a storm, fit in with the arc of justice?

Danny had destroyed the evil of Kopaz. He knew it. Quill had told him that justice bends toward the innocent. Maybe Quill was simply trying to give Danny a pep talk, reassuring him that in the end he would be among the winners of the war of the gods.

Time drifted on. Danny's mind was not still. *Quill doesn't need to give me a pep talk. He knows me. I'll fight to the end for Viracocha, and I'll kill that bastard, Pastor Duncan, Crazy LeRoy, or whoever the hell he becomes. He's going to the Pit of Vulcan along with the rest of those bastards!*

When you're tired, it's funny how the mind plays tricks.

No matter where his thoughts went, they always came back to Jerzom. *Something is wrong. Has the arc of justice bent away from that young man?*

The comfort of sleep finally took over.

CHAPTER 36
Early Morning Fun

"Wake up, sleepyhead!" said Jeannie, shaking Danny back and forth as he lay sound asleep.

She'd crawled on her hands and knees across the large bed to be next to him. Squatting on her haunches, she positioned her body above him and looked down at him with a smile.

His right arm slid under the pillow, and his left he pulled over his head. He squeezed tightly on the soft down cushion under his head to block out noise and light.

That didn't stop Jeannie. It had been a long time since she had had fun with Danny, and she wasn't about to let this opportunity get away.

Straddling his body, a knee on either side, she slid her hand under his arm. Her surprising tickle of his nose brought on an unsuspected flinch.

She giggled. "Come on, sleepyhead! Time to get up up up!"

Rolling over and looking up at her, he grunted. "I'm tired." His voice was barely audible.

"I don't care." And she didn't. She moved off him a bit, swinging her right leg over his body under the blanket.

Without warning, she grabbed the silk edging of the warm blanket that had been his comforter through the long night and yanked it hard. Into the air it went.

Danny had not dressed in the new clothes that the queen's staff had placed in his closet. The clothes that Quill had given him in the wilderness were still on him. The leather strap he used as a belt to keep his loin covering in place had become untied during the night, leaving him without cover.

The blanket went flying into the air like a kite. She leaned back, her fingers clutching the blanket's edge to make sure it could not be used as a cover. She held her hand high above her head and looked down.

Like two giant moons in the sky, Jeannie's eyes flew wide open. They focused. And then, just like her eyes, her mouth fell wide open.

She didn't blink. Her smile began to grow.

Momentarily, Danny was helpless. He didn't have a clue what his next move should be.

She started giggling.

He sat up and tried to grab the blanket from her to pull it over his naked body.

He wasn't fast enough. Jeannie had tossed it to the floor as she said, "*Whoa!* Just look at you! *Oh my!*"

Her giggling didn't stop. In fact, it seemed to get louder as Danny fumbled for words and tried to cover himself with his free hand.

"Whaaa…ah…er…Jeannie, what are you up to?" That was all that he managed to say through Jeannie's cheerful snickering. The mood of the two teenagers lifted.

They had faced hell head on, and through it all, they had emerged as victors, triumphant in the human spirit, valiantly winning the battle of good versus evil. For Jeannie, she was just glad those horrific days were over, and it was now time for fun.

Danny's bloody battle with the goroms only a few hours earlier had not left his body in the state of vulnerability that Jeannie had just managed to create.

She knew it. She loved it.

Fortunately for Danny, he managed to grab a corner of the blanket with his right hand. He pulled it over his legs and abdomen.

That did not stop Jeanne from exploring.

Straddling him again, she looked down with a strange little smile as she said again, "*Oh my!* Your chest and arm muscles are…" She paused and slid her hand under the blanket. With a feathery touch, her fingers moved downward across his rock-hard abs. "Holy cow, you are unbelievably large. I had no idea."

Danny's body tensed as Jeannie explored. She knew exactly what her game plan was, and so she charged on. Her smile grew larger. Holding back the laugh that was bursting to come out of her, she leaned over him, lowering her head to his.

Danny's eyes were now the size of Jeannie's. She moved her lips close to his ear and let her fingers explore farther.

Ever so softly, her breath hot against his ear, she whispered, "*Holy cow! Eeeenorrrrrmus!* You never told me lifting weights would do *that!*"

She lifted her face so she could see his look as her fingers moved gently. "Danny boy, have you intentionally been keeping secrets from me?"

If ever Danny had been rendered speechless, it was now. What could he say? His tongue was tied. His composure was shot. He was in a situation he had never before been in.

Totally uninterested in the frolicking taking place, Yellzor snuggled more tightly in a big furry ball at the foot of the bed. He pulled his crossed paws closer to his chest, never opening his eyes.

Next to him was another ball of fur trying to get a little more shuteye— Zanzee. He was curled with his tail wrapped around his body, nestled comfortably between Yellzor's front paws.

Maybe Danny thought it was time to explore also. Maybe he wanted to let her know that it took two to play this game of love. A slight smile was emerging on his face. It started growing as he looked at her and said nothing.

They never saw the queen walk into the open doorway. Her soft, sheepskin slippers made no sound, not alerting those who were playing— nor those who could care less and just wanted to have a little quiet time so they could enjoy the morning sun on their furry bodies.

Neferapondes had arrived on the scene and stumbled upon the two young lovers embarking on their first course of adventure to explore each other's intimate secrets.

She tried to keep from bursting into laughter as she managed to say, "Breakfast is being served in the royal dining room in fifteen minutes."

Jeannie shot up. Her head spun around.

The bedroom door was open. She saw no one.

Yellzor's ear lifted and then flopped back.

Instantly, Danny's manly voice filled the room with a deep, bass laughter. "You got caught!" Danny said, loudly.

Listening to the young god, Neferapondes stopped. She managed a chuckle. She'd walked only ten feet from the doorway, so his words traveled effortlessly to her ears. Repeating his words in her mind, *You got caught*, the queen grinned, shook her head, and started to make her way to her bedroom.

Neferapondes's smile grew with each slow step. There was no hurry. For the first time in a very long time, she found deep in her soul an excitement waiting to jump out and scream to the world that the joy of young love was back in the royal palace.

CHAPTER 37

The Prince—Where is He?

Delicious aromas filled the air. The royal cooks had been busy since sunrise.

Danny and Jeannie walked into the dining area together. Danny had his hair slicked back. Maybe he was thinking of James Dean and wanted to bring the fifties look to Kopaz.

Jeannie wore a smile that just would not go away—a dead giveaway that she had just found something interesting.

Not knowing what to do, Jeannie waved sheepishly at the queen who was sitting alone at a long table. Most likely, Jeannie didn't care how long the queen had been standing in the doorway and what she had seen.

Her eyes grew brighter, and Jeannie's smile grew larger with a lingering thought she couldn't get out of her mind. *Holy mackerel, does Danny ever…I had no idea!*

Graciously, Neferapondes lifted her hand and smiled as if to say, *Your discovery this morning is a secret that's safe with me.*

Danny was trying to find a place to sit. He could choose from twenty chairs, each beautifully handcrafted from the most spectacular wood he had ever seen.

He didn't have to choose. Neferapondes pointed to the massive chair at the head of the table and then motioned for Jeannie to take the seat next to her.

No sooner had they taken their seats than at least fifteen servants seemed to come out of nowhere—all carrying trays of steaming-hot food.

After a careful watch, Jeannie realized the servant's entrance was to one side of the royal dining room. It was clear that whoever had designed the palace wanted access to the eating area to be convenient and not far from the food preparation area so that the food would stay hot and allow the servants to move as inconspicuously as possible.

In her mind, they'd exceeded their goal, as the most lavish breakfast she had ever imagined was being created before her eyes.

There could be no question in anyone's mind that Danny was the new king of Kopaz.

It was different but exciting. His was a lonesome trail—from a coal miner's son to the most powerful king in the universe. It was an amazing journey that only he and Jeannie could fully appreciate.

It seemed that a relaxing day was at hand. It was welcome, following the chaos that had seized Kopaz not more than ten hours ago.

Having to attend to early morning business, Quill was late to breakfast, but now he walked in. Because he hadn't spent any quality time with Jeannie, he decided they could become acquainted over breakfast. He was about to sit in the seat closest to Jeannie when Danny motioned for him to come to the head of the table.

Quill saw that Jeannie was striking up a conversation with Neferapondes, so he turned and walked to Danny.

Even before Quill had taken his seat, the look on Danny's face prompted him to ask, "What?"

Danny waited for Quill to get situated before responding. He hadn't slept much last night, partly because of this lingering question, and Danny wanted an answer. Now, with a serious look on his face, Danny asked, "If Viracocha does not know he'll win the war, why does he say that 'the arc of justice bends toward good and not evil'?"

Quill listened but said nothing, so Danny continued. "OK, if the arc of justice bent toward evil, that would mean to me that Zuron won. But Viracocha says it won't. It will bend toward good. Do you see my logic?"

"Absolutely *not!* Danny, you are getting tangled up in the weeds. It's breakfast time. A great meal is being served, and what do you get tangled up in? Weeds!"

But Quill could tell Danny had a one-track mind, so he said, "What Viracocha is saying is that if he is the supreme god, he will always bend the arc of justice so it falls on the side of good."

Contemplating what Quill had just said, Danny started to say something but didn't finish. The conversation between Jeannie and Neferapondes stopped him. It had nothing to do with girl talk.

Jeannie was about to enjoy a most welcome meal when the worried mother asked, "Where is he?"

Even spoken softly, Neferapondes's question took center stage.

Silence—thundering like the roar of a stampeding herd of wild buffalo—settled like a hovering fog in a hollow on a cold winter's night.

Her concern was rising, and everyone knew it.

Neferapondes stood. Her look was blank. She spoke. "Never has Jerzom not slept in his bed. Last night he didn't." Her hand moved to cover a tear rolling down her cheek. "Never has he not eaten breakfast. He's not here…something is wrong."

She had hardly finished speaking before Danny was on his feet. He grabbed Quill. "Hurry!" he shouted. They raced toward Neferapondes and Jeannie. "Follow us!" he yelled.

By coincidence, they ran into Handmar in the Grand Hall as they were rushing out of the royal palace.

"Where did Peizar live?" hollered Danny.

"That old house on the banks of the Yellshome River. It's at the third bend in the river downstream."

Not stopping, Danny shouted his thanks over his shoulder. In moments, they were in the courtyard. "Yellzor, come!" Danny bellowed and used his arm to reinforce the command.

With his mouth holding onto a clump of Yellzor's fur, Zanzee was riding high on the wolf, who leaped and bounded across the grassy yard.

Danny's voice elevated to a level conveying the utmost urgency. "*Grab hands…we fly!*"

A beam of green light shot from Danny's ring, and then they were in the air, high in the sky. Quill was at the tail end of the procession, holding tightly to Neferapondes's hand and grabbing Yellzor by his fur. Jeannie was holding Danny's hand for dear life.

In moments, they were standing in front of a dilapidated house. The former queen burst into tears. She could not contain her crying.

Jerzom had on occasion talked of his best friend, Peizar, but she had never thought about the reality. Yet now there could be no shying away from the truth. The shocked mother looked on, trying to comprehend the magnitude of the crime committed against such a poor family. *My god, how could they? How could I have not seen what the goroms did when they blamed the horrible mutilation of Kashom's horse on this poor, innocent family? I don't even think Jerzom knew the truth of what really happened.*

CHAPTER 38

A Dying Prince

Scraping back and forth, emitting *scrrrrraaaa scrrrrreeee saaaaarrreee* sounds, the lone piece of thatch material blowing in the wind was all that was left of the roof. Maybe at one time it had been part of a beautiful roof, but that would be a stretch considering the uneven boards that displayed cracks so wide they could double for small windows.

To any casual observer, it was obvious that whoever had lived in this rambling shack was no longer around. Weeds and vines growing unrestrained all but blocked the entrance to a sad-looking house that had once been called home by the Vassar family. They were gone now, but faithfully, the little house still stood.

"Danny, we've got to hurry," shouted Quill, realizing Danny's mind was drifting.

He couldn't clear his head, and the appearance of the dilapidated house just amplified his thoughts. *The winds of time blow through the vast expanse of endless space, picking up souls like a storm picks up grains of dust, forging the landscape of a fleeting life not unlike the ever-changing dunes of the desert.*

Quill had already cleared a pathway through the vegetation that had been blocking the door. "Come on, Danny! Death is afoot!" yelled Quill.

Turning to Jeannie, Danny said, "You guys wait here."

That was all he had to say. She grabbed Neferapondes's shaking hand.

Danny and Quill stepped in. Words were not needed. "Oh my God," whimpered Danny.

There was a young man lying in the dirt, motionless.

The room they had entered was small. It was one of two about the same size. A fire pit on the floor had likely been the only source of warmth on cold days. An old broken jug sitting on a small wood bench must have been used to fetch water from the river. An iron kettle lying in the dirt was no longer cooking stew. Over the years, it had rolled onto its side, and now it was filled with a rat's nest. Beady eyes peeked out of the kettle to let the strangers know they were not alone.

No windows were necessary. The cracks in the weathered boards let in enough light to manage a makeshift life in that dreary little house on the banks of the Yellshome River.

The wound in Jerzom's leg was bulging with puss. The goroms had used poisoned arrows, and time was not on the victim's side once an arrow found its mark.

The infection was raging, sucking the life out of a helpless young man who had only wanted his friend, Peizar, to help him save his nation from an evil that had no bounds.

Gently, Danny picked up Jerzom's head. There was no sign of life.

Outside, Jeannie waited. The silence was telling. It was not good.

"Help me," said Danny to Quill.

Quill forced his ear next to Jerzom's chest. He heard nothing. "Wait!" yelled Quill. He strained. "Shh," he said. His concentration increased, and he listened harder. "I thought I detected something."

He shook his head. He was on the verge of saying that the boatman had already been there and picked up Jerzom's soul, but Danny spoke first.

"I think his finger twitched," spoke Danny. He lifted his hand from Jerzom's cold cheek and looked sadly at Quill with a blank stare. *Am I imagining that life has not gone from this unfortunate soul?*

"Hurry, Danny! Use your ring!" shouted Quill

The force and power of a god could not be explained. No one tried. Danny had to hunt for a spirit looking to escape a dying body.

No longer a god in training but a young god learning that the ways of justice could not be denied, Danny ripped the emerald ring from his neck and focused a beam of light on Jerzom's leg.

The power entrusted by Viracocha to a young god with yellow hair as bright as the noonday sun and emerald-green eyes as brilliant as his thirty-five carat ring struck Jerzom's soul with such might that the gates to the Land of the Dead slammed shut.

His chest moved. His eyes opened. He tried to speak.

"It's OK," said Danny gently, knowing the pain in this young man's heart was almost beyond the limit that any human could endure.

But Danny was no ordinary human. He was far from it. His relationship with the supreme god was growing more intense with each passing day, and justice was what the young god had in mind.

"I know what happened," said Danny.

"You do?" whimpered Jerzom in a hushed voice.

Jerzom didn't know Danny. How could he? He had no idea that the ways of the gods were mysterious.

Then Viracocha opened his royal prince's mind to a vision of those brutal murders in the Vassar home. The screams, the yells for mercy, the horrifying deaths of a mother and a father were more vivid and real than any Hollywood movie on the giant silver screen. Even for Danny, to see the brutal death of Peizar's parents was almost more than he could bear, but looking at the floorboards, he saw the vision of a small boy hiding.

What Viracocha was revealing to Danny wasn't finished. A young royal prince, Jerzom, on a black stallion, raced to the sad little house. He stopped at the doorway. The scene of horror that just unfolded in Danny's mind was the scene that had greeted the young prince when he walked through the door so long ago.

Danny saw not only the brutal murder of Peizar's parents by the evil band of goroms but also the horrific death that had ended the life of Jerzom's best friend as a result of his loyal allegiance to the prince of Kopaz.

A lone tear fell from Danny's eye, and he nodded his head. "Jerzom, I know all."

Slowly, Jerzom began to talk. "I wanted…wanted to be with my friend."

His mother could not wait anymore. Her son's words sent her bolting to the door.

Quill motioned to her. "Neferapondes, wait there."

Jeannie right behind her, Neferapondes stopped and did as asked. Her eyes could not see through her tears. She listened intently as her son told his story.

"I sent Peizar to his death. He was my best friend. The goroms were plotting to overthrow our kingdom, and I knew not how to stop them."

Exhausted from battling the infection, he had to stop. For a few moments, he breathed. His strength was slow to return.

"My brother once showed me the secret passageway from the royal palace to the Hall of the Goroms. I sent Peizar on a mission. He hid and listened from the secret passage. On the other side of the wall of their hall, he heard the goroms' plan."

He stopped and looked into Danny's eyes. "I didn't know it was yours. I'm so sorry, my royal prince."

Jeannie knew what Jerzom meant, but Neferapondes did not have a clue. She wondered about what her son had just said. *Not yours? What?*

Jeannie listened. It was no mystery to her. Jeannie knew exactly what the conversation was about. *He speaks of Danny's golden watch.*

Neferapondes said nothing. She waited.

Softly, Jerzom continued. "Peizar heard all. He told me that Katchcom said the golden watch was magic."

"When they killed my friend, I wanted to die. I wanted him back so badly." Jerzom struggled to speak between his sobs.

Danny's heart was breaking. Jeannie couldn't stand it any longer. She stepped in front of Quill and came to Danny to sit next to a young god listening to a young man. He was no longer royalty. Now he was a commoner, telling a story that she knew was tearing at the very fiber of Danny's being.

"I thought the watch's magic would bring him back." His words hung in the air.

It is a reality, Danny thought. *Wouldn't it be wonderful if the ravages of time could cease by the gift from the supreme god? Our mountains of hope would stand for an eternity rather than be blown away like the death of a tiny mound of dirt. How beautiful the day when the journey of life will be endless for all time, stretching through the expanse of space.*

He nodded his head as he reached and grabbed Jerzom's hand. He said, "You'll see Peizar again, I promise! That beautiful day will be here soon, when the journey of life is endless for all time, stretching through the expanse of space."

Jerzom's mother moved closer. Yearning to hold her son, she wept. Her eyes swelled, and a stream of tears splattered like tiny raindrops in the dirt next to her folded knees as she sat next to her baby boy. She was going to speak, but as she looked at Danny and watched his smile grow bigger, she waited.

"You didn't know it was mine. How could you? Your efforts helped crush the evil that has gripped your land," said Danny. And then he declared in a loud voice that rang throughout Kopaz, "Well done, mighty prince of Kopaz!"

There could be no denying that the winds of change were coming and that Danny had just bent the arc of justice toward the goodness of a young, innocent man.

CHAPTER 39

A Red Ribbon Tied Around a Princ's Heart

Her bitter sadness had changed to a longing love that only a mother could experience. Their hurried breakfast, which had left them all hungry, had been replaced by an extravaganza of foods that could only be served on a royal occasion. And that it was. Sitting at the head of the table, the young god felt his heart warm watching this mother swell with joy each time she looked at the only one of her children who remained in the land of Kopaz.

Jerzom was tall and extremely handsome. He sat next to his mother, gently put his hand in hers, and squeezed ever so affectionately. "Mom, I just love you." Everyone heard his words. He wasn't looking at Jeannie but at the queen.

Jeannie could not hold back. "Grandma, it is so good to see you smiling." Jeannie beamed. She felt some reverence as she watched the bond of love between a mother and her son growing stronger with each passing moment.

Turning his head slightly, and with a sidewise glance at Jeannie, Jerzom's face grew perplexed. He looked at his mom, then back at Jeannie, and said only one word. "Grandma?" That was enough to express his complete state of bewilderment.

And bewildered he was, but not his mother. She smiled graciously. "Yes, Jeannie is Kashom's descendant!"

"What?" His question hung for a few moments. He looked at Danny, then at Jeannie, and then at his mom. They all looked back at him. No one said anything.

So Jerzom spoke first. "Please, tell me more. I have a cousin?" he quizzed.

"Yes!" said the queen as she looked first at her son and then at Jeannie. "I think it's time. I'm bursting with excitement to hear my granddaughter's stories." Her words let Jerzom know it was not she who had the answers but the strangers.

As the royal staff was picking up the remaining dishes from their welcome feast that left no one hungry, the queen motioned to the others as she spoke. "Shall we retire to the royal library and listen to a story that surely will mend an old queen's heart?"

Danny's announcement a few hours earlier at the Vassar home that Jerzom was still a royal prince was on Neferapondes's mind, but that thought could wait. There was no question that the king of Kopaz was Viracocha's royal prince. That fact no one would dare deny. She was just anxious for the new king and his true love, Jeannie, to fill her heart with enough warmth to crush the wall of defense she had built around herself to shield her heart against the evils of the goroms.

It was interesting that when a good, heartwarming story was about to be told, the sun cooperated and shed an extra measure of light on the four people sitting on soft white-leather couches facing each other. They were trimmed with pure gold braids that stretched along the backs and the arms. The interior designers had had a grand vision, so the sunlight coming through the stained glass windows danced and sparkled on the gold like a most entertaining light show.

When all were comfortable—Jeannie and Danny on one couch, and on the other, facing them, Neferapondes and Jerzom—it was Jeannie who started, as her smile lit her face and made her eyes glow. She did have the most radiant sapphire-blue eyes, which could only have come from the goddess Neferdor. She said, "Grandma, I'm sure you have questions."

Neferapondes could wait no longer to ask her next question. "Is your sacred…"

Perceptively, Jeannie knew what question the queen was about to ask her. Jeannie could not wait to tell the story that had to do with her special name. She cut the queen off. "Please forgive me for rushing in, but yes, your daughter Aerapondes had the same sacred name as I do." She stopped and composed herself. "It is the sacred name given by the goddess, Neferdor."

That was all that was needed. Jeannie looked identical to Aerapondes, including her beautiful, long, shiny black hair and sapphire-blue eyes.

Neferapondes nodded, and Jeannie quickly moved on. "Your son is a great man. He's the father of our people. We are called the Kashome people and have lived in the Scarlet Desert for centuries."

What Jeannie had just said was foreign. That did not matter. Neferapondes would wait to learn about the Scarlet Desert. For now, she wanted to know about her son, Kashom. An expression of joy grew on the queen's face, and a smile erupted. Jeannie could not wait to tell the queen just how great Kashom was. Holding back her emotions, just waiting for Jeannie to tell her about those lost years of a beloved son, it was almost all the queen could bear.

"Even though it has been centuries since Kashom has lived in the desert, he is not much older than I am. You see, Grandma, he, like Danny and I, traveled the Highway of Time, and now time means nothing to us." Jeannie squeezed the queen's hand and smiled.

Even though Danny had already told the queen that she could call him Danny—it was when they had returned from the Pit of Vulcan—Neferapondes was hesitant. She still wasn't sure what she should call the royal prince of Viracocha. She knew Jeannie refers to him by the name Danny.

"When we are alone and in private, can I call Viracocha's royal prince by his name, Danny?" Neferapondes queried.

The queen's question got Jeannie's attention. *I thought Danny already told the queen she can call him Danny…Hmm…Maybe it is some sort of a formal royal thing*, thought Jeannie as she tensed up. *Maybe the queen is not sure and just wants to not come across as being informal.* She turned slightly and gave a quick look to Danny. He nodded, stepped into the conversation, and said, "Neferapondes, it is fine if you call me Danny. You know that Quill has spoken on this and has forbidden anyone to call me by any name other than TRPOV, but since you are the queen, I will allow it, and you may call me Danny."

Danny observed the look of puzzlement on her face. Neferapondes was confused. If Danny was the new king of Kopaz, how could she be the queen? Her mind drifted. *He just called me the queen. Hmm.*

Knowing what was in her mind, Danny politely said, "Yes, you are still the queen. I am the new king, and that sounds strange, but soon I will explain all. It may be a few days, but just be patient." He smiled as he finished speaking and put his hand on Jeannie's leg, which was next to his.

Jeannie wanted Danny to be still. She had much to tell the queen. Trying to be inconspicuous, she moved her hand to pinch Danny softly. *Danny, the queen wants to know about her son...your stuff can wait!*

Danny got her message, and Jeannie charged on.

"After Gorom Mochcom killed Princess Aerapondes, he conned Kashom into using the golden key and the golden watch to venture on the Highway of Time. Kashom and Mochcom ended up in the Scarlet Desert at the Boar's Tusk. That is where I grew up. Shortly after they arrived in the Scarlet Desert, Kashom realized Gorom Mochcom had killed Aerapondes. Kashom fought with Mochcom. Kashom got most of the gifts from the gods away from Mochcom, including my golden key. Mochcom got the top half of the Sun Energy Transformer. It was Danny, our friend Tony—whom Mochcom killed—and I who got the top to the Sun Energy Transformer from the evil gorom."

Out of breath from talking with such emotions, Jeannie stopped and inhaled deeply. The queen waited. "Kashom is the father of our people. Because he never grows old, he is still eighteen. He married a beautiful lady, and they had children. Kashom is my great-great-great-great-grandfather. The evil Gorom Mochcom is also the same age he was when he left Kopaz so long ago."

When Jeannie mentioned the name Gorom Mochcom, a twinge of sadness engulfed Neferapondes. She had hated Gorom Mochcom even before he killed her daughter, and the thought of him still inflicting his evil on people made her shudder.

"The Kashome people know Mochcom still lives in the Scarlet Desert. Danny and I know for a fact that this is true. He killed Danny's mom. He killed our best friend, Tony Lopez."

Jeannie took a short breath. She didn't want to talk about Mochcom, but it was necessary. "Mochcom is the emissary and disciple of the dark god Zuron. It was Zuron who personally gave Mochcom the black ring that protects him. The energy from the ring is a beam of purple light. That is why Kashom was unable to kill him."

And now, Jeannie grew solemn as she stared at the queen, for what she had to say next would be painful. "I know the whole story, and I must tell you this, Grandma, even though it may hurt you."

Neferapondes nodded her head. Jerzom listed.

Jeannie continued. "The gods were furious with the royal family of Kopaz because they failed to protect Aerapondes from the goroms and the precious gifts that are used to open the Highway of Time."

A tear spilled from her eye, and for the first time, Queen Neferapondes was able to express a sigh of relief, knowing her elder son was not a monster. "You have made a mother's spirit soar higher than an eagle in the skies over the Androzes Mountains of Kopaz. Oh Jeannie, thank you!"

The queen choked up as she added, "My husband, the king, could never forgive Kashom. We all knew we had fallen out of favor with the supreme god Viracocha and his wife, the goddess Neferdor. I knew in my heart that it was not just Kashom who was suffering the wrath of the gods but the entire royal family."

She thought of her husband, King Dalvin, the arrow protruding through his robe, and with a lump gathering in her throat, she said, "I wish he could have heard what you just told me."

Watching the tears run down the queen's cheek and splash on her robe, Jeannie smiled comfortingly. "There is more." Now, her voice low and crackling, Jeannie continued. "Someday, because of your son, you will see your family again…all of them."

Holding hands and listing to every word, Neferapondes and Jerzom thought Jeannie's words were strange, but how could they argue with a goddess in training?

Jeannie went on. "As part of his purgatory, Viracocha told Kashom if he were to regain his royal status, he must aid TRPOV and TRPON in the fulfillment of their missions and declare to them who they are."

Jeannie could not get her words out fast enough as she relayed Prince Kashom's instructions to his mother and brother.

"The royal prince of Viracocha is TRPOV, and the royal princess of Neferdor is TRPON." At that point, Jeannie stopped to clarify what she had just said. "Danny is TRPOV, and I'm TRPON. Only when TRPOV and TRPON have killed all of the goroms and thrown their bodies not yet ashes into the fiery depths of CrystalFlame, so their eternity is destined to be everlasting embers in the belly of a dragon, and only then will they together sit on thrones of pure gold alongside the gods at their council table of red worox stone and control the gift of eternal youth for all humans throughout the universe. And to the TRPOV, his beast Yellzor shall devour imposters and throw them into the fiery mouth of CrystalFlame."

Jeannie had finished what she wanted to tell Neferapondes and Jerzom. But there was something that Jeannie wanted to know. She asked, "The red ribbon that is still around Kashom's heart? What does that mean?"

The queen smiled. She knew exactly what was on Jeannie's inquisitive mind.

Neferapondes began her story. "On his twelfth birthday, Kashom got a new friend, a young white stallion. Kashom's birthday is in the seventh moon and on a very special day."

Jeannie very politely interrupted. "Can you hold that thought for one moment?"

"Yes," the queen said. "My story, I'm sure, is connected to what you have to say, and I want your words!" The queen smiled.

Jeannie lifted her arm from Danny's lap. They had been holding hands, fingers intertwined. She bent over slightly so she could get something. Everyone watched curiously as she took her boot off. With her boot held tightly in her hand, she tipped it over and said, "My uncle, my mother's brother, was wise. He must have known the future, as he gave me these boots many years ago, before he got sick and died."

Jeannie lifted one hand to her cheek. She could not hide her emotions as she mentioned her uncle who was like a father to her as her father had died shortly after she was born. "He said, 'Jeannie, someday you will thank me for these boots.' I had no idea they would be the thing that would save my life."

Now she had their attention, even Danny's. As she continued to talk, she was doing something with her boot. "You see, the goroms knew that 'the key dances on the seventh moon for seen far as a distant star.' They wanted it, the key, and I'm sure they knew I had it. If they had found it, they would have killed me. Yet, more importantly, if I no longer had the golden key, Viracocha's GAMMAZEL could not be unlocked! The only reason I'm alive is they needed me to get my key."

Jeannie's reference to Viracocha's GAMMAZEL was a complete mystery to Queen Neferapondes and Prince Jerzom, but it did not matter. They were listening, and enough of the story Jeannie was telling made sense to them.

By now, she had the heel of the boot pivoted on a special pin that held it in place. It was so clever, how her uncle had made the hiding place, that without knowing the pin was there, someone would have had to physically cut the boot in two to get to the hiding place.

Holding her key, Jeannie was about to speak. Then Neferapondes politely interjected. "Yes, your key dances on INTIPRAIMI."

Danny laughed. "Yeah, that puzzle had us going. Fortunately, Jeannie figured it out; otherwise, Mochcom would have killed us all."

"Oh, I'm so sorry," said Jeannie, not paying attention to Danny but looking intently at the queen. "I interrupted your story about the red ribbon that is still tied around his heart."

Jeannie was ready to listen. The queen was ready to talk. Yet she wanted to make another comment before she continued her story of the red ribbon tied around Kashom's heart. "Jeannie, seeing the golden key again warms my heart." She stopped. A tear fell from her eye as she said, "My daughter, Aerapondes, once wore it around her neck."

"My dear queen," said Jeannie, "I know the love you had for Aerapondes, but I believe she is in good hands with the gods."

And with that, Queen Neferapondes continued. "On that day, so long ago, when my son, Kashom, got his birthday gift, quite by surprise, someone showed up unexpectedly in the Grand Hall of the royal palace. We had no idea who it was. He had boxes of gifts. We were celebrating Kashom's birthday. It was a private party with just members of the royal family."

The queen had their attention. Danny had heard many stories from Jeannie many times before, but this was a new story. And hearing it from the queen of the royal family of Kopaz was like discovering a hidden treasure that had been just out of sight and was now in the open for all to see.

"Kashom was outside with his new pony. My twins, Aerapondes and Merapondes, were only six years old. The messenger who showed up surprised us all when he said, 'I'm an emissary from the supreme god Viracocha and his wife, the goddess Neferdor.'"

Neferapondes paused. Jeannie thought about how unlike these leather couches were compared to the old tattered couch in her house in CoalVille, where she would spend hours upon hours talking to her mom about the legends of Kashom. Now she watched the queen sitting directly across from her on a royal couch in a palace. Neferapondes sat so gracefully, so stately and erect. "The messenger was Quill. He laid before us what he described as gifts from the gods. He then told us that we must protect those gifts at all cost from the evils of the disciples of Zuron. We asked him who they were. Sternly, he said, 'Beware of the evil that lurks among you!' His instructions were on a gold note that Viracocha had told Quill to give to us. It outlined our children's—Kashom's and Aerapondes's—journeys to sit at the council table with the gods, and to this day, when I read this note"—she reached into a leather bag, took it out, and held it so all could see—"I can't help but cry, knowing the royal family let down Supreme God Viracocha and Supreme Goddess Neferdor."

At that point, Neferapondes could not stop her tears. She asked, "Does Danny come from royalty?"

"No, my dear grandmother. Danny and I came from poverty, much like Peizar," replied Jeannie. "Although my great-great-great-great-grandfather was a royal prince of Kopaz, my parents were poor. And like Peizar, both of Danny's parents were humble, with few earthly possessions."

Even though Neferapondes did not fully understand what Jeannie had just said, she comprehended the meaning of it. "I'm sure that that is why you and Danny will sit at the council table alongside Viracocha and Neferdor." She looked at Danny and continued. "In the midst of poverty, your triumph—a single-handed triumph, I must add—has destroyed the vile evil that hovered over our land like a black fog for centuries."

She smiled even more graciously as she spoke to Danny. "I see why the supreme god chose you as his royal prince. May the gods be with you as you fight your final battle and kill the most heinous of all, Gorom Mochcom." She turned to Jeannie. "I'm so proud my granddaughter will sit with this most handsome and brave god"—she lifted her arm, pointing to Danny—"at the table with the gods and rule the universe."

It is funny that when a story is being told that so many other facets are interjected. A red ribbon around Kashom's heart. She still didn't know what that was about. Jeannie didn't mind. She loved listening to the queen and patiently waited. Her wait was over.

"The red ribbon?" asked Jeannie, letting everyone know her curiosity was speaking.

The queen turned to Jeannie and winked. She went on. "On Kashom's twelfth birthday, he was not interested in what Quill had brought to the royal family. He wanted his new pony. He raced out of the Grand Hall. There he found a scene of horror that become chiseled on his mind, an indelible memory that would never go away."

Neferapondes stopped, looked to the ceiling to hide her tears, and searched for enough composure to continue. She lowered her head and pressed on with the story. "Screaming, 'Mommy! Mommy! Mommy!' Kashom ran back into the palace. His little hands were red with blood. I picked him up. 'They cut his heart out, Mommy. Zeus, my pony, is dead.'"

A booming silence descended on the royal library like a black storm cloud and reminded those sitting at the couches that evil had lurked in the land of Kopaz.

Through her sobs, Jerzom holding his mother's hand, Neferapondes said, "I threw my arms around Kashom. He was tall for a twelve-year-old, but he was still a little boy—my baby. My husband ordered his royal guard to bury Kashom's pony and immediately called for an investigation."

Jerzom winced, knowing what had happened next. His mother choked up as she said, "The goroms conducted the investigation and concluded that the crime had been committed by the Vassar family. I never questioned my husband or the evil men who had such a stranglehold over Dalvin." She turned to Jerzom. "Thank you for finding justice. You saw what I did not."

As his mother spoke, a knot gathered in Jerzom's throat, thinking of his friend who now resided in the Land of the Dead. *I wish I had Peizar by my side. He gave his life for me. He was a friend like no other.*

She looked back at Jeannie. "It was years later, on Kashom's eighteenth birthday. I planted a large white rosebush outside his bedroom window and tied a red ribbon around it. After his party in the Grand Hall, he and I walked outside. The rosebush bloomed on his birthday, an omen of good things to come. As we walked to the gardens next to his window, he spotted it. He turned and hugged me, saying, 'Thank you, Mom.' With tears rolling down our cheeks, we stood next to the rosebush. 'Mom,' he said, 'I still have a red ribbon tied around my heart for my beloved pony, Zeus.'"

Wow, thought Jeannie, *it certainly was an omen. Those words I spoke as a prisoner changed the course of history! Kashom still has a red ribbon tied around his heart! Mochcom killed Aerapondes, and Ancom killed her twin sister, Merapondes. Your two sons, Kashom and Jerzom, are innocent. The goroms have betrayed you utterly.*

CHAPTER 40
Gold Notes and a Ruby Ring

I t seems some things sometimes happen for a reason. Who knows why, but Neferapondes left her gold note lying on the couch beside her. Maybe it was because it told a story of what might have been, her children sitting at the council table of the gods…and then again, maybe not.

For whatever reason, that golden note was there out in the open. The sunlight was not only dancing on the gold braids that decorated the white leather couches but also reflecting off the polished note's surface. It was déjà vu. Danny remembered how he had just been pulled to the bottom of the pool at the base of Yellshome Falls by a little man. Once he had made it back to the surface, stumbling around in a state of exhaustion on the grassy bank of the river, he had seen a flash of light. It turned out to be a gold note.

Danny staring at her gold note prompted Neferapondes to look at him. It was his beautiful emerald ring that made her want to say something.

Maybe it was the sunlight reflecting from Neferapondes's golden note, which had been given to the royal family by Viracocha, or maybe it was how she stared at Danny's ring. Whatever the reason, it spurred Danny on. He was about to take something else from his leather pouch, something he'd been carrying around everywhere he went.

Before he could, the queen interrupted. "Your ring, Danny. It is identical to another ring, well, almost. Yours has an emerald, and the one

I'm familiar with has a ruby gemstone."

No one paid much attention to the comings and goings of Quill. He had been busy, but now he wandered—along with Yellzor and Zanzee—into the royal library. Upon entering the door, Zanzee took off in a sprint toward the queen and landed in her lap. She lost her concentration. Instantly, she threw her arms around him and pulled him snugly against her chest. "Oh Zanzee! Oh how I've missed you. You would be in my bed, making sure I was up with the sun. Your purr was my alarm!"

Quill took a seat cattycorner from the two couches, where he assumed that Jeannie, Danny, Neferapondes, and Jerzom were deep in conversation. He was content to listen, as his business was finished.

Danny's mind shot to something. *Hmm, the ruby ring?*

Returning to the subject of the ring, he picked up his leather pouch again. Danny pulled his golden note from it. Danny was about to show the golden note to all. Then he hesitated.

"Neferapondes, you are so right. This is how the supreme god communicates. You know this, do you not?" spoke Danny.

He listened intently as Neferapondes answered, "Yes."

At that, Danny clutched the note to his body. He studied every word in his mind:

- ❖ *The girl had sapphire-blue eyes and silky black hair. She was the first Neferzul and was called Aerapondes, and endless time was to be her gift.*
- ❖ *The ruby ring she had with her always—even in death. She was killed by the high priest, Gorom Mochcom.*

  At the last line, Danny stopped. He read it several times to himself. Aware of what it said, he tensed as he reviewed every word carefully.

❖ *The ruby ring holds a secret. Reveal the secret to no one until they reveal the purpose.*

He was not about to show the ruby ring or the golden note to anyone, for fear of retaliation. But he wanted to console the queen.

Puzzled, Danny tried to figure out what the words meant. *I have no idea what the secret is, so how the hell can I reveal it?* He stared at the ceiling as he tightly squeezed his leather pouch that concealed the ruby ring.

No one spoke. It was as if they had lost their tongues. They looked at each other but refrained from conversation.

Then the dam of silence broke as Neferapondes asked, "Jeannie and Danny, do you have the gifts from the gods that were originally given to King Dalvin, me, and the other members of the royal family of Kopaz?"

Danny took note of her question, looked at Jeannie, and waited. Jeannie elected to answer for them both. "We do, Grandma. I think we have them all."

"Do you have the ruby ring?" Neferapondes quickly added.

Puzzled, Jeannie asked, "What ruby ring?"

"Hmm," said the queen. "It was a gift from the goddess, Neferdor. She personally gave it to my daughter, Aerapondes."

The source…she just revealed the source, shot through Danny's mind.

As Danny was deep in concentration, the queen added, "The ruby ring somehow unlocks time. We are not sure exactly how it works, but its purpose is that it is a key to somehow unlock time."

Although his mind was off wandering in a different direction, Danny did catch the queen's statement. Her words echoed in his head. *Its purpose is that it is a key to somehow unlock time.*

Hmm, thought Danny. *The purpose? The ruby ring unlocks time!*

Gently, Danny took the ring from his pouch and put it, along with the golden note he had been holding, on the table between the two couches. The ring he put on a piece of black silk.

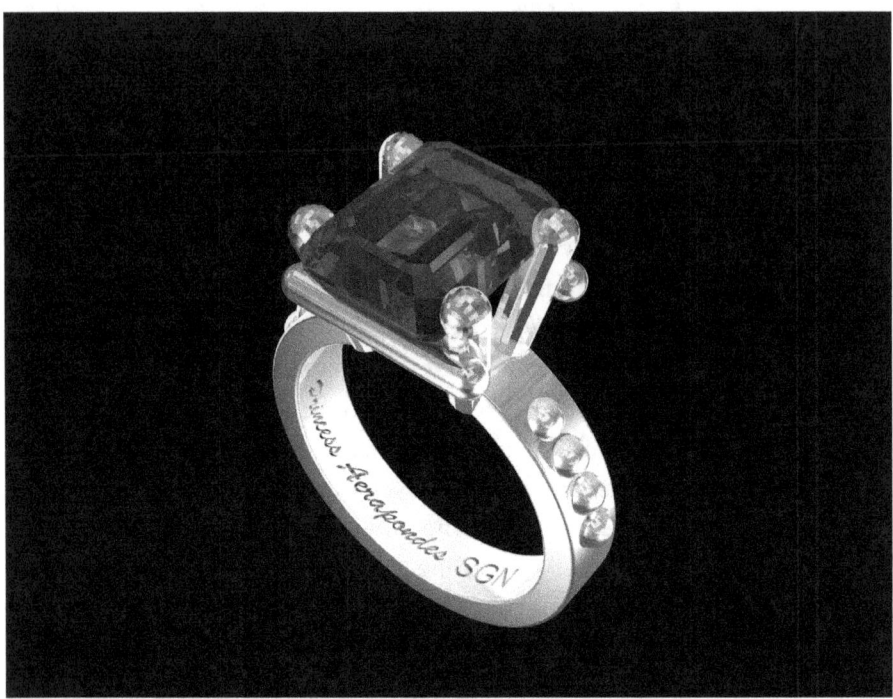

Yet still feeling a sense of caution, Danny covered his gold note with his leather pouch.

With a trembling hand, the queen reached to touch the ruby ring.

Quill stepped up and walked to the couches. Standing next to the table, he said, "You may take your daughter's ring, my dear lady. The supreme goddess Neferdor told me you may keep it until Aerapondes's journey back from the Land of the Dead is complete."

If the dam of silence just a few moments earlier had held back a flood of human voices, it was overshadowed by the stillness that now filled the royal library. What Quill had just said broke all barriers. It dissolved the grip of death that had strangled the human race since the dawning of existence.

For the first time in human existence, the gods had revealed that death had no permanent hold.

Even for Danny, even knowing all that he had learned as a young god, the thought that raced into his mind was very human. *My dad…my mom…*

Tony…I can't believe it. Oh, how great you are, Viracocha!

No doubt, Jeannie, Neferapondes, and Jerzom all had similar thoughts.

Danny had another thought running through his mind. *Is the purpose of the ruby ring to unlock time have something to do with bringing back the souls from the Land of the Dead?*

Bringing souls back up the River Styx was not on Quill's agenda. He had other priorities. "Has the source been revealed, Danny?"

"Yes, Quill!" answered Danny.

"That is good. Show the note to Jeannie, Neferapondes, and Jerzom," requested Quill.

Standing his ground, Danny did nothing. Time pressed on, and silence took over. Quill, although Danny's tutor, become nervous. Danny's look prompted the question, "What?" from Quill.

No one else had apparently entered the room, yet they all heard a voice louder than if it came from the loudspeakers in Dodger Stadium. "Danny, you have *my* permission. And Quill…do not demand of Danny. Ask him next time."

No one had to guess who had just spoken. Only Danny and Quill had actually seen the figure of Viracocha walk in, and they remained silent as to the source of the voice.

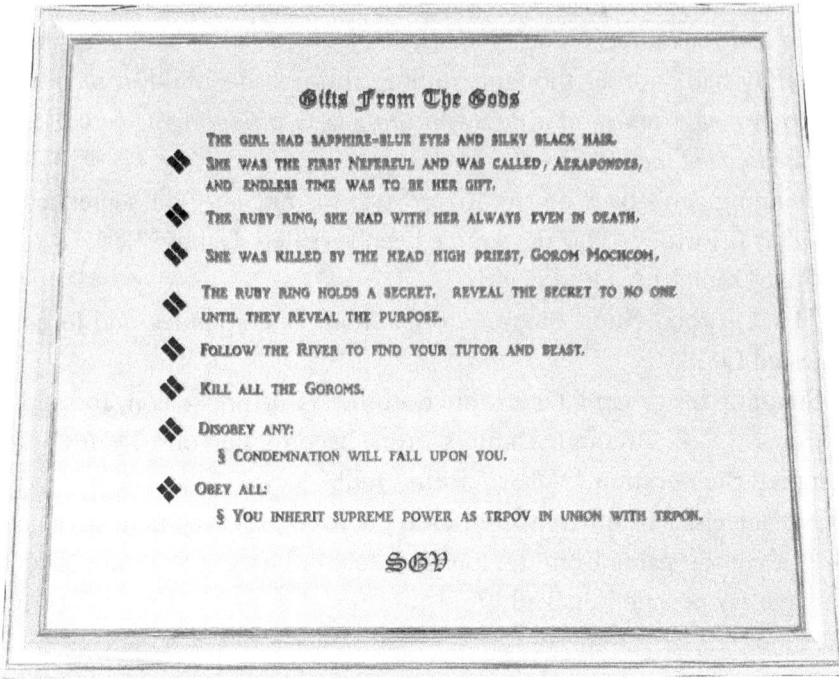

Danny lifted the golden note from under his leather pouch and read it aloud:

> ❖ *The girl had sapphire-blue eyes and silky black hair. She was the first Neferzul and was called Aerapondes, and endless time was to be her gift.*
>
> ❖ *The ruby ring she had with her always—even in death. She was killed by the high priest, Gorom Mochcom.*
>
>   Again, Danny stopped at the last line.
>
> ❖ *The ruby ring holds a secret. Reveal the secret to no one until they reveal the purpose.*

Viracocha's voice once more boomed through the royal library. "The ruby ring of Neferdor was once worn on the finger of the supreme goddess. It holds a secret. Without the presence of the ruby ring, the portal of reality remains closed!" This time not only Danny and Quill saw the supreme god standing before them but Jeannie did as well.

Neferapondes and Jerzom watched Danny, Jeannie, and Quill stare at something they could not see as they listened to the words of the supreme god.

Upon delivering his message, he was gone. Viracocha had just revealed the secret of the ring, but it was doubtful that Danny, Jeannie, Neferapondes, or Jerzom understood its meaning.

"In due time, I will explain the secret of the ring," said Quill, "but for now, all you need to know is this. The veil of time is controlled by the ruby ring."

No one spoke.

And so it was. Neferapondes pulled her only son next to her and whispered, "Soon, my son. Soon." She clutched her daughter's ring with a longing in her heart to see Aerapondes once more gracing the halls of the royal palace.

Jerzom felt his mother's sweet spirit, and his mind had only one thought. *The bonds of death are loosening, and my mom's broken heart is healing.*

CHAPTER 41

Getting Ready

T he coronation of royalty demands pomp and circumstance. Why wouldn't it? The gala, the cheering crowds, the dawning of new rule, the magic of it all lifts spirits to new heights at a new beginning. It always had and always would. The time was at hand. Danny had hinted at something that might be happening in the near future. It had puzzled both Neferapondes and Jerzom, yet they respected the young god, fully knowing his supreme power, both physical and spiritual. His connection with Viracocha was all but cast in stone. His remaining task—to kill Gorom Mochcom and throw his ashes wrapped in the Ancient Shroud of Goroms into the Pit of Vulcan—was yet to be completed.

It would seem simple enough. He would use the gifts from the gods to travel back in time and space over the Highway of Time. He would find Gorom Mochcom, kill him, and bring his ashes wrapped in…something that neither Danny nor Jeannie had the foggiest idea what it was. Jeannie only knew what had to be done because it was clearly laid out in Kashom's golden journal:

TRPOV and TRPON must fulfill the following conditions:

(1)   *They must kill all of the goroms in Kopaz and throw their bodies not yet ashes into the fiery depths of Vulcan—the gateway to hell guarded by CrystalFlame—so their eternity is destined to be everlasting embers in the belly of the outer reaches of darkness.*

(2)   *They must kill Mochcom and wrap his ashes in the Ancient Shroud of Goroms and throw them into the fiery depths of Vulcan so his eternity is destined to be everlasting anguish in the belly of the outer reaches of darkness.*

Then, and only then, shall the TRPOV and TRPON sit on thrones of pure gold alongside the gods at their council table of red worox stone and control the gift of eternal youth for all humans throughout the universe.

Beware that the bodies of the goroms of Kopaz remain not outside the gateway to hell past the evening of the high moon, for if they do, all is lost.

And to the TRPOV, his beast, Yellzor, shall devour imposters and throw them into the fiery mouth of CrystalFlame.

Despite remembering all this, Jeannie remained puzzled about the Ancient Shroud of Goroms.

The final phase of Danny and Jeannie's mission lay before them. Not yet fully comprehending their task, they had to retrieve what was required from the Scarlet Desert, bring it back to the Land of Kopaz, and toss it into the Pit of Vulcan.

As Quill watched the young god making progress, and thinking of his final task that would set him on his journey to the planet Volob at the center of the universe, Quill mused. *In due time, my royal prince of Viracocha, I shall instruct you on your most secret task, which is not as simple as one might think.*

There wasn't a cloud in the sky. It was a deeper blue than an ocean. It was the perfect day, and by midmorning, all were busy. Preparations had been underway for a full week. Danny had proclaimed it to be a day of great celebration and instructed the servants of the royal palace to make ready the occasion.

"Handmar, what more needs to be done?" asked Danny.

"Royal Prince of Viracocha, we have in place the grand stage in the royal courtyard surrounded by the gardens of flowers that would make the gods smile," said Danny's chief guard. No doubt Handmar liked his new boss. His smile was a dead giveaway.

Danny nodded, taking note of the radiant face of Handmar. "OK, what else?"

Ready with the answer, Handmar charged on. "Gold thrones are in place for you, my god and master, TRPON, Neferapondes, and Jerzom. I've made arrangements for one hundred and fifty dignitaries to sit in the first section in front of the grand stage on which you will be seated."

Danny smiled looking out over the royal courtyard and gardens that would make the Super Bowl decorations seem like children's playthings. The outdoor kitchens were in place, out of the main view of the ceremony yet close enough to deliver a royal feast when ready.

"Handmar, let's you and I take one more walk-through to make sure all is as should be for such a great occasion," Danny said.

"Yes, my lord!" shouted the guardsman with military precision.

What should have been a half-hour affair turned into an observation tour lasting an hour and a half, as Danny wanted perfection and expected nothing less. And as they were about to finish walking their final one hundred yards back to the front entrance of the Grand Hall of the palace, Danny's mind wandered into a vault of old memories. It was on a day much like this that Jeannie, Tony, and he had taken Alex's horses and went racing through the Scarlet Desert.

His mind drifted as he recalled each detail. *Jeannie took a chance on the weather that day. Wow! She looked like a million dollars. She had slipped into a pair of tight-fitting shorts, exposing her long legs to the afternoon sun. She loved riding those horses. She kicked Skipper in his sides with her heels, and the sun had warmed up enough so she could finally wear shorts.*

Danny chuckled. Handmar listened and looked but thought Danny's expressions were a comment on the royal ceremony that was to take place in a few hours.

That was not the reason for Danny's inner laughter. "Clutching the reins of CoCo's bridle was so cool as we laughed about stealing the horses for an afternoon adventure," said Danny barely audibly, as his mind continued wandering. *I wonder if anyone from CoalVille ever noticed us take Alex's horses. We didn't care. Whoa—her soft, white, bare legs on Skipper in full gallop. How cool is that!*

"Yes, my lord?" said Handmar, not understanding the English words Danny had just spoken.

Danny heard Handmar, and knowing that the royal guardsman was intently listing to a foreign language, Danny turned his head to look Handmar in the eyes, smiled, and said, "I was just thinking, that's all…just recalling an event from long ago."

Handmar was a bit confused, but he also understood that the royal prince of Viracocha was in charge, and his mind was at ease. His face wore a smile as the guardsman mused, *I think the royal prince of Viracocha is pleased. The royal gardens, the royal seating arrangements…all is good. We are ready.*

As they made their final way along the green marble pathway in the royal gardens, they rounded the corner of the Reflecting Pool of Neferdor. The sun was glistening on the rippling surface. Reflecting the statues of ancient god-like figures, the pool's ripples seemed to make the statues come alive with quivering motions.

And music filled the air. The fountains seemed to be singing songs as they spewed water from their mouths, and it splashed into large stone-layered basins.

With two things on his mind—Jeannie and the final preparations for a royal coronation and the changing of the government—Danny looked at Handmar, put his hand on the guardsman's right shoulder, and said, "Good job! You are excused for now. Take a few minutes of relaxation before the big event this afternoon."

"Anything else, my lord?" asked Handmar, now standing next to Danny.

"No, just get ready," Danny said as he thought about his journey and his true love. *From the Scarlet Desert to the royal palace of Kopaz. On Alex's horses, we raced to White Face Cliff and found the royal palace of Kopaz. Wow, Jeannie! What a journey.*

Knowing his new master had a lot on his mind, Handmar turned to Danny and said, "I'll be here if you need me. We'll be ready for the gala festival!"

With Jeannie still on his mind, Danny slapped Handmar's back, turned, and started his final walk, only a short distance to the front entrance of the royal palace.

Yeah, I remember the day so well. We rounded the hill on our horses, bringing White Face Cliff into spectacular view. The scarlet rays of the afternoon sun set the cliff on fire with breathtaking colors.

Danny's excitement mounted just reliving the past. *My heart was skipping beats not only because I was watching Jeannie's body bouncing up and down on Skipper's back but also because of the legends. I'd always been curious about them—tales of buried treasure in the hills around CoalVille.*

"Are you daydreaming?" Her voice rang through the air.

Danny's head jerked up. Standing in the entrance of the Grand Hall, there she was in tight-fitting shorts.

"Holy crap, Jeannie, you look just like you did on Skipper the day we raced through the desert on Alex's horses," shouted Danny back.

"Danny boy, I have some *big plans for you!*" said Jeannie, twirling her hand toward him.

"What?" That was all Danny could make come out of his mouth.

Her Cheshire cat grin told him she was up to something, but as always, Jeannie was way ahead of Danny.

The morning was all but gone. Danny grabbed Jeannie's hand, and they started walking across the Grand Hall. But as usual, Jeannie had other plans. She started skipping and tugging on Danny's arm. She didn't care that that fifteen royal guardsmen were watching a young girl have fun with her love. Finally, Danny had no choice, and his gait went from a walk to a skipping stride, and that prompted a shout of joy from the group watching from the sidelines, cheering Jeannie on.

And with their last skip, they came to the doorway in the north wall of the Grand Hall. Danny said, "Jeannie, we only have three hours before tens of thousands of people will be shouting in the courtyard as a changing of the guard takes place with a new coronation! We don't have time to play!"

"Sounds like you have a problem, my love," she said, dropping his hand and skipping away from him. She stopped, turned, giggling, and said, "Danny boy, I really do have big plans for you!"

Hmm! thought Danny. *What is she up to?* He watched Jeannie skipping and singing as she made her way down the Grand Hallway leading to her bedroom. Shaking his head, Danny watched as she rounded the corner and entered her room. *She has big plans for me? I wonder what that is all about.*

CHAPTER 42

Little Zeb and the
Changing of the Guard

How could anybody describe such an affair? There could be no words good enough. It would take all the Webster's dictionaries in the world to come up with even a flimsy description of the grand affair that was unfolding in the royal courtyard on that most beautiful afternoon in Kopaz.

Quill had personally brought Danny and Jeannie's ceremonial robes from the pantheon of Viracocha and Neferdor. It was obvious that Neferdor had her hand in the design of the clothing for the royal prince of Viracocha and the royal princess of Neferdor. The goddess must have been schooled at some point in the vast expanse of time on how to make the best of the best in godly robes. Danny's was highlighted with giant emeralds that were framed with gold braiding. In the classiest fashion, the jewels were orchestrated in a stunning design that only Neferdor could have imagined—not only flawless green emeralds but also red and blue diamonds framed with silver braiding, which complemented the gold.

The sun couldn't have been more appropriately positioned, as its rays danced as if with joy on Danny's robe, making the gold, silver, emeralds, red and blue diamonds, sapphires, and rubies come alive in a spectacular early afternoon light show. And Danny's ceremonial robe was in harmony with

Jeannie's. Hers was constructed in like fashion, but where his had emeralds, hers had deep, sky-blue sapphires. The fabric for each was a mixture of fur, silk, and some other godly material that only Neferdor knew.

She had come from a dungeon beneath a pyramid to a seat on a solid-gold throne laden with gemstones and beautiful carvings that had to weigh at least ten tons. Jeannie couldn't care less about its monetary value. It was hers. She was there next to the boy of her heart, a god who sat in his matching golden throne, looking out over a crowd of at least ten thousand cheering citizens of Kopaz.

They had good reason to cheer for the royal prince of Kopaz. He, almost single-handedly, except for Yellzor, at Danny's feet, and Zanzee, in Jeannie's lap, had freed them from the cloud of evil that had inflicted such horrors on them for centuries. The crowd could not refrain from shouts of ecstasy: "*Hail TRPOV! Hail TRPON! Long live the gods! We bow to you! Hail TRPOV! Hail TRPON! Long live the gods! We bow to you!*"

She couldn't help herself. Jeannie reached her hand across the arm of her throne and found an opening in Danny's robe. Since the two center thrones on which Danny and Jeannie were seated were almost touching, her arm was almost undetected. At least that is what she thought.

She flipped her head, her long silky black hair making a *swissssh* sound as she caught a glimpse of Quill. Perfectly aware of what she was up to, he mouthed to her, "Jeannie, leave Danny alone. He has business to attend to. You can have fun with him later!"

No one else saw him or what he was saying under his breath, and Jeannie knew it. By now, her fingers were tickling Danny's side. He fidgeted. She snickered. She covertly took her hand from its hiding place and gave Quill a high five wave. She mouthed back to him. "Quill, this is my time. My business. And you stay out of it."

What could he say other than "OK"?

The cheering crowd had no clue about the strange little interlude that Jeannie had just gone through. They were content to make noise in praise of the gods before them.

On the other hand, Danny's smile, which Jeannie watched grow on his face, told her he knew exactly what she was up to. He slowly shook his head, with his yellow hair blowing in the wind, as he thought, *Jeannie, in a few minutes I have to stand and address ten thousand people, and you are tickling me! That is what I love about you…you never change.*

It was time. Danny stood and slowly took three steps to the front of the massive stage, which had only four people on it—Danny, Jeannie, Jerzom, and Neferapondes. Danny's and Jeannie's golden thrones were together in the center. On Danny's right side was Neferapondes's throne and to Jeannie's left was Jerzom's.

Danny raised his arms above his head, allowing the sleeves of his robe to slide down, exposing his ripped muscles from countless hours of training with Quill. Kopaz had never had a leader who was such a handsome, muscular warrior. Accounts of his bravery had spread like a forest fire traveling up a mountainside, leaving its mark on the landscape. There was not a soul in Kopaz who did not worship their new god.

Maybe they knew his ceremonial robe had just come from the pantheon of Viracocha and Neferdor. Maybe they knew that the supreme god and his wife, the goddess Neferdor, were well pleased with their royal prince and princess, TRPOV and TRPON. For whatever reason, not one person in the crowd could take their eyes off Danny as he stood before them high on the stage. He was their king. He was their savior. He was their god. They loved him. He knew it. Jeannie was in her glory.

"*Great and wonderful people of Kopaz!*" shouted Danny. "*I stand before you as an emissary of the supreme god Viracocha. He bids you good tidings! He sends his blessings! He felt your pains of oppression from the goroms!*"

A deafening cheer broke out. "*Hail TRPOV! Hail TRPOV! Hail TRPOV!*"

For a moment, Danny just watched and smiled down on the crowd.

Maybe it was meant to be. Maybe it was fate. Maybe it was coincidence. For whatever reason, he spotted a mother holding a little boy who seemed to have a stub for an arm. The little guy was trying to hold his half an arm close to his body, so as not to bring attention to it. He did not wear shoes. His clothes were a telltale story and said it all—a tattered pair of pants with patches on the knees and a raggedy old shirt that must have been mended at least one hundred times. His free hand—his little hand—was the only one he had, and it was waving at Danny like a flag in the wind.

As the crowd cheered, Danny started walking to the stairs located center right on the stage. Jeannie was puzzled. She couldn't see the family Danny was focused on.

He spoke not a word as he made his way to the staircase. The crowd cheered louder as he walked down the flight of steps to be in their midst.

As many in the crowd gathered closer, just to be near their TRPOV, Quill took center stage and motioned for them to stand back and let Danny through.

Danny walked to the young mother, who had tears streaming from her eyes. He lifted his hand and gently touched her face as he asked, "And what is this young man's name?"

Although there were thunderous shouts of joy and praise filling the royal courtyard on the warm sunny afternoon, nothing was as loud as the little boy shouting with a giant smile on his face, *"My name is Zeb!"* That was all that Danny heard.

Now the noise of the crowd died down. Their interest was fixed on a young god lifting a young boy in his arms. Danny held Zeb high above his head, to show all in the crowd this smiling boy with half an arm.

Holding Zeb with one hand, he reached and took the young mother's free hand. "And what is Zeb's mother's name?"

Her tears were still falling, and as they ran down her cheeks and over her smile, she softly said, "Nola!"

Nodding his head, Danny said, "Follow me!" He started making his way through the crown back to the stairs. Still holding Nola's hand and carrying Zeb, they walked to the top of the grand stage. Once at top of the stairs, they made their way to center stage.

Jeannie was now standing and waiting for Danny, Nola, and Zeb to reach her.

As he continued to hold Zeb with his left arm, Danny asked him, "How is it, Zeb, that you have only part of an arm?"

Zeb was brave. He was only five years old, yet he had experienced more pain and sorrow than most would in a lifetime. With his head down, looking at the floor, Zeb said, "The bad goroms said my dad was evil and my mom ran out of our house. My dad screamed for her to go back inside. I didn't know what to do. I'm little. They were big."

The words of his little voice carried like the song of a bird in the stillness of the world at daybreak.

A silence filled the Grand Courtyard. Not a breath of wind stirred. The words of a little boy found their way to the ears of ten thousand people listening with all their might.

Zeb continued. "My mom screamed. It was too late. The chief gorom took his knife from his black robe. Two goroms held my dad. The chief put his knife in my dad's heart, and he ventured to the Land of the Dead. I ran. My dad was on the ground. His eyes were open. I started hollering, 'Dad, get up! Dad, get up!' He didn't."

Tears poured from Zeb's eyes, and Danny felt the boy's pain. "I screamed at the bad man that killed my dad: *You are the evil one!*'"

As hard as it was for Zeb to tell his story, he did. "The head gorom started cutting my arm. I screamed! I hurt so badly!" Zeb's little face looked up at Danny as he continued. "My mom saved me. She grabbed me from that evil man and got me back in the house. They left."

No one could see Danny's broken heart. His eyes were bright with tears that wanted to burst forth.

Standing next to Danny, Jeannie sweetly asked, "Zeb, let me hold you, and Danny will make it all better."

Gently, Danny handed Jeannie the small boy. Though she could not see Danny's bleeding heart, she could feel his inner soul wrench with pain just thinking of the horrific scene that had taken place in yet another peasant's front yard.

Zeb's mom didn't understand what Jeannie had just said. Nola just looked on, watching her son in the arms of gods.

"Zeb," Danny said. "You are going to be the royal prince of Kopaz's right-hand man! Can you do that?"

There was a smile on Zeb's little face as he said forcefully, "*Sure!*" Then, in a puzzled way he asked, "What do I have to do to be a right-hand man?"

There was not a dry eye in the crowd. There were smiles everywhere and also a lot of whispering going on.

It was Danny's turn to make a little boy smile. "OK, Zeb, to be a right-hand man for Prince Jerzom, don't you need a right hand?"

"You're fooling with me," said Zeb. "You know I don't have one."

Danny turned to Jerzom who was sitting ten feet behind him on his throne. He motioned for him to come forward. Jerzom stood and walked to where Danny, Jeannie, Zeb, and Nola were. When Jerzom was standing next to Jeannie, who was holding Zeb, Danny asked, "Jerzom, can this little fellow be your right-hand man without a right hand?"

"Nope," replied Jerzom.

"OK, that's it!" said Danny. He pointed at Jerzom's throne and motioned for Jeannie to go there. She did.

Danny grasped Nola's hand and walked alongside her until they were at Jeannie's side.

"Jeannie, put this little prince's right-hand man on the royal throne," Danny said affectionately.

Gently she put Zeb on Jerzom's throne. The crowd shouted, "*Zeb! Zeb! Zeb!*"

There was something going on, but no one except Danny, Jeannie, and Quill had a clue. Those watching with inquisitive wonder didn't care. It was a sight to see. A god making a little boy smile again was bringing joy to everyone's heart.

"Do you like giant wolves?" asked Danny of Zeb.

What could he say except "Yes"?

"Yellzor, come over here and lick Zeb's face," said Danny.

As Yellzor was making his way across the stage, Danny said, "Zeb, Yellzor won't bite you. He may give you a lick or two."

The little boy's smile had started to emerge, and then it disappeared as if to say, "The wolf will lick me?"

Knowing exactly what was in Zeb's mind, Danny asked, "Is that OK?"

A little hesitantly, Zeb lifted his only hand and pointed at Yellzor. "Can I pet him?"

"You bet," answered Danny.

That was a sight to behold in the land of Kopaz—a five-year-old boy with only half an arm sitting in a special golden throne so all ten thousand cheering people could see. He was petting a giant wolf with his little hand—the only one he had. When Yellzor put his massive head next to Zeb's cheek and gave him a lick, the crowd erupted again. "*Zeb! Zeb! Zeb!*"

"Are you ready?" asked Danny over the roar of the crowd.

Having no idea what this giant man was asking—and a giant was exactly how Zeb saw Danny through the eyes of a child—he answered, "Yes."

"Hold your arm out...the one that the bad man cut," commanded Danny, yet in a thoughtful tone of voice.

Little Zeb did as told.

Danny lifted his right hand—the one with his ring—in front of Zeb, and with his left hand, he grabbed his gift from Viracocha, once more displaying the power of the gods that ruled the universe. The beam of green light from Danny's ring hit its mark.

Zeb's heart pounded. His eyes were big as saucers. Nola was trying to hold back her tears of joy as she witnessed the miracle of her only boy, now with two arms and two hands again.

"*Mom, I got two hands!*" shouted the little boy who no longer had a sad heart. He was the main attraction in Kopaz that bright sunny day on a stage that had just thrust him into the limelight, making him a national figure of hope.

"Zeb," said Jeannie, "I think you are ready to be a *right-hand man!* What do you think?"

"I think I'm ready, Miss TRPON! I like you!" burst out Zeb.

"OK, are you ready for your first royal assignment, Prince Zeb?" asked Danny as he reached to shake hands with a little boy who could now do the same.

If there were thundering roars from the crowd up to this point, they were the whispers of silence compared to the roar that now broke loose. "*Prince Zeb! Prince Zeb! Prince Zeb!*"

"What's my royal assignment, Mr. TRPOV?" asked Zeb with more excitement than all the lights and cheers in New York's Times Square welcoming in the New Year.

"Well, you take your mom's hand with your left and Miss TRPON's with your right and stand right there," said Danny as he showed the new prince where to stand for his assignment.

Gracious as she was, Neferapondes watched the episode, content in the knowledge that her broken heart could also be mended by these young gods of Kopaz.

Danny was aware of her feelings of excitement as she witnessed a miracle and also her feelings of sadness about not having her husband, Dalvin, her older son, Kashom, and her daughters, Aerapondes and Merapondes, at this most joyous day. Danny's heart stopped for a moment as he thought, *Soon, honorable mother and wife, you will find joy also.*

Danny motioned for Neferapondes to rise and walk to center stage. Jerzom was at his mother's side.

Anxiously awaiting more news, the crowd looked at the seven people, one giant yellow wolf, and one black cat on stage in front of them.

"Quill has an announcement," proclaimed Danny.

With that, Quill stepped forward, and with a scroll in hand, he prepared to read the official declaration for all the peoples of Kopaz. In a loud booming voice, most unusual from such a small man, he shouted, "The goroms are gone forever! There is no more religious oversight of the government! The Citizens Board is enacted—commoners at the seat of power will rule for the first time in Kopaz! The Citizens Board will be headed up by none other than Peizar!"

A deathly silence fell and a somber mood of understanding was suddenly in everyone's mind, especially Jerzom's, at this last declaration concerning his dead friend, Peizar. The royal prince of Kopaz looked to the sky, his thoughts a jumble of joy, excitement, and puzzlement. *How can it be? My dearest friend, Peizar? How?*

And as the crowd listened in awe, Quill carried on. "Your new queen is none other than Neferapondes! Her son, Jerzom, is the new prince of Kopaz and has joint powers with the Citizens Board! Jerzom and Peizar will report jointly to the queen! The queen has two primary functions. She will report to the people the laws enacted by the Citizens Board, and she will be the commander of the royal army. The board will be made up of an even number of elected representatives from throughout the land. When a vote is split fifty-fifty, Jerzom will break the tie. Jerzom will represent the government of Kopaz, and Peizar, the people of Kopaz."

Quill paused before continuing. "The time is not yet, but soon the boatman on the River Styx will no longer take his passengers on a one-way voyage—from the Land of the Living to the Land of the Dead. There will be those from the Land of the Dead who are waiting, and when their time comes, the boatman will be directed by Viracocha's royal prince to collect them and bring them back to the Land of the Living."

And then Quill made a profoundly important statement. "Only a few who reside in the Land of the Dead will come forth by the grace of TRPOV."

"It's now time," said Danny. "Step forward, Zeb, and be crowned Prince Zeb of Kopaz!"

If ever a small boy had captured the heart of all, not just a few, but *all*, it was at the moment that he asked, "Do I get a crown? A real crown with jewels and gold and…and…I mean, a real one?"

Kneeling, lowering his head to Zeb's, and speaking firmly while looking the excited little boy right in the eye, Danny said, "Would Prince Zeb of Kopaz be crownless? I don't think so!" He smiled warmly.

"Mom, would you do the honor and crown your son?" proclaimed Danny as Quill brought forth a most ornate crown for a young prince.

Then he caught himself. "*Ooops!* Your mom is not royalty yet. Jeannie, would you do the honor and bestow the title of official queen of Kopaz on Neferapondes."

That she did. Quill set Zeb's crown on a golden table at the center of the stage. He then brought forth Neferapondes's crown on a large decorative pillow, completely trimmed with gold and silver braid.

As Neferapondes knelt on one knee at Danny's feet, Jeannie placed the official crown on Neferapondes's head and made the proclamation. "Long live Queen Neferapondes!"

The crowd erupted! "*Long live our queen!*"

"And now, gracious queen of Kopaz, would you do the honor of crowning Nola, your new executive assistant, Princess Nola of Kopaz?"

And with her head held high, her crown catching the rays of the afternoon sun, the queen said most humbly, "Yes, I would be honored to crown Nola as Princess Nola of Kopaz."

Sometimes a little boy's heart beats when he is scared. Sometimes a little boy's heart drops into the depths of anguish and despair when he witnesses the death of his best friend, his dad. But that was not why Zeb's heart was racing. He now had a princess for a mom, and boy, was his heart racing.

"*OK, Mom,* it looks like you have some official business to take care of," said Danny, looking at Nola. He pointed to the crown on the gold table and then at her son.

As Nola placed the golden crown on her son's head, the crowd erupted again. "*Hail Prince Zeb! Long live Prince Zeb!*"

If ever there were a sight for sore eyes, it was this newly crowned peasant boy who had only one pain left in his heart, and that was that his dad was not there. Spirits were on the rise in Kopaz. A new day had dawned, free of the evil that for centuries had smothered their pursuit of a happy and joyful life. But no longer did a fear of horror and death at every corner fill their minds. They looked on and took home the image of a young boy with a miraculous new hand as their "prince of hope."

"OK, Prince Zeb," Danny said. "You have your first official duty to perform! Are you ready?"

Only one word came from little Prince Zeb. "*Yep!*"

And now Prince Zeb's most joyous moment had arrived. Jerzom kneeled in front of Prince Zeb as the newest member of royalty in Kopaz placed a crown of gold on Jerzom's head and said, "I declare you Prince Jerzom, prince of Kopaz!"

On that sunny day, the changing of the guard set a new course for all who lived in Kopaz. The shadow of evil was no more, and the light of good was declared. A new road of hope was paved by a small boy who could not wait to see his dad and tell him, "Dad, I'm Prince Zeb, and we have nothing more to fear!"

CHAPTER 43
A Night to Relax

When all you've ever known for your entire life is a bare-bones existence living in a two-room shack with dirt floors, it's hard to imagine a royal palace as your new home. It not only had a giant soft bed in a room—the bed alone was five times the size of your old house, but also servants to make sure you have anything and everything you want. For a five-year old boy, it was quite a journey.

"Mom, am I dreaming?" little Zeb asked as she was helping his personal assistant get her only son ready for bed.

Between his words, Zeb would look at his new arm and hand and give it a little pinch to see if it was real. It was.

Watching, his mom smiled, knowing that gifts from the gods come unexpectedly.

"No, son, you're not. I don't have all the answers, but what I do believe is that our lives have changed forever," said Nola as she helped Zeb get his old shirt off and watched Katrina holding out a beautiful nightshirt fit for a royal prince.

"Mom, can I keep my crown right here by my bed all night long?" asked Zeb as he rubbed his eyes and looked fondly at his new ensign of power sitting on the green-marble-topped bed stand within arm's reach of where he would lay his head.

"Yes," said Nola, "but you mustn't play with it at night because you don't want to drop it on the floor."

"I won't. I promise. I love you, Mom!" His little eyes were starting to close. "Oh, Mom, I forgot. Can Zanzee sleep with me tonight?" he queried in a sweet little voice.

"I'll ask his owner, TRPON. If she says yes, and Zanzee wants to, well…OK," replied Nola.

In the royal library, there was a meeting going on. It probably didn't start out as a meeting, or not, at least, a serious meeting, but that was what it was turning into. Danny, Jeannie, Neferapondes, and Jerzom were drifting into serious areas of conversation. Even though the queen was reserved, her face was drawn into lines of serious inner pain and introspection.

Jeannie asked, "Grandma, is there something that troubles you?"

Slowly, Neferapondes turned her head to face Jeannie. In this arrangement, Jeannie and Neferapondes were on one couch, and Danny and Jerzom sat on the opposite facing one. Neferapondes looked directly at Jeannie, and there was sadness in her smile.

"Yes," she said, the sorrow clear in her voice. "I want so much to have my children near me again."

It was the first time that Jeannie had seen Neferapondes sobbing. The queen was stalwart and rarely showed outward emotions. Maybe it was the reality that death was not final, but for her family it might be. Maybe it was that she was just a mother who had endured so much pain and sorrow that she could not keep it bottled up inside her anymore. Who knows?

She has a broken heart, and I don't know what I can do, thought Jeannie.

"Do you know, Jeannie, that to get a loved one from the Land of the Dead, the Gravekeeper will demand a lock of hair, and without it, no one leaves?" Neferapondes remarked rhetorically.

"Yes, Grandma, I do," replied Jeannie.

Danny and Jerzom sat quietly listening. Not knowing where the conversation was going, they felt was that silence was good.

Through the open window, the night breeze came as a welcome distraction. It rustled the massive draperies on either side hanging like sentinels to guard against unwanted intruders. The cool breeze felt good and set a blissful mood in the wake of what was turning into a sad conversation.

With a catch in her voice, Neferapondes said, "I never fully believed in the lock of hair story. I blame myself. I will never see either of my beloved girls again."

No one said a thing, as Neferapondes surely had to have been deep in thought as she was organizing her thoughts and was about to say more. She did. "I blame myself, as I should have taken a lock of hair from all my children. I didn't."

"Grandma—" Jeannie tried to break in.

She couldn't. Neferapondes was digging deeper and falling into depression, as it was evident that she was taking all responsibility for shrugging off what she had considered merely folklore or myth. As she managed to say between sobs, "The Boatman will never let them board his vessel again. He is forbidden to let any dead leave the Land of the Dead and return to us without the lock of hair."

"Grandma…Grandma!" half-shouted Jeannie. "Stop!"

Jeannie was about to say something, but someone else beat her to it. "Miss TRPON, would it be OK if Zanzee keeps Zeb company this evening? I think he is a little afraid and even…well, ah, he thinks it might all be a dream," Nola asked in a direct way to bring the conversation to a brighter level.

Jeannie looked at Nola, a thought coming to her mind. *Humor is needed. Nola just provided a welcome break.*

Jeannie was…well, she was Jeannie. She turned her head to look at Nola, who had just walked through the royal library doorway and was looking like maybe she had intruded where she ought not to have.

First Jeannie looked at Nola. Then she looked at Danny, then at Yellzor and Zanzee. They were both curled up in balls beneath the window just soaking up the cool night breeze.

Danny followed her every movement. *Hmm*, he thought. *She's up to something…but what?*

In the sweetest voice she could manage, and with a little smirk on her face that only Danny detected, Jeannie answered, "Why, yes. That would be super for Zeb to have Zanzee spend the night with him." Jeannie hesitated, twisting her chin slightly. She was obviously deep in thought.

Only the breeze made any noise, shuffling a piece of paper that Jeannie had been fiddling with earlier. It had fallen to the floor, and like a skittering spider, it fluttered across the floor and, quite by accident, landed at Danny's feet.

Jeannie watched the paper as she collected her thoughts, deciding what to say next. Danny looked at her and shrugged his shoulders. He didn't have a clue. Jerzom was content to be a bystander.

"Nola, Zeb looked quite content petting Yellzor today, didn't he?" Jeannie asked.

"Why, yes, he really likes Yellzor. I didn't want to say anything, but Zeb thinks Yellzor was a special gift at the coronation today, like a big stuffed animal. He thinks Yellzor is a giant toy that came to life."

More confused than ever, Danny drew his eyebrows down closer to his eyes with a look of "What are you up to, Jeannie?"

Maybe the break was good, because even Queen Neferapondes wore a smile listening to the conversation. Who knows why things happen? Yet this time, Jeannie knew exactly what she was doing.

Nodding her head, Jeannie blurted, "Oh, Nola, both Zanzee and Yellzor would love to sleep in Zeb's bed. He is little. The bed is big…and I know all three would be great company, and little Zeb would have not one but two protectors! So there you go!"

Nola was going to ask, but Jeannie said it first. "*Yellzor, Zanzee!* Go with Nola!"

What is she up to? raced Danny's mind. *I know she has something up her sleeve!*

As Nola walked out the door, with Yellzor walking next to her and Zanzee riding on his back, Jeannie redirected her conversation back to the topic of hair.

"Grandma, let me set your mind at ease," said Jeannie. Maybe it was her mother, Soft Wind, who impressed on her how important it was to save a lock of hair from a loved one. Who knows why, but undetected by anyone, something happened in the Great Pyramid the day Peizar and Merapondes were killed. A black cat, who had once lived in the halls of the Egyptian pharaohs, knew the importance of the lock of hair. When Gorom Ancom made his way back to get Jeannie, his attention was not on a stealthy black cat.

Neferapondes waited. She didn't know what, yet somehow she knew that Jeannie was about to say something that could change destiny.

Characteristically, Jeannie had always carried a bag with pencils, paper, and you name it when she was on adventures with Danny and Tony in the Scarlet Desert. She still had that trait. Standing, Jeannie walked to the table by the door. She had placed something on that table when they had all entered the royal library. She fumbled through her things and spotted her leather pouch. She picked it up and carried it back to the couches.

Standing next to the table between the pair of white leather couches, Jeannie opened her pouch. She was about to take something out of it but stopped and said. "My dear grandmother, I hope I do not cause you sadness with my question." She looked at Neferapondes.

The queen spoke softly. "Jeannie, you fill my heart with hope and love, so please ask your question."

"I did not know that Aerapondes had a sister. It was never mentioned by Kashom in his journals. I met her in the pyramid before she was murdered and saw so much love in her eyes. I had no idea she existed. Why do you think Kashom did not talk about his other sister?

The queen smiled. "Merapondes was the younger twin. Maybe it was that Aerapondes was the older of the twins and that is why she was the first Neferzul. Maybe the fact that Aerapondes and Merapondes were identical in all respects was the reason the gods granted me twins. Maybe it was to help protect the first Neferzul from the evil goroms, as they did not know which of the two was slated to become a goddess. We, the royal family, did not have all the answers. That could be why I suspect Kashom never spoke of his beloved younger sister, Merapondes. He probably wanted to protect her from any more evil or harm because he was well aware that Gorom Mochcom had figured out who was the Neferzul, and you know the rest."

As the queen talked, Danny listened but said nothing as he recalled his vision of Merapondes just before he and Jeannie were attacked and overpowered on the banks of the Yellshome River the day that they had arrived in Kopaz. It was Danny's way of being reverent, and so he let Jeannie and Neferapondes discuss this delicate subject.

Jeannie waited for the queen to finish, and then she took something from her leather pouch and said, "This is Merapondes's hair, and this is Peizar's. We can thank Zanzee for this! He got locks from Princess Merapondes and Peizar when Gorom Ancom chased me down the dark hallway in the Great Pyramid," Jeannie said quietly, knowing the very sight of the hair was almost more than Neferapondes and Jerzom could bear.

With trembling hands, Neferapondes reached to touch the strands of hair, each tied with beautiful ribbons of pink and blue. As she held them in her hands, it was evident to the queen that Jeannie had taken great pains to make bows that would remind anyone who looked at them of how much their owners had been loved.

As Neferapondes held the two locks of hair tied neatly with bows, Jeannie wrapped her hands around the queen's and said, "Grandma, my mother, Soft Wind, has Aerapondes's lock of hair hidden in a secret hiding place in our home in the Scarlet Desert."

The queen was speechless, but Jeannie wasn't. "Grandma, hope is a good thing! I used to tell Danny this, especially after his father was buried alive, and Gorom Mochcom murdered his beloved mother, Darla. It was so sad. Danny and I know that hope is a good thing."

Tears streamed from Neferapondes's eyes. Jeannie wrapped her hands more tightly around the queen's as she continued. "I know that you will see your children again. I only met Merapondes briefly, but the love in her heart was like a beacon of light that spread warmth to the whole world. I promise with all my heart that you will see your daughters again."

And for the first time that evening in the royal library of the royal palace, Queen Neferapondes smiled and said, "I hope so."

CHAPTER 44
A Mother Wants Her Son

When the night breeze blew back the curtains, Neferapondes caught a glimpse of the moon as it briefly showed its face. The mood in the royal library had lifted a bit. Yet there was a sadness that Neferapondes could not shake.

Maybe it was time. Maybe it was the only time. Who knows? For whatever reason, Quill walked in. The somber mood was not invisible to him. But that was not a concern to him. He had more pressing things on his mind.

Looking at Jeannie first, then the queen, and then at Quill, Danny was sure that time was not on their side. He was about to break into a conversation that Jeannie was having with her grandmother, who, heartbroken as she was, wanted nothing more than her children all back in the Land of the Living.

Jeannie had just said, "Hope is a good thing." Yet words were far from reality, and Jeannie, looking at the deep lines of sadness on Neferapondes's face, knew all too well that action and not words was needed.

What Jeannie was about to say was preempted by Quill. "Tomorrow, Danny and Jerzom must go!"

That certainly was not what Jeannie was about to say. That took them all by surprise.

Danny nodding his head slowly seemed louder than the shouts of a warrior in the midst of battle. For battle was at the very core of what Quill had just said.

For now, Quill said no more. It was Danny who explained. "The war of the gods is raging, and the power of the universe is teetering. Gorom Mochcom is at the heart of this war, and time is quickly running out."

If the mood had been somber prior to Quill's entrance, an atom bomb of somberness just exploded. There could be no turning back. Once more, Quill took center stage. His voice was low and solid as he firmly laid out the course of destiny for the universe. "The plan is set. On the morrow at dusk, Danny and Jerzom leave for the Scarlet Desert. Their two-fold mission must not fail. First they must capture Gorom Mochcom. Second, they will kill the last gorom by the order of Viracocha."

All eyes and ears were on Quill, even Danny's. Although Danny knew most, Viracocha had reserved the details to which even Quill was not privy. All he had were the words from the supreme god, and so he proclaimed them word for word: "On top of my high tower, when my glory is at its high point, the first Neferzul will thrust my knife of zedite into the beating heart of Mochcom as he lies on the Ancient Shroud of Goroms with a finger bone of my wife's first prized possession deep in his throat!"

They were puzzled. Why wouldn't they be? Even the strange look on Quill's face was a dead giveaway that he dared not open his mouth to suggest a plausible explanation.

Well, that certainly was a bunch of gobbledygook, thought Jeannie. *I sure hope someone turns that word-trail-of-wonderment into a successful game plan, 'cause it appears that killing Mochcom is not going to be as easy as just killing the monster with a plain old knife to the heart! Oh well, it's Danny's problem to figure out. Tonight is going to be a surprise!*

She had other plans, and right now she was not the least bit interested in all that high-towers, glory-at-high-point, shroud-of-goroms stuff.

"Well, why don't we call it a day? Head for the sack and take on tomorrow when the sun comes up," Jeannie said, knowing all too well the magnitude of the danger that was yet ahead. Even so, tonight, she had other plans.

CHAPTER 45
Night of Love

It was most likely a motherly trait—at least that's what a casual observer might deduce from afar. For anyone who has experienced that most precious gift from the gods, a young child, there can be no denying that a child can easily entwine the hearts of others in the bonds of love. Their innocence captures the triumph of the human spirit. Such was Zeb, and all loved him, especially his mother, Nola. Yet for Jeannie, like others who yearn for that most precious gift of bringing forth life, there was no denying the bond of affection she had for another's small boy. Her desire to bring forth and protect life only intensified when she watched Zeb, who had just been thrust onto the battlefield of the gods. Whether or not she knew it yet, the young goddess, Jeannie, who was TRPON—the chosen one of Supreme Goddess Neferdor—was yearning to bring forth her own new life. Was she aching for her own child like five-year-old Zeb? Or was she worried that Danny's intervention had just thrust Prince Zeb onto a dangerous stage populated by those who were playing for the existence of a new human race? Was this what tugged at the heart of this young girl… or was it not?

The hour was late, and the night birds were singing. It seemed that when the sun goes to bed and the vast black sky of the night takes over, nightingales come to life in search of lovemaking. And with a full moon next to the endless ribbon of the Milky Way, it was a perfect time to serenade the one you loved.

Figuratively speaking, it seemed that the plans Quill had announced were set in concrete. Was there a way to turn back? Well, most likely not without consequences. But that was a subject that could wait for the dawning of a new day when the sun brought warmth to all who struggled with grand challenges that would forge the course of destiny for all creatures in the universe. For the present, the sun was resting, and the night was beckoning. Time was fleeting, and the moment was now.

With the meeting wrapped up and plans made for Danny and Jerzom to journey into the mysterious realm of time and space, the moments quietly ticking away reminded everyone that the travelers must ready themselves for their unknown adventure—and that meant sleep.

Weighing heavily on Jeannie's mind was the bleak reality of losing, even temporarily, the one she would spend the eternities with, and it was a thought that she could not bear. She stood in the hallway outside the royal library, inches from Danny. She looked on longingly as he smiled back. Her hands were on his cheeks. Her sparkling eyes searched every minute facet and expression of his face, and her heart yearned for the battle of time to be over. There was no other course. Soon he would say, "Good-bye, my love."

"Danny, I love you so much! I don't even think the gods at the council table know the secrets of my heart..." As she struggled for words, her fingers tightened of their own accord, and she moved her lips closer to his.

He tenderly embraced her, his arms massive beyond human comprehension, arms that could crush the life out of a giant. Gently he pulled her trembling body closer to his. His bare chest muscles pressed tightly against her small breasts beneath her T-shirt.

She felt his warmth as her struggle for words became even greater. "Danny, I...I...I don't...wah...aaa...how can..."

His lips found hers. There was silence.

For what seemed like a lifetime, two gods were no longer in training. They were lost in their fantasy of an escape from an unknown future that was moving closer.

From her doorway, fifty feet down the hallway, Neferapondes watched the silhouettes of two young lovers finding warmth in each other's most intimate affections. Her heart pounded just recalling similar precious moments she had with Dalvin, who now had voyaged to a land beyond the grave.

Hard as it was, Danny pulled back. As his bedroom was in the opposite direction from Jeannie's, he looked down the hallway, where the only motion was flickering shadows from the candlelight dancing on the walls.

"I think I had better say good night, my love. It will be OK," he said as he dropped her hands.

Taking another step backward, they were starting the final leg of their conquest that leads to golden thrones at the council table of the primeval gods.

She couldn't take it any longer. She stepped forward, reached, and touched his face. Quickly, she turned and started walking away, a stream of tears pouring from her eyes that he could not see.

Maybe it was planned. Maybe it was coincidence. Maybe it was fate. Who knows? For whatever caused it to happen, Jeannie's room was located right next to one that had been unoccupied, at least up until that night. But on this night, five-year old Zeb, who had known nothing but dirt floors as a peasant boy, was the new owner of the room in the royal palace of Kopaz.

Passing his door, she couldn't help but stop and walk in. There they were. It was picture-perfect, with the light of the full moon streaming through the window and landing on them. In the middle of the bed, on top of the covers, Yellzor was curled in a giant ball. And tucked between his paws, next to his warm furry stomach, was Zeb, also curled up. His sweet little hands, both of them, were wrapped around one of Yellzor's front paws. And next to Zeb's head was Zanzee—snug as a bug in a rug.

Jeannie tiptoed to the bed. Then she laughed softly. On Zeb's head, tilted slightly to the left, was his crown. *How sweet*, she thought. She decided to move it, as she did not want his golden crown and precious gems to accidently hurt him during the night.

She wanted to get closer. But there was a problem. The bed was big! For a wolf that stands six feet tall when on all fours to have plenty of room in a bed, while leaving room for others, the bed had to be really big.

Jeannie's problem was how to give Zeb a good-night kiss.

Hmm, she thought. *Do I get on the bed and crawl like a stealthy cat after a mouse to get to them? Yep, that's it!*

And that she did. As she was on her hands and knees with her head over Zeb's, she caught the lid on a large green eye opening for just a moment and then it closed. Yellzor made no more sounds or movements. He was content to know that Jeannie had a fond spot in her heart for the peasant boy who was now Prince Zeb of Kopaz. Although Yellzor shrugged his shoulders a bit and made himself more comfortable, there was a distinct purring sound that could come from no one except Zanzee. He was happy, and his way of saying "All is well!" was a loud purr

Jeannie slowly let her head drop so she could kiss Zeb's forehead. He was never the wiser.

She gently lifted his crown from its resting place, stuck between Yellzor's big furry belly and Zeb's little head. She set it on the nightstand and walked out.

Danny couldn't get to sleep. His mind raced like an Indy 500 car on its last lap. From time to time he looked at his watch. It was eleven o'clock at night. It was midnight. It was one in the morning. Finally he drifted off into a deep sleep.

Always on guard, something didn't seem right. Danny was on his left side. Although Danny was six foot three, he had tons of room to roll around in a bed so big that it could only be found in a royal palace.

On his left side, facing the wall with three large windows, he felt a weird sensation tingle through his body. He had pulled the drapes on the two end windows closed, but the middle window he had left open to let the moonlight create a mood in the room that would invite love.

It was more than instinct and perception. For Danny, he knew something was up. Slowly he slid his right arm behind him. He stretched it out. He touched something warm and soft.

Jerking like a finger that just touched a hot stove, Danny's arm recoiled a bit. Nothing happened, so he reached again…this time exploring.

His hand felt bare skin.

He fumbled more letting his hand move down to discover two bare legs.

He moved his hand up the person's legs. He found no clothes.

He knew who it was.

As his hand moved around, he said, as he turned over, "My god! Jeannie, you are bare-assed naked!"

She gently touched his lip with a finger. And as if she might say something, her lips parted. The moonlight glistened on them, shining like the skin of a ripe red apple. She said not a word.

He blurted, "What the hell is going on?"

"Danny, shh…no talking!" she whispered.

He was completely caught off guard. Defenseless, he froze.

She scooted closer. Her warm chest pressed against him.

Snug against him, he could feel her small breasts, sending a jolt through his body as though he had been struck by a bolt of lightning.

His breathing intensified. His heart took off. Her hand was now on his belly button. Her fingers ever so lightly slithered over his skin. Jeannie's fingers grasped the silk night shorts that the queen's servants had prepared for him. She gently pulled on them. Nothing happened.

Her hot lips were over his. His eyes shot wide open. His mind was exploding, *Oh my God, Jeannie!*

She moved her head slightly back, and in a sweet voice, she whispered, "Danny, you have a goofy set of silk shorts wrapped around you. Take them off!" She pulled at his shorts again.

Massive in structure and solid on the marble floor, the royal bed never moved, although its occupants found pleasure in motion.

The light of the moon was the only visitor to that royal bedroom. Jeannie's careful planning earlier had given a new prince some warm furry friends to sleep with. This was Jeannie's moment. She had waited. Knowing it would be the last for a long time, she wanted it to last.

The night drifted on—minutes turned into hours, and the hours into ecstasy. For those precious moments of experiencing the special joy of first love, the hours were kind.

The nightingales maintained their lovemaking serenade and provided an enchanting melody as two young gods dreamed of holding on to the rapture of that first night for an eternity. Maybe they could. Forever young they would be. It was a gift from the gods for all those who traveled the Highway of Time, and Danny and Jeannie already had that gift.

And so it was on that warm summer's night in Kopaz. Could it be that new life was in the making—the start of a new human race?

CHAPTER 46

Farewell Once More

The sun peeked through his window. Danny rubbed his eyes and rolled over. He looked for Jeannie, but he was all alone.

Where is she? I didn't dream what happen last night…did I? He struggled to wake up.

Every other morning, he got a big slobbery lick on his face from his furry friend. That didn't happen.

He jumped out of bed and realized he was naked. He looked and then spotted it—his silk shorts were on the floor at the foot of the bed.

Yeah, it did happen, thought Danny, his face displaying the biggest smile his face had ever worn. *She made sure the animals were farmed out to a little guy. Oh my gosh!*

With the new day upon him, Danny, even though he would give anything to stay with Jeannie, had no options.

Figuratively speaking, it seemed that the plans were set in concrete. If the question was "Could he turn back?" the answer was "No such luck." So even though his fondest desire would be to stay and have fun with Jeannie, he could not.

Unknown to all, even Quill, Danny, and Jeannie, the power struggle between two warring factions of the primeval gods who had ruled the universe since the dawning of time was on the threshold of a climactic ending. Either Supreme God Viracocha or Dark God Zuron would be triumphant in a winner-take-all conquest. The war of the gods had boiled down to two issues. One, there was a traitor in the supreme god's inner circle, and two, they lacked the answer to a riddle: *The site of the black pit defines the color of the scent.*

As would become known in the future, Viracocha was blind to a traitor in his circle. And that riddle—*The site of the black pit defines the color of the scent*—had stumped them all for eons, even the most learned and noble gods at the council table. The answer was still elusive, and now the balance of power in the universe was at stake.

For humans to intervene and successfully address both of these issues would be profound, as it would change the outcome of the war and redirect the destiny of all living creatures in the universe over the expanse of unending time.

Heavy stuff for a young boy from CoalVille whose dad had been buried alive in a mining accident and whose mom was brutally murdered by Gorom Mochcom, disciple of the dark god Zuron. You might say it was a heavy load to carry, especially when Danny had no clue about this most important element of his assignment.

As Danny was fumbling to untie the knot in one of the legs of his shorts, he thought, *Jeannie was up to her old tricks! She tied this goofy thing up in knots!* He chuckled. And as he stood there naked, he thought he heard something or someone. He turned quickly and saw nothing—only an open doorway. *Hmm, it must have been the breeze coming through the open window.*

He smiled as he thought, *That darn Jeannie left my door wide open on her way out!*

He got dressed, and then he decided he wanted to take the next ten for himself.

But for a young god, in those early morning hours, all alone in his room, his mind on this day seized on a single reflection. *What is it all about? On top of my high tower, when my glory is at its high point, the first Neferzul will thrust my knife of zedite into the beating heart of Mochcom as he lies on the Ancient Shroud of Goroms with a finger bone of my wife's first prized possession deep in his throat!*

Staring out the window, deep in thought, Danny was startled by a sweet voice behind him.

"Danny, breakfast will be served in half an hour. Jeannie and Zeb are outside with the animals. I think Jeannie really likes that…it is so sweet to watch them." The queen hesitated momentarily and then added, "Jeannie will be in the royal dining room in ten to fifteen minutes."

She wanted to stay, but she turned to walk out.

Before she had a chance to take one step, Danny said, "Do you have a minute?"

"Oh yes, Danny, for you, I have all the time you need," she answered softly.

His first thought as she came farther in was, *Wow, I'm glad she didn't stop by a few minutes ago…me in my birthday suit.*

As she made her way to the large leather couch against the west wall, she smiled and said, "I am glad you asked for a conversation. I haven't had time to talk about so many things that are on my mind. I have tons of questions."

Thinking that the queen was concerned about her only remaining child, Danny carefully put his thoughts into words. "I'll have Jerzom back to you as soon as we have accomplished what I need him to do."

That she didn't expect. Yet Danny could only imagine the pain she would go through if she lost all her children to the evil of the goroms. He continued, "My dear queen, the most precious person in the world to me I entrust to your care."

There was silence as Neferapondes listened. Sitting next to Danny, she placed her hand on his leg and said, "I treasure Jeannie like my daughter." Now there were tears. "She is my flesh and blood, and so you can feel like she is with her mother as you are away."

Her hand was warm on his leg. Danny put his hand on hers and said, "Our challenge is great, but Viracocha is with us. And fortunately, I know Gorom Mochcom's weakness."

Danny's statement took the queen by surprise. Her face was drawn into lines of curiosity as she asked, "Why is that?"

"It's his ring! Without it, he is helpless!" said Danny, smiling. Not waiting for her to respond, he proceeded, "Your son, Kashom, will help me, for he knows more than I do about how to defeat Mochcom, and I know together we shall prevail!"

What Danny just said gave Neferapondes comfort. Her mind was drifting. *Oh my darling Kashom, if only you could help Danny, how great that would be in the eyes of all who condemned you!*

With her soul at peace, she asked a profound question. "Would you care to talk about your parents, as I know nothing of them?" Perceptive as she was, the expression on Danny's face was a sure giveaway. She asked sincerely, "Did I say something to offend you, my lord?"

"Oh no, Neferapondes, you did not. How could you know? My best friend, my father, Johnny, was buried alive in a mining accident. We were incredibly poor. My beloved mother, Darla, was beside herself, and she turned to Pastor Duncan, the leader of our little community church. Then she was brutally murdered, and I found her."

Danny stopped. His eyes swelled up. He could not stop the tear that escaped. As it rolled down his cheek, Neferapondes lifted her hand and touched his face.

Slowly, Danny went on. "After the loss of my mom, I also turned to Pastor Duncan for comfort. He gave me five hundred dollars. I know that is meaningless to you, but it was a little money. The house I lived in had been taken away by the coal company that owned it, and so my friend Tony, who had also lost his father in a mining accident, opened his house so I would have a bed to sleep in and food to eat."

She listened and waited. Collecting his words, Danny proceeded. "My venom for Mochcom is beyond description. Gorom Mochcom was masquerading as Pastor Duncan, and so I hate myself for being deceived. It was Mochcom who murdered my mom. In a final race with death, just before Jeannie and I escaped the murderous hands of Gorom Mochcom, he killed my best friend, Tony. My friend Tony was to me like Peizar was to Jerzom."

Now taking both of Danny's hands, she squeezed tightly and said forcefully, "I know why the supreme god chose you as his royal prince. There could be no other...not Kashom, not Jerzom, no one. Danny, you are the hope of all mankind, and I am sure that watching you in action, killing the goroms and ridding our land of evil, could not have been more pleasing to Supreme God Viracocha."

She stopped, took a deep breath, and continued. "An impoverished boy coming from a bleak existence who has integrity, honesty, and compassion… yes, I watched closely your touching kindness and the gift you gave Zeb and Nola. Yes, there could be no other to fill the responsibilities of the royal prince of Viracocha!"

Danny nodded and said, "So, my dear queen, what is waiting for our palates?"

A surprised look crossed her face. Neferapondes asked, "Waiting for our palates?"

Danny laughed. "Sorry for my lack of proper words. What's for breakfast?"

"You come and see." The queen rose and made her way to the door.

"You go, and I'll be there in a minute. I have just a few things to do," said Danny as the queen exited through the doorway to his bedroom.

The little smirk on Jeannie's face was a dead giveaway to even the untrained eye. When Danny walked into the royal dining room, Jeannie's eyes followed his every movement. And between her smirk and his smile… well, the obvious question was to wonder what was going on.

There was one who knew. Well, not one but two—the first being Neferapondes and the second, Jeannie. Earlier, Jeannie and the queen were holding hands, walking down the hallway, and as they walked by the open doorway into Danny's room, they stopped. Although Danny did not see them there, Jeannie and the queen had an opportunity to catch a glimpse of a naked Danny looking for something. Neferapondes had meant to have a few moments with Danny, but under the circumstances, she chose to continue down the hall with Jeannie. Jeannie was snickering under her breath, and that did not go undetected by the queen, as she squeezed tightly Jeannie's hand.

The queen had planned on having a conversation with Danny about Jeannie, but with Danny in his compromising state of undress, it was not the right time. Yet something tugged at the queen's heart. Maybe she wanted comfort, knowing that the royal prince of Viracocha would be with her son on the most important mission of all time. Who knows? For whatever reason, after Neferapondes dropped Jeannie off in the royal dining room, she walked back to Danny's room. It was then that she had her private conversation with the young god of Kopaz.

Although Jeannie was snickering when Danny walked into the royal dining room, one thing was for sure—Danny was clueless, and we'll leave it at that.

"Good morning, Danny," said Queen Neferapondes, as he took his seat at the head of the table. "I trust you had a good night?" She smiled at Jeannie.

Considering the magnitude of what was coming up, there were more important things to take care of than dwelling on small talk.

All eyes went to the next guests of honor arriving for breakfast. It was an unusual sight. Between a six-foot-tall yellow wolf and a black cat that was at most ten inches in height was a small boy with a royal ornament on his head. His steps were carefully calculated so as not to disturb the golden crown adorned with hundreds of precious gemstones that he wore on his head.

The queen nonchalantly rose and went to help him steady his most prized possession. Once seated at the royal dining table, there was a shout of "Welcome, Prince Zeb!" by all.

Far be it for the old guard of the royal family, Queen Neferapondes and her son, Jerzom, to say a word on the protocol of wearing crowns. That bit of schooling could wait for a more appropriate time. Zeb, in due time, would be and act as a model royal prince, and his crown would be reserved for only state occasions.

And speaking of protocol, Danny feeding Yellzor from the table was also not addressed by any. Who would dare?

And Zanzee sitting on Jeannie's lap at the royal table, well, that was OK, as he had learned that habit from Kashom so long ago.

Time marched on. Breakfast passed, and all were pleased with the morning's royal feast. The morning and afternoon slipped away. Soon there would be final farewells. And to prepare for that final sendoff, the royal servants were busy preparing an evening meal to be served on the banks of the Yellshome River two hours prior to sunset.

The five-mile journey from the royal palace was half an hour by royal carriage. And the event was done in a grand style. A Hollywood movie set would have done well to model the occasion for a fantasy adventure.

A team of white stallions pulled the queen's carriage, in which sat the queen, Jerzom, Zeb, and Nola. They followed an even more spectacular carriage pulled by a team of black stallions. Danny and Jeannie were in the front carriage and had time to spend alone.

As each mile passed, the somberness of their mood increased.

Jeannie had so much to say but couldn't think of how to say any of it. She remembered how, so long ago, at Danny's dad's funeral, she had felt this very same way. Back then, she had focused on his sad countenance. She had been standing next to her mother in the old wooden pews of the chapel. A strikingly beautiful teenage girl with silky black hair and sapphire-blue eyes, Jeannie had watched a tall, strong, handsome boy walk by—he hadn't noticed her. Her mind on that day had filled with thoughts similar to those she now had. *Oh, Danny, will it be OK? My wonderful Danny! How can I help you? I wish I could go with you and hold you in my arms, your body next to mine, and make the pain in your heart go away.*

Sitting across from Danny in the royal carriage, tears spilled from Jeannie's eyes as a knot gathered in her throat.

It seemed the roles had changed. She was the one who was struggling.

Feeling the tenseness grow with each passing moment and watching his love fall into a hole of depression, Danny searched his mind for words of comfort.

"Jeannie, do you remember the day we found the rock with a hand on it?"

"Yes, Danny, I do," said Jeannie wistfully.

"Do you remember what I asked you?" he queried.

"Yes, Danny, I do," said Jeannie again. "You asked me, 'Jeannie, do you really think some mystery person is trying to communicate with us?'"

"And you said, '*Yep!*' as you were hopping over the little brook," said Danny.

Danny recalled more of their conversation on the day their adventure took off.

"And then you looked at me and said, 'Danny, I don't know. I guess all we can do to find out is do our best. If we don't find anything, well…what have we lost? These things are for sure—someone put those markings on White Face Cliff, and we have the Biblia Reina-Valera references, and they describe this small brook we're following to a T—is that not correct?'"

Jeannie nodded wistfully, and Danny continued. "I listened to you and kicked a rock. It rolled down a small incline onto an anthill. You watched, and I chuckled to myself as I thought, *Little red creatures…you just got a big knock at your door!*"

"Evidently I had a frown on my face because you kind of got upset with me and said, 'Danny, put a smile on your face!'"

Danny then entwined his fingers, locking his hands together. He covered his face with them. He slowly slid his locked hands up his face, exposing a smile.

Jeannie laughed. "Yes, Danny and this is what I said to you: 'That's good, Danny…real good! Seriously, Danny, I guess all we can do is hope— hope that we'll find the rock with a hand on it—hope that we're led to something worthwhile—hope is what we have. Do you know that hope is a good thing? Hope is the defining factor between having a good life and having a bad life. Danny, if we have hope, I believe the gods will step in and help us!'"

And like she had on that day in the Scarlet Desert, Jeannie studied the expression on Danny's face. They had found the rock with a hand on it. They had found the gifts from the gods. They had escaped from Mochcom using the treasure of gemstones and the power of the sun that opened the Highway of Time. And like that day so long ago when it all started, she was reminded again that she didn't have to philosophize to him. *Yes, even after all we have been through*, she thought happily, *Danny is the one with hope—his hope is really the driving factor behind our quest for adventure, and ultimately, our dream will come true. I know from the bottom of my heart. It will come true!*

It was different now. Their love had started as a bud and now had opened into a blossoming flower. Maybe it was just the thought of not having him near her that brought the cloud of depression upon her. His allegiance to the supreme god Viracocha and the goddess Neferdor was unquestionable. There could be no doubt that the young man sitting opposite to her in the carriage would ultimately, with her by his side, triumph over the last evil monster, Gorom Mochcom. Jeannie was sure that she and Danny would win the most glorious prize of all—golden thrones at the council table of the primeval gods.

But sadly, Jeannie knew all too well that that glorious prize for now was as elusive as a butterfly in the wind.

"Danny, I will miss you so much. I...I...you have no idea how much I love you, and just the thought of not having you near me is sad, yet I know your mission will change the course of existence for all creatures throughout the universe over the expanse of unending time." She spoke in almost a whisper.

"Wow! That was profound." He selected his words carefully. "You know, Jeannie, it's not just me who is going to do this...*it is us!* And I am sad because I told you I would never leave you again. You remember when I saw you for the first time in the palace?"

And with hope in her voice, she charged on. "Oh, Danny, it will be OK! We were selected. And in response, we're reaching for the ultimate goal—seats at the council table of the primeval gods, and with the grace of Viracocha, we'll be there!"

Sensing his unquestionable confidence, she smiled wistfully and loved him even more deeply.

They arrived at the gentle waters of the Yellshome River, on the riverbank next to the lone tree. But it was a very different place than when Danny and Jeannie had first arrived. As only Queen Neferapondes could have orchestrated, the gala affair of a royal sendoff picnic was in the making. Everywhere they looked there were decorations and lavish arrangements—farewell signs, royal tables laden with food fit for a king, entertainers, dancers, and all the trappings of the grandest possible good-bye—that no one but Neferapondes could have come up with.

Danny and Jeannie created quite a lot of excitement when they retrieved the treasures they had hidden. Having taken Sun Energy Transformer from its vault at the base of the lone tree, they set that treasure, a gift from the gods, on a green-and-white marble table. Zeb couldn't keep his hands off it. His new hand was his pride and joy, and he let everyone know it.

"See, everyone, I can lift the emerald star box!" Zeb shouted as he grasped it tightly and raised it four or five inches off the table.

However, the queen had a bad scare. Quite by chance, Neferapondes was sitting next to Zeb as he was playing with the Sun Energy Transformer, and she noticed a canvas bag. She was curious as to what was in it. She pulled out Danny's high school annual, the Pirate Log of 1958.

All eyes turned to the queen when she screamed. Danny raced to her, thinking the worst—that something dreadful was happening. He reached to hold her hands and asked, "What is the matter?"

She was shaking. Her words were faint. It seemed to Danny that she was scared to death for some reason. She tried to point at something. Danny, in his sweetest tone of voice, asked her again, "Did something hurt you?" She relaxed as Danny squeezed her hands.

Now she was able to point at the Pirate Log. She whispered, "There are little people trapped in there! Who are they? How did they get there?"

It was hard. Danny was about to bust a gut laughing, but he refrained. His smile, however, was broad. "My dear queen, there is no one in there, but when you and Jeannie get back to the royal palace, she will have an assignment to explain what this is all about."

He stopped and motioned for Jeannie to come to where they were. "Jeannie—" was the only word he managed to say before she interrupted and said, "I'll take care of it! Not to worry!"

It's interesting how things happen that change a person's entire perspective and how what was imagined to be one thing can turn out to be totally different. Moments earlier, there had been a panic in the making. And although Danny had softly said, "No one is in there," and Jeannie had said, "Not to worry!" the queen was still frightened. Those strange words fell on deaf ears. However, the child changed everything.

Still wearing his golden crown, Zeb came to the table where Danny, Neferapondes, and Jeannie were, as curiosity was a powerful motivator for a small boy. Not paying attention to the newcomer at first, Neferapondes did not see Zeb leafing through Danny's Pirate Log. Zeb looked at one page and turned to the next. When she did notice him looking, she realized that nothing was happening. All seemed peaceful.

Neferapondes thought, *Hmm! If he doesn't get hurt, maybe Danny and Jeannie are right.*

For the next hour, all enjoyed a royal picnic on the banks of Yellshome River.

As the time to depart grew closer, everyone's anxiety rose. And as the sun kissed the horizon of the Vulcan Mountains, the departure of Danny and Jerzom was at hand. The sun must still be in the sky for the Sun Energy Transformer to work. Preparations were complete. The dials on it were set. All that remained was to turn the key, the brass arrow.

As it was a solemn occasion, only a small group gathered: Danny, Jeannie, Jerzom, Neferapondes, Zeb, and Nola. The rest of the party, the royal guardsmen, and the servants had been sent upriver to wait.

"Zeb, come here," said Danny. He bent down so his head was level with Zeb's. "You can be a right-hand man, right?"

"Right," answered Zeb.

Who knows why? It was quite by coincidence that Danny sat on the marble bench with the Sun Energy Transformer only a few inches behind his back. As Danny was looking away from the table while holding Zeb on his lap, he missed something.

Trying to have a serious discussion with a five-year-old was a challenge, especially when an object of curiosity was within the child's reach. Zeb found a way to explore something that caught his eye. Unperceived by Danny, Zeb innocently moved one of the dials that had so piqued his interest.

Meanwhile, the discussion between the young god and the young prince continued. With his new hand back on his lap, Zeb smiled at Danny. "Right, Mr. TRPOV! I can be a right-hand man!"

"Good," said Danny. "In a few moments, Prince Jerzom and I will be gone. We will be traveling the Highway of Time." As Zeb nodded, Danny moved the conversation forward. "You will be the only royal prince in Kopaz, and that is a big responsibility!"

"I know that, Mr. TRPOV. I will do my duty as a royal prince," replied

Zeb.

From the mouths of babes comes the wisdom that rules the world. And that is what happened. Zeb asked most earnestly, "Will you bring my dad back with you?"

Now that was a challenging question. What was the answer?

The winds of change were blowing throughout the universe, and Danny was at the eye of the storm. At that moment, with a five-year-old sitting on his lap, how could Danny know that the dawning of a new human race was in the making or that the boy he held would play a role?

"You will see your dad again, I promise," answered Danny.

What could Jeannie, Neferapondes, Nola, and Jerzom say? How could they argue with a god? They could not, yet the moment was growing closer and so was the lingering question—how would they find solace?

Taking Jeannie's hand, Danny pulled gently, letting her know they needed a few private moments. "I want to hold your hand," said Danny. Jeannie nodded, and they walked along the river's edge, their fingers entwined, their hands swinging freely back and forth.

It was only a short walk. With only the sounds of the rippling waters making their journey to the brink of Yellshome Falls not far downriver, they stopped and faced each other. Their lips met. With strong embrace, Jeannie held him tightly for a few short moments.

Kolar was approaching the western horizon, letting Danny know his departure must be before the last rays of daylight vanished behind the Vulcan Mountains.

Danny took something from his pocket and handed it to Jeannie.

She read slowly his words.

To My One and Only Love

A boy from the Scarlet Desert at a time long ago met the Neferzul.
She's from royal blood and now lives in the
Valley of the Mountains in the land of Kopaz.

And it shall be that henceforth these young sweethearts will be bound
together by the powerful force that is love, as they embark upon their
journey of eternal life, knowing endless life is a gift from the gods that
will linger throughout the ages and fill the depths of their souls with
the rapture of that divine love until the end of time.

And to my love, the girl left behind in the Valley of the Mountains in
the land of Kopaz, although this road I soon will travel will ofttimes
be thorny and rocky, I'll carry your heart with pleasure next to mine,
no matter where my trail of joy and sorry leads me, until I cross the
final bridge over troubled waters to find that blissful life of endless
youth with you, my true love!

May Viracocha and Neferdor hold you in the palms of their hands
until we meet again.

The boy from the Scarlet Desert,

Danny Roberts

What could she say? Her words were hidden deep inside her. In tears,
she lifted his note and held it in the fingers of one hand; with the other,

she took her pencils and paper from her little bag. It was a Jeannie thing to always have her colored pencils and notepaper close by.

He watched her write. She handed it back to him. He silently read her words.

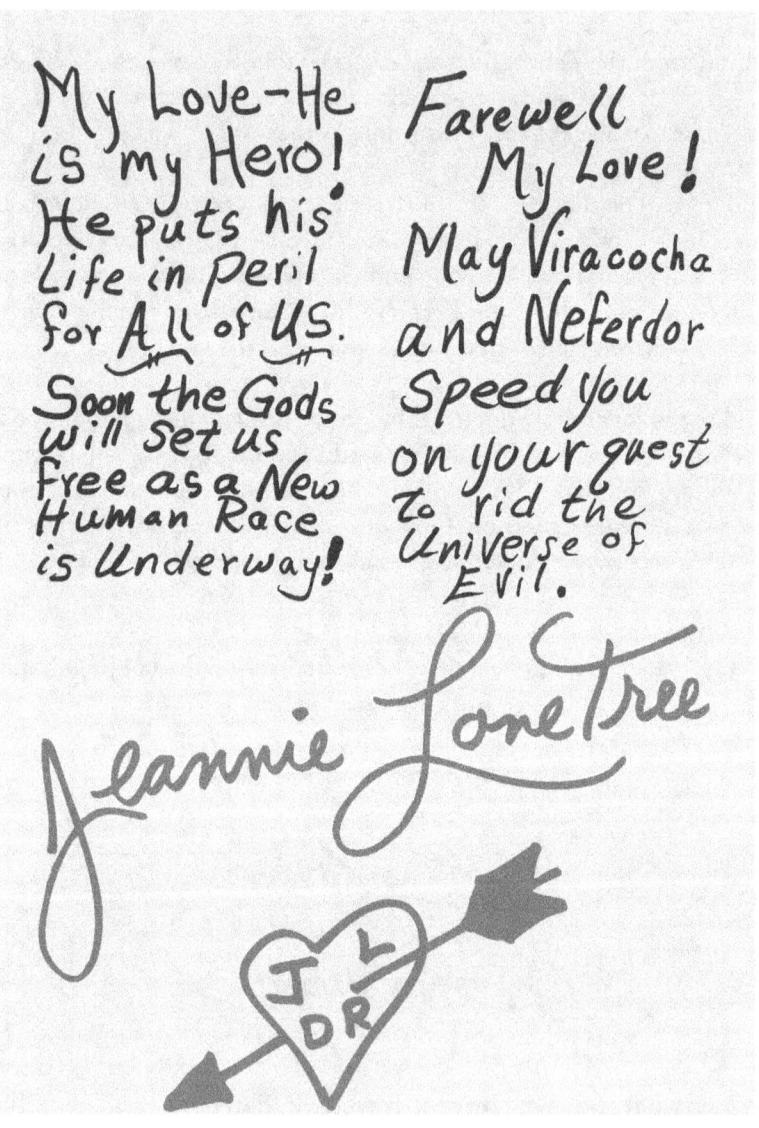

My Love—He is my Hero! He puts his Life in Peril for All of US. Soon the Gods will set us Free as a New Human Race is Underway!

Farewell My Love! May Viracocha and Neferdor Speed you on your quest To rid the Universe of Evil.

Jeannie Lone Tree

As he read, Jeannie grabbed Danny's free hand. Softy she said, "Farewell, my love. May the might of Viracocha be with you!"

The time had come. Jerzom was standing by the Sun Energy Transformer—dials set correctly, or so he thought. No more words or tears. Danny lifted his fingers to his lips. He threw a kiss to the girl he was leaving behind.

Danny and Jerzom grabbed the green handle. He let Jerzom turn the arrow in the keyhole, and they were gone.

Then there were only Jeannie, Neferapondes, Nola, and Zeb standing next to the lone tree on the banks of the mighty Yellshome River. Jeannie's farewell kiss from her first and only love was still warm on her lips, but his lips were no longer in Kopaz.

That absence weighed heavy on Jeannie as she stood next to the lone tree. The queen, along with Nola and Zeb, waited patiently as she watched and listened. In the twilight still of the evening, Jeannie sweetly sang a song:

> Soon the night will take him far;
> My love will be my distant star.
> He travels through a time unknown,
> In search of answers all alone.
> Somewhere out there in a desert's night,
> He'll chase his dreams of pure delight.
> Fleeting as the dust that's blown,
> My love will wander on his own.
> *Hold me softly, hold me tight.*
> *Hold me in your arms tonight.*
> *Soon the gods will set you free*
> *And take my love away from me.*
> *Will the road that crosses time*
> *Bring my love back home to me?*

Watch for the next adventure in the Kopaz Series

—WAR OF THE GODS—

Yellshome Falls

Dale Groutage

Dale Groutage was born and raised in Reliance, Wyoming, a poverty-stricken coal camp in the state's southwestern desert. His childhood reading inspired him to pursue a better life, leading to BS, MS, and PhD degrees from the University of Wyoming.

Groutage served as a senior scientist for the US Navy, developing missile guidance and submarine silencing technology. He was inducted into the University of Wyoming Engineering Hall of Fame for his service to his country and honored as one of the top ten engineers in federal government by the National Society of Professional Engineers.

Now retired, Groutage is married with three kids. The former adjunct professor for the University of California and the University of Washington lives in Neenah, Wisconsin.

www.ingramcontent.com/pod-product-compliance
Lightning Source LLC
Chambersburg PA
CBHW072331020726
47503CB00013B/754